I0575350

Samuel Hall

Homes and haunts of the wise and good

Samuel Hall

Homes and haunts of the wise and good

ISBN/EAN: 9783337203030

Printed in Europe, USA, Canada, Australia, Japan

Cover: Foto ©Andreas Hilbeck / pixelio.de

More available books at **www.hansebooks.com**

HOMES AND HAUNTS

OF

THE WISE AND GOOD,

OR

Visits to Remarkable Places

IN ENGLISH HISTORY AND LITERATURE,

BY

MRS. S. C. HALL, WM. HOWITT, THOS. GRATTAN, PROF. RHOADS, REV. THOS.
BRAINERD, D.D., PROF. JNO. S. HART, REV. JOSEPH BELCHER, D.D.,
REV. THEO. L. CUYLER, J. G. WHITTIER, REV.
JOEL PARKER, D.D.

Profusely Illustrated.

PHILADELPHIA:
J. W. BRADLEY, 48 N. FOURTH STREET.
1860.

Preface.

THERE is no more common mistake than that of supposing that Americans are, as compared with other nations, without national recollections. Though our republic is young, our nation is old. We have an inheritance in John Milton and Oliver Cromwell, in Shakspeare and Spenser, and Chaucer, and Wickliffe, and Alfred, and Caedmon, in the Long Parliament, and Battle Abbey, and Doomsday Book, and in all the other great names and events of early English history, just as inalienable as that of the most loyal subjects of Queen Victoria. Every great stream has a delta at its mouth. England is one, we are the other, of the two main channels through which the long stream of Anglo-Saxon life is emptying itself into the great ocean of modern civilization. This delta commences with the reign of George III., less than a century ago. All the long centuries before that, all the glorious achievements in literature, in arms, in the growth of liberal ideas, and the establishment of civil rights, are a joint inheritance. Such being the case we need not apologise for introducing the following sketches of some of our most illustrious ancestors, and the places made interesting by their associations. The articles are from both English and American writers well known on both sides of the Atlantic. The illustrations are principally from the designs of Mr. Fairholt, and made by him upon the spots delineated.

Contents.

William Caxton.

BY PROFESSOR RHOADS.

CARDINAL WOLSEY, in a letter to the Pope, written not long after the introduction of the art of printing into England, expressed his grief at the numerous evils which the new invention had already produced, and the deleterious influences it was destined still to exert. One passage in this letter is very remarkable. He says, "If men were once persuaded that they could make their own way to God, and that prayers in their own native language might pierce heaven as well as in Latin, how much would the authority of the mass and of ecclesiastics fall." The same forebodings existed in his mind respecting the effects of a general diffusion of knowledge upon affairs of state. He had an acute perception of the means which influence human action. And when the gray-haired William Caxton began at Westminster to labour with his types, his ink-balls, and his rude press, it was evident that a new power was established in England, stronger than cardinals or statesmen, popes or kings. The calculating prime minister, and the enthusiastic, persevering printer, both recognised its might; but one anticipated incalculable good, the other incalculable

(9)

evil from its exercise.   Let the condition of the world now, compared with what it was then, tell which was in the right.

ANCIENT PRINTING PRESS.

Little is known of the early life of Caxton.   Even the time of his birth is uncertain; but it was probably about 1410.   The honor of being his birth-place has been claimed for the little town of Caxton, in Cambridgeshire, because of coincidence of name, rather than from any evidence of the fact.   He himself tells us in his " Prologue to the History of Troy," that he first drew breath in the weald of Kent. He afterwards served an apprenticeship under Robert Large, an eminent London mercer. Of the correctness of his conduct during this period, we may judge from a clause in his master's will. This will is still preserved in the English Prerogative office, and a legacy of twenty marks shows that Caxton was favorably remembered.

For nearly thirty years after the decease of Large, Caxton resided in the Netherlands, as agent for the Mercer's Company of London; in which service he continued over twenty years. During this time he acquired so high a reputation for integrity and abilities, that he was appointed one of two commissioners to negotiate a treaty of commerce between his sovereign, Edward IV., and Philip, Duke of Burgundy. Subsequently he obtained, probably through acquaintance formed while thus engaged, a situation in the household of Philip's son, Charles; whose wife, Lady Margaret of York, sister of Edward IV., afterwards became distinguished as his patroness.

Notwithstanding his other engagements, Caxton had found time to make himself practically acquainted with the new art, just put into successful operation by Guttenberg, Faust, and Schöffer. At the request of Lady Margaret, he published at Cologne, in 1471, in folio, a work which he himself had translated from the French. This was the first book printed in the English language. Such copies as are still preserved, are now considered very valuable. In 1812, the Duke of Devonshire purchased a copy at public sale, for £1060 10s. The title page of this book is quaint and curious :—" Here begyneth the volume intituled the Recuyell of the Hystorye of Troye ; composed and drawen out of dyverse bookes of Latyn into Frensshe, by the right venerable persone and worshippful man, Raoul le Fevre, preest and chapelayn unto the right noble, gloryous, and myghty prince in his tyme, Philip, Duc of Buorgoyne, of Braland, &c., in the yeare of the incarnation of our Lord God, a thousand, four hundred and sixty and foure, and translated and drawen out of Frensshe into English by William Caxton, mercer, of the cyte of London, at the commandment of the right, hye, mighty, and vertuouse Princesse, his redoughtyd Lady Margarette, by the grace of God, Duchesse of, &c., which sayd translacion and work was begonne in Burgis, in the countre of Flaunders, the fyrst day of Marche, in the yeare of the incarnacion of our sayd Lord God, a thousand, foure hondred and sixty and eight, and ended, fynyshed, in the holy cyte of Colon, the xix day of September, the yeare of our said Lord God, *a thousand, foure hondred, sixty and eleven.*" Caxton further informed the readers of his book, that "It

CAXTON'S CIPHER.

is not written with penne and ynke, as other books ben, for all the bookes of this storye, named the Recule of the

Hystorye of Troyes, then emprynted as ye here see, *were begonne (begun) in oon (one) daye, and fynyshed in oon daye.*" Besides their long titles, the printers of olden time were accustomed to inscribe their ciphers in the books they issued. The cut on p. 12 represents that of Caxton. It consists merely of his own initials, with the Arabic numerals 74, noting the year of the 15th century, in which he introduced the art of printing into his native country.

CAXTON'S HOUSE.

It was at Westminster that the printing-press was first used in England ; and the *Game and Play of Chess*, dedi

2

cated to the Duke of Clarence, was the first typographical work executed there. Until within a few years, a house continued to stand in Little Dean Street, London, pointed out by tradition as the house occupied by Caxton while engaged in his labours at Westminster. It was a timber and plaster structure, three stories high; the last story having a wooden balcony resting on the projecting windows below.

Though Caxton was sixty-four years old when he published the Game and Playe of Chess, he continued to labour earnestly and diligently at his favourite pursuit for nearly twenty years longer; sending forth from his press during that period between fifty and sixty volumes, most

CAXTON'S MONUMENT, WESTMINSTER.

of which were composed or translated by himself. About 1492 he died; and was buried at Campden, in Gloucester, according to some accounts, but according to others, at St. Margarets, Westminster. A monument (see p. 14) has been erected to his memory at the latter place. The inscription is as follows:

TO THE MEMORY

OF

WILLIAM CAXTON,

WHO FIRST INTRODUCED INTO GREAT BRITAIN

THE ART OF PRINTING,

AND WHO, A. D. 1477, OR EARLIER,

EXERCISED THAT ART.

IN THE ABBEY OF WESTMINSTER,

THIS TABLET,

IN REMEMBRANCE OF ONE

TO WHOM

THE LITERATURE OF THE COUNTRY IS SO LARGELY INDEBTED,

WAS RAISED,

ANNO DOMINI MDCCCXX,

BY THE

ROXBURGHE CLUB,

EARL SPENCER, K. G., PRESIDENT.

The Printing-Office of William Caxton.

THE PRINTING-OFFICE OF

William Caxton.

BY MRS S. C. HALL.

CONSIDER how many hours of our existence are spent in reveries! in that waking sleep, that dream-like condition, apart from present life, yet recalling lives and scenes over which we may have just closed some venerable volume. How we envy those old worms! small atoms full of wisdom, wriggling their way through black-lettered tomes, unable to endure any light but that of other days; full of what they can neither impart nor comprehend. For aught we can tell they have their own literary *cliques*, which like other cliques can see no good beyond their own narrow circle—the circle which, no larger than might be covered by a silver twopence, forms *their* world! Roll away, little fellow, we cannot replace you in your nest; you have eaten a good round hole out of old Caxton's book upon chess—that combination of brown and faded leaves which our old housekeeper calls 'rubbish.' Rubbish! how precious in our eyes are those mouldering pages; how carefully we turn them over and mend them here and there with soft smooth paper, tending them as mothers do their children, and laying sheets of foolscap between

(19)

each page, close the volume carefully, and then sink into
a reverie, in which things and scenes of old, float, and
pass, and dimly crowd around us. Man may philosophise,
and closing his eyes upon the material world, dream on,
and by the magic and strength of imagination, that refin-
ing essence of immortality, which stirs within us, active, ennobling, and invigorating—by that mighty power—he may
create new wonders and new worlds; but the wonders of
the *future* will hardly surpass the wonders of the *past*.
If we had but the power to open afresh the bowels of
the earth, to call upon the sea to give up its treasures and its mysteries, to command that lost ART may be
restored, how should we be shorn of our self-sufficiency and
pride! Every moment of our lives we are enjoying the
benefits of past improvements, and yet suffering ourselves
to be carried away by anticipations of those that are to
come. Yet surely we may be too prone to overvalue the
past. We have arrived at that period of life when memory
is stronger than sympathy, and a habit of wandering
amongst old places, and pondering over old works, and
thinking about the people of old—the olden world—may,
perhaps, render us not so alive, as an immortal spirit should
be to the future. The past is more tranquil and pleasant
to dwell with than the present; we do not perceive those
blemishes through the mist of years which offend us now.
The people themselves, the great and mighty ones, do not
come before us with their palpable faults to undeceive our
conceptions, and we can comfort ourselves with the belief,
that their errors, when recorded, have been exaggerated
by the harshness of the historian.

This train of thought has been encouraged as we have

been pondering over the eventful and not unromantic life of one of whom we know little—yet nothing that is not honorable to human nature; one to whose memory we owe much more than we can pay, or are even disposed to pay ; for who, upon opening a book, thinks upon blessing the memory of WILLIAM CAXTON, *the first English printer?* Of truth, his cypher should be inscribed in every English school-room, and scholars should doff their caps as they pass it by; while such as feel bound to honour the *first* who introduced, practised, and communicated this most useful art into our country, should not forget that it was a WOMAN, the Lady Margaret of York, King Edward the IVth's sister, who passing as a bride to the Duke's court at Bruges, entertained William Caxton in her retinue,* and encouraged him in the practice of an art, of which he had learned, according to his own simple account, "a good deal at considerable expense."

He was born in the weald or woody part of Kent, during the latter part of the reign of Henry IV., and apprenticed to one of London's worthy citizens, by trade a mercer ; and thus laid the foundation of his commercial

---

* Caxton notes that he received a yearly fee and "other many goode and grete benefets," which proves he stood high in her favor, though in what rank or quality he served the Duchess is not known with certainty. Dr. Dibdin says, "he should suppose him to have held no regular employment, or rather that he was a gentleman of her household, in a sinecure situation, receiving an annual salary." That he was entrusted by King Edward IV. on important missions is proved by his being connected with one Richard Whetehill, in concluding a treaty of trade and commerce between that Sovereign and the Duke of Burgundy, whose son afterwards married King Edward's sister, the Lady Margaret named above.

knowledge.   His taste led to the acquirement of considerable proficiency in penmanship and the knowlege of languages,* which, doubtless, forwarded his interest in obtaining the situation he held in the Lady Margaret's "retinue."
We are informed that he " stuck painfully" to the task she
gave him, bringing forth the work under the title of
" The Recuyell of the Historye of Troye, &c.," which is the
first book, at least in being, or which we know of, ever
printed in the English tongue.   The title-page, and some
other portions of the first edition of this book, are printed
in red ink ; but its most charming portion is the evidence
of Caxton's modesty, as he apologises for his small knowledge of the French language, and his imperfectness in his
own, *having lived out of England* nearly thirty years.   It
is impossible also not to sympathise with our first printer
when he concludes with this gentle appeal to our sympathies :—" Thus," he says, " end I this booke, and for as
moche as in wrytynge the same my penne is worne,
myne hande wery, and eyen dymmed with overmoch
lookyng on the whyte paper, and that age creepeth on me
daily and feebleth all the body."   And he goes on to say
how he had promised this book to divers gentlemen, adding, " It is not wretton with penne and ynke as other bookes
ben to thende that all men may have them att ones, for

* Dr. Dibdin informs us that the mercers of those days being
general merchants, frequently had commissions for books ; a cargo
of Indian spices and Greek manuscripts sometimes came together
to the Medici, their great fellow traders.   The original French composition of " The book of Good Manners" was delivered to Caxton
by a special friend of his, *a mercer* of London, named William Pratt ;
and Rodger Thornye, also *a mercer*, at a later period induced Caxton's successor, Wynkyn de Worde, to print the " Polychronicon."

all the other bookes of this storye named the Recule of
the Historys of Troye then emprynted as ye here see,
were begonne in oon day and fynyshed in oon day." What
astonishment this declaration must have excited in the
literati of old ; quite as much as our steamboats, and rail-
roads, and daguerreotypes, and a score of other things have
produced in the present. What will our friends the Edinburgh Chambers say to this, who issue their hundreds
of thousands of " bigger books" weekly !

Although Caxton so touchingly complains of his advanced years when he had fulfilled the wise and gracious
command of his royal patron, " the sovereign Lady Margaret," yet three years elapsed before he brought his art
into England, during which period we have no record of
Caxton's proceedings ; " the Game of Chess," which was
elaborately dedicated to the Duke of Clarence, who ' made
his exit about four years after. in a butt of malmsey,' is
believed by many to have been the first book he printed in
this country.

Our very pearl of favourites, old John Stow, in his
"Survey of London," says that " in the Eleemosynary or
Almonry (at Westminster Abbey), now corruptly called the
Ambry, for that the alms of the Abbey were there distributed to the poor, John Islip, Abbot of Westminster,
erected the first press of book-printing that ever was in
England, and Caxton was the first that practised it in the
said Abbey." Whoever authorised him (and the *who* is a
disputed point), it is very certain that *he did* practise it
there, at the entrance to the Abbey, from which circumstance a printing-room is to this day called in technical

phrase, a *chapel*.* Stow, all wonderful as he was, was not
infallible, and there are others who prove from certain
documents that Doctor Thomas Milling was abbot in those
days; he was succeeded by the bountiful John Estney,
who survived him, so that if he established Caxton in his
printing-office, it must have been before he achieved the
mitre of Westminster.

The first book printed by Caxton at Westminster (which
contains an absolute date "fynysshed the xviii. day of No-
vembre, and the sevententh yere of the regne of King
Edward, 1477") was a translation by the unfortunate and
accomplished Earl Rivers, containing seventy-five leaves,
called the "Sayings of the Philosophers." At the end of
this work are three pages of Socrates' saucy sayings
about women, passed over by the noble translator, but
added—with an apology—by the printer himself, which
made the matter worse. He declares that the women of
this our England are altogether different from the Xan-
tippes of Greece, being here "right good, wise, playsant,

* Dr. Dibdin says: "It is most probable that Caxton, after the
manner observed in other monasteries, erected his press near one of
the chapels attached to the aisles of the Abbey, and his printing office might have superseded the use of what was called the Scrip-
torium of the same, which was the chamber in which the younger
monks were constantly employed in transcribing books." No remains of this once interesting place can now be ascertained; indeed, there is strong presumption that it was pulled down in making
preparation for Henry VIIth's Chapel. For if Henry made no
scruple to demolish "the Chapel of the Virgin," in order to carry
into effect his own plans for erecting the magnificent one which goes
by his name, the office of our printer stood little chance of escaping
the same fate.

humble, discrete, sobre, chast, obedient to their husbondis, treue, secrete, stedfast, ever busy and never idle, attemperate in speaking, and vertuous in all their workes."

Very good, Master Caxton, and for so much your countrywomen are greatly your debtors; but mark the context—the stamp of an old bachelor, or a man rejoicing in liberty, regained by widowhood, is upon it: "*or at least sholde be so*," they are so " or sholde be so." This is, perhaps, as good an example as we can give of the half pleasant, half ironical style, of our rare old printer. But that it would occupy too much of our space, we might insert a list of Caxton's works; for he imparted his knowledge unto others, and he printed more rapidly after a time than he had done at first. The art made its appearance in 1479 at Oxford, and the following year Caxton sent forth three works from his press in Westminster.

Caxton having been the first to *print* that King John was poisoned by a monk, at the Abbey of Swineshed, near Lincoln, he drew upon him much monkish abuse; yet he only printed it from a chronicle, of which we are told several MSS. are still in existence; one, for instance, in Benet College Library. Doctor John Parkman, in his life of the King, in Speed's Chronicles, believes the tale; for, he says, " an author more ancient and unexceptionable than all the rest, even King John's son and successor in his kingdom, averred it," when the Prior of Clerkenwell saucily told him, being in that house, " that as soon as he ceased to do justice towards his prelates he should cease to be king," to which his Majesty, enraged with his traitorous threats, replied, " What! mean you to turn me out of my kingdom, and afterward to murder me, as my father

3

was dealt with ?"   About the same time that printing was introduced at Oxford, a schoolmaster set up a press at St. Albans ;* and truly the knowledge of the art, which is knowledge, spread amazingly, for it was patronised by the nobility and by the church; the latter, indeed, were the great preservers, though not the diffusers, of literature, and promoters of art during the darker ages; enriching their monasteries with the treasures of printing, and taking care of what otherwise would have been destroyed.   At first, the church did not apprehend any evil to itself from the extension of knowledge, and it was evident that Caxton feared none ; his labors were those of a man of passing industry, devoted to his art, and most anxious to make it the means of fostering and spreading abroad a love of religion, virtue, and good manners.   His great age seems not to have abated his constant application at a period when nature, worn out by the cares and trammels of life, seeks repose.   He continued indefatigable, laboring with the vigor, and more than the perseverance of youth, in an occupation which, at its very commencement, he found painful, "as his frame was worne, his hande weary, and his eyes dimmed with looking on white

* The ancient printing-press, engraved on page 10, is copied from one of the earliest representations of this "mighty engine" known. It is seen in the title-page of a book printed in 1498, by Jodocus Badius Ascensianus. It is curious, as it shows the printer at work, attended by his boy inking the dabbers, and the compositor seated on one side, with his composing stick and manuscript before him. On a shelf above his head are various books. It also shows how little improvement was made in the printing-press comparatively until our own times. This cut may be received as a picture of Caxton's office at the end of his industrious life.

paper." His last days were eminently characteristic of
his life and character, for he employed them in transla-
ting from the French a large volume of the 'Holy Lives
of the Fathers Hermits living in the Deserts;' a work
full of the solemn stillness of its subject, and calculated,
while it weaned his heart from all worldly attachment, to
exalt it above the vain solicitude of life.

Wynkyn de Worde, who was Caxton's pupil,* informs
us that this work was translated in 1491, and that he
finished it *the last days of his life.* Events often supply
proofs that the Almighty permits the spirit to linger in
its frail tenement for the accomplishment of some great
object. Certainly the body wrestled with the spirit, and
the old man accomplished his task, and then quietly and
calmly departed. There is no record of his having been
married, but his funeral expenses are rated in the War-
den's account books of St. Margaret's, Westminster; six
shillings and eightpence being charged for four torches,
and sixpence for tolling the bell.

Cardinal Wolsey tolled an alarum bell to his memory
which sounded beyond England, when he wrote to the
Pope, "that his holiness could not be ignorant what divers
effects the new invention of printing had produced;" and
after complaining of its having occasioned schisms and

---

* He was a native of Lorrain, and came into England either
along with Caxton, or was afterwards invited by him. He was a
man of superior talent and skill, and was employed as Caxton's
assistant until his death. He continued in his office as his successor till between the years 1500 and 1502, when he removed his
printing-office to the sign of the "Sun," in the Parish of St. Bride's,
Fleet Street, where he died in 1534, after greatly improving his art.

sects in Germany, he arrives at the conclusion "that if men were persuaded once that they could make their own way to God, and the prayers in their own native language might pierce heaven as well as in Latin, how much would the authority of the mass fall? how prejudicial might this prove to all ecclesiastical orders."' But the power of the press once manifested, could not be restrained; the revolutions that have been effected by its influence, whether for good or evil, are registered in history; and it would be difficult for us to imagine the interests, occupations, or business of a world, without books. Caxton, an old man with white hair, and of a simple and steadfast, rather than a brilliant or comprehensive mind, effected more towards illuminating England, than all the mighty powers that preceded him for centuries.

We had a curiosity to visit the Almonry in Westminster, to look upon the house traditionally said to have been his residence; we have pictured it (on page 13) as it was previous to its demolition at the end of last year; but before we describe the *house*, let us say something of the place.

The Almonry is so termed from the foundation of an almshouse for poor women, by Margaret, mother of King Henry VII. The old Chapel of St. Anne also stood here, and the place was called the Eleemosynary or Almonry, because there also the alms of the Abbey were anciently distributed to the poor. The whole of the ground for a considerable distance around this spot was covered by the buildings of the monastery, the Great and Little Sanctuary, and the Gate-house adjoining the Almonry. The Sanctuary was celebrated as a place of refuge for offenders from the earliest period; some writers supposing that it obtained that privilege from Edward the Confessor. A violation of sanctuary perpetrated by Thomas of Wood-stock and Sir John Cobham, in the reign of Richard II., who dragged from thence Tresilian, the Lord Chief Justice of the King's Bench, and hanged him at Tyburn, was so loudly complained of by the abbot, that the offending parties were obliged publicly to ask the abbot pardon and absolution. In the reign of Henry VI., Eleanor Cobham, wife to Thomas of Woodstock, Duke of Gloucester, fled there; but being charged with witchcraft and high treason, (crimes imputed to her in Shakspeare's delineation of this lady) she was refused harborage. In the reign of Henry VII., the privileges of the Sanctuary were restricted, and Elizabeth brought it under regulations so that no persons but debtors could avail themselves of it; and such were obliged to take oath that they claimed it not for fraud, but only for safety till they would pay their debts. They were then made to give up all their accounts honestly, and an inventory of all their debts and effects, which, if not sufficient to pay, they were to labor to do so by all honest means. They were to attend daily prayers, be obedient to the dean, wear no weapons, or be out of the Sanctuary before sunrise or after sunset. The Gate-house was a prison for offenders in general. Here Colonel Lovelace, the poet, was confined, as were many of the royalists in the time of Cromwell. The last relic of the building was removed a few years since; it was a portion of the old wall with an ancient pointed arch; it stood at the en-trance to the Dean's Yard, where the way is now to the schools.

The Little Sanctuary included that portion of ground
3 *

opposite St. Margaret's Church where now stands the ses-
sions-house, the hospital, and mews. It consisted, as lately
as 1806, of a cluster of streets with gabled overhanging
old plastered houses, partially decayed, and exhibiting their
timber framework in a tottering condition. Upon pulling
them down, the original gates leading to the Sanctuary
were discovered, which then formed the entrance to a
narrow way that received the appellation of 'Thieving
Lane,' so given, probably, because down that lane felons
were led to the old Gate-house prison ; but the inhabitants
may have occasioned the bestowal of the title upon the
street they inhabited, for it is recorded as being haunted
by the worst of characters, and a harbour for filth and
pestilence.

The Almonry recently was literally worse than it *can*
be represented. Prepared as we were for all that was vile
and revolting in its miserable inhabitants, we were not,—
could not, be prepared for all we there saw. To say that
it was the St. Giles's of the west end, is saying nothing ;
its dark and unclean streets were the abodes of infamy.
Those who, impelled by a holy wish to save from sin,
visited it by day, crept cautiously along, shrinking from
the haggard faces or thievish hands, that found refuge there
when they could find it nowhere else. The impure district,
called by a name so redolent of charity, consisted of a
cluster of small streets, buried as it were between the
greater thoroughfares of Westminster ; which, however,
had no direct communication with them but by narrow
alleys and courts still narrower, several of them being mere
doorways that formed dark passages in the close and
murky streets, whose dim and shattered windows let the

cold blast in, and the fumes and voices of maddening
and most degrading dissipation out. Ragged and blear-
eyed children, serving to show how hideously sin can de-
form even a child, peered at, and cursed us as we passed.
Rushing like a pestilence, from beneath an antique door-
way, came a woman intoxicated, followed by a still more
intoxicated man, brandishing a broom, with which he had
not power to strike; some of their " neighbors," in their
savage pleasure at the chase, expressed their satisfaction by
loud oaths and shouting; and a costermonger, while load-
ing his poor donkey from a cellar with more wood than a
horse ought to carry, assured a heap of moving blackness—
a sweep, we believe—who was half drowning kittens in a
broken crock, taking them out to see if they were dead,
and then putting them in again, not heeding that their tail-
less mother expressed her agony by every means in her
power,—" that he'd leave the place next week—no one
could stand it." Having made our way from this open den,
we fell to conversing with ourselves as to why our righteous
folk did not purify what was, in the very olden time, a
district sacred to deeds of love and holiness; and at last
we got into Little Dean Street, by which, we afterwards
learned, we might have reached Caxton's house without so
much annoyance as we had experienced, and which, truth
to say, somewhat damped our antiquarian ardor for the
time; for the day was dark, and the miserable people we
encountered darker still.

Much of this unwholesome district has since our visit
been removed; a new street, of great width, is opened
through its densest lanes. The squalid inhabitants have
passed, we hope, to healthier localities. We now continue

to describe the place as it was before the alterations, and the house called Caxton's was standing.

Passing down Little Dean Street, the distance of some dozen houses, the lane suddenly widened, as if it were aware that, bad as it was, it contained something worth looking at ; and so it did, for there stood the remarkable house engraved on page 13—a timber and plaster erection, of three stories in height, the last story having a wooden balcony resting on the projecting windows below, with doors leading on to it ;—which has been traditionally called the house of William Caxton. Its antiquity cannot be safely ascribed to so early a date as the period when our printer lived, but it may have stood upon the site or have been altered from the original structure.

The Roxburghe Club did themselves much honor when they erected a monument to this hero of letters, in the church where he lies buried, St. Margaret's, Westminster.

But England has not yet discharged its duty to its great citizen—its mighty benefactor : surely it is high time that a monument worthy of his fame, and of his country, should perpetuate the memory of one to whom England owes so large a debt of gratitude.

Shakspeare.

Shakspeare.

BY WILLIAM HOWITT.

SHAKSPEARE is not merely a dramatic poet. Great and peerless as is his dramatic fame, the very elements, not of dramatic art and fame alone, but of universal poetry, and that of the highest order, are so diffused throughout all his works, that the character of poet soars above the character of dramatist in him, like some heaven-climbing tower above a glorious church. Every line, almost every word, is a living mass of poetry; these are scattered through the works of all authors as such exponents of their deepest sentiments as they cannot command themselves. They are like the branches, the buds, the flowers and leaves of a great tree of poetry, making a magnificent whole, and rich and beautiful as nature itself, down to its minutest portions. To leave out Shakspeare were, indeed, to play Hamlet with the part of Hamlet himself omitted; it were to invite guests, and get the host to absent himself. In the Walhalla of British poetry, the statue of Shakspeare must be first admitted and placed in the centre, before gradations and classifications are thought of. He is the universal genius, whose presence and spirit must and will pervade the whole place.

(35)

And yet, where are the homes and haunts of Shakspeare in London ?   Like those of a thousand other remarkable men, in the accidents and the growth of this great city they are swept away.   Fires and renovation have carried every thing before them.   If the fame of men depended on bricks and mortar, what reputations would have been extinguished within the last two centuries in London!   In no place in the world have the violent necessities of a rapid and immense development paid so little respect to the " local habitations" of great names.   The very resting-places and tombs of many are destroyed, and their bones, like those of Chatterton, have been scattered by the spades of the unlettered laborer.

We may suppose that Shakspeare, on his coming up to London, would reside near the theatres where he sought his livelihood.   The first appears to have been that of Blackfriars.   It has long been clean gone, and its locality is now occupied by Play-house-yard, near Apothecaries' Hall, and the dense buildings around.   Play-house-yard derives its name from the old play-house.   In Knight's London, it is suggested that this theatre might be pulled down soon after the permanent close of the theatres during the Commonwealth, by the Puritans ; but the real old theatre of Shakspeare must, had that not been the case, have perished entirely in the fire of London, which cleared all this ground, from Tower-street to the Temple.   If Shakspeare ever held horses at the theatre door on his first coming to town it would be here, for here he seems to have been first engaged.   The idea of his holding horses at a theatre door, bold and active fellow as he had shown himself in his deer-stealing exploits, and with friends and acquaintances

in town, has been scouted, especially as he was then a full-
grown man of twenty-three. The thing, however, is by no
means improbable. Shakspeare was most likely as independent as he was clever and active. On arriving in town,
and seeing an old acquaintance, Thomas Green, at this theatre, he might, like other remarkable men who have made
their way to eminence in London, be ready to turn his
hand to anything till something better turned up. Green.
who was a player, might be quite willing to introduce
Shakspeare into that character and the theatre ; but it had
yet to be proved that Shakspeare could make an actor of
himself, and, till opportunity offered what so likely to seize
the attention of a hanger about the theatre, as the want of
a careful horse-holder for those who came there in such
style, which appears was then common enough. We have
the statement from Sir William Davenant, and therefore
from a cotemporary, admirer, and assumed relative. We
are told that the speculation was not a bad one. Shakspeare, by his superior age and carefulness, soon engrossed
all this business, and had to employ those boys, who had before been acting on their own account, as his subordinates ;
whence they acquired and retained, long after he had
mounted into an actor himself, within the theatre, the
name of Shakspeare's boys. That he become "an actor at
one of the play-houses, and did act exceedingly well," Aubrey tells us. He is supposed to have acted Old Knowell
in Ben Jonson's " Every Man in his humor ;" and Oldys
tells us that a relative of Shakspeare, then in advanced age,
but who in his youth had been in the habit of visiting London for the purpose of seeing him act in some of his own
plays, told Mr. Jones, of Tarbeck, that he had a faint re-
4

collection of having once seen him act a part in one of his
own comedies, wherein, being to personate a decrepit old
man, he wore a long beard, and appeared so weak and
drooping, and unable to walk, that he was forced to be
supported, and carried by another person to a table, at
which he was seated among some company who were eating, and one of them sang a song." This is supposed to
have been in the character of Adam, in " As You Like It,"
and hence it has been inferred, in connection with his acting the Ghost in Hamlet, and Old Knowell, that he took
chiefly old or elderly characters.

Every glimpse of this extraordinary man, who, however
much he might have been acknowledged and estimated in
his own day, certainly lived long before his time, is deeply
interesting. That he was estimated highly we know from
Jonson himself:

> " Sweet swan of Avon, what a sight it were
> To see thee in our waters yet appear,
> And make those flights upon the banks of Thames
> That did so take Eliza and our James."

When the two monarchs under whom Shakspeare lived
admired and patronized him, we may be sure that Shakspeare's great merits were perceived, and that vividly,
though the age had not that intellectual expansion which
could enable it to rise above its prejudices against a player,
and comprehend that Shakspeare's dramas were not merely
the most wonderful dramas, but the most wonderful ex-
positions of human life and nature that had ever appeared.
People were too busy enjoying the splendid scenes presented to them by this great genius, to note down for the

gratification of posterity the daily doings, connections, and whereabouts of the man with whom they were so familiar. He grew rich, however, by their flocking to his theatre, and disappeared from among them.

In this theatre of Blackfriars he rose to great popularity, both as an actor and dramatic author, and became a proprietor. It was under the management of Richard Burbage, who was also a shareholder in the Globe Theatre at Bankside. To the theatre at Bankside Shakspeare also transferred himself, and there he became, in 1603, the lessee. There he seems to have continued about ten years, or till 1613; having, however, so early as 1597, purchased one of the best houses in his native town of Stratford, repaired and improved it, and that so much that he named it New Place. To this, as his proper home, he yearly retired when the theatrical season closed; and having made a comfortable fortune, when the theatre was burned down in 1613, retired from public life altogether.

Bankside is a spot of interest, because Shakspeare lived there many years during the time he was in London. It is that portion of Southwark lying on the river side between the bridges of Blackfriars and Southwark This ground was then wholly devoted to public amusements, such as they were. It was a place of public gardens, play-houses, and worse places. Paris Garden was one of the most famous resorts of the metropolis. There were the bear-gardens, where Elizabeth, her nobles, and ladies used to go and solace themselves with that elegant sport, bear-baiting. There, also, was the Globe Theatre, of which Shakspeare became licensed proprietor, and near which he lived. The theatre was an octagon wooden building, which has been

made familiar by many engravings of it. In Henry the
Fifth Shakspeare alludes to its shape and material :

> " Can this cockpit hold
> The vasty fields of France ?　Or may we cram
> Within this *wooden* O the very casques
> That did affright the air at Agincourt ?"

It was not much to be wondered at that this wooden
globe should get consumed with fire, which it did, as I have
already stated, in 1613. Shakspeare's play of Henry VIII.
was acting, a crowded and brilliant company was present,
and among the rest Ben Jonson, when in the very first act,
where, according to the stage directions, " drums and trumpets, chambers discharged," cannons were fired, the ignited
wadding flew into the thatch of the building, and the whole
place was soon in flames.　Sir Henry Wotton thus describes the scene in a letter to his nephew : " Now, to let
matters of state sleep, I will entertain you at present with
what happened this week at the Bankside.　The king's
players had a new play, called All is True, representing
some principal pieces from the reign of Henry VIII., which
was set forth with many extraordinary circumstances of
pomp and majesty, even to the matting of the stage ; the
knights of the order, with their Georges and garters ; the
guards, with their embroidered coats, and the like ; sufficient, in truth, within a while, to make greatness very familiar, if not ridiculous.　Now, King Henry making a mask
at Cardinal Wolsey's house, and certain cannons being shot
off at his entry, some of the paper or other stuff wherewith one of them was stopped, did light on the thatch,
where, being thought at first but an idle smoke, and their

eyes more attentive to the show, it kindled inwardly and
ran round like a train, consuming within an hour the whole
house to the very ground. This was the fatal period of
that virtuous fabric, wherein yet nothing did perish but
wood and straw and a few forsaken cloaks; only one man
had his breeches set on fire, that perhaps had broiled him,
if he had not, by the benefit of a provident wit, put it out
with bottle ale."

Fires seem to have menaced Shakspeare on all sides, and
he had narrow escapes. As there is no mention of his name
in the accounts of the Globe Theatre in 1613, nor any in
his will, it is pretty clear that he had retired from the proprietorship of the Globe before, and escaped that loss ; but
in the very year after it was burned down, there was a
dreadful fire in Stratford, which consumed a good part of
the town, and put his own house into extreme danger.

These were the scenes where Shakspeare acted, for
which he wrote his dramas, and where, like a careful and
thriving man as he was, he made a fortune before he was
forty, calculated to be equal to £1000 a year at present.
He had a brother, also, on the stage at the same time with
himself, who died in 1607, and was buried in St. Savior's
Church, Southwark, where his name is entered in the
parish register as "Edmund Shakspeare, a player."

The place where he was accustomed particularly to resort for social recreation was the Mermaid Tavern, Friday
street, Cheapside. This was the wits' house for a long
period. There a club for *beaux esprits* was established by
Sir Walter Raleigh, and here came, in their several days
and times, Spenser, Shakspeare, Philip Sydney, Jonson,
Beaumont and Fletcher, Massinger, Marlowe, Selden, Cot-

4 *

ton, Carew, Martin, Donne, Wotton, and all the brave
spirits of those ages.   Here Jonson and Shakspeare used
to shine out by the brilliancy of their powers, and in their
" wit combats," in which Fuller describes Jonson as a *Span-
ish great galleon*, and Shakspeare as the *English man-of-
war.* "Master Jonson, like the former, was built far higher
in learning; solid, but slow in his performances.   Shakspeare, with the English man-of-war, lesser in bulk, but
lighter in sailing, could turn with all tides, tack about, and
take advantage of all winds, by the quickness of his wit
and his invention."   Enough has been said of this celebrated club by a variety of writers.   There can be no doubt
that there wit and merriment abounded to that degree, that,
as Beaumont has said in his epistle to Jonson, one of their
meetings was enough to make up for all the stupidity of
the city for three days past, and supply it for long to come;
to make the worst companions right witty, and " downright
fools more wise."   There is as little doubt, however, that,
with Jonson in the chair, drinking would be as pre-eminent
as the wit.   The verses which he had inscribed over the
door of the Apollo room, at the Devil Tavern, another of
their resorts, are, spite of all vindications by ingenious pens,
too indicative of that.

> "Welcome all who lead or follow
> To the oracle of Apollo:
> Here he speaks out of his pottle,
> Or the tin-pot, his tower bottle:
> All his answers are divine;
> Truth itself doth flow like wine.
> Hang up all the poor hop-drinkers,
> Cries old Sam, the king of skinkers.

He the half of life abuses
That sits watering with the Muses,
Those dull gods no good can mean us:
Wine—it is the cream of Venus,
And the poet's horse accounted:
Ply it, and you all are mounted.
'Tis the true Phœbian liquor,
Cheers the brain, makes it the quicker;
Pays all debts, cures all diseases,
And at once the senses pleases.
Welcome all who lead or follow
To the oracle of Apollo."

There is not any reason to believe that Shakspeare, lover of wit and jollity as he was, was a practical upholder of this pernicious doctrine. He may often make his characters speak in this manner, but personally he retired as soon as he could from this bacchanal life to his own quiet hearth at Stratford; and if we are to believe his sonnets addressed to his wife, and they possess the tone of a deep and real sentiment, he seriously rued the orgies in which he had participated.

" O, for my sake do you with Fortune chide,
The guilty goddess of my harmful deeds,
That did not better for my life provide
Than public means which public manners breeds:
Hence comes it that my name receives a brand,
And almost thence my nature is subdued
To what it works in, like the dyer's hand:
Pity me, then, and wish I were renewed.
While, like a willing patient, I will drink
Potions of eyesell,* 'gainst my strong infection.

* Vinegar.

No bitterness that I will bitter think,
    No double penance to correct correction,
Pity me, then, dear friend, and I assure ye
    Even that your pity is enough to cure me."

We cannot read these and many other portions of his
sonnets ; we cannot see Shakspeare retiring every year,
and, as soon as able, altogether from the bacchanalian and
dissipated habits of the literary men of the day, to the
peaceful place of his birth, and the purity of his wedded
home, without respecting his moral character as much as
we admire his genius. The praises and the practice of
drunkenness by literary men, and poets especially, have
entailed infinite mischief on themselves and on their followers. What woes and degradations are connected with
the history of brilliant men about town, which have tended
to stamp the general literary character with the brand of
improvidence and disrespect—jails, deaths, picking out of
gutters, sponging-houses, and domestic misery—how
thickly do all these rise on our view as we look back through
the history of men of genius, the direct result of the absurd
rant about drinking and debauch ! With what a beautiful
purity do the names of the greatest geniuses of all rise
above these details, like the calm spires of churches through .
the fogs and smokes of London ! How cheering is it to
see the number of these grow with the growth of years !
Shakspeare, Spenser, Sidney, Milton, Cowper, Scott,
Wordsworth, Southey, Shelley, have all been sober and domestic men ; and the sanction which they have given by their
practice to the proprieties of life, will confer on all future
ages blessings as ample as the public truth of their teaching. The Mermaid Tavern, like the other haunts of Shak-

speare, has disappeared. It was swept away by the fire. If any traces of his haunts remain, they must be in the houses of the great, where he was accustomed to visit, as those of the Lords Southampton, Leicester, Pembroke, Montgomery and others. These are, however, now all either gone, or so cut up and metamorphosed that it were vain to look for them as abodes hallowed by the footsteps of Shakspeare. If it be true that he was commanded to read his play of Falstaff in love—the Merry Wives of Windsor—to Queen Elizabeth, it would probably be at Whitehall or St. James's, for Somerset House was comparatively little occupied by her.

The very places in London more particularly illustrated by his genius have too much followed the fate of those in which he lived. It is true, the Tower, Westminster Palace, and some other of those public buildings and old localities where the scenes of his national dramas are laid, still remain, spite of time and change; and the sites of others, though now covered with wildernesses of fresh houses, may be identified. But the Boar's Head in East Cheap is annihilated; it, too, fell in the great fire, and the modern improvements thereabout, the erection of New London Bridge, and the cutting of King William-street, have swept away nearly all remaining marks of the neighborhood. It is supposed that the present statue of William IV. stands not very far from the spot where Hal reveled, and Sir John swaggered and drank sack.

Over London, and many a spot in and about it, as well as over a thousand later towns, forests, and mountains, of this and other countries, wherever civilised man has played his part, will the genius of Shakspeare cast an undying glory; but to see the actual traces of his existence we must resort to the place of his nativity and death. There still stand the house and the room in which he was born; there stands the house in which he wooed his Ann Hathaway, and the old garden in which he walked with her. There stands his tomb, to which the great, and the wise, and the gifted from all regions of the world have made pilgrimage, followed by millions of those who would be thought so, the frivolous and the empty; but all paying homage, by the force of reason, or the force of fashion, vanity and imitation, to the universal interpreter of humanity. It is well that the slow change of a country town has permitted the spirit of veneration to alight there, and cast its protecting wings over the earthly traces of that existence which diffused itself as a second life through all the realms of intellect.

There is nothing missing of Shakspeare's there but the house which he built, and the mulberry-tree which he planted. The tree was hewn down, the house was pulled down and dispersed piecemeal, by the infamous parson Gastrell, who thus "damned himself to eternal fame" more thoroughly than the fool who fired the Temple of Diana. There only a few miles distant, is the stately hall of Charlecote, whither the youthful poacher of Parnassus was carried before the unlucky knight. There, too, and, oh shame! shame to England, shame to the lovers of Shakspeare, shame to those who annually turn Stratford and their club into a regular "Eatanswill," on pretence of honoring Shakspeare; there, too, live the descendants of the nearest relative of Shakspeare—of his sister Joan—in unnoticed and unmitigated poverty! Seven years ago, on my visit to this place, I pointed out this fact; and now, that the disgraceful fact still remains, I will once more record the words I then wrote.

"As I went to Shottry, I met with a little incident, which interested me greatly by its unexpectedness. As I was about to pass over a stile, at the end of Stratford, into the fields, leading to that village, I saw the master of the national school mustering his scholars to their tasks. I stopped, being pleased with the look of the old man, and said, "You seem to have a considerable number of lads here; shall you raise another Shakspeare from among them, think you?' 'Why,' replied the master, 'I have a Shakspeare now in the school.' I knew that Shakspeare had no descendants beyond the second generation, and I was not aware that there was any of his family remaining. But it seems that the posterity of his sister, Joan Hart, who is mentioned in his will, yet exist; part under her marriage name of Hart, at Tewkesbury, and a family in Stratford, of the name of Smith.

"'I have a Shakspeare here,' said the master, with evident pride and pleasure. 'Here, boys, here!' He quickly mustered his laddish troop in a row, and said to me, 'There now, sir, can you tell me which is a Shakspeare?' I glanced my eye along the line, and instantly fixing it on one boy, said, 'That is the Shakspeare.' 'You are right,' said the master, 'that is the Shakspeare; the Shakspeare cast of countenance is there. That is William Shakspeare Smith, a lineal descendant of the poet's sister.'

"The lad was a fine lad of, perhaps, ten years of age; and, certainly, the resemblance to the bust of Shakspeare in the church at Stratford is wonderful, considering he is not descended from Shakspeare himself, but from his sister ; and that the seventh in descent. What is odd enough is, whether it be mere accident or not, that the color of the lad's eyes, a light hazel, is the very same as that given to those of the Shakspeare bust, which, it is well known, was originally colored, and of which exact copies remain.

" I gave the boy six-pence, telling him I hoped he would make as great a man as his ancestor—the best term I could lay hold of for the relationship, though not the true one. The boy's eyes sparkled at the sight of the money, and the healthful, joyous color rushed into his cheeks ; his fingers continued making acquaintance with so large a piece of money in his pocket, and the sensation created by so great an event in the school was evident. It sounded oddly enough, as I was passing along the street in the evening, to hear some of the same schoolboys say one to another, ' That is the gentleman who gave Bill Shakspeare six-pence.'

" Which of all the host of admirers of Shakspeare, who has plenty of money, and does not know what to do with it, will think of giving that lad, one of the nearest representatives of the great poet, an education, and a fair chance to raise himself in the world ? The boy's father is a poor man ; if I be not fanciful, partaking somewhat of the Shakspeare physiognomy,* but also keeps a small shop, and ekes out his profits by making his house a ' Tom-and-Jerry.' He has other children, and complained of mis-

* Ireland, when, in 1793, he collected his " Views on the Avon," was much struck with the likeness of this bust in Thomas Hart, one of this family who then lived in Shakspeare's house.

fortune. He said that some years ago Sir Richard Phillips
had been there, and promised to interest the public about
him, but that he never heard any more of it. Of the man's
merits or demerits I know nothing: I only know that in
the place of Shakspeare's birth, and where the town is
full of the 'signs' of his glory; and where Garrick made
that pompous jubilee, hailing Shakspeare as a demi-god,
and calling him 'the god of our idolatry;' and where thousands, and even millions, flock to do homage to the shrine
of this demi-god, and pour out deluges of verse, of the most
extravagant and sentimental nature, in the public albums;
there, as is usual in such cases, the nearest of blood to
the object of such vast enthusiam are poor and despised:
the flood of public admiration, at its most towering height,
in its most vehement current, never for a moment winds
its course in the slightest degree to visit them with its re-
freshment; nor of the thousands of pounds spent in the
practice of this devotion, does one bodle drop into their
pockets."

5   D

A Day at Stratford-on-Avon.

A Day at Stratford-on-Avon.

BY THE REV. THOMAS BRAINERD.

We read travelling sketches as our children play with their kaleidoscopes. Nothing new can be exhibited—but as each revolution of the instrument developes new combinations, so every traveller has his own mode of shadowing forth his recollections. If ambitious of novelty, I should select scenes of miner interest; but sufficient reasons move me to lead the reader to the most familiar spots in Old England—to ground made classic ages ago—to scenes illustrated by the pens of biographers, poets, and philosophers—for the same causes which have consecrated these shrines still exist to create excitement and stimulate curiosity. As the very announcement of the subject stirs a responsive chord in the hearts of all, my task is as easy as that of the Arab who is guiding the caravan towards well-known springs of pure water.

I love Old England! Two hundred years ago my ancestors left her shores, because they there found, according to their convictions, no "Freedom to worship God." But if England finally exiled, she first made the Puritan stock—and where else in Europe could a race of such intelligence and manly virtues have found an origin? The intolerance which exiled the Pilgrims, was an heir-

5

loom of ages, which even the fathers of New England were slow to surrender.

England is Old America—and America, Young England. The national antipathy between the two is a family rivalship. Each is very proud of the other, except when their paths cross; and then is heard a right oldfashioned family scolding—more unrestrained and clamorous from the near relationship of the parties.

During the war of words on "Oregon boundary," I saw stuck up in the windows of London, a caricature of *John Bull and Jonathan.* John was, as usual, a stout, burly, ruby-cheeked old fellow, whose glorious "British Constitution" had been enlarged and invigorated by free indulgence in roast beef and plumb pudding. His hat was set on proudly. His watch-chain dangled ostentatiously from his portly chest. His boots were double-soled, (or, as Mrs. Kirkland pertinently says, "hoof-like,") implying not alone the solid foundation beneath him, but that the impulsive force of his lower extremities was admonitory! He stood bolt upright, with a stout cane in hand, before Jonathan, and gave him a look in which irritation, jealousy, impatience, and pride struggled,—with a little of the relenting and respectful air of relationship and good-will, while he said—"*Boy, will you strike your own daddy ?*"

Jonathan, a tall, overgrown, but well-knit and hardy youngster, was looking up impudently, and flourishing his fist, as if he asked no odds, but had fairly set up for himself. It did my heart good to see even in this caricature that the parental and filial relation was still recognised by British satirists, in those days when the madness of politicians came near involving us in war.

England, yet covetous of dominion, anticipates the growing decline of age, and is querulous. Young America looks forward to her own rising power and final supremacy, and is impertinent and reckless. This is the position of the two nations. I am happy to believe, however, that in both countries, the ties of blood, language, commerce and religion, absorb and annihilate among thousands, the jealousy and alienation which the peculiar condition of the two nations is likely to engender. This is certainly the case with the middle class in England, who have nothing to fear, but much to hope from the example and tendency of our free institutions. I had the honor to address crowded assemblies, and know that no sentiment could enkindle so sudden and rapturous enthusiasm—an enthusiasm which British audiences are not slow to indicate by clapping and shouts—as allusion to the common origin, and the perpetual harmony of England and America—the Anglo-Saxon race of the East and of the West. As an American, my eyes often moistened while crowds before me acknowledged their paternal relation to my countrymen, and their desire for perpetuated good-fellowship. As Americans, we need feel no envy in view of what England, by the growth of a thousand years, *now is*, and we hope that our British brethren will rejoice and not repine at the anticipation of what America is yet *to be*. Her noble achievements in the past are our common heritage ; and in the final elevation which our national youth and opportunities promise, our triumphs will be her victories—our expansion over the continent of the West, the diffusion of her race, her literature, her language, and her religion.

I love to speak thus kindly of Old England—for I have

many a debt of gratitude to discharge for the open-handed
hospitality of her citizens.   To estimate a cordial welcome
in one's own language in a foreign land, one must know
the solitude of a stranger.   An agreeable incident of this
kind occured at Leamington, in Warwickshire, the geo-
graphical centre of England.   My friend, Mr. C—— of
London, was about to spend a week with his friend Mr.
P——, a merchant of Leamington, and invited me to share
in the excursion.   Common sympathies in the cause of
temperance led to our acquaintance, and he persuaded me
to believe that I might be useful as well as pleased by the
jaunt.   It was in August, 1846, when we visited Leamington—and were most hospitably received by his friend,
who, with his family, spared no pains for our entertainment.
This family consisted of Mrs. P—— and some six children.
In systematic arrangement, tidiness, comfort, courtesy,
and unobtrusive but sincere piety, it was a model household—such as may often be found in England.   I felt at
home, and yielded myself delighted to the benevolent plans
adopted for making my visit agreeable.

As is my custom, I first explored Leamington itself.   It
was formerly only a small village, overshadowed by the
pretensions of the more ambitious Warwick and Kenilworth.   The modern tendency to congregate at watering-
places for recreation, has given it an impulse, so that it
has the air of a modern, ruralized city of twenty thousand
inhabitants.   Its hot springs, celebrated for three centuries
past, as well as its contiguity to places made classic by
historical or poetic association, concentrate in winter a
crowd of the aristocracy, whose taste is gratified by all
the conveniences and embellishments deemed essential by

the most fastidious class in Europe.   But it is not of Leamington itself, that I desire to speak.   When the reader is told, that at Leamington he is only three miles from Warwick, six from Kenilworth, and ten from Stratford-on-Avon, he will readily conclude that we found more pleasure in outside excursions, than in the town itself, beautiful and charming though it be.

Our excursion to Stratford-on-Avon was a day to be remembered.   No sun ever rose more beautiful.   And here I will vindicate English weather from scandal, by asserting that for all the month of August, 1846, we had but two rains and no fogs.   Mr. P.—— had arranged that we should travel post, if that term can be applied to a ten miles' journey.   At an early hour our carriage made its appearance.   Its solid heavy aspect, contrasted strangely with the gaudy and monkey-like dress of our postilion. Imagine a fat, animalized man of thirty, with a close-fitted cloth cap, tasseled,—closely fitted and button-bedizened blue jacket—white cravat, and white short-clothes—long, tasseled boots, from which project enormous spurs—and whip in hand, which ever and anon he flourishes with a *coachee* air, and you have our redoubtable postilion.   But to see him in his glory, you must let him mount—and casting a responsible look behind him, apply whip and spur, while he goes bobbing up and down in the saddle, according to the most approved transatlantic model of horsemanship.

Our company consisted of Mr. and Mrs. C——, Mr. and Mrs. P——, myself, and Miss P——, a sweet little maiden of ten summers, who was a pet of the party.   Emerging from town, we entered the vale of the Avon, and near the old castle and town of Warwick we crossed that quiet, classic stream, on a massive and wide bridge. We entered and passed through the gates of Warwick—for that remarkable city has two gates of entrance and departure, but no *walls*. We must not detain the reader at Warwick, because we may make a special pilgrimage to it for his benefit—provided always, we ever fairly bring him to and from Stratford-on-Avon. Leaving Warwick, we had nothing to interrupt the full impression of the rural beauty around us. All along we luxuriated in the vision of the velvet, deep green lawn, peculiar to the British Isles; the well-trimmed hedges chequering the fields, and clustering with flowers and autumnal fruits; the elms, rich in drapery, so thickly planted as to seem forest-like, yet opening here and there to reveal rich pastures, on which cattle and sheep of unsurpassed beauty and thrift were grazing; the road, nicely graded and white with pulverized rock, making a line of silver over hill and dale, before and behind us; the Avon and its little tributaries, now hidden by hills, now indicated only by the livelier green and richer shrubbery fringing their border—and now glancing out, like mirrors, to reflect a summer sun; cottages frequent, always of stone, white-washed and embowered with green; here and there an aristocratic mansion, like its owner, recluse and unapproachable, but sublime in its solitude and frowning magnificence;—this is English scenery, and it is found nowhere else but in Old England. In jaunting amid such scenes, our young dreams of the Fatherland are realized; and to an Anglo-American traveller, romance is made reality.

In England, it would seem that almost every road is a *turnpike*. While John Bull thus levels mountains and ele-

vates valleys to make smooth paths for his subjects, it will
readily be believed that he does not spare their pockets.
But if turnpike gates occur with marvellous frequency in
his dominions, they are not such outlandish bars and posts
as we meet in the United States.   The English enjoy the
enduring public works of past centuries, and when they
build, they build for centuries to come.   An English turnpike gate is a graceful and massive structure, refreshing
to the eye of taste, if not to the vision of avarice.   Its neat
cottage, too, around whose doors and windows ivy creeps
and flowers nestle; its garden with its miniature subdivisions
marked by clipped box; and, above all, its keeper, a little
inflated, as all English, high or low, are with office;—but
not, like the servants of the nobility, having the arrogance
of rank without its courtesy

But I will now bring the reader through these turnpike
gates, which have so impeded his progress.   An hour and
a half of pleasant travelling brought us to the sight of
Stratford-on-Avon.   It is a beautiful town in prospect, as
it quietly reposes on the margin of its classic river, with
its noble church spire piercing the sky.   Its four thousand
inhabitants, like those of all towns thronged by genteel
visitors, have more than an average share of civility of manners, and sharpness in a bargain.   Its chief glory is its
giving birth to Shakspeare;—its chief treasures, his
natal mansion and his sepulchre.   Though it rests beautifully in the vale of the Avon, and unites the venerable-
ness of age with something of the neatness and briskness
of a modern village,—yet separate the great name of
Shakspeare from it, and no one would think it worth a
paragraph.   The citizens feel this.   Boys meet you in ad-

vance with the inquiry, " Will you see the *house ?*" " Shall
I show you to the *church ?*"—assuming that all travellers
are pilgrims to the shrine of Genius.   For this impression
they have abundant reason.   While to them the birthplace
and grave of Shakspeare are commonplace things, they
see strangers, without distinction of nation, rank, or sex,
possessed by a common enthusiasm on this classic ground.
Kings, Queens, Princes, Nobles, Hierarchs, Statesmen,
Philosophers, Poets, and Theologians, here bow with profound reverence before the majesty of the great creative
intellect which has thrown its scintillations broadcast
over the earth.   Nor is their interest more intense, nor
their devotion more sincere than that of tradesmen, me-
chanics, and rustic laborers, who mingle gratitude with
their admiration of one who, rising from their own level,
beat down all accidental distinctions in his way to greatness, and retained, in the eye of the world, the simple
habits, the love of nature and of man, which he bore from
his native village.

Milton, Pope, Dryden, Cowper, Scott, Wordsworth,
Coleridge, Southey, Moore, and Byron, have each roused
an enthusiastic admiration, and had devoted worshippers.
But world-wide and enduring as the influence of each has
been and is, it has been limited to certain classes.   It has
given rise to poetic schools and cliques, and elicited literary affinities and antipathies.   Each has been worshipped
and hated—adored and despised, according to the mental
structure, education, taste and character of those who have
sat in judgment.   Not so with Shakspeare.   Trained at
the feet of no literary or poetic Gamaliel, he had no master to imitate ; and writing with no ambition or expectation

of fame, he stretched himself to the "iron bed" of no clique, class, or faction.   His perception of "what was in man," seemed to be almost intuitive, and has never been surpassed on earth, save by Him, the Infinite—with whom to compare the finite, would be irreverent presumption.   A poet by nature, and great by endowment rather than human instruction, he bowed to no earthly authority—but, like a spirit of another world, above human partialities, wrote not for a class, but a race.   When the nature of the subject allowed it, he diverges from the strict claims of the matter in hand, to utter grand moral principles, which have been made the proverbs of moralists and merchants, of statesmen and soldiers, of poets and ploughmen.   The fact that his eye penetrated every strata of society—that he felt the universal pulse of human passion, and enriched universal human nature, accounts for the common affection and enthusiasm with which he is regarded.   He not only is not the property of a class, but no nation nor age can claim him.   His memory is the treasure of his race.   If it be suggested that his writings are exceptionable in reverence for sacred names, and often indelicate—it is only saying that he adapted himself to the object he had in view, and to the standard morality and taste of his age.   In his period, a dramatist would feel himself justified in adopting for the stage expressions not then deemed improper for the lips of bishops and queens.   We must hold him responsible for the taste of his own times, not ours—and may well marvel, that one who wrote professedly only for the *amusement* of mankind, strewed the path of pleasure with gems of sober and enduring truth.

But enough of digression.   We have not yet reached

6

Stratford-on-Avon. Indeed, we are in danger of imitating the New York Dutchman, so facetiously described by Washington Irving, who ran a long way to get an impulse to leap a wall, but when he reached it was out of breath, and *crawled* over it.

On arriving at Stratford, we were driven at once to the house where Shakspeare was born, and having alighted, and ordered the carriage to the " *Red Horse Hotel*," took a survey of the premises. It is the only ancient house in its block. All the others are modern erections, towering above it, and rendering its antique peculiarity more striking. It is two stories in height, and low at that. In its erection, like some ancient houses among our early Germans, a frame was first put up, and then filled in with stone and mortar—still leaving the timber visible, like a rough mosaic. Its windows are venerably small—but the panes of glass redeem in number what they lack in size, so that some light actually enters the interstices of the huge sash. The lower window, by the side of the door, is without sash or glass, but longitudinal in its position, and furnished with a trap-door opening outward, on which a butcher exhibits his meat on market days. If the expression be not Hibernian, I would say that the lower rooms are *floored* with stone—which is about as even and beautiful as the first stone paving of a city in Iowa, or Wisconsin ; and though it may give a prosaic chill to the poetic admirers of the great Bard, the truth must out, that the house where Shakspeare was born is a *meat-shop!* If any consolation is available for this, it may be found in rejoicing that it is no worse. I entered the house at Ayr, where *Robert Burns* drew his first breath, and found it a *dram-shop!*—filled with those who resembled " Scotia's sweetest bard" only in the habit which injured his character and happiness, health and life.   The only other room on the ground floor of the Shakspeare house, is used as a kitchen for the widow and daughter who claimed proprietorship of the mansion.   The back chamber, on what we call the second floor, and Englishmen the first floor, was the dormitory.   The front chamber of this story—the Shakspeare birthplace, specifically—is the family parlour. Since the poet's time, it has passed through many hands. Of its original furniture nothing remains—though its place has been supplied with articles of like age.   A visitor is amazed at the lowness of the ceiling, which allows men of ordinary stature to reach and write their names on it. The room never had any paper ; but this was fortunate— as it has given thousands an opportunity to aspire to immortality, by there inscribing their names.   Above, around, all over, every inch is covered with autographs of visitors. You may be sure the Yankees are fairly represented.   It is amusing to see, indicated by various tricks of chirography, an effort to make a name "stand out from the mass." Our cicerone seemed to regard the great majority as an incumbrance, but she took much pride in pointing to some royal signatures.   This place must be a paradise to autograph hunters.

The *Album* is an old book, "tattered and torn," but still legible.   It has many impromptu effusions, among which that of Wasington Irving is regarded as the best, not only from its originality, but because it is richly spiced with the laudation so grateful to English ears.   It is free from a vice most prominent in many of these effusions, an

effort to magnify one's self while professing to laud Shakspeare.

It is said that the *earthly* immortality of those who have
inscribed their autographs on these walls, was once put in.
fearful jeopardy. A female tenant, who had long enjoyed
the profits of this show-room, unwilling to pay an increased
rent, was warned to leave the premises. She devised a
right feminine but most Vandal scheme of vengeance.
Having hired another house, to which she conveyed the
Album, and all the Shakspeare relics, she next took a
brush, and if not " at one fell swoop," by repeated appli-
ances covered the whole with a coat of whitewash ! Those
victimised by this ebullition of feminine anger, might well
say,

> "Absurd to think to overreach the [*brush*],
> And from the wreck of names to rescue ours."

They passed away,

> " Like the baseless fabric of a vision,
> Leaving no [*scratch*] behind."

What her successor said on first entering the denuded
and blank apartment, history does not tell us; perhaps
because none but the great Bard himself could depict her
rage. But thanks to the progress of science, some Oxonian,
or somebody else, gave her a chemical solvent, which
removed the villanous lime, and released the imprisoned
names of these Shakspearian martyrs from their tempo-
rary eclipse.

> "I tell the tale as 'twas told to me!"

This house formerly had a great rival. It is known when
Shakspeare returned from London, in the height of his

fame, and moderately rich, he fitted for his residence a large and beautiful edifice, in which to spend the remainder of life. This, in contrast with the old mansion, was called the *New House*. As this was the chosen abode of the dramatist, and bore in all its internal and external arrangements and decorations the impress of his mature taste; as here he held intercourse with the wits of his day, and the troops of friends whom his genius and fame had attracted; as here he lived and here had died, this house was justly the pride of his native village and the shrine of his admiring countrymen. In process of time it became the *Manse*—the property of the incumbent rector. He quarrelled with the inhabitants of the village, and on removing from town, in order to mortify his old parishioners, deliberately tore down, utterly demolished, and annihilated Shakspeare's *New House*. Pity that some one had not suggested to the wrathful and revengeful parson, the old admonition of sacred writ: "Rend your heart and not your garments,"—nor your *house!* But no considerations of his sacred profession; no desire to perpetuate the mind of Shakspeare, as he had inscribed it in the plan and ornaments of his dwelling; no reverence for objects enshrined in the hearts of his countrymen; no fear of the curses of future generations, restrained his ruthless hand. Over all, his wrath triumphed. "Hoc censeo *domum*, esse delendum," was his word, and the house was demolished. Like Eratostratus, Jack Ketch, Guy Fawkes, and Judas Iscariot, he has made himself to be remembered. Perhaps this was his object, and if so, we have aided his purpose by introducing his malicious outrage to the attention of our readers.

6 *   E

While the world was execrating the demolition of the
New House, no doubt, if the truth were known, the owner
of the *old* house (the birthplace) secretly congratulated
himself that its rivalry was ended.   As an illustration of
the increasing wealth of the times, and of augmented
regard for the great poet, the old house, which had once
been sold for £250, is now held at £4000.   Our cicerone,
the daughter of the owner, told us that at the death of her
mother, it was to be sold, and she hoped to get £4000 for
it.   Her mother has since died, and the daughter has
disposed of it to an association of contributors, who, to
prevent its demolition or decay, united to purchase it.   It
is now beyond the reach of private cupidity or caprice, in
the custody of the friends of literature.   The world owes
to this association its gratitude.   May the *Old House* stand
a thousand years !

Our next pilgrimage was to the school-house where
Shakspeare received his education.   It is a large apartment with a low ceiling, miserably lighted, and worse
ventilated.   It is paved with stone laid on the bare earth.
Its benches or forms are of the rudest construction, and
would be by no means out of place in a western camp-
meeting.   About thirty right English boys were present,
with their demure looks and cherry cheeks, who tried ex-
periments on optics in our presence to see if they could
seem to study their books, while in reality they watched us.
The place derives its main interest from the fact that
to this humble place Shakspeare came—

> " The whining schoolboy,
> With his satchel and shining morning face,
> Creeping like snail unwillingly to school."

After what I have said of the place, his "*unwillingness*" is not surprising.

Our next visit was to the church, in the chancel of which the Poet was buried. This edifice is a Gothic structure, of great magnitude and beauty, surrounded by a large yard, studded with graves and monuments. It is approached by an avenue, about thirty rods in length, of lime trees, which have been bent, clipped, and trained, until they form a perfect arch, with a green and rustling but well-defined roof, about three feet in thickness. We have nothing like it in the United States. Forming a sweep around the churchyard, is the Avon, to whose edge it extends. The bank, about fifteen feet high, is protected by a perpendicular wall, which rises about two feet above the level of the yard, forming a most charming terrace in the interior, from which the whole vale for a great distance, up and down the stream, is brought under the eye. This terrace is the most charming spot in Stratford. Here, seated on the wide wall—our feet hanging over the stream, the old church lending its shade—our lady friends opened their treasures, and regaled us with *sandwiches*. This is characteristic. An American party would have bespoken a *good dinner* at the "*Red Horse.*" The English of the highest rank are economists on the road. And besides this, their solitary, exclusive, and fastidious modes, make them reluctant to mingle with the crowd in hotels. At the hazard of being thought deficient in Shakspearian enthusiasm, I must say our *sandwiches* had a fine relish. Our hospitable friends, perhaps, were mindful that

> " You take my life, when you do take
> The means whereby I live."

Hence they were careful to provide "visible means of support" for the excursion.

The old church is the very one where Shakspeare worshipped. The old Bible, formerly attached by a chain to the reading desk, that parishioners, having none of their own, might read, but not abstract it, is still kept, chain and all, in the vestry. Its chain indicates a period when the sacred volume was inaccessible to those who have the most need of its consolations; and it illustrates the blessedness of the press, and those associations which have *unchained* the Bible, and made Heaven's truth as free and universal as Heaven's air.

The monument of Shakspeare, attached to the wall, is an object so beautiful and unique, that I desire to give to others the pleasure which it afforded me, and therefore have furnished a drawing of it to the reader.

His dust is covered by a single flat stone in the chancel. An effort was once made to remove his bones to Westminster Abbey. Never was a town in such an uproar. The abstraction of the sacred relics from St. Peter's in Rome would agitate less the good Catholics of the Eternal City. The proposition outraged at once the romance, ambition, poetic veneration, and avarice of all classes. The clergy preached against it as a sacrilege; the lawyers declared it illegal; the hotel-keepers, hack-drivers, and porters, the shopmen and milliners, if they could not make a show of argument, disclosed a disposition to guard the grave of their great townsman by show of physical force—of clubs and fists. Whatever secret influence might have slept under the surface, prompting a zeal like that which protected "Diana of the Ephesians," the great

argument was that *Shakspeare himself had forbidden it.*
Whether he distrusted his neighbours, who had exiled him
in youth for deer-stealing, or whether he dreamed of a
glorious fame which would invest his bones with interest,
it matters not, he had caused to be inscribed on the flat
stone which covers his ashes the following couplet, tran-
scribed verbatim:

> " Good Friend, for JESVS sake forbeare
> To digg T-E dvst EncloAsed HERE
>
> Blest be T-E Man $\frac{T}{Y}$ Spares ᛏ-hs Stones,
>
> And cvrst be He $\frac{T}{Y}$ moves my bones."

The Poet's curse, his townsmen averred, would light
upon them, if they suffered his bones to be removed, even
to Westminster Abbey. The Londoners had with them,
perhaps, the argument. Where should the great Poet
rest but with England's mightiest dead? But the Strat-
fordians had *possession*—and interest and force to retain
it. For once the great Metropolis had to surrender. All
the influence of aristocracy, wealth, great names, and
even good intentions, were powerless, before an aroused
rustic community, determined to resist, if need be, by
force. The plan was abandoned; but one influence of
that discussion still remains. The rustic population are
afraid to put their feet on the tombstone, lest they should
incur the malediction of disturbing their Poet's bones.
They will thus protect his epitaph, which had become
almost illegible. This is as it should be. The village to
which Providence gave the birth of Shakspeare, and to

which his own simple affections led him back in the prime of manhood, to find a home, rest, and a grave, has a right to retain his ashes.

But I may not protract this article. We remained at Stratford until late in the afternoon; and as the lengthened shadows began to throw a pensiveness over the landscape, returned leisurely to Leamington. The sole alloy to my recollection of that day, is in the fact that the only Americans whom I met at Stratford, were the Rev. Dr. Hopkins, of Buffalo, N. Y., and his lady. My friends invited them to spend the evening with us at Leamington, and it passed pleasantly away. I saw them, full of hope, leave in the morning by coach for Blenheim and Oxford. And I shall see them no more! Mrs. H. died on the homeward passage, and her husband also now sleeps in death.

My recollections of Stratford-on-Avon are mingled with musings of sadness, that two of those who shared with me in its excitements—and who united with an admiration of genius and poetry, the holiest purposes and most affluent charity, have passed from a world which they longed and labored to bless. With the exception of a reminiscence so painful, I recall my excursion to Stratford-on-Avon with the liveliest pleasure. May I hope that I have shared in a slight degree this pleasure with my readers.

Shakspeare's Minor Poems.

Shakspeare's Minor Poems.

BY PROF. JOHN S. HART.

To the observer of our literary history one object ever
stands proudly eminent—an object not unlike the Pyramid
of Cheops—which, whether you go up or down the Nile,
whether you penetrate its rich valley from the east over the
sand-hills of Arabia, or from the west across the trackless
desert of Zahara—from whatever quarter you approach—
is the first object to strike, the last to recede from the vision.
So it is with the object which we have indicated. Whether we
approach it travelling backward from the names of Wordsworth and Coleridge, and Byron and Scott, or descend towards the same point from Cædmon, Chaucer, Sidney, and
Spenser—whether we cross the current of our literature
by a transition from that of France or Germany, the
Norseland or the South of Europe—from whatever quarter
of the literary horizon we direct our gaze towards the point
indicated—one name rises spontaneously on every tongue—
the greatest name in all English, in all modern, perhaps I
may say absolutely, in *all* literature. Shakspeare may
possibly not be read as much now as he once was. The
time will come, I believe, when he will be read still less.
But he is studied all the more. His fame is steadily in

the ascendant. It is confessedly higher now than it was at the beginning of the present century. It has made a perceptible rise even within the last ten years.

The minor poems of Shakspeare, besides the Sonnets, are the Passionate Pilgrim, the Lover's Complaint, Venus and Adonis, and the Rape of Lucrece.

The Passionate Pilgrim was first published in 1599. It is not, like the other three that have been named, a connected poem, but a name given to a small collection of Sonnets and Songs on various subjects, but mostly of a passionate character. The publisher had evidently found these pieces circulating in manuscript, and proposed to profit by the rising reputation of the author by collecting them into a small volume for sale. He made however many extraordinary mistakes, such indeed as to prove incontestably the surreptitious character of the publication. Several of the pieces in the collection were ascertained afterwards not to be Shakspeare's, but the work of different authors. Some appear elsewhere as parts of other works of Shakspeare's. Others, that do not appear elsewhere, and that may reasonably be accepted as Shakspeare's, are yet not of a character to entitle them to much consideration. On the whole, therefore, the collection is of little value, and need not be farther noticed.

The Lover's Complaint was originally published as an appendix to the Sonnets. This was the case in the original edition of 1609, and in the second edition of 1640. They are generally so printed now. This however is merely an incidental connection, adopted originally probably for bookselling convenience, and followed since from custom. There is no connection in form or subject. The

Lover's Complaint is a continuous narrative poem, in the seven-line stanza or Rhythm Royal of Chaucer and the elder poets. This was the favorite stanza, particularly for romantic poetry, through the fourteenth, fifteenth, and sixteenth centuries. It is a modification of the Italian ottava rima, and an evident improvement upon it. Chaucer, who first domesticated, if he did not invent it, has written in this form the Court of Love, Troilus and Creseida, the Complaint of the Black Knight, the Flower and the Leaf, besides four of his Canterbury Tales. Spenser used it also in the Ruins of Time and the Hymns of Love and Beauty. The capabilities of this stanza for poetical effect, with all due deference to the craft, have not been sufficiently considered by our living poets. But to return.

Of incident in the Lover's Complaint there is very little, almost nothing—less even that in Longfellow's Kavanagh, of which so many have complained, because forsooth the author was better advised than to make a shilling novel for the newsboys. The poem, in fact, though narrative in its form, is chiefly speculative and intro-versive. The story is of a female, now past the meridian of life, who had been deceived and deserted in youth. She is described as a half-crazed being, with some remains of beauty and of comely apparel still cleaving to her, sitting alone on the margin of a gentle streamlet, bewailing in melancholy tones her sad history.

The story opens with the following scene. The poet represents himself as reclining upon a gentle hill, listening to the echo from a "sistering" vale. The echo thus brought to his ears was a "plaintful" story, which on directing his eyes thither, he found to proceed from the half-crazed person already described.

7 *

" From off a hill whose concave womb rewarded
　A plaintful story from a sistering vale,
　My spirits to attend this double voice accorded,
　And down I laid to list the sad-tuned tale:
　Ere long espied a fickle maid full pale,
　Tearing of papers, breaking rings a-twain,
　Storming her world with sorrow's wind and rain.

" Upon her head a platted hive of straw,
　Which fortified her visage from the sun,
　Whereon the thought might think sometime it saw
　The carcase of a beauty spent and done.
　Time had not scythed all that youth begun,
　Nor youth all quit; but, spite of heaven's fell rage,
　Some beauty peeped through lattice of seared age.

" Oft did she heave her napkin* to her eyne,
　Which on it had conceited characters,†
　Laund'ring‡ the silken figures in the brine
　That seasoned wo had pelleted§ in tears,
　And often reading what contents it bears,
　As often shrieking undistinguished wo,
　In clamours of all size, both high and low.

" Sometime her levelled eyes their carriage ride,
　As they did battery to the spheres intend:
　Sometime diverted their poor balls are tyed
　To the orbed earth; sometime they do extend
　Their view right on; anon their gazes lend
　To every place at once, and nowhere fixed,
　The mind and sight distractedly commixed.

" Her hair, nor loose, nor tied in formal plat,
　Proclaimed in her a careless hand of pride;
　For some, untuck'd, descended her sheav'd‖ hat,

* *Napkin*, handkerchief.　　　† *Conceited characters*, fanciful figures.
‡ *Laund'ring*, washing.　　§ *Pelleted*, formed into pellets or small balls.
‖ *Sheaved*, made of straw collected from sheaves.
　7 *

Hanging her pale and pined cheek beside;
Some in her threaden fillet still did bide,
And, true to bondage, would not break from thence,
Though slackly braided in loose negligence.

"A thousand favours from a maund* she drew,
Of amber, crystal, and of bedded jet,
Which one by one she in a river threw,
Upon whose weeping margent she was set;
Like usury, applying wet to wet,
Or monarch's hands, that let not bounty fall
Where want cries 'some,' but where excess begs all.

"Of folded schedules had she many a one,
Which she perused, sigh'd, tore, and gave the flood:
Crack'd many a ring of poised gold and bone,
Bidding them find their sepulchres in mud:
Found yet more letters sadly penned in blood,
With sleided silk feat and affectedly
Enswathed, and sealed to curious secrecy.

"These often bathed she in her fluxive eyes,
And often kissed, and often 'gan to tear:
Cried, O false blood! thou register of lies,
What unapproved witness dost thou bear!
Ink would have seemed more black and damned here!
This said, in top of rage the lines she rents,
Big discontent so breaking their contents."

At this point an incident occurs, if incident it may be
called, the only one in the poem. An aged man of venerable aspect approaches. He had been in early life a
courtier, but had retired to the green fields to spend the
quiet close of life, a simple herdsman. From the neighboring fields he observed the strange conduct and appear-

* *Maund*, basket.

ance of this half-crazed female. His gentle manner and his reverend age win her confidence, and he draws from her the story of her wrongs.

> " So slides he down upon his grained bat,
>   And comely-distant sits he by her side ;
>   When he again desires, being sat,
>   Her grievance with his hearing to divide :
>   If that from him there may be aught applied
>   Which may her suffering ecstacy assuage;
>   'Tis promised in the charity of age."

Thus invited she recounts to him the story of her grief. It is the old story.   But when, before or since, was it told with such perfection of beauty ?   Listen to her description of her youthful lover.

> " His browny locks did hang in crooked curls,
>   And every light occasion of the wind
>   Upon his lips their silken parcels hurls.
>   What's sweet to do, to do will aptly find :
>   Each eye that saw him, did enchant the mind ;
>   For on his visage was, in little drawn,
>   What largeness thinks in paradise was sawn.*

> " Small show of man was yet upon his chin ;
>   His phœnix down began but to appear,
>   Like unshorn velvet, on that termless skin,
>   Whose bare out-bragged the web it seemed to wear ;
>   Yet showed his visage by that cost more dear ;
>   And nice affections wavering stood in doubt
>   If best 'twere as it was, or best without.

> " His qualities were beauteous as his form,
>   For maiden-tongued he was, and thereof free ;
>   Yet if men moved him, was he such a storm,

---

* *Sawn*, sown (Boswell), or seen (Malone).

As oft 'twixt May and April is to see,
When winds breathe sweet, unruly though they be,
His rudeness so with his authorized youth,
Did livery falseness in a pride of truth.

"Well could he ride, and often men would say,
  'That horse his mettle from his rider takes;
Proud of subjection, noble by the sway,
  What rounds, what bounds, what course, what stop he makes.'
And controversy hence a question takes,
  Whether the horse by him became his deed,
  Or he his manage by the well-doing steed.

"But quickly on his side the verdict went,
  His real habitude gave life and grace
To appertainings and to ornament,
  Accomplished in himself, not in his case:
All aids, themselves made fairer by their place,
  Came for additions; yet their purposed trim
  Pierced not his grace, but were all graced by him.

"So, on the tip of his subduing tongue
  All kind of arguments and question deep,
All replication prompt, and reason strong,
  For his advantage still did wake and sleep:
To make the weeper laugh, the laugher weep,
  He had the dialect and different skill,
  Catching all passions in his craft and will;

"That he did in the general bosom reign
  Of young, of old; of sexes both enchanted,
To dwell with him in thoughts, or to remain
  In personal duty, following where he haunted:
Consents bewitched, ere he desire, have granted;
  And dialogued for him what he would say,
  Asked their own wills and made their wills obey.

F

" Many there were that did his picture get,
  To serve their eyes, and in it put their mind;
  Like fools that in their imagination set
  The goodly objects which abroad they find
  Of lands and mansions, their's in thought assigned;
  And labouring in more pleasures to bestow them,
  Than the true gouty landlord which doth owe them:

" So many have, that never touched his hand,
  Sweetly supposed them mistress of his heart.
  My woful self, that did in freedom stand,
  And was my own fee-simple, (not in part)
  What with his art in youth, and youth in art,
  Threw my affections in his charmed power,
  Reserved the stalk, and gave him all my flower."

The sad maiden goes on then to describe the various
arts by which her affections and her confidence had been
won, and ends her woful tale with the following genuine
touch of nature.

" Who, young and simple, would *not* be so lovered?
  Ah me! I fell; and yet, do question make
  What I should do again for such a sake.

" O, that infected moisture of his eye,
  O, that false fire which in his cheek so glowed,
  O that forced thunder from his heart did fly,
  O that sad breath his spongy lungs bestowed,
  O all that borrowed motion (seeming owed),
  Would yet again betray the love-betrayed,
  And new pervert the reconciled maid!"

The single and particular beauties in this poem are as
numerous as the lines, almost as the words. It has been

my object rather to give to readers who may not be familiar with the poem—am I wrong in supposing there are such?—some general impression of the character of the poem as a whole.

Shakspeare calls his Venus and Adonis " the first heir of his invention." I have seen no sufficient reason why we should not take this expression in its obvious import. If so, the poem is to be regarded as the author's first and earliest literary performance. There seems indeed but little doubt that it was composed on the sweet banks of the Avon, and before the author had left Stratford for the great metropolis. The poem has about it all the freshness of country air, all the warmth of youthful passion.

It is founded upon a well-known Grecian legend. That imaginative people invented for almost every abstract mental idea some material and concrete symbol, for every emotion and passion of the soul some graceful tale of life and action. Grecian fable is only Grecian logic, Grecian science Grecian opinion personified. Among the ideas thus embodied in action are two that seem to be in some respects the counterparts of each other, although this correlation, so far as I am aware, has not been heretofore observed. As was Diana among women, so was Adonis among men—each having every perfection except that which is most characteristic. The same inventive fancy, which formed the idea of a woman possessed of every gracious and womanly quality except the desire to be acceptable to the other sex, conceived also the idea of a man, in all respects manly and noble, beautiful and brave, but utterly and absolutely indifferent to what is after all man's ruling passion. The Adonis of early Græcia was simply a passionless boy. He was one who could love a woman only as he loved his sister, his mother, or his brother. It was not guile, used to decoy more victims. It was not affectation, to hide the real state of his heart. It was not vanity, to show his own importance by apparently contemning that which others prized so highly. It was simply sheer, absolute indifference. Love, in the special application of that term, was to him a thing unintelligible, He could form no more idea of it, than can a blind man of colors, or a deaf man of sounds, or a cherub of the feelings of humanity. Yet was never cherub more beautiful or more enchanting. The flush of health was on his cheek, the pride of intellect was on his brow, the strength of manhood was in his arm. Such was the Adonis of the graceful and imaginative Greek; such, with disagreeable abatements and additions, was the Syrian Thammuz, worshipped with foul and disgusting rites by the daughters of Israel during the degenerate days of the later prophets.

Numberless are the incidents framed by the poets out of this general idea. The most common is that celebrated by Shakspeare in the present poem. It is briefly this. Venus, the Goddess of female beauty, becomes enamored of the beautiful boy, but her admiration is not returned; he forsakes her for the more congenial sports of the chase, where he is killed by a wild boar, leaving her to lament in bitter wailings his untimely fate. Such is an outline of the story. In the main incidents and in the leading idea, there is nothing original. All the creative power is in the filling up. Here the poet distances all competitors, ancient or modern. The various scenes are painted with

a distinctness—a sort of visibility—not surpassed even by
Spenser, while there is throughout a compactness and
force of expression of which Spenser was entirely incapable.   The actors stand out to the mind's eye with all
the distinctness of a group of statuary.

One peculiarity, first observed I believe by Coleridge,
is worthy of note.   The poem is not marked by stirring
action, but by a series of minutely finished pictures.   In
other words, it is descriptive, not dramatic.   Yet the
character of these descriptions is precisely that which
would indicate the possession of the dramatic power
Drama is action.   That the action may be consistent and
suitable, the dramatist while composing must have the
actors and the scene of action most vividly and palpably
before his own mind.   He must be present to every scene
and every soul, as really as though he were at the moment
actually on the stage, surrounded by the characters whom
he has summoned into existence.   He must therefore
have the power of conception in the highest degree.   The
fact to be noted is, that this power is equally shown in
the Venus and Adonis.   In other words, a poem essen-
tially and characteristically undramatic evinces at the
same time the possession of high dramatic power.   The
pictures given to the reader in the poem are such as must
be ever present to the mind's eye of the poet while writing
a drama.   Shakspeare's descriptions in his Venus and
Adonis raise in our minds just such scenes as I suppose
always existed in his own mind while putting language
into the mouth of his dramatic characters.

The scene in which the horse of Adonis breaks loose
from him may be cited in illustration of this peculiarity:

8

"Imperiously he leaps, he neighs, he bounds,
And now his woven girths he breaks asunder,
The bearing earth with his hard hoof he wounds,
Whose hollow womb resounds like heaven's thunder:
   The iron bit he crushes 'tween his teeth,
   Controlling what he was controlled with.

" His ears up-pricked ; his braided hanging mane
Upon his compassed crest now stands on end ;
His nostrils drink the air, and forth again,
As from a furnace, vapours doth he send :
   His eye, which glistens scornfully like fire,
   Shows his hot courage and his high desire.

" Sometimes he trots, as if he told the steps,
With gentle majesty, and modest pride ;
Anon he rears upright, curvets, and leaps,
As who should say, lo! thus my strength is tried ;
   And thus I do to captivate the eye
   Of the fair breeder that is standing by.

" What recketh he his rider's angry stir,
His flattering ' holla,' or his ' stand, I say ?'
What cares he now for curb, or pricking spur ?
For rich caparisons, or trappings gay ?
   He sees his love, and nothing else he sees,
   For nothing else with his proud sight agrees.

" Look, when a painter would surpass the life,
In limning out a well-proportioned steed,
His art with nature's workmanship at strife,
As if the dead the living should exceed ;
   So did this horse excel a common one,
   In shape, in courage, colour, pace, and bone.

" Round-hoof'd, short-jointed, fetlocks shag and long,
Broad breast, full eyes, small head, and nostril wide,
High crest, short ears, straight legs, and passing strong,
Thin mane, thick tail, broad buttock, tender hide :
   Look, what a horse should have, he did not lack,
   Save a proud rider on so proud a back.

" Sometimes he scuds far off, and there he stares ;
  Anon he starts at stirring of a feather ;
  To bid the wind a chase he now prepares,
  And whêr he run or fly, they know not whether ;
     For through his mane and tail the high wind sings,
     Fanning the hairs, who wave like feather'd wings."

The accuracy of Shakspeare's descriptions has lately
received a very striking illustration.   A few years since
there was published in London a volume, entitled " Essays
and Sketches of Character, by the late Richard Ayton,
Esq."   These essays contain, among other things, a paper
on hare-hunting.   It is curious to observe the similarity
between the descriptions of this professed hare-hunter,
and those of the poet, even when the latter are most
highly idealized.

" She (the hare) generally returns to the seat from which she
was put up, running, as all the world knows, in a circle, or something sometimes like it. . .   At starting, she tears away at her
utmost speed for a mile or more, and distances the dogs halfway :
she then returns, diverging a little to the right or left, that she may
not run into the mouths of her enemies—a necessity which accounts
for what is called the circularity of her course.   Her flight from
home is direct and precipitate ; but on her way back, when she has
gained a little time for consideration and stratagem, she describes
a curious labyrinth of short turnings and windings, as if to perplex
the dogs by the intricacy of her track."

Shakspeare says:

" And when thou hast on foot the purblind hare,
  Mark the poor wretch, to overshoot his troubles,
  How he outruns the wind, and with what care
  He cranks and crosses, with a thousand doubles :
     The many musits through the which he goes
     Are like a labyrinth to amaze his foes."

Mr. Ayton:

"The hounds, whom we left in full cry, continue their music without remission as long as they are faithful to the scent; as a summons it should seem, like the seaman's cry, to pull together, or keep together, and it is a certain proof to themselves and their followers that they are in the right way: on the instant that they are ' at fault,' or lose the scent, they are silent. . . The weather, in its impression on the scent, is the great father of ' faults;' but they may arise from other accidents, even when the day is in every respect favourable. The intervention of ploughed land, on which the scent soon cools or evaporates, is at least perilous; but sheep-stains, recently left by a flock, are fatal: they cut off the scent irrecoverably—making a gap, as it were, in the clue, in which the dogs have not even a hint for their guidance."

Shakspeare:

"Sometime he runs among a flock of sheep,
　To make the cunning hounds mistake their smell,
And sometimes where earth-delving conies keep,
　To stop the loud pursuers in their yell;
　　And sometime sorteth with a herd of deer;
　　Danger deviseth shifts; wit waits on fear.

"For there his smell with others being mingled,
　The hot scent-snuffing hounds are driven to doubt,
Ceasing their clamorous cry till they have singled
　With much ado the cold fault cleanly out;
　　Then do they spend their mouths: Echo replies,
　　As if another chase were in the skies."

Mr. Ayton:

"Suppose then, after the usual rounds, that you see the hare at last (a sorry mark for so many foes) sorely beleaguered—looking dark and draggled, and limping heavily along; then stopping to listen, again tottering on a little, and again stopping: and at every step, and every pause, hearing the death-cry grow nearer and louder."

Shakspeare :

"By this, poor Wat, far off upon a hill,
   Stands on his hinder legs with listening ear,
   To hearken if his foes pursue him still;
   Anon their loud alarums he doth hear;
      And now his grief may be compared well
      To one sore-sick, that hears the passing bell.

"Then shalt thou see the dew-bedabbled wretch
   Turn and return, indenting with the way;
   Each envious briar his weary legs doth scratch,
   Each shadow makes him stop, each murmur stay:
      For misery is trodden on by many,
      And being low never relieved by any."

Adonis, regardless of the entreaties of the Goddess of
Love, goes forth to pursue the wild boar. By accident,
while in close pursuit, he fell from his horse and was
overrun by the ferocious beast. The protruding tusk of
the "grim, urchin-snouted boar," penetrated the groin
of the beauteous boy, and killed him outright, goring him
horribly. The anguish and distraction of Venus on
seeing his mangled body, is another of those striking
pictures with which the poem abounds.

"She looks upon his lips, and they are pale,
   She takes him by the hand, and that is cold;
   She whispers in his ears a heavy tale,
   As if they heard the woful words she told;
      She lifts the coffer-lids that close his eyes,
      Where, lo! two lamps, burnt out, in darkness lies."

Passion always exaggerates. The spectator of a tragedy
may be accurate and precise; the actor never. In wo, or
rage, no man stops to measure his words, or correct his

8*

images.   The boldest metaphors in his mouth seem tame;
forced and even artificial comparisons become natural.
They indicate an excited, an unnatural, an "artificial"
state of mind.   They are the efforts of a drowning man
grasping at straws.   No one ever understood this principle
better than Shakspeare.   When Venus sees the flowers
and grass drenched in the blood of Adonis, they seem to
her to be bleeding in "sympathy," or to have "stolen"
the precious drops.   Indeed, the whole scene describing
the lament of Venus over the dead body of Adonis is
exquisitely beautiful.   Every line shows the hand of a
master.

> "No flower was nigh, no grass, herb, leaf, or weed,
>   But stole his blood, and seem'd with him to bleed.

> "This solemn sympathy poor Venus noteth;
>   Over one shoulder doth she hang her head;
>   Dumbly she passions, frantickly she doteth:
>   She thinks he could not die, he is not dead.
>   Her voice is stopped, her joints forget to bow;
>   Her eyes are mad that they have wept till now.

> "Upon his hurt she looks so steadfastly,
>   That her sight dazzling makes the wound seem three;
>   And then she reprehends her mangling eye,
>   That makes more gashes where no breach should be;
>   His face seems twain, each several limb is doubled,
>   For oft the eye mistakes, the brain being troubled.

> "'My tongue cannot express my grief for one,
>   And yet,' quoth she, 'behold two Adons dead!
>   My sighs are blown away, my salt tears gone,
>   Mine eyes are turned to fire, my heart to lead:
>   Heavy heart's lead melt at mine eyes, as fire
>   So shall I die by drops of hot desire.

"'Alas, poor world, what treasure hast thou lost!
What face remains alive that's worth the viewing?
Whose tongue is music now? what canst thou boast
Of things long since, or any thing ensuing?
        The flowers are sweet, their colors fresh and trim:
        But true-sweet beauty lived and died with him.

"'Bonnet nor veil henceforth no creature wear!
Nor sun, nor wind will ever strive to kiss you:
Having no fair to lose, you need not fear;
The sun doth scorn you, and the wind doth hiss you.
        But when Adonis lived, sun and sharp air
        Lurk'd live two thieves to rob him of his fair;

"'And therefore would he put his bonnet on,
Under whose brim the gaudy sun would peep;
The wind would blow it off, and, being gone,
Play with his locks; then would Adonis weep:
        And straight, in pity of his tender years,
        They both would strive who first should dry his tears.

"'To see his face, the lion walked along
Behind some hedge, because he would not fear* him;
To recreate himself, when he hath sung,
The tiger would be tame, and gently hear him:
        If he had spoke, the wolf would leave his prey,
        And never fright the silly lamb that day.

"'When he beheld his shadow in the brook,
The fishes spread on it their golden gills;
When he was by, the birds such pleasure took,
That some would sing,.some other in their bills
        Would bring him mulberries, and ripe-red cherries:
        He fed them with his sight, they him with berries.

* *Fear him,* frighten him.

" ' But this foul, grim, and urchin-snouted boar,
  Whose downward eye still looketh for a grave,
  Ne'er saw the beauteous livery that he wore :
  Witness the entertainment that he gave ;
      If he did see his face, why then I know,
      He thought to kiss him, and hath kill'd him so.' "

The mind, highly excited on any subject, is easily and
rapidly carried from one passion to another. The disappointment and grief of Venus prepare the mind of the
reader for the intense bitterness and spite that follow.

" ' Since thou art dead, lo ! here I prophesy,
  Sorrow on love hereafter shall attend ;
  It shall be waited on with jealousy,
  Find sweet beginning but unsavoury end ;
      Ne'er settled equally, to high or low ;
      That all love's pleasures shall not match his wo.

" ' It shall be fickle, false, and full of fraud ;
  And shall be blasted in a breathing-while :
  The bottom poison, and the top o'erstrawed
  With sweets, that shall the sharpest sight beguile ;
      The strongest body shall it make most weak,
      Strike the wise dumb, and teach the fool to speak.

" ' It shall be sparing, and too full of riot,
  Teaching decrepit age to tread the measures ;
  The staring ruffian shall it keep in quiet,
  Pluck down the rich, enrich the poor with treasures ;
      It shall be raging-mad, and silly-mild,
      Make the young old, the old become a child.

" ' It shall suspect, where is no cause of fear ;
  It shall not fear, where it should most mistrust ;
  It shall be merciful and too severe,
  And most deceiving when it seems most just,
      Perverse it shall be, when it seems most toward,
      Put fear to valour, courage to the coward.

" ' It shall be cause of war and dire events,
  And set dissension 'twixt the son and sire ;
  Subject and servile to all discontents,
  As dry combustious matter is to fire ;
    Sith, in his prime death doth my love destroy,
    They that love best, their love shall not enjoy.' "

The Venus and Adonis is by all the critics regarded as betraying marks of youth, and it is expressly called by the author "the first heir of his invention." Yet no one, I think, can read it without being struck with the ease and sweetness of the versification, the splendor and polish of the diction, the concentrated energy of expression in some places, and the extraordinary command of language through-out*—in short, with a high state of finish in the style, and a thorough · mastery of the art of composition, which we rarely expect to find except in the practised writer.

In the dedication of the Venus and Adonis, Shakspeare promises, if the work proves acceptable to the noble Earl, to take advantage of all idle hours till he has honored his patron with some graver labor. This promise he redeemed by the production in the following year of another narrative and descriptive poem entitled " The Rape of Lucrece." This poem is in many respects the fellow and counterpart of the other. It is in the seven-line stanza, or "Rhythm-Royal," which has been already noticed. It is considerably longer than the Venus and Adonis, and is much graver in its cast. It is, like the other, remarkable for its fulness and accuracy in painting minute details. The author takes an incident as free as possible from all

---

* " A perfect dominion, sometimes *domination*, over the whole world of language."—Coleridge.

complication of plot.   There is no unravelling of difficulties, no solving of mysteries, no exciting of curiosity, (which in a tale of fiction is one great source of interest—sometimes the only one,) no multiplication of actors or changing of scene.   It is a story which every school-boy knows by heart ; a story containing but few actors and few incidents ; nor does the author seek to create an interest by multiplying these.   On the contrary, he leaves it apparently as bare as possible of all the ordinary sources of interest in a narrative poem.   The effect which he seems to seek is that of the painter of nature, who invites attention not by novelty or the glare of his colours, but by the fidelity with which he gives back to the eye a familiar scene.

The story is this.   Collatinus, a noble Roman, boasts in camp of the matchless beauty and the incorruptible virtue of his wife Lucretia.   Tarquin, the king's son, incited partly by pique and partly by lawless passion, steals away privately from camp, and goes to Collatium, to the house of Collatinus.   There by the hostess he is courteously and hospitably entertained over night, as became the prince royal and the friend of her husband.   His fiendish end accomplished, he returns next day to camp.   The wretched victim of his violence, frantic with despair, despatches a messenger to camp with a letter, urging her husband's instant return on account of some deep grief, but without relating what it was.   Collatinus, his father-in-law Lucretius, his friend Brutus, and other followers, repair forthwith to Collatium. Lucretia meets them in the threshold, relates the horrid crime which had been committed, makes them first swear vengeance on the criminal, and then, uttering his name, plunges into her heart a fatal dagger in attestation of her

innocence.   The agony-struck husband and father give way
to a violent and benumbing grief, from which they are
first roused by a sudden suggestion of Brutus.   He sees
that the critical moment has come, and drawing from the
wound the yet bloody steel, made all present kneel, and
severally kissing the still reeking dagger, swear by it to
expel the insulting Tarquins from the throne, and abolish
the monarchy.   This is the whole story.

   In respect to the general character of the poem, I said
it was in many respects the fellow of its predecessor.
And yet, if I mistake not, there is one perceptible difference.   They are both paintings; but the one is more a
painting of external, visible, material objects; the other,
of things internal, invisible, immaterial.   In the Venus
and Adonis, there is more of what strikes the senses.   In
the Lucrece, there is the minute, microscopic anatomy of
crime and passion.   When Tarquin steals along at dead
of night on his fiendish errand, we see indeed the torch
that lights his guilty path, and the threatening falchion in
his hand; but we are made to see still more clearly, with
our mind's eye, the workings of his soul, as he is agitated
successively by conscience, honour, pity, pride, and passion.
And never probably was there such a complete anatomy of
grief, as in the description of Lucretia's feelings during
those few hours intervening between her injury and her
death.   These actings of the mind turning inward upon
itself, are made by the poet to supply the place of external
incident.   It is this power of describing minutely the
processes of thought, which is, in my opinion, the chief
characteristic of the poem.   Thoughts, passions, motives,
and acts of the mind, are in the Lucrece made to occupy

the place occupied in most narrative poems by material and external scenes and actions. The reader who takes up the poem with the expectation of that sort of interest which arises from novelty, or from lively and rapid narrative, will soon lay it down in disappointment. But he who comes to the perusal prepared to feel an interest in tracing minutely the workings of passion, who knows already something of the psychology of crime and grief, and who would receive still farther revelations of its mysteries at the hand of one who has sounded the soul of man through its whole diapason—such a reader will find the Lucrece a poem of abounding and most enchaining interest.

John Bunyan.

Birth-Place of John Bunyan.

BY MRS. S. C. HALL.

THE pilgrim who approaches a SHRINE without devotional reverence—reverence which stimulates the pulsations of his heart, and suffuses his eyes with unbidden tears—can have no "calling," so to say, to his pilgrimage. Instead of bearing the worldly "fardel" of doubts and unbelief, he must go forth with genuine faith and cordial enthusiasm—faith in the virtues of him before whose shrine he seeks to offer the homage of mind and heart. Without this, he can neither comprehend the *actions* nor appreciate the *motives* of the mighty dead; he becomes entangled in a net of so-called "reasons," leading to unworthy and treacherous "doubts." One, who is still with us—a great mystic yet a mighty teacher—asks—" Does not every true man feel that he is himself made higher by doing reverence to what is really above him?" That steady and sturdy faith in all high and glorious things, is one of the first great steps towards the Heaven which shall be revealed hereafter.

We do not expect those who are born of the flesh to be without those weaknesses and failings which are the lot of humanity, but where there is a strong and lofty spirit, doing battle honestly and openly with what is wrong, and,

(99)

above all, warring against himself, and lashing his own
frailties with a rigorous and unsparing hand—we tender
the homage of FAITH to his good intent and unflinching
purpose, and ask for him to be judged, not by the burs
that cling to his garment, but by his high attributes and
the holy PURPOSE of his MISSION. This "purpose" we
should never lose sight of when doing pilgrimage. The
worthiest thinkers and writers of modern times have offered
tributes to the genius which breathes throughout the " Pilgrim's Progress." " New editions," " illustrated editions,"
" lectures on," " lives," and even " records," of the author,
pour forth from the press, each stimulating the other; and
few would make pilgrimage to the drowsy city of Bedford,
but for the interest created for it by the once despised and
persecuted, but now universally appreciated, advocate of
Puritanism, whom the poet Cowper, with all his admiration
for his genius, even in his day feared to name.

It had long—indeed, ever since our childhood—been
with us an earnest desire to visit the place of Bunyan's
birth. It has been said, that when God's will crosses
man's will, man calls it disappointment. We had often
been " disappointed" of our projected journey to Bedford.
At last, however, it was accomplished, and we felt how
much better it was that we had not visited it previously.
The railroad offers facilities to those who have not much
time to spend in travel, which atones for its destroying a
great deal of the picturesque beauty of our country, and
leaving but little trace of the primitive habits and manners of our ancestors.

No one, we have said, would visit this midland town for
its own sake. The locality calls to mind that of one of those

heavy Flemish towns where there is literally no landscape; but where all is dark and flat, and rich with heavy vegetation—not even a mound of earth higher than a church-yard-grave to animate the torpid scene. The Ouse creeps lazily here through fertile meadows, sunning its lake-like waters without the relief of a single shadow from mountain or small hill. Cultivation does its utmost to atone by abundance for lack of beauty; and the sleepy locality is not devoid of historical interest.*

But that which renders Bedford a shrine, and elevates the whole neighborhood into a place of intense interest, is the memory of a persecuted and imprisoned man, John Bunyan, the author of some sixty volumes of the outpourings of his own heart under various forms; many of these, however, evincing the strong hardy spirit of the fearless

---

* As far back as the reign of our Sixth Edward, a grammar-school was here founded: but it was endowed in 1566 by Sir William Harpur (a native of Bedford and Lord Mayor of London), and by "Dame Alice, his wife," with a house and premises in Bedford, and land situate in Middlesex. This land, in the heart of London, has so increased in value, and the trustees have made such use of their funds, that all Bedford seems one huge charity, and every householder in the city has a free education for his son. The increase of the value of London land is curiously exemplified in Harpur's gift. He purchased 13 acres and a rood of meadow land in Holborn, which he obtained for 180*l.* This had produced, in 1668, the yearly rent of 99*l.* to the funds of his charity; but the progress of building rapidly augmented it, and it is now of the annual value of 12,000*l.*

Howard, the philanthropist, in later times, was stimulated by the state of his county (Bedford) jail, to investigate and model the prisons of Europe, and was most liberally supported in carrying out his glorious projects by Mr. Whitbread, whose descendants possess considerable property in the neighborhood.

9 *

man, are only regarded as curiosities; for the oppressions and other circumstances that called them forth, have long since passed away, and are now matters of history; but the "Pilgrim's Progress" is sacred in every Christian home, and will exist as long as the spires of our holy temples point to the skies, or a knee remains to bend in prayer at any house of Christian worship.

It seems strange to us that Southey, whose memoir is full of feeling for his subject, never visited Bunyan's birthplace, and Mr. Philip must have looked upon what is still called the Pilgrim's Cottage with a poet's eye, when he suffered the *vignette décorée*, which certainly adds to the pictorial beauty of his book, to be considered as a faithful representation of the cottage at Elstow.*

It was a day of mingled sunshine and showers, when we arrived at Bedford, and after crossing the new bridge, which has been erected on the site of the old one, where Bunyan passed a portion of his captivity, we drove to the village rendered celebrated as his birth-place. We first paused at "the green," still the "play-stow" or play-place of the village children; when we pushed back the gate and entered, we stood on the self-same "green" where Bunyan stood more than two centuries ago, when he sought to dis-

---

* The old edition of his works, as first published by Charles Doe, thus quaintly narrates his early history:—"Our Excellent Author, by the Abundant grace of God, Mr. John Bunyan, was born at Elsto, a mile this side of Bedford, about the year 1628, (his father was mean, and by trade a mender of pots and kettles, vulgarly called a Tinker, and of the national religion, as commonly men of that trade are,) and was brought up to the Tinkering trade, as also were several of his brothers, whereat he worked about that country, being also very profane and poor, even when married," &c.

perse, by the wildness of a game at "cat,"* the conviction
of the evil of sabbath-breaking, which had struck upon his
heart from a sermon, preached within the church, looking
so gray and weather-worn amid those venerable trees; here
he was arrested in the midst of that game, under the peculiar circumstances which he describes in his " Grace
Abounding;" from this well-worn and time-beaten sward
which joins the church-yard, is the best view of the
"steeple-house," or church tower, which is detached from
the church, and in which Bunyan, even after his marriage,
assisted the ringers, until " his conscience beginning to
get 'tender,' he thought such a practice was but vain, and
therefore forced himself to leave it." We wandered into
the church avenue, and leaning against the worn buttresses
of the tower, looked upwards to where hung the identical
bells, which Bunyan feared might fall upon him in judgment for his sins; the church must at one time have been
of monastic extent, and two hundred years ago exhibited
more of the remains of catholicity than appears at present.

We thought of the time when Bunyan first began to
worship earnestly within those walls, before the commencement of his hatred of prelacy, and when his great heart
expanded towards every particle, even of the dress worn
by the officiating clergyman; in this church *beginning* his
devotional existence, where, after his marriage with a

---

* *Cat, or tip-cat,* is a game still played by children. The cat
being a piece of wood tapering from the centre like a double cone;
so that the blow struck at either end occasions "the cat" to fly upwards with considerable force; the impetus given to which denotes
the ability of the player, as well as his dexterity in hitting it again
in its ascent.

woman whose only portion was two books—of which we shall speak hereafter—his earnest enthusiasm adored, to use his own language, " all things, both in the high place, priest, clerk, vestments, service, and what else belonged to the church, counting all things holy that were therein contained, and especially the priest and the clerk, most happy, and therein greatly blessed." " And, certainly," says an unnamed writer, who honors the locality where Bunyan transferred his overwhelming energy and burly activity into his master's vineyard, " certainly the spirit of the place might well work on a mind unenlightened and imaginative as was that of the glorious dreamer of Elstow. The building is large and lofty, hallowed by antiquity, and well calculated to interest and impress the romantic spirit of a young rustic. The door-way is a fine specimen of the round Norman arch, and above it is a rude representation of our Saviour's charge to St. Peter; and the body of the church contains two large brasses, commemorating a former Abbess of Elstow,* and another female, who probably filled the same office." When we came out of the church the rooks were flying low, and cawing loudly, and the dark heavy clouds, separated at intervals by streaks of light, told of the coming shower; but though, as in

---

* Here, in the old time, was an Abbey of Benedictine Nuns, founded by Judith, niece to William the Conqueror, and wife to Waltheof, Earl of Huntingdon. It was dedicated to the Holy Trinity, the Virgin Mary, and Helena, the mother of Constantine the Great. At the Dissolution, its revenues were valued at 284l. 12s. 11¾d. The brass mentioned above, to the memory of Elizabeth Harvey, Abbess of Elstow, (temp. Henry VII.) is remarkable as being the only representation extant of an Anglican Abbess *in pontificalibus.*

sacred duty bound to do, we had given our first attention
to the temple, where so important a change had been
wrought in Bunyan's mind, we desired to return to "the
green" and see how time had dealt with the "Green-house,"
while we recalled to mind the passages in Bunyan's life,
recording how his life was spent in the self-same spot,
when the trees were striplings that now are tending towards
decay. Doubtless, the remnant of the cross, which might
not in his early days have been converted into a stand for
a sun-dial, excited his indignation, after he became a rigid
nonconformist; it is now but the wreck of both, and tells
neither of faith nor time. Nearer to the village is the
"Green-house," or house upon the green, a large substantial
building, now used as a rural school; its massive timbers,
its low pointed door-way, and its antique character, prove
that it is far older than the days of Bunyan; it might
have been one of the barns or milk-houses, or stables, in
which the good old Bedford Puritan wept and prayed; he
asks of his spiritual children, in his introduction to "Grace
Abounding," "Have you forgot the close, the milk-house,
the stable, the barn, where God did visit your souls?"
After a few drops of large full rain, during which we
ascended the creaking stairs, and passed through the low-
ceiled rooms, the clouds rolled away, and the rich mellow
sunset faded into the soft grey light of evening. We
could imagine the village boys roystering upon the green,
and indulging in words of riot, which, in after times, the
excited and over-wrought imagination of the sensitive Puritan exaggerated into terrible sin. We agree with the poet
Southey in his opinion that the heart of the "glorious
dreamer" was never hardened; the "self-accusations of

such a man are to be received with some distrust, not of
his sincerity, but of his sober judgment.' It would seem
that he ran headlong into the boisterous vices which prove
fatal to so many of the ignorant for want of that necessary
and wholesome discipline which it is the duty of government
to provide ; but he was not led into those sins which infix
a deeper stain.

Pious enthusiasts are just as prone in our own day to
self-condemnation as was John Bunyan; they plough up
their hearts, if we may so express it, and discover sins
which the world could never suspect bu for their own ad-
mission ; as long as this self-knowledge causes a deep and
earnest watchfulness over themselves, and renders them
charitable, it is in all respects a most merciful dispensa-
tion ; sometimes it is so uncharitable to its fellow-sinners,
that it seems to us a species of self-glory—a satanic pre-
eminence which fosters pride. Bunyan's great and early
sins were sabbath-breaking and swearing, perverting the
power of speech—the happiest gift of God—to blasphemy
instead of blessing ; his strong emotions sought the relief
of words, and imprecations continually burst forth until
he was brought by divine grace to see the wickedness of
sabbath-breaking and evil speaking. Frequently in his
boyish life he had some remarkable escape: and his grateful nature could not but recall how, when he forced open
the adder's mouth to extract the poison, he received no
wound; his affections were all right, and towards his wife
he was not only loving, but permitted her to read to, and
reason with him, so that he was not so utterly degraded as
many would have it, as if to make the shining light of his
conversion the more brilliant and marvellous.

He was but nineteen when he married, and if there was no prudence, so called, in a marriage even without humble means, there was in the woman the wisdom which leadeth to salvation.

But we must on upon our pilgrimage, leaving "the green" to walk through the village, after taking our last look at the "ancient" house where the "glorious dreamer" may both have rioted and prayed. We could not but observe, how beautifully and tenderly the light caught up various portions of the trees, darting its beams amid their depths, and leaving much in obscurity: then flinging long spectral shadows on the grass, and imparting a strange unearthly character by its "flitting" to the old church tower, which just at the moment tolled out eight in its deep sepulchral voice. Before the chime was finished, the whole character of the place was changed; the "flitting" light was concentrated into a halo round the grim, grey tower of the venerable pile. There are few traits in the character of Bunyan more engaging than his exquisite relish for the works of Nature; he loved to meet God in the loveliness of his own world, and many times had walked the path on which we trod, perchance, after his spirit had been refreshed and strengthened by a sense of the wondrous beauty and harmony of Nature, and passed from that to the contemplation of the power of Christ's atonement. Those who are read in the outpourings of his heart will remember how, when he had struggled through the Slough of Despond, and escaped the chains of Doubting City, after hearing one comforting sermon, he exclaims, "I could not tell how to contain myself till I got home, I thought I could have spoken of HIS love, and have told of

HIS mercy towards me, even to the very crows that sat upon the ploughed lands before me, had they been capable to have understood me!"

Although the shadows of evening were drawing in more closely, the women were still plying their busy bobbins over their lace cushions, as they sate at their cottage doors; the village is as rambling and as picturesque as a village can be, that has no back-ground; although the cottages must have been nearly all rebuilt since Bunyan's time, some are even now so old as to need repair to prevent their falling to decay;—thus the associations between past and present are astonishingly close, and contribute much to the actual feeling that this is really the Elstow of Bunyan's time.

We must pause at the threshold of his cottage, for though no vestige remains of the actual *walls* that heard his infant wail when he entered into this world of strife and tumult, yet the *site* and materials are undoubtedly the same; for no builder of modern cottages would have bestowed such massive beams on such a structure.

A group of women arose from their lace pillows that we might enter the once dwelling of him who, according to an old chronicle, was one of the men "that in those times were enabled of God to adventure farre in showing their detestation of the bishops and their superstitions:" he was born within a few feet of where we stood, in 1628; the dates he has immortalized occurred to our memory one by one. He began to preach about the year 1656, was ordained pastor 21st of October, 1671, and died on the 31st of August, 1688. What a marvellous change in the circumstances of the tinker's child! who struggled into exist-

ence beneath so humble a roof,* and the termination of
HIS life, who triumphed over most bitter persecutions and
bequeathed to the world, for all time, a monument such as
the "Pilgrim's Progress."   The cottage raised upon the
ruins of that which he occupied is of the poorest description, with the exception of the beams, which, in their
thickness and the lowness of the ceiling, reminded us
of the cottage at Chalfont, where Milton sheltered during
the plague; it is in nothing remarkable, except, perhaps,
being more dilapidated than many of the neighboring cottages; but if Captain Smyth's communication needed con-
firmation, it would be in the fact that the cottage presents
the appearance of want of care, rather than extreme old
age: Mr. Fairholt, as we have said, sketched both; and
the cottage as it *was*, and *is*, illustrates what we have
written.   The little garden is dank and tangled; it was
overgrown partly by weeds and partly by vegetables, but

---

* An eminent divine, writes thus of the cottage and its locality ;—
"The house he (Bunyan) lived in at Elstow was a favorite haunt
of mine, when I was curate of that parish, on account of its historical associations as well as because there were two very old persons
living in it who took delight in showing the very forge at which
Bunyan worked—so they believed, and so did I.   It is all gone now,
the cottage having been pulled down some ten or twelve years ago.
I send you a sketch made from an old drawing of mine done upon
the spot, under some foreboding fears that the time would not be long
before the fate which has now come upon it would befall it."   The *old*
cottage was of far more importance in appearance than the *new*, the
shed at the side being what is so often mentioned as "*the forge*"—the
word "forge" leading us to believe that to the "tinker's" humble
calling might be united that of the "smith," a more manly and honorable trade.

10

both were neglected. "It was a dear place to live in,"
the lace-maker said, "and prices for lace so low; they all
worked at the pillow, but they earned little, work they ever
so late or ever so early : strangers often came to see the
cottage, but the townsfolk did not think much about it."
It is to be hoped the quiet people of quiet Bedford do not
deserve this character ; for ourselves, we can only say that
those it was our good fortune to meet on our pilgrimage
shared our enthusiasm.   It was wrong to be disappointed
that the poor lace-makers did not feel the influence of
the sacred ground upon which they dwelt ; it was, however,
a comfort that they were free from the jargon of sight-
showers, and suffered us to muse on what we saw—or did
not see ; not disturbing the enjoyment of that holy SILENCE
which subdues tumultuous feelings by its solemn stillness,
and calls up the dearest and purest memories to confirm
or disprove those fancies which, though the offspring
of facts, are frequently unworthy their descent.   Some
might count that as the very walls were not those that
sheltered Bunyan, we had gained nothing by our pilgrimage—not so ; had the whole place been desolate we still
had trodden the self-same place where most of his days
were passed ; and we still had to visit the scenes of his
imprisonment and his preaching.   It is, moreover, a holy
and elevating exercise to recall the past and its people,
and dwell with them, even in their silent tombs and mouldering graves.

When he was on the verge of eighteen he was most sig-
nally preserved from death, at the siege of Leicester ; but
this in nothing changed his life, though, doubtless, the providence took good root in his mind, to bring forth fruit in

due season; soon after this Bunyan married the wife whose father was "counted godly," and who was dowered with two books, "The Plain Man's Guide to Heaven," and "The Practice of Piety;" this young woman knew her duty, and neglected it not, but wiled her husband tenderly and lovingly into the right path, bearing with his frailties, and yet steadfast in her faith and in her love; meek and patient, yet having the great end of his conversion in view, despite his Sabbath-breaking even after his church-going, despite his oaths, that would break forth, though he considered himself improved in Christian knowledge; despite these, she persevered, she *believed* in him, she loved him, doubtless as a Christian wife: she prayed for him, earnestly, faithfully; and at last, his often stricken imagination heard the solemn voice on that very "green" we have just quitted, saying "Wilt thou leave thy sins and go to heaven, or have thy sins and go to hell?" When his soul was really aroused, and his conscience awakened, he never halted or turned back. Oh! what then must have been the joy of his faithful wife, when she saw him put away all worldly strength and vain glory, and kneel with bending head and contrite spirit, meekly, at the foot of the cross; it is beautiful to observe the strong-hearted man, with his vigorous intellect and gorgeous imagination, distrusting himself, putting away his own wisdom, continuing instant in prayer, and stimulating his righteousness by the constant perusal of Holy Writ; he at one period looked for sudden impulses, and direct signs and revelations, but after a time—and a long time it was—of turmoil and trial, his fiery spirit became subdued, and, as Doctor Cheever most beautifully says, when writing of him, "his piety not only grew elevated and glowing, but strong and impregnable, and of a deep, ripe, serene, and heavenly character, that fitted him as a wise master-builder, for his work with other souls, and as an experienced guide, to mark for others the road that leads to the Lamb."

Mr. Scott, in the life of John Bunyan affixed to one edition of the "Pilgrim's Progress," says it is not advisable to recapitulate those impressions which constitute a large part of his religious experience. "But to admire him as he deserves to be admired," says Southey, "it is necessary that we should be informed not only of the coarseness of his youth, but of the extreme ignorance out of which he worked his way, and the stage of burning enthusiasm through which he passed, a passage not less terrible than that of his own pilgrim in th valley of the shadow of death."

In time, weaned from the church which had first awoke him to a sense of his spiritual darkness, he became a member of the Baptist congregation of which a Mr. Gifford (whose character had also undergone a great spiritual change) was pastor at Bedford, and after his death Bunyan went frequently forth as a preaching itinerant to neighboring villages. In the year 1653 Bunyan was first received into this handful of Baptist Christians—and strangely enough the same year, 1653, Cromwell was declared Lord Protector of these realms—there was much similarity in the characters of these two men, but of that we have not space to write, yet the coincidence is singular. Bunyan's wanderings during the Protectorate, over his native county, must have been extensive, as there are traditions of him in numberless villages. He was, like all teachers of his class and time, for a considerable period, an Alarmist rather than a Comforter, but his experience rendered him, as he became older, more hopeful. We have no record of his domestic life during this period—indeed few "preachers" have any to record—and thus it may be that what others consider their "home duties," are so frequently unfulfilled; but that he tenderly loved his wife and children there can be no doubt; there is no record of the date of his first wife's death, no telling how or when her simple, chastened, and believing spirit was called to HIM, who had so ordered her pilgrimage on earth as to be peculiarly instrumental in awaking her husband to a sense of sin, and a knowledge of the way, the truth, and the life. That he entertained a truly Christian belief in the instrumentality of women in Christian purposes, is evident from the position he gave to "Christiana" in the "Pilgrim's Progress." Certainly before the commencement of the public persecutions against him, in the reign of the second Charles, he had married a second wife—of whom hereafter. Even during the Protectorate he suffered much from calumny, as all men do who become remarkable by peculiar gifts; but the reign of the dissolute Charles had commenced, and many remembered the daring words of the nonconformist, and how he had served in the Parliament's army— and so he was arrested at a place called Samsell in Bedfordshire, while addressing a congregation; and after being examined by a "Justice Wingate," committed to Bedford jail, there to remain until the quarter sessions.

While his mittimus was making out, a Doctor Lindale,

10 *

H

whom the nonconformist considered a "great enemy to
the truth," rather jested with him, and said he had read
of one Alexander the coppersmith, who troubled the
Apostles. "Aiming this at me," said Bunyan, "because
I was a tinker;" upon which I answered, "that I had
read of priests and pharisees who had their hands in the
blood of our Lord."

Mr. Philip gives the renown of Bunyan's imprisonment
to the city prison, which in his (Bunyan's) time stood on the
bridge; but those persons in Bedford with whom we conversed, seemed inclined to the belief, that the greater part,
if not the whole, of his twelve years' confinement, was
passed in the *county* jail—which is now a modern structure.
We stood upon the bridge, and looked along the sluggish
waters of the Ouse on the left; on the right is the Swan
Inn; not the "Swan," in a room of which the nonconformist's second wife so heroically pleaded her husband's
cause, but a new building, standing as the old one did, on
the site of the ancient castle of Bedford.

It seems to us more likely that Bunyan, having been
arrested *not* in the city, but in a country village, should
have waited for his trial at the quarter sessions in the
county jail. A ring,* believed, and with excellent show

---

* This valuable relic is in the possession of the Dean of Manchester,
and we are kindly permitted to transcribe the Dean's own account
of the ring:—"As to the ring, the history of it is curious. The old
prison in which Bunyan was confined for twelve years after his trial
before Hale, stood upon the centre of Bedford bridge, which was
pulled down in 1811. A friend of mine, Dr. Abbot, was present
day by day while the work of delapidation was going on, and in the
course of time, out of the floor of the old prison, the ring was dug

of reason, to have been Bunyan's, was found in the floor of the old prison on the bridge, when it was pulled down in 1811.

It might be that after his examination at the quarter sessions, he was committed to the city jail, having first been imprisoned in the county; be that as it may, there is nothing more touching in his whole history than when he says, referring to that committal, "before I went down to the justice I begged of God, that if I might do more good by being at liberty than in prison, that then I might be set at liberty, but if not, His will be done; for I was not altogether without hopes that my imprisonment might be an awakening to the saints in the country; therefore I

up. Abbot bought it, and wore it until within a short time before his death, in 1817, when he took it off from his own finger, and placed it upon mine, charging me to keep it for his sake. Dr. Abbot never doubted its genuineness, nor does there appear to be any reason for doing so. The place where it was found was undoubtedly Bunyan's dwelling-place for many years. Persecuted as we may consider him to be, there can be no doubt that he was, in his own days and by his own party, looked upon as a victim of State persecution: and there is evidence to show that he was not unkindly treated, but, on the contrary, found his friends increasing as his sufferings were supposed to be undeserved. His imprisonment was probably not much unlike that of St. Paul at Rome, bating that he was kept within the prison walls; but there were no visiting justices in that day, and no doubt his friends and others had access to him; and it may be that the ring was given to him by some person of condition, as a token of regard. I am inclined to think this must have been its history, as the letters I. B. appear to have been inserted after the ring was made. They were punched in probably by Bunyan himself. Indeed, the whole of the indents seem to have been made by punching; they are not cut in by any graving tool."

could not tell which to choose; only I in that manner did commit the thing to God; and verily, at my return, I did meet my God *sweetly in the prison again*, comforting of me and satisfying of me, that it was HIS will and mind that I should be there."

Three months of imprisonment followed, and then the clerk of the peace went to him by desire of the magistrates to see if he could be persuaded to obedience—which "obedience" inferred relinquishing his calling as a preacher; this he refused to do; it is evident from this courtesy that Bunyan was then regarded with no common respect even by his enemies. The coronation of Charles took place on the 22d of April, 1661, shortly after this interview, and when the next assizes came, Bunyan's wife presented a petition to the judges that they would impartially take his case into consideration, and that he might be heard, and threw a second petition into the coach to Judge Twisden. It is not difficult to imagine the trembling but eager hand of the devoted wife flinging this entreaty at the judge's feet, as he was preparing to descend from his carriage, and proceed to "the Swan Chamber,"—doubtless many in the crowd were filled with anxiety as to the result—and when glancing his eyes over the contents he told her that her husband was a convicted person, and could not be released unless he promised to preach no more, how must hope, strangled by despair, have expired within her bosom as she turned her eyes towards the prison likely to become his tomb.

"Heaviness may endure for a night, but joy cometh in the morning;" Elizabeth was so constituted as to be the worthy wife of the author of the "Pilgrim's Progress" as well as the help-mate of John Bunyan, the tinker of Elstow; Sir Matthew Hale had expressed sympathy towards her, and the high sheriff (whose memory for this one act deserves a record more ennobling than his civic dignity) encouraged her to make another effort for her husband before the judges left town; accordingly "with a bashed face and trembling heart," she entered the "Swan chamber" where the two judges and many magistrates and gentry of the county were in company together. We wish that one of those artists who immortalize noble deeds with a true and vigorous pencil, would think of this as a subject worthy to be recorded :—

The quaint "Swan chamber," its open windows admitting a view of the jail on the bridge, and the heavy waters which passed slowly beneath this "bridge of sighs;" the contrast between Judge Twisden and Sir Matthew Hale, the varied grouping and expression of the "magistrates and gentry of the county." The nonconformist's "young wife, with a bashed face" and righteous purpose.* Let it not be thought irreverent to the memory of one of the unsullied glories of England, the Lady Rachel Russell, if we remember that Lady Rachel craved to be her husband's secretary, but that Bunyan's wife, lowly born, lowly bred, but of lofty heart, became her husband's advocate. She had previously been to London to petition the House of Lords

* The Rev. J. Scott, in his life of Bunyan, prefixed to the edition of the "Pilgrim's Progress," states that he was married in 1658 to his *second* wife, by whom he had *no* children. His family (four) were by the first wife; thus he had been only three years married at the time of the Restoration, and this accounts for him speaking of her as his young wife.

in his behalf, and one, whom she called *Lord Barkwood*, had told her that they could do nothing, but that his releasement was committed to the next assizes, and the assizes having come she stood there to plead her husband's cause.   The painter, as is his gift, could throw her soul into her face, and illustrate any one of her replies by that expression: "I am come to you," she said, "and you give neither releasement nor relief;" and then appealing to Sir Matthew Hale, she complained that her husband was detained unlawfully in prison, for the indictment was false, and he was imprisoned before there were any proclamations against the meetings.   One of the judges said he had been lawfully convicted, and thus aroused, she indignantly answered, " *It is false !*" and then reasoned why, according to her belief.   " Will your husband leave preaching ?" said Judge Twisden ; "if he will do so, then send for him." " My lord," was her faithful reply, faithful to her God as to her husband ; " My lord, he DARES NOT LEAVE PREACHING AS LONG AS HE CAN SPEAK."

And now either in the city jail on the bridge, or the county jail in the town, Bunyan was a fast prisoner, and although his jailer was his friend, and gave him opportunities of going forth, particularly at night, and meeting little bands of his own faith, beside the sluggish waters of the Ouse,—or in the thickness of dark shadowing trees,—or, farther away, in unsuspected dells, where the footsteps of the midnight congregation fell on the pliant moss, and the winking stars or pallid moon were silent witnesses to the outpourings of his prayers, and the torrent of his eloquence ; sinking, as it did, into the hearts of his hearers —still he was in captivity ; and in the day-time, his blind child sitting at his feet, he might be seen tagging the laces woven by his family, that they might sell them to buy bread. And here in his prison-house, his tenderness for his family was expressed in language so touching that few parents, we believe, could read it without tears.

It was most interesting to see the actual agreement entered into between Josias Ruffhead, brushmaker, and John Bunyan, brazier, by which Bunyan and his friends purchased "*a Barn*," with a piece of ground adjoining it, in the parishes of St. Paul and St. Cuthbert, or one of them, of Ruffhead, for 50*l.*, in 1672. The present minister believes that this "barn" was the building for which the license was granted, and which was afterwards permanently occupied by this Church as its place of meeting for many years. Mr. Jukes maintains his opinion that this "barn" remained in its natural state until after it pleased God to remove Bunyan from the ministry.*

As no vestige of the old barn remained, but all external

---

* The Rev. Mr. Jukes has published a very interesting little history of Bunyan's Church, compiled chiefly from the records of the old meeting. No lover of the "Pilgrim's Progress" should be without it. Bunyan was called to the pastoral office, October 21, 1671, during the eleventh year of his imprisonment. Captain Smyth has favored us with the following interesting notices of the preacher and his Church in his time:—"He had a family by his first wife, one of whom died before him; but Fowitt Thomas Bunyan, rather a captious body, was admitted into the Congregation in 1673. Fowitt's children—Katherine and John—were entered in the same meeting, the daughter in 1692, the son in the year following. John is often mentioned in the records of the sect, one of the last entries being his mission to reprove Brother Steven White, in April, 1718. Shortly afterwards the dynasty seems to have expired in him, for we trace no more Bunyans in the Bedford documents."

things were new, it was a great pleasure to hear from the
worthy minister that a spirit of love, and peace, and charity, dwelt with the descendants of the "old meeting,"
and that while firmly united together they are in harmony
and friendship with the "mother church;" which, dearly
as we love the establishment, we confess, was at times
much too severe in the punishments she awarded her tru-
ant children; and thus, not adhering to the principles of
her Divine Originator, who decreed that even offences
which numbered "seventy times seven" should be forgiven,
she provoked them both by harshness and neglect to forsake the shelter of the spire and the music of the church
bell, and wander forth until new tabernacles sprang up in
the wilderness of the world, not to be re-united to her until the great day when all minor distinction shall be swept
away, and all—sheltering beneath the broad banner of
Christian faith—rejoice that there is but "one fold and
one Shepherd."

Again, "heaviness may endure for a night, but joy
cometh in the morning;" it was pleasant to see the dark
clouds passing as the morning dawned, and to turn our
attention from the scenes of his trials to those of his triumphs. We sought the dwelling of the Baptist "Interpreter," to see the relics preserved in connection with the
"old meeting." It seemed as though we had passed
through a storm, and had just found a harbor of shelter,
when we entered the cheerful parlour of Mr. Jukes, the
far down successor of John Bunyan in the ministry, and
saw upon his table a venerable volume and a small cabinet
which were once in the possession of the author of the
"Pilgrim's Progress." The volume was Bunyan's church-

book,—the cabinet was probably used for various purposes; it is not larger than what a lady would choose to
keep ribands and gloves in.   At all events, the fact of its
having been HIS, sanctified it in our esteem; and next to
the church-book, it is the relic we should most value.   Mr.
Jukes then accompanied us to the new Baptist chapel,
erected on the site of the " old meeting."   It is a large
building; the interior plain, light, and cheerful, with ample
space to seat 1200 persons ; the minister who ascends the
pulpit, can see nearly every individual in the congregation, and all the congregation can see him.   How the
spirit of Bunyan would have rejoiced in such a goodly
meeting, assembled—in peace and safety—on the plot of
ground, where his persecutor, Charles the Second, after so
many years of suffering, licensed him to preach the Gospel in his own fashion.

The vestry contains Bunyan's chair, and we had hoped that
his pulpit was preserved there also ; but Howard the philanthropist gave thirty pounds for it, and a new pulpit.*   We
have a great reverence for the memory of Howard; but
we think he ought to have permitted Bunyan's pulpit to
remain in the " old meeting."

We should like to see all the authenticated relics of
Bunyan, preserved at this record of his triumph in Jesus,
the "old meeting ;" and it seems a pity that there is not suffi-

---

* With regard to the pulpit, an old resident in Bedford says:—
" The celebrated John Howard presented a new pulpit in the room
of the old one, which was cut up : of part of the wood a table was
made which now belongs to Mrs. Hillyard, the widow of the late
Mr. Hillyard, who was minister of the chapel for fifty years, and
died about eight or nine years ago."

11

cient unity of purpose in his admirers to devote each relic
they possess to that purpose; there should be no "mine," or
"thine" in such a case. Mr. Philip mentions "a Mr.
Hillyard," as having a table made from the pulpit, upon
which he sometimes places "Bunyan's cup;" one tradition
says that his "broth" was carried to him in prison in this
cup; another that his "broth" was brought to chapel in it,
for his Sunday dinner in the vestry.*

There is an old engraving of the great nonconformist
over the mantel-shelf in the vestry, which, with one exception, is more like the ideal of Bunyan than any other
likeness we have seen; the eyes are deep and expressive,
the nose firm set, and large, but not coarse, the mouth
expressive of great humour, and the chin ample and
benevolent. The head is of a noble shape.

It was deeply interesting to us, as we wandered through
the town or looked from the windows of the "Swan" upon
the Ouse, reflecting the passing clouds, to endeavour to
realize Bunyan's position and spirit, "while he was thinking
for the world and writing for all time"—with few external
objects to divert his attention, while his secret soul was
filled with the ever-glorious dream of the "Pilgrim's
Progress." The calm waters reflecting the multitudinous
stars, the suggestive music of a dipping oar, the splash
and sparkle of a fish setting the waters trembling beneath

---

* This is also in the possession of Mrs. Hillyard. There is in the
Baptist Library at Bedford, a Concordance of Bunyan's, although
not that he had in prison. Mr. Philip also mentions another chair,
" now in the possession of the Polehill family;" and another in the
Whitbread family, who have also his pulpit Bible.

a moonbeam, the bark of a distant watch-dog, were once sounds and objects of interest to him during a portion of his prison time; and however damp it might and must have been, for the sake of the mysterious waters, which have ever tales to tell to the thoughtful and the imaginative, we would rather have had him imprisoned on the bridge than in the town—we would rather think of him *there* than in the closed up town; pass the waters ever so slowly, still there is freedom in the very bubbles that float upon the stream.

But we may indulge the remembrance that the last four years of Bunyan's imprisonment was little more than nominal confinement; for during that period he regularly attended the Baptist meeting, his name being always in the records, and in the eleventh year of his "incarceration," the congregation chose him for their pastor.

His character had obtained respect; his books, notice and renown. Dr. Barlow, then Bishop of Lincoln, and other prelates, are believed to have sympathised with his sufferings, and assisted in procuring his enlargement. This might be considered an OMEN of the future universality of his fame—the highest fame mortality can hope to achieve.

In the full grave-yard of the meeting-house, there is but one tablet which bears the name of Bunyan; it is to the memory of Hannah Bunyan, a great-grandchild of Bunyan, who died in 1770, aged 76 years,—there is no record of the burial of either of his wives:*—we went to see the

---

* We are told in the old edition of his works by Charles Doe—"As to his family, he left his widow, Elizabeth, and three sons; John, Thomas, and Joseph, and three daughters, Elizabeth, Sarah,

spot where his house in Bedford stood, and which was indeed a shrine, for he lived there during the greater part of his *permitted* ministry ; and it will be always matter of regret, that it was not purchased and preserved by the members of the " old meeting," when it was offered them before its destruction.

Bunyan had many friends in London, and frequently journeyed thither, and whenever his preaching was announced, the meeting was crowded to suffocation by his admirers.   He was never free from apprehension of what might befall him from the powers that were ; and, soon after James II. came to the throne in 1685, Bunyan conveyed the whole of his property to his wife by a singular deed, which still exists ; whatever evil he may have feared from the second James, he experienced none ; but worked on by word of mouth and power of pen, by the body and by the spirit, until his fine constitution quailed beneath over-labor.   He suffered from what was called the " sweating distemper ;" and while his health was much impaired by its effects, undertook a journey to Reading, to reconcile a young friend to his father.   The exertion proved too much for his strength ; and after an illness of ten days, at the age of sixty years, " his strong man bowed under him," and his burden was laid at the feet of his Saviour.

Bunyan's son Thomas succeeded him in the ministry ; but though he won *respect*, he never achieved admiration ; indeed, no son of Bunyan's could shine while the glory of his father was remembered.   Of his other children

and Mary ; but his blind daughter (of whom he writes in his " Grace Abounding") died some years before him, and his widow died 169 ."

nothing is recorded, and even the exact spot of the Pilgrim's rest, in Bunhill Fields, seems undecided.

An old lady, whose testimony is always sound, told us, that in her girlish days she has stood by the side of John Bunyan's grave in Bunhill Fields; she remembers it perfectly; the first time she ever saw it, it was shown her by her maid, a pious young person, who induced her, when she was little more than a child, to go and hear John Wesley preach—early—early on a summer's morning, to a hundred ministers who were about to proceed to various parts of the world; and, after the sermon, this girl took her to see the grave of the author of "The Pilgrim's Progress;"—it was, she says, a decayed-looking grave, some brick-work fallen down, and a sort of head stone, green and mouldering, upon which was what she calls *faintly* carved, "Here lies John Bunyan." Often in days long past, when the "Pilgrim's Progress" was laid in her lap, and we read therein, has she told us of this humble grave, and promised when we went to London we should see it: it was associated in our mind with the dead in Westminster Abbey and St. Paul's; but, when we did see it, and described to her that it was a fair large tomb, she was greatly pained in the belief that his body had been removed—a belief which Mr. Philip inclines to.

The vault beneath the tomb that bears his name, is that of his friend Strudwick, a grocer on Snow Hill, at whose house, after his journey to Reading, he was taken ill—and perhaps he died there.

He would rather, we think, have chosen to repose where his wife Elizabeth could have been placed beside him, than in the stately vault of his friend; and the relation in

which he stood to the Lord Mayor of London, at the time
of his death—being his chaplain, or, as Southey proves
from Ellis's Correspondence, his "teacher"—would entitle
him, if nothing else did, to a resting-place of his own.
Mr. Philip believes he was originally interred in the
"Baptist corner" of the burying-ground at Bunhill Fields;
but the fact of his being interred "somewhere" within the
"place of tombs" sanctifies the enclosure, though we regret that the old stone bearing the inscription is nowhere
seen.   Our venerable informant is positive as to the words
—"Here lies John Bunyan," as she frequently visited the
grave, and speaks of it to this day.   Mr. Philip says that
none of Bunyan's descendants are now in England; we
have reason to believe that this is an error; when we were
in Bedford, Mr. Jukes gave us the address of a very old
lady in London, who claims to be a descendant of John
Bunyan, and is possessed of a portrait of her ancestor,
which she has left by will, to be given after her death to
the "old meeting;" on our return to town we set forth to
seek her, and drove to the "Angel" at Islington, within
a few doors of which we were told she resided.   We only
arrived in time to be too late; Mrs. Sanigear had quitted
her lodgings the day before; the landlady assured us she
did not know where she was gone.   "She was so very
odd—she liked none but her own people, the same as John
Bunyan's.   Yes; she left yesterday, and took *the old
preacher's picture with her.*"   We saw there had been a
feud between the ladies; and must confess our informant
lost in our good opinion, by referring to the picture we so
much wished to see, in so irreverent a manner; so we
drove away, wrote to Mr. Jukes, who very kindly procured

for us Mrs. Sanigear's new address, and the next time we
went to town, we paid her a visit.   The name of the "old
meeting" was an "*Open sesame*," and she pointed to the
portrait of her ancestor with evident pride.   "It is not an
original," she said; "but was copied from an original that
was painted on glass;" adding, "so they said when I was
a girl many years ago, for in six months I shall be eighty-
eight years old."   Despite her years, there is fire in her
dark deep eyes, and an expression of both humor and severity in her mouth.   We observed how very like she was
to the portrait; she admitted that "every one said the
same, they all said she was like to it: she might have
been once, but not now, for he died *young*, only sixty,
quite young, but she was nearly ninety, only wanted two
years and six months to be ninety all out.   She was his
great, great, grand-daughter, and we understood her to
say, she had a nephew who bore the name of Bunyan; we
felt inclined to question as to which of the nonconformist's
children she was descended from, but she did not like
being questioned, at least she did not like the trouble of
reply; she spoke of the "old meeting" with animation,
and looking at the picture repeated more than once, "He
was a great pilgrim, a faithful pilgrim!"   She told us she
had left THE PICTURE to the "old meeting," but added
that no one from the town of Bedford had ever called
upon her, until Mr. Jukes had done so.   She was kind
and even cordial, but there was a natural severity in her
tone and manner which savored of the Puritans of old
times.   She would not permit the little maid who showed
us up, to attend us down stairs, but did so herself, standing at the open door after an assurance of how glad she
would be to see us again.

She is not easily forgotten; her formal dress, close cap, and snowy neckerchief—pinned down as you see in portraits of some sixty or seventy years ago—and above all, the earnest steadfast expression of her face, telling of firmness of the most immovable kind, softened by a world of affection in her deep brown eyes.   She was a singular link between the present and the past ; and we make no doubt, would at this moment be willing to suffer imprisonment or death for the sake, not only of her general faith, but for any one point thereof. We ought to have inquired of her about the tomb ; but have a great unwillingness to press questions on old age, and every one who passes Bunhill Fields burying-ground, whatever doubts may arise as to this spot or that, may safely say—

There lies JOHN BUNYAN.

LIFE AND WRITINGS OF

John Bunyan.

BY THE REV. JOSEPH BELCHER, D. D.

No one of our readers will object to a little talk about John Bunyan; for who has not read and admired his "Pilgrim's Progress?" Not a few remember the intense interest with which, in their childhood, they traced the steps of the heavenly Pilgrim through all the perils and difficulties of the narrow path, and learned to desire that, like him, they might at length find a home in the celestial city. Others will look back to the commencement of their Christian life, when they found, in Bunyan's metaphorical narrative, instructions, encouragements, and cautions, adapted to their conditions, and derived from it impressions which they hope never to lose till they have passed the dark river, and are beyond the reach of their enemies. For ourselves, we remember that, in very early childhood, we read it with intense and tearful interest; and though too young to understand its spiritual import, we followed Christian from scene to scene with rapture, and at the close asked, trembling for the answer, whether he ever came back from the celestial city.

As it is quite possible that here and there may be found

a reader who yet knows but little of our spiritual hero,—
for the day in which he lived, the prince of preachers and
the Shakspeare of divines,—we will transcribe, as our
introduction, the opinions of men whose character and
standing will command attention. And though the testimonies relate chiefly to his Pilgrim, they apply to his less-
known productions, especially to his " Holy War," a work
which others beside the late Dr. Andrew Fuller placed
even higher than his better-known and more admired
volume.

LORD KAIMES, who did not at all sympathize with Bunyan in his estimate of Christianity, admires the Pilgrim's
Progress as being composed in a style enlivened like that
of Homer, by a suitable mixture of drama and narrative.

MACAULAY says that " Bunyan is indeed as decidedly
the first of allegorists as Demosthenes is the first of
orators, or Shakspeare the first of dramatists.   Other
allegorists have shown equal ingenuity, but no other alle-
gorist has ever been able to touch the heart, and to make
abstractions objects of terror, of pity, and of love."

DR. SAMUEL JOHNSON, who has been properly called
" the unwieldy and uncouth leviathan of English literature," and certainly far enough from Bunyan's theology,
according to Mrs. Piozzi's account, described the Pilgrim's
Progress as " a work of original genius, and one of the
very few books which every reader wishes had been
longer;" and BOSWELL says, "Johnson praised John Bunyan highly : his Pilgrim's Progress has great merit, both
for invention, imagination, and the conduct of the story ;
and it has had the best evidence of its merit, the general
and continued approbation of mankind."

GRAINGER, one of the high-church party, in his Biographical History of England, calls it "Bunyan's masterpiece; one of the most popular, and, I will add, one of the most ingenious books in the English language."

COLERIDGE, in his last and best days, wrote: "I know of no book, the Bible excepted, as above all comparison, according to my judgment and experience, I could so safely recommend as teaching and enforcing the whole saving truth, according to the mind that was in Christ Jesus, as the Pilgrim's Progress. It is, in my conviction, the best *Summa Theologiæ Evangelicæ* ever produced by a writer not miraculously inspired."

MONTGOMERY, in his admirable Lectures on General Literature, says: "There is no long allegory in our literature at all comparable to Bunyan's Pilgrim's Progress; and one principal reason why this is the most delightful thing of the kind in the world is, that though written 'under the similitude of a dream,' there is very little of pure allegory in it, and few abstract qualities or passions are personified." "It will continue," says the same author, "to be a book exercising more influence over minds of every class, than the most refined and sublime genius, with all the advantages of education and good fortune, has been able to rival, in this respect."

Omitting the eulogiums of COWPER, of BYRON, of SCOTT, of MACKINTOSH, of SOUTHEY, and a multitude of others, we quote a line or two from our own Franklin, and then commence our narrative.

FRANKLIN, whose sound judgment no man disputes, says: "Honest John Bunyan is the first I know of who has mingled narrative and dialogue together, a mode of

writing very engaging to the reader, who in the most
interesting passages finds himself admitted, as it were, into
the company, and present at the conversation."

We now introduce our hero to the inspection of the

BUNYAN IN PRISON.

reader, and though he will be found in prison, probably
engaged on his great work, the scene is not less interesting.
It may be as well, before we proceed, that we should

give from a friendly contemporary a description of his personal appearance :—"He appeared in countenance to be of a stern and rough temper, but in his conversation mild and affable; not given to loquacity or much discourse in company, unless some urgent occasion required it; observing never to boast of himself or his parts, but rather to seem low in his own eyes, and submit himself to the judgment of others. He had a sharp, quick eye, accompanied with an excellent discerning of persons, being of good judgment and quick wit. As for his person, he was tall of stature, strong-boned, though not corpulent; somewhat of a ruddy face, with sparkling eyes; wearing his hair on his upper lip, after the old British fashion; his hair reddish, but, in his latter days, time had sprinkled it with gray; his nose well set, but not declining or bending, and his mouth moderately large; his forehead somewhat high; and his habit always plain and modest."

Such was "the outward man" of one who mingled with our Pilgrim Fathers, and probably did not a little to encourage their holy enterprise: one who was numbered with those who secured England from Popery, and restored her fading freedom. Though not of our land, he is our common property, with Milton and Shakspeare, and with the other giants who lived in that eventful period. Let us look now at the facts of one who far more than Dryden deserved the epithet of "GLORIOUS JOHN," and see the influence of events on his character.

All my readers know that Bunyan was a tinker, and the son of a tinker, and that poverty, illiteracy, and profanity, marked his early life. He was born in a small village called Elstow, about four miles from Bedford, in the year

12

1628. It was but little of education which the poor of that day could obtain ; but it seems that John's father sent him to school, where he was taught to read and write. His general information, however, in his youth, was very small ; and, as Macaulay says, " he knew no language but the English, as it was spoken by the common people. His spelling was bad. He frequently transgressed the rules of grammar." Though profane, proverbially so, he never was a drunkard, a libertine, or a lover of sanguinary sports. What gave Bunyan notoriety in the days of his ungodliness, and which made him afterwards appear to himself such a monster of iniquity, was the energy displayed in his conduct. He had a zeal for idle play, and an enthusiasm in mischief, which were the perverse manifestations of a forceful character. Dr. James Hamilton thus beautifully presents a scene, which every one who has seen Elstow will be ready to recognize and confirm. Here is " a quiet hamlet of some fifty houses, sprinkled about in the picturesque confusion, and with the easy amplitude of space, which gives an old English village its look of leisure and longevity. And it is now verging to the close of the summer's day. The daws are taking short excursions from the steeple, and tamer fowls have gone home from the darkening and dewy green. But old Bunyan's donkey is still browsing there, and yonder is old Bunyan's self—the brawny tramper, dispread on the settle, retailing to the more clownish residence, taproom wit and roadside news. However, it is young Bunyan you wish to see. Yonder he is, the noisiest of the party, playing pitch-and-toss— that one with the shaggy eyebrows, whose entire soul is ascending in the twirling penny—grim enough to be th.

blacksmith's apprentice, but his singed garments hanging round him with a lank and idle freedom which scorns indentures; his energetic movements and authoritative vociferations, at once bespeak the ragamuffin ringleader. The penny has come down on the wrong side uppermost, and the loud execration at once betrays young Badman. You have only to remember that it is Sabbath evening, and you witness a scene often enacted on Elstow green two hundred years ago."

But even then Bunyan had a faithful conscience, and often trembled as he thought of his sins. His nights were frequently terrified with dreams,—such as that the day of judgment had come, and that the quaking earth was opening to admit him into eternal punishment; and his days were often gloomy with forebodings of the wrath to come. He would try to persuade himself that there was no future punishment, and then would wish himself a devil, that he might torment others, hoping thus to escape himself. But as he grew older, his heart hardened, and he could sin without remorse; except that now and then his strong feelings would return, and then he would flee from the belfry, where he was fond of ringing the bells, in fear that they might fall and kill him.

The early life of Bunyan was marked with several striking interpositions of the providence of God on his behalf. At one time he fell into the sea, and at another, into the river Ouse, at Bedford; and each time was in danger of drowning. One day he was walking in the fields with a companion, when an adder glided across their path; Bunyan's ready switch stunned it in a moment, but with the daring consistent with his whole character, he forced open its mouth, and plucked out the sting—a specimen of foolhardiness, which, as he himself observes, might, but for God's mercy, have brought him to his end. Several years after this, when he had entered the Parliamentary army, he was selected to go to the siege of Leicester; but when ready to start, a comrade offered to take his place, which he was allowed to do, and while standing sentry in that town, the said comrade was shot through the head and died. These manifestations of Divine kindness produced, however, at the time, no salutary impression on Bunyan's mind.

At about the age of eighteen, Bunyan was married to his first wife. To this step he was advised by friends who thought it would tend greatly to his reformation; nor were their hopes disappointed. Bunyan and his wife were both poor, so that he says, "this woman and I came together as poor as poor might be, not having so much household stuff as dish or spoon betwixt us." But she had been differently and better educated than her husband; her father had the reputation of being a godly man; and she carried to her new home two religious books which her father had left her when he died. These books Bunyan read, and was pleased with them; but the conversation of his wife, in which she had the prudence to tell him in an unassuming and wise way of the consistency of her father's conduct, produced a strong impression on his mind as to his sinfulness, and consequent danger of eternal punishment. He mistook superstition, however, at that time, for religion, and gave his reverence to the church-building, the priest, and even the surplice. Several years elapsed before he became truly devoted to God and holiness.

This change was chiefly effected by overhearing the pious conversation of some poor women in the town of Bedford.

There was at that time living at Bedford a remarkable man named Gifford. He had been a staunch royalist, and was concerned in the rising in Kent. He was arrested; and with eleven of his comrades, was sentenced to die. The night before the day fixed for his execution, his sister came to visit him. She found the guard asleep, and with her assistance, Gifford made his escape. After a time, he removed as a stranger to Bedford, and commenced the practice of physic; but was still abandoned to habits of recklessness and vice. By reading a pious book, his conscience became restless, and at length he was led to rest his hope of salvation on the atoning sacrifice of Christ. He soon after began to preach; and a small Baptist church was formed, of which he remained pastor till his death. Into this church, Bunyan was baptized in 1653; and two years afterwards, was encouraged by them to preach the gospel of Jesus Christ. Dr. Southey says that none but the Baptists would have suffered an illiterate man like Bunyan to preach; and he is right, for all other denominations of Christians at that period made a collegiate education an indispensable qualification for the pulpit. At first he did not venture farther than to address his friends in their private meetings; but his warm-hearted friends, even the most judicious of them, urged him forward, somewhat against his will, to more public services. Though his education was rude, God had given him from the first a strong, athletic mind, and a glowing heart,— that downright logic and teeming fancy, whose bold strokes and burning images heat the Saxon temper to the welding

12 *

point, and make the popular orator of the English multitude. As Southey has remarked, "His was a homespun style, not a manufactured one. It was a clear stream of current English—the vernacular of his age; sometimes, indeed, in its rusticity and coarseness, but always in its plainness and strength." To this natural style Bunyan was partly indebted for his popularity; but his low origin, and rough, wild history, still more forcibly attracted attention. If, indeed, he had exchanged a leathern apron for a silken one, or scrambled from the hedge-side to the high places of the church, they might have suspected his motives, and despised his character; but no man could now deny the truth of his religion, or the disinterestedness which influenced his conduct. All Bedford went to hear him, and all men felt an interest in his ministry. Not a few were unspeakably benefitted; while in some other instances persecution became rampant. "Some lewd fellows of the baser sort" would sometimes amuse themselves by following home the preacher, stoning or pelting him with rotten eggs or apples all the way. As an old and scarce print has preserved a view of his cottage, now partly removed, we copy the engraving on the opposite page.

Every one knows that at the time of which we are writing, and for some years afterwards, persecution raged in England, and a determination was shown, alike by church and state, to put down all worship and preaching which were not in accordance with the established church. But before we proceed to narrate instances in connection with Bunyan, illustrative of the tyranny of that age, it may be well to describe still more fully the character of his preaching, that thus we may learn what it was which excited the

EXACT VIEW OF BUNYAN'S HOUSE.

From a rare print.

139

jealousy and cruelty of the clergy. That preaching was
not incoherent rant. Words of truth and soberness formed
the staple of every sermon, and his burning language and
startling images were only the electric scintillations along
the chain of his scriptural eloquence. Though the common people heard him gladly, he had occasional hearers
of a higher class. Once on a week day he was expected
to preach in a parish church near Cambridge, and a con-
course of people had already collected in the churchyard.
A gay student was riding past, when he noticed the crowd,
and asked what had brought them together. He was told
that the people had come out to hear one Bunyan, a tinker,
preach. He instantly dismounted, and gave a boy twopence (four cents) to hold his horse, for he declared that
he was determined to here the tinker *prate*. So he went
into the church, and heard the tinker; but so deep was
the impression which that sermon made on the scholar,
that he embraced every subsequent opportunity to attend
Bunyan's ministry, and he himself became an eminent
preacher of the gospel in Cambridgeshire.

When Bunyan preached in London, it is said that he
was frequently heard by the eminent Dr. Owen, Vice-
Chancellor of Oxford University; and that when Charles
the Second once upbraided him for hearing "that illiterate
tinker prate," the Doctor replied, "Please your majesty,
could I possess that tinker's abilities for preaching, I
would most gladly relinquish all my learning." Dr.
Southey says, that in London "his reputation was so
great, that if a day's notice were given, the meeting-house
at Southwark, at which he generally preached, would not
contain half the people." And Bunyan's warm friend,

Charles Doe, says, "I have seen, by my computation, about twelve hundred persons to hear him at a morning lecture, on a working day in dark winter-time. I also computed about three thousand that came to hear him at a towns-end meeting-house; so that half were fain to go back again for want of room; and there himself was fain, at a back door, to be pulled almost over the people to get up stairs to the pulpit."

Alas for England that such a man should be considered a criminal! It was impossible for him to conceal his light under a bushel, and it seemed equally impossible that the enemies of truth should permit such a light to remain unextinguished, if they could put it out. On the 12th of November, 1660, he had engaged to preach in a private house at Samsell, in Bedfordshire. He was apprised before the meeting of the fact that a warrant was out to seize him; but he felt that he owed it to the gospel not to run away at such a time. Three years before this an attempt had been made to imprison him and had failed, but now, only five weeks after the restoration of the king, it was determined to make an example which should, if possible, strike terror into the hearts of the Dissenters. Mr. Francis Wingate, a well-known justice of the peace, issued his warrant, and ordered the constable to keep a strong watch about the house where the meeting should be kept, "as if we that were to meet together in that place did intend to do some *fearful* business to the destruction of the country; when, alas! the constable when he came in, found us only with our Bibles in our hands, ready to speak and hear the word of God; for we were just ready to begin our exercise. Nay, we had begun in prayer for the bless-

ing of God upon our opportunity." When the constable
had seized him, he had only time to say to the people,
" You see we are prevented of our opportunity to speak
and hear the word of God, and are likely to suffer for the
same. But be not discouraged. It is a mercy to suffer
for so good a cause. We might have been apprehended
as thieves or murderers, or for other wickedness; but
blessed be God it is not so. We suffer as Christians for
well doing; and better be the persecuted than the persecutors." On the following morning he appeared before the
justice, and as he boldly refused to cease from preaching, no
bail could be taken, and he was committed to Bedford jail
till the quarter sessions. The jail and the bridge on which

BEDFORD JAIL AND BRIDGE.

it stood have long ago been demolished, but we rejoice
that we can copy a drawing which will long perpetuate
their recollection.

The men who, like Bunyan, were placed in prison for what was deemed the high crime of preaching, were a noble race, including not a few distinguished for talents and learning. Ivimey, one of Bunyan's biographers, tells us that belonging to the church at Bedford were no less than seven preachers. One of these, named Nehemiah Coxe, was a grandson of a bishop; and though only a shoemaker was an eminent scholar. He was tried at the Bedford Assizes for preaching, and pleaded first in Greek and then in Hebrew. The judge was astounded, and called for the indictment. In that Coxe was styled a cordwainer. The judge told him that none of the lawyers could answer him. Coxe, however, claimed his right to plead in whatever language he pleased; this was conceded, and he was released. It is said that the judge enjoyed the discomfiture of the lawyers, and said to them, as Coxe left the court, "Well, gentlemen, this cordwainer has wound you all up."

Perhaps we ought before this to have introduced our readers to Bunyan's domestic circle. His first wife, in the midst of trials and poverty, had been removed to a better world, leaving behind her four children, one of whom was blind. Another, named Elizabeth, soon after, in the year 1658, took her place, and proved a wife worthy of her husband, and a mother such as his children needed. She was every way a noble woman, who was loved by her husband's friends, and respected even by his enemies. When Bunyan was unjustly confined in prison, and she was advised by wise men of the illegality of this fact, and knew for herself that what was called his trial was a scene of injustice, she determined to do all that a woman could do to obtain his release. She was indeed a heroine of no ordinary stamp, in so trying a situation. She went to London with a petition for the release of her husband,

BUNYAN BEFORE THE JUDGES.

which was presented to the House of Lords, but in vain. Time after time she appeared in person before the judges, and although a delicate young woman of retiring habits,

13   K

pleaded the cause of her husband and his children in language worthy of counsel of the most eminent talent; but all her entreaties were fruitless, although Chief Justice Hale was evidently affected by her powerful appeal, and felt much for her. Dr. Cheever has admirably said, "This courageous, this fine, high-minded English woman, and Lord Chief Justice Hale, and Bunyan, have long since met in heaven; but how little could they recognise each other's character on earth! How little could the distressed, insulted wife have imagined that beneath the judge's ermine there was beating the heart of a child of God, a man of humility, integrity and prayer! How little could the great, the learned, the illustrious, and truly pious judge have dreamed that the man, the obscure tinker, whom he was suffering to languish in prison for want of a writ of error, would one day be the subject of greater admiration and praise than all the judges in the kingdom of Great Britain! How little could he dream, that from that narrow cell where the prisoner was left incarcerated, and cut off apparently from all usefulness, a glory would shine out, illustrating the government and grace of God, and doing more good to man than all the prelates and judges of the kingdom put together had accomplished."

Shall we look at our hero in his jail? There we see him, as one of some eight thousand, who it is said were confined for their nonconformity to tyrannical ecclesiastical law, during the reign of Charles the Second. His indictment runs, that he "devilishly and perniciously abstained from coming to church to hear divine service, and is a common upholder of several unlawful meetings and conventicles, to the great disturbance and distraction of the good subjects of this kingdom." And can he by no means be released? This was a subject more than once discussed between him and his enemies, the justices and judges; and truly amusing is it to read the remarks of these *learned* men, and to see how easily the tinker disposes of all they can say. After Bunyan had confessed to Judge Keeling, that he with his friends "' had many meetings together, both to pray to God, and to exhort one another,' ' Then,' said Keeling, ' hear your judgment. You must be had back again to prison, and there lie for three months following; and at three months end, if you do not submit to go to *church*, to hear divine service, and leave your preaching, you must be banished the realm; and if, after such a day as shall be appointed you to be gone, you shall be found in this realm, &c., or be found to come over again, without special license from the king, &c., you must stretch by the neck for it, I tell you plainly;' and so he bid my jailer have me away." But what said Bunyan as he was returning to the prison, where he must remain for more than twelve years? " I told him as to this matter, I was at a point with him; for if I were out of prison to-day, I would preach the gospel again to-morrow, by the help of God." Noble confessor! Here was conduct worthy of Paul or of Luther!

We are ready, as Americans, to ask why, under these circumstances, he did not join the Pilgrim Fathers, and remove to New England. Gentle readers, stay, and recognize the hand of God:—*John Bunyan had to write the Pilgrim's Progress in Bedford Jail!* Who can tell the usefulness of this book, the propriety of the publication of which was once doubted, but which has since been

translated into more languages than any other volume, the
Bible excepted.

> " *Bunyan,* O thy precious dreaming,
>   How it charms the listening ear!
> Young and old, with faces beaming,
>   Group the *Pilgrim's* tale to hear;
> Learning from the lessons given
> All the wondrous ways to heaven."

Here then we see the object of our esteem immured for
twelve long weary years in a prison. But even here he
has enjoyment. His family were permitted to visit him,
and his most beloved blind daughter often cheered his solitude and her own. As Dr. Hamilton says, " He had his
Bible and his ' Book of Martyrs.' He had his imagination
and his pen ;—above all, he had a good conscience. He
felt it a blessed exchange to quit the ' iron cage' of despair
for a ' den' oft visited by a celestial comforter; which,
however cheerless, did not lack a door to heaven." What
books he wrote in prison cannot be certainly known, excepting his " Grace Abounding" and his " Pilgrim's Progress."

There were other alleviations in his captivity. God had
blessed him with a cheerful temper, and a love of wit.
Here is an instance. One day a friendly Quaker visited
him in jail, thus introducing himself, " Friend Bunyan,
the Lord hath sent me with a message to thee, and I have
been searching for thee everywhere." " Nay, friend,"
said Bunyan, "if thy message to me had been from the
Lord, he would have told thee *where* to find me; for I
have been long here." We have somewhere met with
another specimen of his wit. He was greatly opposed to

the observance of the fasts and festivals appointed by the
Church of Rome. A friendly neighbor thought somewhat to entrap him on this subject, and at Christmas time
sent him a mince pie, which John ate with a hearty relish.
His friend expressed his surprise that he should sanction
the day by eating Christmas pie; "Oh," said John, "that
matter is soon explained; I have long ago learned to dis-
tinguish between Christmas and pie."

But that which gave to Bunyan the greatest enjoyment
during his long imprisonment, was the humanity and kindness of his jailer, with whom, like Joseph of old, he found
favor. This worthy man even allowed him frequently to
leave the prison to visit his family, and to preach, which
he often did at midnight; and for more than three years
he regularly attended the week evening church meetings
of his brethren. On one occasion, some of the bishops,
who had heard a rumour of the unusual liberty conceded
to him, sent a messenger from London to Bedford, a distance of fifty-six miles, to ascertain the truth. The officer
was instructed to call at the prison during the night. It
was a night when Bunyan had received permission to stay
at home with his family; but so uneasy did he feel, that
he told his wife that he must go back to his old quarters.
So late was it that the jailer blamed him for coming at
such an untimely hour; but a little afterwards the messenger arrived. "Are all the prisoners safe?" "Yes." "Is
John Bunyan safe?" "Yes." "Let me see him." Bunyan was called, and the messenger went his way. When
he was gone, the jailer said to his prisoner, "Well, you
may go out again just when you think proper, for you
know when to return better than I can tell you."

13 *

While yet in prison the church at Bedford elected him as their pastor. The following entry appears on their records, " On the 24th of August, 1671, the church were directed to seek to God about the choice of Brother Bunyan to the office of elder or co-pastor; to which office he was called on the 24th of the tenth month, in the same year, when he received of the elders the right hand of fellowship."

Not long after this, while yet in prison, as the result of the wily king's "Act of Indulgence," Bunyan received license to preach. He seems not to have belonged to the large number of those who saw the design of that "Act," and refused its benefits; but probably felt it his duty to preach whenever and wherever he could. Not long since some curious manuscripts were discovered in the record room at Leicester, many miles from Bedford, which are now carefully preserved by the Town Council; and among the rest is a small scrap of paper whereon the following sentences are written :—"John Bunyon's License bears date the ninth day of May, 1672, to teach as a congregational parson, being of that persuasion, in the house of Josias Roughead, in the town of Bedford, or in any other place, room, or house licensed by his Majestie.—Memorand. The said Bunyon showed his License to Mr. Mayor. Mr. Overinge, Mr. Freeman, and Mr. Browne, being then present, the 6th day of October, 1672, being Sunday."

In September of that year Bunyan, with many others, was released from prison. It was long supposed that Bishop Barlow was the agent by whom his freedom was obtained, but the whole affair was involved in mystery, till within a very few years past, when all the documents relat-

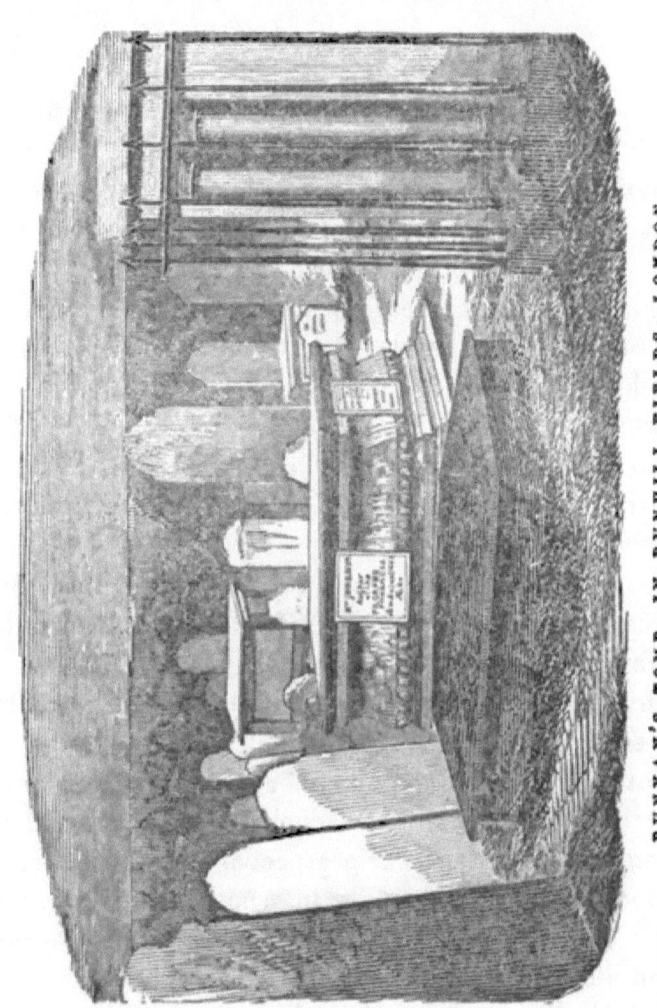

BUNYAN'S TOMB, IN BUNHILL FIELDS, LONDON.

Drawn on the spot in 1837.

(152)

ing to it have come to light; and we learn that it was effected by the influence of George Whitehead, a leading member of the Society of Friends, who included his name in a list of Quakers and others, to the number of four hundred and ninety, whose release he obtained from Charles. The original patent of release, with the great seal attached to it, is carefully preserved by the Society of Friends, in their archives at Devonshire House, London.

But we must draw to a close. For sixteen years after his release, did Bunyan pursue his ministerial labors in Bedfordshire, Cambridgeshire, Huntingdonshire, and the neighboring counties, where many prosperous congregations still exist, who claim him as their founder. Whitefield used to call him a bishop, and assuredly no man who has ever borne that title labored with more zeal or success. In 1688, the year of the glorious Revolution, he died. The last act he performed was characteristic of the man. A young gentleman, who lived in his neighborhood, had fallen under his father's displeasure, and was much grieved at his father's estrangement, as well as at the prospect of being disinherited. He implored Bunyan's friendly interposition to propitiate his father, and prepare the way for his return to parental favor and affection. The kind-hearted man undertook the task, and having successfully achieved it, was returning from Reading to London, some fifty miles, when he was thoroughly drenched with excessive rains. He arrived, cold and wet, at the house of his friend, Mr. Strudwick, a grocer on Snow Hill, in the city of London. Here he was seized with violent fever, and after ten days' sickness, his pilgrimage ended, "and he went in by the gate into the city," August 31, 1688, in the sixty-first year of his age. His precious remains repose in the vast burying-ground of Bunhill Fields, with those of many thousands of "the excellent of the earth."

We will not, fascinating as the subject is to ourselves, weary the attention of the reader by an analysis of the mental character of this extraordinary man. This has been often done, and done well. We will, therefore, only utter a few words more on what he has accomplished. Dr. Hamilton, the most recent writer on the subject, in his beautiful little sketch, says, "None has painted the beauty of holiness in tints more lovely, nor spoken in tones more thrilling to the heart of universal humanity. At first the favorite of the vulgar, he is now the wonder of the learned; and from the obscurity, not inglorious, of smoky cupboards and cottage chimneys, he has been exalted up to the highest places of classical renown, and duly canonized by the pontiffs of taste and literature. The man whom Cowper praised anonymously,

> "Lest so despised a name should move a sneer,"

has at last extorted emulous plaudits from a larger host of writers than ever conspired to praise a man of genius, who was also a man of God. In the same sentence, Bunyan has a word for the man of sense, and another for the man of fancy, and a third for the man of feeling; and by thus blending the intellectual, the imaginative, and the affectionate, he speaks home to the whole of men, and has made his works a lesson-book for all mankind."

> Thou wast a tinker; but the hallowed fire
> Of God baptized thy spirit, and thenceforth
> Thou wast a flaming prophet. Heaven and earth

Rang with the symphonies of thy sweet lyre,
Whiles the vibrations of the ecstatic wire,
'Neath thy discoursive touch, embodied forth
Forms of no vain or transitory worth;
Whose truth, when all sublunar things expire,
Gorged in infinitude's profound abyss,
Shall be the song of angels.   Every gleam
Of that pure flood that sparkles through thy dream.
Is light from heaven shot from the bowers of bliss.
Thou an apostle by the holy beam
That fired thy soul to speak God's mysteries.

John Bunyan.

BY REV. T. L. CUYLER.

THE question, wherein lies the charm of the world-known Pilgrim's Progress, does not admit of a *single* answer. It does not lie alone in the exquisite simplicity of the language, or in the liveliness of the conceptions, or in the clearness of the theological truth presented, or only in the beauty and force of its practical teachings. It is the combination of them all which throws the immortal charm over the allegory: and for this wondrous combination he was indebted to one book. It was his *only* book. He had indeed read one or two volumes of the martyr history of Christ's Church, and his wife brought him, among her marriage portion, two more volumes—the "Practice of Piety," and the "Plain Man's Pathway to Heaven." But the Bible was to him the "book of all learning." He had read little poetry save the sublime breathings from the inspired lips of David and Isaiah; and he has himself written a poem glowing with the loftiest imagery. He had studied no theology but that which he learned directly from Moses and the Prophets, and which fell from Him who spake as never man spake; and yet he

(156)

has produced a 'body of divinity' second to none but his great original.

It is to the study of the English translation of the Bible that he is mainly indebted for the strength and purity of his language. His English is undefiled. His dialect is the old unpolluted dialect of England's heroic days, which the most illiterate may understand, and which the most learned cannot improve. It is the dialect which Shakspeare found rich enough to meet all the varied wants of all his characters, from eloquent senators and courtly ladies, down to the clownish peasant and the lisping child. It is the prevailing dialect of Taylor—"Taylor, the Shakspeare of divines"—of Macauley, the most brilliant of modern essayists—of Webster, the purest in style of our American orators.

The poetical language of Scripture, Bunyan seems to have completely mastered. What an oriental splendor falls upon his land of Beulah, where the "sun shineth night and day, and the flowers appear every day, and the voice of the turtle is heard in the land." We imagine him to ourselves at this moment, bending over his oaken table in the Bedford prison cell. By the light of his solitary lamp, we can discern the ruddy face and the sharp twinkling eyes, the broad forehead, and the large mouth with the tuft above it, which "he wore after the old British fashion." He is adding the last lines to the immortal allegory. The book of books is before him—opened at the Apocalypse. He has lingered over John's wonderful visions until his soul is lifted into a devotional rapture, and as he is borne along in rapt enthusiasm, his thoughts pour forth in a constant flow of scripture imagery. He seizes his

14

pen and writes—"Now I saw in my dream that the two
pilgrims went in at the gate; and lo! as they entered they
were transfigured; and they had raiment put on that shone
like gold.   Just as the gate was opened to let in the men,
I looked in after them, and behold the city shone like the
sun!   The streets were also paved with gold, and in them
walked many men with crowns on their heads, and golden
harps to sing praises withal.   There were also of them
that had wings, and they answered one another without
intermission, saying, 'Holy, holy, holy is the Lord! And
after that they shut up the gates; which, when I had seen,
I wished myself among them."

Among character painters, Bunyan deserves a place in
the highest rank.   Shakspeare had to do with living men,
and Bunyan with personifications; yet in the wonderful
tinker's hands these impersonifications *become* living men.
To all who read the Pilgrim's Progress, old and young,
unlearned and learned, the multitude of characters that
throng its pages are actual persons.   We take but a short
walk with Mr. *Ignorance*, who came out of the town of
Conceit, but we see enough of him to know that he is the
perfect counterpart of a dozen good-for-nothing fellows in
our own neighborhood.   Mr. *Byends* and My *Lord Time-
server*, we have often seen in legislative halls.   Mr. *Talka-
tive* has pestered us a thousand times.   Mr. *Selfwill* has
long been a thorn in our flesh : and we never meet with a
faint-hearted brother, with his head bowed down like a
bulrush, without thinking of poor Mr. Fearing, who lay
moaning so long beside the Slough of Despond, and who
went down with trembling steps at last into the deep river.
Thrice blessed dreamer! thou hast lain for more than a

century and a half in Bunhill fields, but no lapse of years
can destroy the spell which thou holdest over the strongest
minds! Thy audience grows with the advance of time.
In a country which thou knewest only as a trifling colony,
thy immortal allegory lies on the tables of ten thousand
drawing rooms arrayed in crimson and gold, and lives, too,
in the inner heart of God's struggling church!"

Says Macauley—"The Puritans were men whose minds
had derived a peculiar character from the daily contemplation of superior beings and eternal interests. Not
content with acknowledging, in general terms, an overrul-
ing Providence, they habitually ascribed every event to the
will of the Great Being, for whose power nothing was too
vast, for whose inspection nothing was too minute. To
know him, to serve him, to enjoy him, was with them the
great end of existence. They rejected with contempt the
ceremonious homage which other sects substituted for
the pure worship of the soul. Instead of catching occasional glimpses of the Deity through an obscuring veil,
they aspired to gaze full on the intolerable brightness, and
to commune with him face to face. Hence originated their
contempt for terrestrial distinctions. The difference between
the greatest and meanest of mankind seemed to vanish
when compared with the boundless interval which separated the whole race from Him on whom their eyes were
constantly fixed. They recognised no title to superiority
but His favor; and confident of that favor, they despised
all the accomplishments and all the dignities of the world.
If they were unacquainted with the works of philosophers
and poets, they were deeply read in the oracles of God.
If their names were not found in the registers of heralds,

they felt assured they were recorded in the Book of Life.
If their steps were not accompanied by a splendid train of
menials, legions of ministering angels had charge over
them.   Their palaces were houses not made with hands:
their diadems crowns of glory which should never fade
away !   On the rich and the eloquent, on nobles and priests,
they looked down with contempt: for they esteemed themselves rich in a more precious treasure, and eloquent in a
more sublime language ; *nobles by the right of an earlier
creation, and priests by the imposition of a mightier hand.*
The very meanest of them was a being to whose fate a
mysterious and terrible importance belonged—on whose
slightest action the spirits of light and darkness looked
with anxious interest—who had been destined, before
heaven and earth were created, to enjoy a felicity which
should continue when heaven and earth should have passed
away.   Events which short-sighted politicians ascribed to
earthly causes, had been ordained on his account.   For his
sake, empires had arisen, and flourished, and decayed.   For
his sake, the Almighty had proclaimed his will by the pen of
the evangelist and the harp of the prophet.   He had been
rescued by no common deliverer from the grasp of no
common foe.   He had been ransomed by the sweat of no
vulgar agony, by the blood of no earthly sacrifice.   It was
for him that the sun had been darkened, that the rocks
had been rent, that the dead had arisen, that all nature
had shuddered at the sufferings of her expiring God !"

John Bunyan.

BY J. G. WHITTIER.

" Wouldst see
A man i' the clouds, and hear him speak to thee ?"

WHO has not read PILGRIM'S PROGRESS? Who has
not, in childhood, followed the wandering Christian on his
way to the Celestial City? Who has not laid at night his
young head on the pillow, to paint on the walls of darkness pictures of the Wicket Gate and the Archers, the Hill
of Difficulty, the Lions and Giants, Doubting Castle and
Vanity Fair, the sunny Delectable Mountains and the
Shepherds, the Black River and the wonderful glory
beyond it; and at last fallen asleep, to dream over the
strange story, to hear the sweet welcomings of the sisters
at the House Beautiful, and the song of birds from the
window of that "upper chamber which opened towards
the sunrising?" And who, looking back to the green
spots in his childish experiences, does not bless the good
tinker of Elstow?

And who, that has re-perused the story of the Pilgrim
at a maturer age, and felt the plummet of its truth sounding in the deep places of the soul, has not reason to bless
the author for some timely warning or grateful encourage-

14*   L   (161)

ment ?   Where is the scholar, the poet, the man of taste
and feeling, who does not, with Cowper,

> " Even in transitory life's late day,
> Revere the man whose PILGRIM marks the road,
> And guides the PROGRESS of the soul to God !"

We have just been reading, with no slight degree of
interest, that simple but wonderful piece of autobiography,
entitled " GRACE ABOUNDING TO THE CHIEF OF SINNERS,"
from the pen of the author of Pilgrim's Progress.   It is
the record of a journey more terrible than that of the
ideal Pilgrim ; " truth stranger than fiction ;" the painful
upward struggling of a spirit from the blackness of despair
and blasphemy, into the high, pure air of Hope and Faith.
More earnest words were never written.   It is the entire
unveiling of a human heart ; the tearing off of the fig-leaf
covering of its sin.   The voice which speaks to us from
these old pages seems not so much that of a denizen of
the world in which we live, as of a soul at the last solemn
confessional.   Shorn of all ornament, simple and direct as
the contrition and prayer of childhood, when for the first
time the Spectre of Sin stands by its bedside, the style is
that of a man dead to self-gratification, careless of the
world's opinion, and only desirous to convey to others, in
all truthfulness and sincerity, the lesson of his inward
trials, temptations, sins, weaknesses, and dangers ; and
to give glory to Him who had mercifully led him through
all, and enabled him, like his own Pilgrim, to leave behind
the Valley of the Shadow of Death, the snares of the
Enchanted Ground, and the terrors of Doubting Castle,
and to reach the land of Beulah, where the air was sweet

and pleasant, and the birds sang, and the flowers sprang up around him, and the Shining Ones walked in the brightness of the not distant Heaven. In the introductory pages he says: "I could have dipped into a style higher than this in which I have discoursed, and could have adorned all things more than here I have seemed to do; but I dared not. God did not play in tempting me; neither did I play when I sunk, as it were, into a bottomless pit, when the pangs of hell took hold on me; wherefore, I may not play in relating of them, but be plain and simple, and lay down the thing as it was."

This book, as well as "Pilgrim's Progress," was written in Bedford prison, and was designed especially for the comfort and edification of his "children, whom God had counted him worthy to beget in faith by his ministry." In his introduction he tells them, that, although taken from them, and tied up, "sticking, as it were, between the teeth of the lions of the wilderness," he once again, as before, from the top of Shemer and Hermon, so now, from the lion's den and the mountain of leopards, would look after them with fatherly care and desires for their everlasting welfare. "If," said he, "you have sinned against light; if you are tempted to blaspheme; if you are drowned in despair; if you think God fights against you; or if Heaven is hidden from your eyes, remember it was so with your father. But out of all the Lord delivered me."

He gives no dates; he affords scarcely a clew to his localities; of the man, as he worked, and ate, and drank, and lodged, of his neighbors and contemporaries, of all he saw and heard of the world about him, we have only an occasional glimpse, here and there, in his narrative.　It is the story of his inward life only that he relates.　What had time and place to do with one who trembled always with the awful consciousness of an immortal nature, and about whom fell alternately the shadows of hell and the splendors of heaven ?　We gather, indeed, from his record, that he was not an idle on-looker in the time of England's great struggle for freedom, but a soldier of the Parliament, in his young years, among the praying sworders and psalm-singing pikemen, the Greathearts and Holdfasts whom he has immortalized in his allegory ; but the only allusion which he makes to this portion of his experience is by way of illustration of the goodness of God in preserving him on occasions of peril.

He was born at Elstow, in Bedfordshire, in 1628 ; and, to use his own words, "his father's house was of that rank which is the meanest and most despised of all the families of the land."　His father was a tinker, and the son followed the same calling, which necessarily brought him into association with the lowest and most depraved classes of English society.　The estimation in which the tinker and his occupation were held, in the seventeenth century, may be learned from the quaint and humorous description of Sir Thomas Overbury.　"The tinker," saith he, "is a movable, for he hath no abiding in one place ; he seems to be devout, for his life is a continual pilgrimage, and sometimes in humility, goes barefoot, therein making necessity a virtue ; he is a gallant, for he carries all his wealth upon his back ; or a philosopher, for he bears all his substance with him.　He is always furnished with a song, to which his hammer, keeping tune, proves that he

was the first founder of the kettle-drum; where the best
ale is, there stands his music most upon crotchets. The
companion of his travel is some foul, sun-burnt quean, that,
since the terrible statute, has recanted gypsyism, and is
turned pedlaress. So marches he all over England, with
his bag and baggage; his conversation is irreprovable, for
he is always mending. He observes truly the statutes,
and therefore had rather steal than beg. He is so strong
an enemy of idleness that in mending one hole he would
rather make three than want work; and when he hath
done, he throws the wallet of his faults behind him. His
tongue is very voluble, which, with canting, proves him a
linguist. He is entertained in every place, yet enters no
farther than the door, to avoid suspicion. To conclude, if
he escape Tyburn and Banbury, he dies a beggar."

One day, while standing in the street, cursing and blas-
pheming, he met with a reproof which startled him. The
woman of the house in front of which the wicked young
tinker was standing, herself, as he remarks, "a very loose,
ungodly wretch," protested that his horrible profanity made
her tremble; that he was the ungodliest fellow for swearing she had ever heard, and able to spoil all the youth of
the town who came in his company. Struck by this
wholly unexpected rebuke, he at once abandoned the practice of swearing; although previously he tells us that "he
had never known how to speak, unless he put an oath
before and another behind."

One day, he tells us, a sudden rushing sound, as of wind
or the wings of angels, came to him through the window,
wonderfully sweet and pleasant; and it was as if a voice
spoke to him from heaven words of encouragement and

hope, which, to use his language, commanded, for the
time, "a silence in his heart to all those tumultuous
thoughts that did use, like masterless hell-hounds, to roar
and bellow, and make a hideous noise within him." About
this time, also, some comforting passages of Scripture
were called to mind; but he remarks, that whenever he
strove to apply them to his case, Satan would thrust the
curse of Esau in his face, and wrest the good word from
him. The blessed promise, "Him that cometh to me, I
will in no wise cast out," was the chief instrumentality in
restoring his lost peace. He says of it: "If ever Satan
and I did strive for any word of God in all my life, it was
for this good word of Christ; he at one end, and I at the
other; oh, what work we made! It was for this in John,
I say, that we did so tug and strive; he pulled, and I
pulled, but, God be praised! I overcame him; I got sweetness from it. Oh! many a pull hath my heart had with
Satan for this blessed sixth chapter of John!"

Who does not here call to mind the struggle between
Christian and Apollyon in the valley! That was no fancy
sketch; it was the narrative of the author's own grapple
with the Spirit of Evil. Like his ideal Christian, he "con-
quered through Him that loved him." Love wrought the
victory: the Scripture of Forgiveness overcame that of
Hatred.

He never afterwards relapsed into that state of religious
melancholy from which he so hardly escaped. He speaks
of his deliverance, as the waking out of a troublesome
dream. His painful experience was not lost upon him;
for it gave him, ever after, a tender sympathy for the
weak, the sinful, the ignorant, and desponding. In some

measure, he had been "touched with the feeling of their infirmities." He could feel for those in the bonds of sin and despair, as bound with them. Hence his power as a preacher; hence the wonderful adaptation of his great allegory to all the variety of spiritual conditions. Like Fearing, he had lain a month in the Slough of Despond, and had played, like him, the long melancholy bass of spiritual heaviness. With Feeble-mind, he had fallen into the hands of Slay-good, of the nature of Man-eaters; and had limped along his difficult way upon the crutches of Ready-to-halt. Who better than himself could describe the condition of Despondency, and his daughter Much-afraid, in the dungeon of Doubting Castle? Had he not also fallen among thieves, like Little-faith?

His account of his entering upon the solemn duties of a preacher of the gospel is at once curious and instructive. . He deals honestly with himself, exposing all his various moods, weaknesses, doubts, and temptations. " I preached," he says, "what I felt; for the terrors of the law and the guilt of transgression lay heavy on my conscience. I have been as one sent to them from the dead. I went, myself in chains, to preach to them in chains; and carried that fire in my conscience which I persuaded them to beware of." At times, when he stood up to preach, blasphemies and evil doubts rushed into his mind, and he felt a strong desire to utter them aloud to his congregation; and at other seasons, when he was about to apply to the sinner some searching and fearful text of Scripture, he was tempted to withold it, on the ground that it condemned himself also; but, withstanding the suggestion of the Tempter, to use his own simile, he bowed himself like

Samson to condemn sin wherever he found it, though he brought guilt and condemnation upon himself thereby, choosing rather to die with the Philistines than to deny the truth.

Foreseeing the consequences of exposing himself to the operation of the penal laws by holding conventicles and preaching, he was deeply afflicted at the thought of the suffering and destitution to which his wife and children might be exposed by his death or imprisonment. Nothing can be more touching than his simple and earnest words on this point. They show how warm and deep were his human affections, and what a tender and loving heart he laid as a sacrifice on the altar of duty:

"I found myself a man compassed with infirmities; the parting with my wife and poor children, hath often been to me in this place, as the pulling the flesh from the bones; and also it brought to my mind the many hardships, miseries, and wants, that my poor family was like to meet with, should I be taken from them, especially my poor blind child, who lay nearer my heart than all beside. Oh! the thoughts of the hardships I thought my poor blind one might go under, would break my heart to pieces.

"Poor child! thought I, what sorrow art thou like to have for thy portion in this world! thou must be beaten, must beg, suffer hunger, cold, nakedness, and a thousand calamities, though I cannot now endure the wind should blow upon thee. But yet, thought I, I must venture you all with God, though it goeth to the quick to leave you. Oh! I saw I was as a man who was pulling down his house upon the heads of his wife and children; yet I thought on those 'two milch kine that were to carry the ark of God into another country, and to leave their calves behind them.'

"But that which helped me in this temptation was divers considerations: the first was, the consideration of those two Scriptures, 'Leave thy fatherless children, I will preserve them alive; and let thy widows trust in me:' and again, 'The lord said, verily it shall go well with thy remnant; verily I will cause the enemy to entreat them well in the time of evil.' "

He was arrested in 1660, charged with "devilishly and perniciously abstaining from church," and of being "a common upholder of conventicles." At the quarter sessions, where his trial seems to have been conducted somewhat like that of Faithful at Vanity Fair, he was sentenced to perpetual banishment. This sentence, however, was never executed, but he was remanded to Bedford jail, where he lay a prisoner for twelve years.

Here, shut out from the world, with no other books than the Bible and Fox's Martyrs, he penned that great work which has attained a wider and more stable popularity than any other book in the English tongue. It is alike the favorite of the nursery and the study. Many experienced Christians hold it only second to the Bible; the infidel himself would not willingly let it die. Men of all sects read it with delight, as in the main a truthful representation of the Christian pilgrimage, without indeed assenting to all the doctrines which the author puts in the mouth of his fighting sermonizer, Greatheart, or which may be deduced from some other portions of his allegory. A recollection of his fearful sufferings, from misapprehension of a single text in the Scriptures, relative to the ques-

15

tion of election, we may suppose gave a milder tone to the
theology of his Pilgrim than was altogether consistent with
the Calvinism of the seventeenth century. "Religion,"
says Macaulay, "has scarcely ever worn a form so calm
and soothing as in Bunyan's allegory." In composing it,
he seems never to have altogether lost sight of the fact,
that in his life and death struggle with Satan for the
blessed promise recorded by the Apostle of Love, the ad-
versary was generally found on the Genevan side of the
argument.

Little did the short-sighted persecutors of Bunyan
dream, when they closed upon him the door of Bedford
jail, that God would overrule their poor spite and envy,
to his own glory and the world-wide renown of their victim. In the solitude of his prison, the ideal forms of
beauty and sublimity, which had long flitted before him
vaguely, like the vision of the Temanite, took shape and
coloring; and he was endowed with power to reduce them
to order, and arrange them in harmonious groupings. His
powerful imagination, no longer self-tormenting, but under
the direction of reason and grace, expanded his narrow
cell into a vast theatre lighted up for the display of its
wonders. To this creative faculty of his mind might have
been aptly applied the language which George Wither, a
contemporary prisoner, addressed to his Muse:

> "The dull loneness, the black shade
> Which these hanging vaults have made,
> The rude portals that give light
> More to terror than delight;
> This my chamber of neglect,
> Walled about with disrespect,—

From all these, and this dull air,
A fit object for despair,
She hath taught me by her might,
To draw comfort and delight."

That stony cell of his was to him like the rock of Pa-
dan-aram to the wandering Patriarch. He saw angels
ascending and descending. The house Beautiful rose up
before him, and its holy sisterhood welcomed him. He
looked, with his pilgrim, from the Chamber of Peace.
The Valley of Humiliation lay stretched out beneath his
eye, and he heard "the curious melodious note of the
country birds, who sing all the day long in the spring
time, when the flowers appear, and the sun shines warm,
and make the woods and groves and solitary places glad."
Side by side with the good Christiana and the loving
Mercy, he walked through the green and lowly valley,
"fruitful as any the crow flies over," through "meadows
beautiful with lilies;" the song of the poor but fresh-faced
shepherd boy, who lived a merry life, and wore the herb
heart's-ease in his bosom, sounded through his cell:

"He that is down need fear no fall,
He that is low no pride."

The broad and pleasant "river of the Water of Life"
glided peacefully before him, fringed "on either side with
green trees, with all manner of fruit," and leaves of heal-
ing, with "meadows beautified with lilies, and green all
the year long;" he saw the Delectable Mountains, glorious
with sunshine, overhung with gardens and orchards and
vineyards; and beyond all, the Land of Beulah, with its
eternal sunshine, its song of birds, its music of fountains,

its purple clustered vines, and groves through which
walked the Shining Ones, silver-winged and beautiful.

What were bars and bolts and prison walls to him, whose
eyes were anointed to see, and whose ears opened to hear,
the glory and the rejoicing of the City of God, when the
pilgrims were conducted to its golden gates, from the
black and bitter river, with the sounding trumpeters, the
transfigured harpers with their crowns of gold, the sweet
voices of angels, the welcoming peal of bells in the holy
city, and the songs of the redeemed ones? In reading the
concluding pages of the first part of Pilgrim's Progress,
we feel as if the mysterious glory of the Beatific Vision
was unveiled before us. We are dazzled with the excess
of light. We are entranced with the mighty melody;
overwhelmed by the great anthem of rejoicing spirits. It
can only be adequately described in the language of Milton in respect to the Apocalypse, as "a seven-fold chorus
of hallelujahs and harping symphonies."

Few who read Bunyan now-a-days think of him as one
of the brave old English confessors, whose steady and
firm endurance of persecution baffled, and in the end overcame the tyranny of the established church in the reign of
Charles II. What Milton and Penn and Locke wrote in
defence of Liberty, Bunyan lived out and acted. He made
no concessions to worldly rank. Dissolute lords and
proud bishops he counted less than the humblest and poorest of his disciples at Bedford. When first arrested and
thrown into prison, he supposed he should be called to suffer death for his faithful testimony to the truth; and his
great fear was, that he should not meet his fate with the
requisite firmness, and so dishonor the cause of his Mas-

ter. And when dark clouds came over him, and he sought
in vain for a sufficient evidence that in the event of his
death it would be well with him, he girded up his soul
with the reflection, that, as he suffered for the word and
way of God, he was engaged not to shrink one hair's
breadth from it. "I will leap," he says, "off the ladder
blindfold into eternity, sink or swim, come heaven, come
hell. Lord Jesus, if thou wilt catch me, do; if not, I will
venture in thy name!"

The English revolution of the seventeenth century,
while it humbled the false and oppressive aristocracy of
rank and title, was prodigal in the development of the
real nobility of the mind and heart. Its history is bright
with the footprints of men whose very names still stir the
hearts of freemen, the world over, like a trumpet peal.
Say what we may of its fanaticism, laugh as we may at
its extravagant enjoyment of newly acquired religious and
civil liberty, who shall now venture to deny that it was
the golden age of England? Who that regards freedom
above slavery, will now sympathize with the outcry and
lamentation of those interested in the continuance of the
old order of things, against the prevalence of sects and
schism, but who, at the same time, as Milton shrewdly
intimates, dreaded more the rending of their pontifical
sleeves than the rending of the church? Who shall now
sneer at Puritanism, with the "Defence of Unlicensed
Printing" before him? Who scoff at Quakerism over the
Journal of George Fox? Who shall join with debauched
lordlings and fat-witted prelates in ridicule of Anabaptist
levellers and dippers, after rising from the perusal of Pilgrim's Progress? "There were giants in those days."

15*

And foremost amidst that band of liberty-loving and God-fearing men,

> "The slandered Calvinists of Charles's time,
>   Who fought, and won it, Freedom's holy fight,"

stands the subject of our sketch, the Tinker of Elstow. Of his high merit as an author there is no longer any question. The Edinburgh Review expressed the common sentiment of the literary world, when it declared that the two great creative minds of the seventeenth century were those which produced PARADISE LOST and the PILGRIM'S PROGRESS.

John Hampden.

Burial Place of John Hampden.

BY MRS. S. C. HALL.

JUST at the close of the summer of 1848, it was our privilege to sojourn at a hospitable old English house in Hertfordshire; a stately mansion with abundant space, and yet withal so comfortable and suggestive! every nook fitted with old story-telling cabinets, or great high book-cases, crammed with rare books, books that conjure up old memories, talk in quaint language, and have a dark-determined-knowledge-look. The walls, too, were impressive teachers, hung with fine portraits—Vandyke, Lely, and Sir Joshua, speaking from the canvass. And when our eyes were uplifted from the page, it was so delightful to us, city dwellers, to gaze out of the large windows into the green park, diving through dark recesses and deep hollows—beneath huge "Patrician trees." So still, so solitary, was the dwelling, that, but for the hallowing view of the Church tower, and the smoke from the adjacent village of Aldbury, we might have believed ourselves detenus in "the happy valley." It was so delicious to watch the clouds gathering over Moneybury Hill: to canter through the never-ending green drives of Ashridge—to wonder at the tameness of the forest deer—to speculate on the geological formation of

M   (177)

Incombe-hole, where giants might play at bowls—to creep among the venerable box-hedges, and appreciate the taste of the old monks of Aylesbury, who here established a Health-house for such of the brethren as were " sick in the flesh"—to pause still longer on the " Beacon Hill" that rises boldly and verdantly above the village of Iving-hoe, and recall much that we have read, or tradition tells us, of the times of England's bitter struggle between Des-potism and Liberty,—when upon that very hill was kindled the beacon-fire, which told to Harrow the issue of the fight at Edge-hill, that Harrow might tell it to eager and anxious London !   What fearful times—fearful to read of even now—most fearful to those who knew that the freedom of future England was in their keeping ; when one of the hard Iron men, in whose high bravery and truth of purpose our utilitarian age finds it no easy matter to have faith, ex-claimed, in the Commons House of Parliament, " We must fight as in a cock-pit—we are surrounded by the sea—we have no stronger holds than our own skulls and our own ribs, to keep out our enemies !"

Pacing further back, we recalled the old rhyme—

> "Tring, Wing, and Ivinghoe
> From the HAMPDENS did goe,
> For striking the Black Prince a blowe."

The three sisters were within our ken, while we stood on the Beacon Hill, and, without pausing to consider whether History confirms or contradicts the legend, THE NAME, thus suggested, reminded us that the home and the grave of the truest—the purest—the best—of England's Patriots, was nigh at hand, among the far-famed Hill of the Chiltern

Hundreds.* A morning drive would take us there, through
the quaint villages and green lanes of Buckinghamshire—
all tranquil and grateful for the abundant realities of a full-
lapped autumn ; and then we might have some hours to
ramble amid scenes the great and high-hearted Patriot
loved so well; thus continuing our purposed pilgrimages
by a visit to one of the most interesting of England's many
hallowed shrines.

We passed that evening with Lord Nugent's interesting
history of the patriot, to whose dwelling we had vowed a
pilgrimage, calling in, occasionally, to council, one of the
Old Chronicles, or consulting a volume of grave Parliamentary Reports—resolved to strengthen and refresh our
memory, before presuming to look upon the honored urn
that contains the ashes of John Hampden.

We learn that he was born in the year of 1594 ; that
the city of London was his birth-place, and that he mani-

---

* From these Chiltern Hills is derived the celebrity of three of
the hundreds of Buckinghamshire, viz., Stoke, Desborough, and
Bonenham, which constitute a district very frequently referred to
in the proceedings of Parliament, by means of the well-known
phrase, "taking the Chiltern Hundreds." It is a mere ceremony,
a legal fiction, expressed by the words accepting the situation of
steward or bailiff of Her Majesty's Chiltern Hundreds—an office
purely nominal; for though, perhaps, the claim to some fees might
be enforced, if duties were performed, yet as no functions are ever
discharged, so no rewards are acquired by the holder; it is therefore only "in the eye of the law" that it is an "office of emolument."
No such office can be conferred by the Crown on a member of the
House of Commons without his thereby vacating his seat ; and it is
only by obtaining office that any person *qualified* to sit in Parliament can rid himself of the duties which any body of constituents
may impose, even without his consent.

fested an early love of letters, overcome only by those stern duties of the times to which taste and pleasure must unmurmuring yield.   His reputation for scholarly attainments must have been considerable, for he was chosen to write the Oxford gratulations on the union of the Elector Palatine with the Princess Elizabeth.   Strange destiny, that Prince Rupert, the issue of that marriage, should have led the troops at Chalgrove by whom John Hampden was slain!   We found him, in 1613, studying the law in the Inner Temple; there acquiring the knowledge to which he afterwards gave practice, to the salvation of that law.   Yet this study in no degree hardened his nature; nor did it ever become stern under Puritan ascendancy : he loved worthily, and at twenty-five years old—in 1619—married whom he loved—Elizabeth, the daughter of Edmund Symeon, Lord of the Manor of Pyrton, in Oxfordshire. His lineage was old and honorable, his fortune more than ample, his love successful, his mind nurtured to perfectness by severe and thoughtful studies, and enriched and adorned by the higher delights of poetry; while his healthful frame enabled him to enjoy all country sports amid the delicious scenery he loved—as fathers love their children—where he cherished, as twin-born, the home affections and the Liberty that glorifies the name of England. How clearly we felt, while tracing out the vast possessions that made him, perhaps, the richest Commoner in the kingdom, and revelling over the little of either conversations or correspondence that remains to those who would have sat at his feet for instruction—how clearly we felt that he was *forced* by troublous times from the privacy he loved; appearing suddenly, as Sir Philip Warwicke says, "with all great qualities ripened about him, of which he had never given a crude or ostentatious promise." He was, indeed, compelled to raise the standard by what, among many high and noble qualities, was the highest and noblest quality of his nature—a deep, stern, true, unquailing love of Justice! Although in Parliament during a portion of the reign of the first James, his fame, filling all England, is based upon the occurrences of the last few years of his great life; like his cousin Cromwell, he entered the arena when the blaze of youth had sunk into the deep burning fire of middle age; he had numbered forty years before he was recognised as "the Patriot Hampden." There is no record of his having bowed in the ante-room of the coarse and faithless James, for the title his mother coveted for her son; he had nobler aspirations—nobler company, than that which waited there; the chronicles are radiant with the glorious names of those who constituted with him the GREAT MOVEMENT—the Parliamentary party. How they echo through the vaults of history! Wentworth, and Pym, and Eliot, and Selden! But we write not a chronicle—though tempted to dwell upon strange records of strange times—often with natural indignation, when we read how James, scrambling through his dignity more like an idiot-baby than an anointed king, could offer insults to men like these!

We glanced rapidly over the early reign of his successor, the first Charles; dignified by some high virtues; disfigured by lack of forethought and want of truth; born out of season; belonging to the past, unwilling to advance, if not incapable of moving, with the times that rose and swelled about him! Then the gathering of Parliaments—

16

dark clouds heralding a tempest—now dispersing—now collecting—outraged in their dearest rights and privileges—struggling for their constituents, as men struggle for life, against "imposts" and "levies," and the worse mockery of "loans," which no man was free to refuse; Hampden with his friends—laboring with them to the

THE GATE HOUSE.

death, yet seeking no self-glory. As the horizon darkens, as the storm gathers, so does this great spirit come brightly forward—suffering imprisonments even in the GATE HOUSE;*

---

* Hampden was confined in the Gate-House for his opposition to the forced loans endeavored to be imposed on the country in 1625. This prison, which obtained much celebrity during the civil wars on account of the incarceration of so many eminent men within its walls, was erected in the reign of Edward III., and was originally the principal approach to the inclosure of the Monastery at Westminster from the open space in front of the western towers of the Abbey.

but never swerving for a moment from the path of honorable, though perilous, duty. How glad were we to find him again free; and though retaining his seat for Wendover, once more listening to natural thunder from the depths of his own deep woods—watching the increasing breach between the King and the people, but surrounded by his home affections, while upholding the Puritan doctrines in which he trusted, and pondering the means of checking the tide of unlawful prerogative. Strange minglings of good and evil!—inseparable from all destinies. He had suffered persecution, indignity, imprisonment: but he was at home—with the wife of his bosom—the children of his love! Trusting in God—trusting, yet prompt for action. We rejoiced with him in his enjoyment of the free air, and in his strong hope of the future—the strongest of all strengths; but there and then, a sorrow came upon him that, for a time, obliterated the past—put aside for awhile the public wrongs that wrung his heart; for even more full of agony than the wail of oppressed England, was the deep-toned bell of that little church—where they all sleep now—when it knelled out to hill and valley, that the mistress of Hampden, the beloved and cherished of its lord—the wife and friend of his youth—had been called away from him, when her counsel, tenderness and affection were needed most.

It was converted into an ecclesiastical prison shortly afterwards, and was used for criminals on the suppression of monasteries. It was pulled down in 1777, at which period it had become a debtor's prison. Our view is from a drawing published in the Gentleman's Magazine for 1836.

It takes brief time to read, or tell, of these events. Alas! the seeds of civil war were sown and nurtured, both by King and Parliament, who, wearied of each other, sought not peace. If the olive branch were held out, it was stripped of its leaves, and showed but as a dry and sapless twig. The patriot's energy was summoned from retirement by another blow struck at the country's liberty—by the issue of a writ for the levying of " SHIP MONEY." SHIP MONEY !* words steeped in the best and bravest

* The resuscitation of levies for furnishing ships to the king was one of the last acts of the life of Noy, the Attorney-General, who, by similar researches among obsolete usages, had already embroiled the court and country. He did not live to see this act enforced, but his friend the Lord Keeper Coventry, warmly approving all means of extortion, revived a practice which had only existed in the earlier stages of English government, before the rights of the sovereign and people had been clearly defined ; and which had in these distant days been but sparingly resorted to. Finding that sea-port and other towns had occasionally been called upon to furnish ships for the service of the crown, it was determined to revive the forgotten power which had been abrogated by Magna Charta, and make it the means of raising a direct and heavy-tax over the whole kingdom, subject to the king's will alone. The pretended reason for the rate was the aggressions of Turkish and other pirates ; yet was the money obtained by this unpopular and unconstitutional tax so badly applied, that the Algerines took many English vessels, and made captives of nearly 5000 Englishmen, while the Dutch seized two ships (East Indiamen) valued at £300,000. At no period of our country's history were the British flag and the sovereignty of the sea less respected. The bold opposition of Hampden struck a death-blow to this levy, which had been enforced and obtained, owing to the fears of some, and the lukewarmness of others, who looked less at the great principle involved in the right of arbitrary taxation in the crown, than at the sum required from each person, and the trouble and danger of opposition.

blood of England; words to which we owed eleven years of nearly uninterrupted civil war! At the head of the resistants to this new impost, stood John Hampden; the eyes of the court and the people were alike turned upon the champion now ungloved; the subject fighting *for* the law—the monarch *against* it: the King and the commoner pitted against each other—to the death; all Europe abiding the issue! The commoner was overthrown, but not in fair fight; the "court rescue" was the establishment of general discontent; the King and the people were separated for ever, by a matter of thirty-two shillings and sixpence!

Turning over the leaves of old and modern histories, we found that ancient worthies of the Chilterns differ as to the exact spot upon which the money was levied; many localities contending for the glory. No matter the place; there is no doubt as to who piloted English liberty through this particular storm. After its lull, brief as it was, Oliver Cromwell and John Hampden would have sailed, with a chosen band of Puritan friends, to Connecticut; but the doomed King forbade their departure! Well for us that it was so. Truly, enjoying as we were, that evening, the freedom of free speaking, thinking our own thoughts, and uttering our own words, without dread of STAR-CHAMBER,* or GATE-HOUSE, we carried back these *thoughts* to

---

* This building may be considered as the focus of Charles's despotism. From hence issued all the extortionate loans and levies which ended in the great civil war. So frightful in the end did it become, that its name infused terror, and to be "Star-chambered," was applied as a term indicative of the severest and cruelest infliction of semi-legal tyranny. In this court were men summoned by extra-judicial right, fined mercilessly and extravagantly, branded as

16 *

THE STAR CHAMBER.

things those grand old champions of our liberty wrought
for us.   Why do we utter hard words against these iron
men in ungarnished helmets ?   Staunch, stern, true, deep-

felons, their noses slit, and ears cut off, for acts and words less strong
than many in use daily by the Press at the present time.   The Star-
chamber stood on the eastern side of New Palace Yard, and was originally a portion of the royal palace.   It obtained the name of
Camera Stellata, from the walls or ceiling having been ornamented
with stars; but the building in use for the meetings of this court
from the end of the reign of Elizabeth until its abolition in 1641,
although probably built on the site of the elder chamber, was evidently of the Elizabethan era, as the letters E. R. and the date 1602
appeared over one of the doorways.   It was pulled down in 1836
for the erection of the New Houses of Parliament.   Our view exhibits the interior of the principal room, from a sketch made immediately previous to its demolition.

hearted men,—enthusiasts, as all must be who work great changes,—men combating with themselves as well as with their foes; fighting with the arm of flesh, and yet at war with those passions which lead strong men captive,—heroes in a double sense—as against others and themselves!

How rapidly, with those old books as our guides, did we pass over an interval of some ten or eleven years, and then again find Hampden married to Letitia Vachel; but she could have had but little contentment with her great lord; his habits of life were changed; she never resided with him in the sweet bowers of the Chiltern Hills. He lived for the people's service, not his own pleasure; and during the time passed in London they resided, as we read, in "lodgings near the house occupied by Pym in Gray's Inn Lane." *

The night was passing, and we were anxious about our next day's pilgrimage; we looked out into the park, the moon was shining brightly upon the upland woods, and the termination of the avenue to Ashridge showed like a huge spectre on the brow of Moneybury hill. We felt it was time to restore to their shelves the venerable councillors

---

* When Mr. John Forster was writing the lives of some of those great lights, he sought in vain for vestiges of their dwellings. They were probably "garden houses" with a pleasant look-out towards the country. John Gerard dates the dedication to his *Herbal*, published in 1597, "from my house in Holborne, in the suburbs of London." Gray's Inn Lane was at that time one of the principal roads into London, and was connected by the old bridle-ways with the great north roads at Highgate. In such suburban districts the old aristocracy lived, and the Lord Gray of Wilton having a mansion here in the reign of Edward III., gave name to the *Inn*, which became celebrated as the residence of some of our greatest lawyers.

who had revived our knowledge of the past; replacing a
volume is like saying adieu to an old and dear friend; and
there seemed an almost interminable number of last words
to speak before we parted; in them all we saw, pitted
against each other—the KING and HAMPDEN—the former
preserving his natural dignity and courtliness of bearing;
unsparing of his own toil and presence to work out purposes unworthy;—the latter, having thrown away the
scabbard when he drew the sword; chiefest among those
who added to their rigid morals a noble and simple vigor;
having put on, as Sidney says, " the athletic habit of liberty
for the contest." And yet, during the short remainder
of his great days, how bitterly was "the Patriot" tried;
domestic sorrows loosening the cords of life ! The funeral
plumes that waved over the coffins of his beloved daughter,
Mrs. Knightly, and his eldest son, were stirred by the
trumpet blast, the howls of ruined villages, and the still
more agonizing pangs of treachery—the treachery of re-
latives in whom he trusted ! The motto on his banner

" Vestigia nulla retrorsum,"

marked well his public course, and marshaled him, at the
head of his troop, clad in the ancestral color of his house,
the Lincoln green, to the various fields of Coventry,
Southam, Worcester, Evesham, Edge Hill, Reading, Chalgrove ; one by one those old chronicles were replaced; yet
still we lingered in memory over pages eloquent with facts.
   It was impossible to dismiss them from thought without
again and again thanking GOD for the many blessings we
enjoy in our age and generation—contrasting England of
the present with England of the past; without rejoicing

that the best lessons we receive in all high, all true, and
more especially all womanly virtues, issue from the
throne; knowing that no English woman of rank, elevated
or humble, can have loftier aims or nobler ambitions, than
to regulate a household, to bring up children, to study all
domestic duties, in close imitation of her whose example
is of far weightier force in her kingdom than all the precepts
of her servants in divinity and law. The times in which
we live may abound in difficulties; "the arts of peace" may
have been cultivated to ruinous excess; we may have to
guard against the enervating effects of luxury on the one
hand, and the debasing inroads of poverty on the other;
but we have liberty of conscience, no evil influences in
high places, no civil war to ravage our lands and desolate
our homes. Our task is but to preserve the freedom,
purchased by the bold hearts, great heads, and iron arms
of our forefathers—and to be grateful.

Early on the following morning we left the pretty village
of Aldbury far behind, passed the town of Tring, and
drove through those actual hamlets of old times,—unchanged
as their quaint names,* "Aston-Clinton" and "Weston-
Turville,"—where the cottages are shaded by noble trees,

---

* Much that is curious is connected with the names both of places
and persons in many of our English counties, and striking peculiari-
ties, indicative of remote antiquity, frequently arrest attention.
While Cornwall tells of early British location, Kent speaks of Saxon
rule in such names of persons as Fordred, which appears on the
coinage of that people; or of places, as Offham, (the house of Offa),
Wodensborough, (the hill of Oden,) &c. The names above quoted
are equally indicative of Norman rule, and the settlements awarded
to the followers of William the Conqueror

or peep, like toy-houses, out of boquets of monthly roses
and holyoaks, and wildernesses of clematis.   We strongly
desired to spend an hour in the beautiful church of Kimble,
which formerly belonged to the Hampdens; for those
village churches are full of interest; brasses and time-worn
tombs are to be met with in their sanctuaries; an old
morion above a tattered flag, or some hallowed name stamping
a blue slate with immortality; and Kimble tempted us,
looking so full of conscious glory, upon its steep, above
the tree-tops; but we had a long day's work before us at
Great Hampden.   We passed "The Chequers" in heroic
self-denial—for the present; and while we admired the
tinted woods and uprisings of the Chiltern Hills, we
became grievously perplexed by the net-work of lanes and
drives that, as we got deeper into the country, cross and
recross, and seem to diverge everywhere, and in all directions; the crows evidently considering their right to the
shorn harvest field indisputable.   Our driver was in happy
ignorance of Hampden, either the patriot or the house,
yet affirmed it was "somewhere hereabout;" and but for
a pretty cheerful girl, a miracle of intelligence, at a place
we believe called "Brockwell Farm," we might have wandered vainly among the hills, and valleys, and paths, until
the day was done.   We had not heard that the fine red
brick Elizabethan house of the Hampdens had been
stuccoed into whiteness, and we passed it without recogni-
tion; for the church, which we knew almost joined the
dwelling, is concealed by trees.   We drove on, however,
to what an honest-looking smith, who wielded his iron as
lightly as if it were a quarter-staff, told us was the
"Patriot's" village, and that the clerk of the church

THE VILLAGE OF GREAT HAMPDEN.

(197)

resided there. Hampden village consists of an irregular
line of very primitive cottages, straggling along one side
of a small common, from which their gardens have been
taken, bit by bit; it is backed by rising and well-wooded
ground.   An old and ragged tree, nearly opposite the gate
that separates the road from the common, attracted our
attention ; and a peasant, whose appearance bespoke little
of what we term "comfort," seemed much astonished at
our visit to "so poor a place."   He shook his head gravely,
and told us—"The people dead and gone said that tree
stood there in the "Patriot's" time, but the clerk of the
church knew it all ; he could tell all about the "Patriot,"
and everything : he would call him in a minute ; when
gentry did come to see so poor a place, they ought to know
everything."   The clerk soon came—a tall, thin man, who
stooped rather, and looked perhaps older than his years.
His calm intelligent face lit up when Hampden's name was
mentioned, and he knew the nature of our errand.   "Ay,"
he said, "that tree had heard the blast of Hampden's
trumpet, sure enough !"   No doubt it was *there*, under the
woody brows of his own Chilterns, he first issued the command to gather the militia of his own county, which had,
long before, caught the spirit of its great leader.   We
imagined the parishers and hundreds with their preachers
at their heads, marshaling up a defile to the right, to meet
him who had so bravely struggled for their liberty !   "Not
only the tree," resumed the worthy clerk, "but the cottage
in which I live, was standing then," and he invited us to
look at the beams, "they were so thick."   When we
entered, he pressed upon us pears and plums, the fruit of
his garden ; and his wife selected the largest from her store,

17   N

and took no little pride in the thickness of the low oak beams. She regarded us with respect when she found we had come from London to see and hear all about "The Patriot," which no one, she assured us, could tell better than her husband; "we must have great curiosity!" She had heard that Tring was twelve miles off; she had lived in this cottage forty years, but had never been so far. She confessed, with a quiet smile, "she was no great traveller." This Dorcas had bright eyes beneath her white hair, and was withal kindly, courteous, and intelligent, with abundant health, and was well learned in simple garden and house craft, and better still in that lore which renders wise unto salvation; yet, from the time of her youth, she had never been twelve miles from that most lonely and primitive village in which she was born!

Yes; nothing is more likely than that Hampden mustered his men upon that common; for the broad and beautiful table-land, spread in front of the house, which now commands so glorious a view of the surrounding country, was then intersected by quaint hedges and garden fantasies, suited to the taste of the period; no place, therefore, could have been more fitted or appropriate, as a muster-ground for the Hampden men, than Hampden Common, which almost adjoins the house. We turned back; leaving the common, and passing again through the green lanes, and by the forge, we came to the gate opening to a winding drive that leads through the park to the entrance of both church and dwelling—separated only by a narrow road, over-arched by stately trees and almost as stately evergreens: on the right, a small garden gate admits, by a back path, to the house, flower-garden, and lawn, where

the Patriot spent his happiest days: on the left, is the
entrance to the sacred church, where his remains repose.
It is very rarely that thus, within, as it were, the compass
of a ring, a great man's FIRST and LAST are gathered
together. It is impossible to imagine anything more still
than this hallowed spot, hid away at the back of that chalky
range, the Chilterns, which bound on one side the rich vale
of Aylesbury. The flower-garden, through which we
passed, seemed as if called into existence by the wand of
an enchanter; the lingering roses, the heavy-headed
dahlias, the bright-toned autumn flowers, looked so lonely
in their beauty. We almost feared to speak in such deep
solitude. A human footstep, the bark of a dog, the song
of a bird, the tinkle of a sheep-bell, would have been a
relief—until we had drunk deeply of the spirit of the
place, and then, as thoughts and memories crowded around
us, we felt the luxury of its solemn quiet, and that sound
here would be as sacrilege. Passing a low sort of postern
entrance we walked beneath an arch, starred over by jessa-
mine, and stood in front of the extensive mansion, added
to and enlarged by various proprietors, and at one time
displaying some goodly architecture of the age of Elizabeth; the stucco, as if ashamed of its usurpation, beginning to drop away from the red brick, of which the house
is built. Save the "natural decay" which must progress
in all uninhabited dwellings, we saw nothing that told of
the "ruin" which comes of carelessness or neglect.

The hall is of that gloomy character, once considered necessary for grandeur of effect; the suite of rooms consists
of a library, two dining-rooms, a drawing-room, a sort of
small presence-chamber, and a bed-room, that enjoys the re-

putation of having been especially furnished for Elizabeth by Griffith Hampden, when her gracious Majesty visited this

JOHN HAMPDEN'S HOUSE.

favored spot; the gallant high sheriff paid his Queen right royal homage, cutting a passage through the woods, which is still called "the Queen's gap." The furniture, however, of her Majesty's bed-room, has nothing about it of the

Elizabethan era; it is no older than the time of the second Charles. In the library is a curious Bible, once the property of Philip, uncle of Oliver Cromwell; it contains detailed entries of the births of many of the Cromwell family.

There is a very celebrated portrait of the Protector on the stair-case, and another of one of the family of Hampden,—we believe the "Patriot's" son,—who, wearied of the world he knew, rushed unbidden to that which he knew not. All memory of the sleeping-chamber of John Hampden is lost; but that of the tragedy is well-known;—what house is there without its skeleton!—yet what dwelling in all England more sacred than this lonely one, to the hearts of Englishmen? In one of the reception-rooms is an interesting portrait, believed to be of the Patriot; it hung unnoticed on the stairs, until Lord Nugent undertook to exhume the remains of Hampden, with a view to ascertain whether he had died by the effect of the bursting of his own pistol, or from the shot of the carabine, which, according to other historians, shattered the shoulder of the hero on Chalgrove field. The body, of which the grave was despoiled in a ruder manner, and for a longer period than appears to have been at all necessary, was found perfect, except that a shattered hand was rolled in a separate cerement beside it: the features, when discovered, "bore so strong a resemblance to this hitherto neglected portrait, that it was taken down and cleaned, and in a corner the name was discovered;"*—it has since been placed in a

* Such, at least, is the motive assigned for its removal, by the household; but upon very unsatisfactory grounds. It is much to be lamented, and certainly not to be accounted for, that Lord Nu-

17 *

wortnier position.   It is deplorable that this noble mansion, honored by time and circumstance, contains no other
record of *the* one who has given it immortality ; no papers,
no documents, no scrap of his hand-writing, no table upon
which his hand rested, no chair, as the master of the household often has appropriately called " his own ;" no room
—nothing except a doubtful portrait ; the very character
of that dwelling changed, rendering it a whited sepulchre
rather than a glorious Mausoleum, where everything
connected with him should be found ; and where the youth
of England might learn how to live and how to die for
their country.   And yet his presence was with us wherever

gent, in his " Life of Hampden," published some time after the exhumation, takes no notice whatever of the circumstance ; not attempt-
ing to account for the fact that in the " rummage" to which the
grave was subjected no body was found exhibiting wounds on the
shoulder, while that which his lordship and his friends disinterred
was without the hand, which, wrapped in a separate cerement, was
by its side.   Lord Nugent quotes the statement, (which rests upon
doubtful authority,) that " at Chalgrove field his pistol burst and
shattered his hand in a terrible manner ;" a story which his lordship's search would seem to confirm, but which he quotes and leaves
without comment.   Soon after the appearance of this article in the
Art-Journal the author was subjected to a severe " questioning" in
the *Athenæum*, where the accuracy of the statement was assailed ;
in reply, she gave her authorities—John Martin, the Parish Clerk,
and the steward of the Earl of Buckinghamshire, both of whom
were present at the disinterment ; she has since again visited the
locality, and her impressions were confirmed by conversations with
others : the point at issue—the manner of Hampden's death—cannot fail to interest many—who may take up the controversy with a
better grace than the author of this work ; and for the facts glanced
at, reference may be made to several persons of the district, whose
testimony would be beyond suspicion.

GREAT HAMPDEN CHURCH.

we turned; the scene was so entirely his own, that he moved with us, among the old places, in the sunshine and the shade.

The view of the house opens through a long vista; a lawn of noble width, and carpeted with the richest verdure, slopes on, until lost beneath the shadows of magnificent trees, judiciously cleared so as to afford one of the richest views in the midland counties of England; the atmosphere was so transparent that the prospect over hills and into deep valleys and dark woods, and down dells, clothed in juniper, and beech, and chestnut, seemed interminable; a very empire of beauty and of silence! It was better to picture Hampden *there* than within the precincts of that whited house. What a region for thoughts and works! Woe to those poor spirits who have no ideas, but those they can vent in sound! Truly the scene before us was worthy of its name; worthy to be noted from the old times to the present; worthy of its patriot-master; worthy to own no other lord than him whose name is as a beacon of liberty—a sacred unquenchable fire. Here were his great thoughts conceived; here nourished; not developed rashly or flung unadvisedly to the world, but nurtured by observation and in quiet. It is only in the magnificence of silence that the soul can commune with its God! The babbler knows nothing of the holiness, the uplifting, up-looking nature of this great privilege. We turned our footsteps towards the church; the clerk waited to receive us; the edifice is well cared for by the proprietor, the rector, and last, not least, the honest clerk, who looks upon it with the increasing affection begotten by the serving and tending of forty years. It is a beautiful specimen of an

old English house of worship, carefully preserved;* and
the clerk was a fitting guide to its solemnities, thankful to
be inquired of concerning what he so much loved, but
saying no word too many; speaking not at all when he
saw us full of thought.   The church doors were open, but
extra doors of iron net-work prevented the entrance of
birds or boys; by this means the fresh breezes of the
Chiltern Hills passed through the sanctuary, laden with
the perfume of the flower garden of Hampden's house, so
that the porch and aisle were fragrant with the scent of
mignonette and clematis.   Upon a young tree planted, as
the clerk told us, "near eighteen years past by his own
hands, to live when he was gone," a robin was rehearsing
its autumn song, at intervals, as if it were too early to
begin, and yet time to have it ready.   The day was changing; a soft misty rain commenced, and rude gusts of wind
swept through the trees, scattering the golden-tinted leaves
on the green grass.   We were now within the porch that
Hampden had so often entered; within the sanctuary in
which he communed with his God!   The pews of the
church are low and open; there is no gallery, and the
organ, a gift of the late Lord Buckinghamshire, is placed
amongst the seats, nearly opposite the communion-table.
It was a privilege to stand within the sacred temple where
Hampden lies, uncenotaphed, but unforgotten; to know
that we were sheltered by the same roof that covered the

---

* It is a primitive structure, consisting of a nave with side aisles
and chancel.   The pillars and arches of the nave are early English,
and of considerable beauty, exhibiting the purest features of the
original architecture.   The clerestory windows and roof are of the
latest perpendicular style, merging into the Tudor.

remains of the purest of England's patriots; the offspring of an unbroken descent from the confessor; of a line famous in chivalry, and often entrusted with state services,

INTERIOR OF HAMPDEN CHURCH.

yet sufficient of himself to stamp a name with the truest immortality, had all his progenitors been peasant-born. On the right hand, close to the communion-table, is the

simple monument* inscribed with his own words to the
memory of his wife; and within the rails his own remains
were deposited; it was his own hand that traced the
tribute to her virtues—the "truly vertuous and pious,"
the "tender mother of nine hopeful children."

> "In her pilgrimage
> The staie and comfort of her neighbors,
> The love and glory of a well-order'd family,
> The delight and happiness of tender parents,
> But a crowne of blessings to a husband
> In a wife, to all an eternall paterne of goodnes
> And cause of joye whilst shee was in her dissolution."

Opposite to this monument "in perpetual testimony of
conjugal love," is a far more sumptuous tomb to the
memory of a lesser John Hampden,† here described as
"xviiii. hereditary lord of great Hampden," who, "dying
in 1754, bequeathed his estates and name to the Hon.
Robert Trevor," his kinsman by descent from Ruth,
daughter of *the* John Hampden. Issue here failing, the

---

* The monument erected by Hampden to the memory of his
wife is a plain black marble tablet in a simple frame of lighter
marble, and is placed between the windows on the south wall of
the chancel, close to the spot traditionally pointed out as his last
resting-place.

† This monument is a characteristic example of the taste which
prevailed during the last century in monumental decoration, when
weeping children were so unsparingly used. In this instance we
have one perched at each angle of the cenotaph. One holds a
countryman's hat on a staff, (an adaptation of the classic cap of
liberty,) the other, a sealed roll, (perhaps intended for Magna
Charta.)

heritage passed to the children of another daughter: the Hobarts, Earls of Buckinghamshire, now own the house and lands of the Patriot: they own them, nothing

more. This tomb is gorgeous with armorial bearings; and contains in low relief a sculptured tablet, which describes the Patriot's fall on Chalgrove field.* A faded morion,

* This portion of the upper part of the tomb is given in our cut; it is well executed in white marble, but exhibits that inattention to costume which was prevalent in the last century. The stem of the

18

with the crest, surmounts the tomb; and this is all that recalls to us the name of Hampden in the place to which he has given eternal fame.

In memory of John Hampden, there is no monument of any kind in Hampden House, Hampden Church, or Hampden village! No single sentence has been written anywhere to say that here he lived, and here was he laid

in death; but for a memorial to the greatest man of a great period of British history, let us borrow an inscription from one of the humblest gravestones in the church-yard—

> "Praises on tombs are idly spent,
> His good name is his monument!"

Yet what a host of memories were conjured up, as we

genealogical tree, and the principal shield of arms, appear above the falling figure of the Patriot: this tree, laden with shields properly emblazoned, fills the larger part of the oval tablet, and being cut in white marble, stands in bold relief from the dark-veined marble which forms the substructure.

THE MONUMENT ON CHALGROVE FIELD.

(207)

stood in the chancel of that small village church, beside the vault which holds the ashes of the Patriot.

On the 25th of June, 1643,* the body, without the soul, entered this church, and was interred inside this altar, where had been gathered the dust of so many of his progenitors. It had been removed hither from Thame, the village in which he died, on the 24th of June, of the wound received at CHALGROVE, on the Sabbath morning of June 18, 1643.†

---

* The following is extracted from the Register of Burials, Great Hampden, 1643. It was copied for us by the clerk, William Martin, to whose courtesy we have elsewhere made reference, and who deserves the highest praise for the neatness and order in which he keeps the church.

"1643. John Hampden, Esquire, Lord of Hampden, buried June 25. Robert Renthall, Rector.

† Chalgrove field is about twelve miles from Oxford and ten from Thame. The field itself is a large open plain, intersected by four cross roads, as seen in the sketch. It was allotted in different appointments some short time since, and the spot where the monument is erected was appropriated to Dr. Hampden, now Bishop of Hereford, a descendant of the Patriot. The monument is of brick, coated with stone. It is in an unfinished condition as far as the original design is concerned, which was, to have ornamented this pedestal with an obelisk seventeen feet high: omitted—*for want of funds*. As the pedestal now stands, it is about fifteen feet wide on each side. The east side has a sculptured medallion figure of Hampden, with his motto, *Vestigia nulla retrorsum ;* the same motto with his arms on the west side ; the south side is devoted to the names of those who subscribed to this memorial, and is dated "June 18, 1843." The north side has a long inscription, setting forth that "this stone was raised in reverence to his memory," in the "two hundredth year" from the day on which he received his death-

18 *   O

Hampden was seen for the first time turning his back upon the battle-field before the fight was done, "a thing," writes Clarendon, "he never used to do;" hence it was

A CARABINEER.

concluded he was "hurt." He had been "struck in the shoulder with two carabine balls,* which, breaking the

wound. It is a poor and paltry affair; conferring a renown by no means enviable upon the wealthy noblemen and gentlemen, who commenced a miserable monument and left it unfinished.

* The carabine was a small gun, slung at the back of a light horseman by a leathern belt, which passed across the shoulders, and had a hooked swivel at the end, sometimes fancifully ornamented, through which the barrel of the carabine passed, as shown in our cut; the men were armed with back and breast-plate, helmet and

bone, entered his body, and his arm hung powerless and shattered by his side." He left his friends and soldiers not at a time of victory, but in a moment of defeat; he left them to die, as was said by Sidney on a memorable occasion, for " THE OLD CAUSE."

Slowly riding, " his head bending down, and his hands resting on his horse's neck," his first impulse was to seek the village of Pyrton, the house in which, a high-hearted and hopeful man, he had wedded the wife of his affections thirty years before; but the brilliant Rupert—the mirror of chivalry, according to the Cavaliers—the Prince-robber, according to the Roundheads—with his fierce cavalry, interposed. "In great pain and almost fainting" he reached Thame, distant about ten miles from Chalgrove, and found shelter in the HOUSE OF ONE EZEKIEL BROWNE.* His wounds were dressed, but he knew they were mortal; and he addressed himself to die, not merely with the grace and dignity of the old Roman, but with the fortitude and trusting faith of the true Christian—first despatching

sword, and were named Carabineers, from the principal weapon with which they were equipped. They are first mentioned in 1559, but became an important portion of the army in the Civil Wars.

* This interesting building is still pointed out by village tradition, and is represented in our wood-cut as it now appears. It was formerly the Greyhound Inn, and is now divided into two shops— one a butcher's, the other an ironmonger's. The exigencies of modern residents have, in a great degree, interfered with its original features; but its connection with one of England's purest patriots must ever invest its humble walls with interest. It is necessary to state, however, that the honor is claimed by other old houses in the village, although the balance of evidence is in favor of this.

"letters of counsel to the Parliament," and then receiving the sacrament at the hands of the Rector of Chinnor, according to the forms of the Church of England, declaring "he thought its doctrine in the greater part primitive and conformable to God's Word, as in Holy Scripture revealed." At length, being "well-nigh spent, and labouring for breath," he turned himself to die in prayer; and

THE HOUSE IN WHICH HAMPDEN DIED.

his last words were, "O Lord, save my bleeding country Have these realms in thy special keeping. Let the king see his error, and turn the hearts of his wicked counsellors." So died

"The noblest Roman of them all!"

He died at the moment when the issue of the contest was very doubtful, and when his generous and considerate counsels were needed most. The best tributes to his character are not those of his friends, but of his personal opponents and political enemies. Charles himself, it is said, offered to send his own surgeon to the Patriot's bedside; and Clarendon, in after years, bore testimony to his genius, his courage, and his integrity. "Many men observed," writes Clarendon, "that Chalgrove field, the place on which he received his death-wound, was the same place in which he had first executed the ordinance of the militia, and engaged that county, in which his reputation was very great, in this rebellion." Strange if it were so! strange that he should, like the hunted stag, return to die where he was roused.*

Had he lived to see the final issue of the contest for liberty, there is little doubt that the one dismal act for which two centuries have vainly sought an excuse, would have been avoided. "He was, in truth, a very wise man, and of great parts; temperate in diet, a supreme governor

* Such of the soldiers of the Parliament as could be spared from the several adjacent quarters of the army were gathered together to accompany the corpse of their honored leader to his grave, in Hampden Church; they marched to the sad music of the muffled drum, and with reversed arms, through the lanes and over the hills of the Chilterns: as they conducted the body to the grave, the soldiers chaunted the 90th psalm:—

"In the morning they are like grass which groweth up: in the morning it flourisheth and groweth up; in the evening it is cut down and withereth."

On their return from the interment, they sung the 43d Psalm:—

"Judge me, O God, and plead my cause against an ungodly nation: O deliver me from the deceitful and unjust man.

"Why art thou cast down, O my soul? and why art thou disquieted within me? Hope in God; for I shall yet praise Him, who is the health of my countenance and my God."

over all his passions and affections;" and it is clear that the king lost far more than he gained by the death of John Hampden. Such is, indeed, the testimony of the friends as well as the enemies of the unhappy king, whose fate deducts so largely from the heroism of a remarkable epoch; an epoch fertile of strong minds and great hearts, in men who, whatever may have been their errors, truly and deeply loved the country for which so many of them perished on the scaffold and in the field.

Surely this village, this house, and this church, are shrines which all Englishmen should visit as pilgrim-students. Great acts from high motives may be taught here: in the patriotism of this patriot there was no atom of self-ishness; no self-glory stirred him on; the "rare modesty" by which he was distinguished when "the business of ship-money" made him "the argument of all tongues," marked him through his whole career; no thought had he of a monument to record his mighty services to his country—as little as his descendants who have given him none!

The pilgrim to this shrine will, however, find memories of Hampden all about him—memories that cannot perish, for they exist with Nature.

And what a holy scene it was when the veterans, and the young men, of his regiment bore across the Chilterns the body of John Hampden, to lay it under foot in this lonely village church! chaunting psalms as they marched; a sad funeral procession of true mourners; their arms reversed, their drums muffled, and their heads uncovered. It was no hard task upon imagination to recall this solemn scene as we looked along the landscape towards Oxfordshire, and traced the route they must have taken; a band of steel-clad men with their boy comrades by their sides—branches and saplings of the old tree of British freedom. Weeping aloud, and not ashamed of tears, they enter this church— fill it, as it was never filled before nor since ; deposit there the body of their great leader, and retire—again singing the words of the psalmist, and wending their way to another battle-field.

John Hampden.

BY PROFESSOR RHOADS.

TRULY has it been said, that less learning makes a learned man at one age of the world than at another. It will not, perhaps, be so generally admitted, that it takes much more greatness to make a great man at one time than at another, but it is equally true. At some periods in the progress of almost every nation, great men are so scarce that even mediocrity becomes illustrious, while at others, there is such a flow of talent, that none but the stronegst can rise into view.

When Napoleon led the armies of France to victory, a long line of marshals and generals served under him, whose names grace the pages of history merely as efficient subordinates, any one of whom, if he had lived a century earlier, would have attained a place in the front rank of the mighty ones. These facts should be kept constantly before us when we are endeavoring to appreciate properly the men whom history introduces to our acquaintance; for he who wins his laurels from powerful competitors, deserves much more our

(216)

applause than one who merely gathers them because they lie invitingly in his path. The season which produced John Hampden, the subject of this memoir, was a season of plenty. Never was there a more brilliant array of statesmen and patriots than that which the love of English liberty brought in the middle of the seventeenth century to the battle against the encroachments and despotic aspirations of the first two Stuart kings. It is one of the compensating principles in the natural organization of nations and other communities, that times of distraction and tumult serve always to draw out and expand the latent talent of the people.

Then flourished Eliot, and Pym, and Vane, and Cromwell, and a host of other noble spirits. Such men as these are usually produced but one at a time, and but once in an age. And yet the era of the "Great Rebellion" teemed with them. Even to serve under men like these is honorable. Hampden led them; and had his life been spared until the day of triumph, he would probably have secured for them and for the rest of his countrymen, a happier termination for their labors. Be this as it may, his exertions in the cause of his country, and the perfect self-devotion, the eminent ability, and majestic integrity which made them so efficacious, have secured for him a place in the regards of the generations which have succeeded, higher than any of his co-workers in the same cause; have emblazoned his name brightest on the most glorious page of his nation's history, and have singled him out from the crowd of patriots, who ennobled his age, as "*the* patriot."

To condense within the limits of a short article, a complete account of his life is impossible; to give even an

19

intelligible abstract of it is scarcely less. It would require an investigation of the motives and characters of thousands, and a record of the actions of a whole generation of Englishmen; it would form the most important volume of a great nation's history. I purpose, therefore, to attempt nothing further than to state a few of the prominent points in his personal history, and to call attention to a few of the personal relics of him which remain to us. Here, far from being embarrassed by a superabundance of materials, we are struck with their scarcity. Though estimable in private life, it was the public life of Hampden that made him renowned, and himself sacrificing everything private to the public weal, his cotemporaries seem to have, at least partially, forgotten that there could be a private history of such a man.

John Hampden was born in 1594. It is generally believed that London has the honor of being his birth-place, though the people of Buckinghamshire, who adored his name, long denied this claim, asserting that he was one of themselves, born at the manor-house at Hoggestone, in the hundred of Cottlesloe, in their county. His family was an ancient one, able to trace its descent, in an unbroken line, from the times before the Norman conquest. The estate and residence in Buckinghamshire, from which the name Hampden was derived, was conferred upon the family by Edward, the Confessor, and was transmitted in direct male succession to the patriot. It is said that, in the fourteenth century, the Hampdens were one of the most opulent families in England. Besides the extensive domains in Buckinghamshire, they had large possessions in Berkshire, Oxfordshire, and Essex. In the time of

Edward I., one of them was obliged, in order to escape the loss of his hand, to surrender three valuable manors, as penalty for striking the Black Prince in a dispute at tennis. This surrender is commemorated in the traditionary lines

> "Tring, wing and Ivanhoe
> For striking of a blow
> Hampden did forego
> And glad he could escape so."

Notwithstanding other losses during after years, the estate to which "the patriot" succeeded was very large. The mother of "the patriot" was Elizabeth Cromwell, sister of Robert Cromwell, who was the father of the great Protector, and a descendant of a sister of Thomas Cromwell, the prime minister and favorite of Henry VIII., who succeeded to Wolsey's power and to a similar downfall. But 'tis superfluous to speak of John Hampden's ancestry. The noblest could add nothing to his worth; the meanest, such as his could ennoble.

Hampden was not four years old when the still ample estates of the family descended to him in consequence of the death of his father. The story of his boyhood, and of his early manhood, as far as it has been transmitted to us, possesses but little interest, and will claim but few words. It is to be regretted that we have not fuller accounts of his early life, for it is almost impossible that such a man as he should live to middle age, before doing anything worthy to be recorded. The care of his education was entrusted, after his father's death, to Richard Bouchier, master of the free grammar-school at Thame, in Oxfordshire. He remained with Bouchier for several years, and then entered, in 1609, as commoner at Magdalen College, Oxford. Here he pursued his studies with the same indomitable energy and persevering zeal which he afterwards displayed in the great battle of life. He consequently gained considerable reputation for scholarship, the first fruits of which was his being one of those chosen to write the Oxford poems of gratulation on the marriage of the Elector Palatine and the Princess Elizabeth. It is worthy of remark, that among his associates upon this occasion, was William Laud, afterward Archbishop of Canterbury, who became as celebrated for his thorough support of the arbitrary measures of Charles I., as did Hampden for his opposition to them. The last three lines of the verses produced by their joint labors, expressed a hope, or prophecy, that from this marriage, a progeny should rise, such as should be unequalled in the whole world. These lines are, as Lord Nugent suggests, indeed remarkable, when it is remembered that from this marriage sprang Prince Rupert, who led the royalist troops by whom Hampden was slain at Charlgrove.

In 1613, he was admitted to the Inner Temple as a student of law. Here he gained a reputation less enviable than that he had acquired at Oxford, and we fear not less justly awarded. Clarendon probably referred to this epoch, when he charged him with having led, in his earlier years, " a life of great pleasure and license." To what extent he allowed lively temperament and fascinating manners to betray him into the dissipations of the times, cannot now be determined. His errors were not, probably, very serious ones, else they would have sapped his taste for literary labors, and have, in some degree at least, incapacitated him for intellectual efforts. That they did not do so, we have not only the evidence of his later career, but the positive testimony of one not likely to speak more favorably of him than he deserved. Sir Philip Warwick declared that before leaving the Inner Temple, he possessed "great knowledge, both of scholarship and law."

But, whatever may have been his irregularities, they were soon thrown aside. On the 14th of June, 1619, he married; and, as we are informed by the same author who charges him with "the license and pleasure," he suddenly "retired to a more reserved and melancholy society," from that time forward leading a life of "extraordinary sobriety and strictness, but retaining his usual cheerfulness and affability." His wife was Elizabeth, only daughter of Edward Symeon, Lord of the Manor of Pyrton, in Oxfordshire.

For several years after his marriage, though not altogether inattentive to public affairs, in which he was destined soon to take so conspicuous and honorable a part, he lived in retirement on his estate in Buckinghamshire. Having no private interest to promote, no personal vanity to indulge, no craving desires, no uneasy ambition to gratify, he shunned the strife of politics, and sought for happiness in the society of his wife, and in efforts for the welfare and improvement of his numerous tenantry. The house in which he resided during this tranquil period of his life, is still standing, and is now owned by the Hobarts, Earls of Buckinghamshire.

In the immediate vicinity of this beautiful spot, from
19 *

which it is separated by a narrow road, is the church, where, during the happy season of peace which succeeded his marriage, the patriot so often knelt, and in the interior of which his remains now repose. The church, like the dwelling, is well kept, and in good repair, and affords a specimen of the old English house of worship. But the particular spot where rests what was mortal of the great Hampden, is not certainly known. No proud monument is reared where the patriot sleeps, not even a simple stone to tell us, Here he lies. Tradition, however, points to a spot close to a plain tablet of black marble, dedicated to his wife, who died on the 20th of August, 1634.

Hampden made his first appearance on the stage of public life in 1620; when he took his seat in the House of Commons of the British Parliament, as member for Grampound, then a borough of wealth and importance. This was the crisis of his life, the point when it became necessary to decide, whether, by joining the courtiers, he should attain honor and advancement, or, by attaching himself to those who were resisting the tendency of the government to despotism, he should receive only pains and penalties in this life, and look to the life to come for rewards. He did not hesitate. He threw himself at once into the arms of the popular party, and, with steady integrity, he always afterwards adhered to it. This decision was a sad disappointment to his poor mother, who, proud of his great talents and acquirements, longed to see her son a peer of the realm. There is preserved in the British Museum, a curious letter from this lady, in which the following advice is sent to Hampden, but without effect: " If ever my sonn will seeke for his honour, tell him nowe to come ; for heare is multitudes of lords a making—Vicount Mandville, Lo. Thresorer; Vicount Dunbar, which was Sr. Ha. Constable; Vicount Falkland, which was Sir Harry Carew. These two last of Scotland; of Ireland, divers; the deputie a vicount, and one Mr. Fitzwilliams, a barron of Ingland; Mr. Villers a vicount, and Sr. Will. Fielding a barron. . . . I am ambitious of my sonne's honour, which I wish were nowe conferred upon him, that hee might not come after so many new creations." But the path which this beloved son entered, was not that leading to titles and preferment. Its course lay rather toward persecution and the prison. He aimed not to profit by the power of the government, but to resist its encroachments upon the liberties of the people of England.

Though, in the earlier Parliaments, of which he was a member, Hampden took no distinguished part in the proceedings, it was neither from want of interest, nor of ability, but rather from an innate modesty, which withheld him from assuming to lead, except when circumstances required it. This was proved when the crisis came. When danger thickened around the patriots, and many began to falter, then he pressed firmly on at the head of those who feared not the encounter. It was thus that, from being a man comparatively unknown, he suddenly claimed the admiring applause of a whole nation. Thus it was that, when first he attracted public attention, he had already, as Sir Philip Warwick expresses it, "all great qualities *ripened* about him, of which he had never given a crude or ostentatious promise."

Immediately after the dissolution of the second Parliament of Charles I., letters were issued by order of Council,

under the privy seal, for forcing private persons to lend
money to the government. These loans were exacted in
most cases from members of the popular party. One of
the requisitions was addressed to Hampden, who positively
and resolutely refused the loan. Upon being asked why
he was so unwilling to contribute towards the King's necessities, he gave the memorable answer, "That he could be
content to lend as well as others, but feared to draw upon
himself that curse in Magna Charta, which should be read
twice a year against those who infringe it." In consequence of this refusal he was arbitrarily committed to a
close and rigorous imprisonment in the Gate House. This
prison was built in the reign of Edward III., and was
originally the principal approach to the enclosure of the
monastery of Westminster. It obtained much celebrity
during the civil wars in England, on account of the incarceration of so many eminent men within its walls. From
the Gate House he was sent into private detention in
Hampshire.

Hampden had now suffered persecution; it had its usual
effect. He no longer stood in the ranks of the patriots.
He placed himself at their head. From a faithful follower
he became at once transformed into a skilful leader. In
the new Parliament, which met in March, 1628, this change
was remarked by all. Lord Nugent informs us, that
"Scarcely was a bill prepared, or an inquiry begun on
any subject, however remotely affecting any one of the
three great matters at issue—privilege, religion, or the
supplies—but he was thought fit to be associated with St.
John, Selden, Coke, and Pym on the committee."

Upon the dissolution of this Parliament in May, 1629,

Hampden retired to his estate in Buckinghamshire, to
entire privacy, but not to inactivity. He was diligently
engaged in preparing himself for further efficient action
in the struggle which he foresaw must soon re-commence.
History and politics claimed his chief attention.   Davila's
History of the Civil Wars of France was his favorite, "as
though in the study of that sad story of strife and blood-
shed, he already saw the parallel which England was to
afford so soon." There was, however, one thing remaining which might have unfitted him for the desperate display
of determination, which the crisis now rapidly demanded—
the strength of his domestic ties.   But God, in his wisdom,
saw fit at this time to break them.   On the 20th of August,
1634, died "the patriot's" wife.

In the latter part of 1635, the celebrated ship-money
writs were sent into Buckinghamshire. The English kings
of the olden times, had claimed the right of requiring the
maritime towns to furnish the royal navy with a certain
number of ships for the defence of the coast.   Charles I.
endeavored to make this antiquated and obsolete claim,
the foundation of a right in the King to raise, without the
authority of Parliament, a tax in money from all parts of
the kingdom, inland as well as maritime.   Had he
succeeded he would have been entirely independent of
Parliament, and have had power to tax the people at will.
England owes a great debt of gratitude to the noble spirits
of the time, that he did not succeed.   The next year the
sheriffs were required to proceed by distress, in case of
refusal or delay of any one to pay the ship-money.   Here
Hampden planted himself immovably in opposition.   The
terrors even of the merciless Star Chamber disturbed him

not. The amount of his tax was only thirty-one shillings and sixpence. But it was to the principle of the exaction that he objected. He reasoned as did the fathers of the American Revolution. "The right to take one penny implied the right to take a thousand." He denied the right. He refused to pay. Proceedings against him were immediately instituted in the Exchequer. The case was solemnly argued before the twelve judges. They decided in favor of the Crown by a majority of eight to four. But Hampden, though condemned by venal judges, was in reality triumphant. He had attained his object; he had aroused the people. Even Lord Clarendon was constrained to testify, that "the judgment infinitely more advanced him, Mr. Hampden, than the service for which it was given. He was rather of reputation in his own county, than of public discourse or fame in the kingdom, before the business of the ship-money; but then he grew the argument of all tongues, every man inquiring who or what he was, that durst, at his own charge, support the liberty and property of the country, as he thought, from being made a prey to the court." The same writer notices his manner during the trial. "His carriage, throughout this agitation, was with that rare temper and modesty, that they who watched him narrowly to find some advantage against him, to make him less resolute in his cause, were compelled to give him a just testimony."

Hampden had hitherto, though firm, been gentle and moderate; he now became stern and impetuous. He had hitherto been merely for reform and protection; he now became, in the language of the times, "a root and branch man." Instead of seeking to lop off rotten boughs, he now aimed to destroy entirely the corrupt tree. At the opening of the Long Parliament in November, 1640, " the eyes of all men were fixed upon him as their Pater Patriæ, and the pilot that must steer the vessel through the tempest and rocks which threatened it." The persecutions which he had endured, and the universal belief in his honesty of purpose, and devotion to the public good, made him the most powerful man in the kingdom. The first use to which he applied this power was in zealous support of the impeachment of Lord Stafford; but when the Commons changed the course of proceeding, by introducing a bill of attainder, he ceased to take part either way. He has been censured for this. Why, it has been asked, did he not, if he disapproved the attainder, oppose it as resolutely as he supported the impeachment? Lord Nugent has well answered the question. "In a case doubtful to him only as a matter of precedent, but clear to him in respect to the guilt of the accused person; in a case in which the accused, in his estimation, deserved death, and in which all law, except that of the sceptre and the sword, was at an end if he had escaped it; when all the ordinary protection of law to the subject, throughout the country, was suspended, and suspended mainly by the councils of Stafford himself, Hampden was not prepared to heroically immolate the liberties of England, in order to save the life of him who would have destroyed them."

Through all the important scenes and acts which followed, Hampden took a leading part. He was one of the five members accused of treason, whom Charles undertook to seize in the House of Commons, January 6, 1642; but instead of being intimidated, from this time "his nature

and carriage" became fiercer. When, finally, the power
of the sword was asserted for Parliament by the Ordinance
of Militia, and the Committee of Public Safety was formed,
he became a member of the committee; the King issuing
his Commission of Array, raised his standard at Notting-
ham, and thus the struggle was made to be hereafter one
of arms.

Hampden was one of the first of the patriots to take
the field. He hastened to Buckinghamshire, and tradition
says, on Hampden Common he mustered and marshaled
the militia of his native county. Other, and perhaps
better authority, designates the field of Charlgrove as the
place of muster. He devoted both purse and person to
the cause. Besides raising a regiment at his own expense,
he subscribed £2000 to assist the Parliament, and accepted
the commission of Colonel. He joined the army of the
Earl of Essex, over whom his powerful mind soon obtained
such an ascendency, that the enemies of both charged
that he was really the commander, placed by Parliament
as superintendent over the Earl. Well would it have been
for the cause, if this really had been the case. But with
all his influence he could not make that individual an energetic general. At the battle of Brentford, during the
first campaign, after his troops and those of Lord Brooke,
in support of the London regiment under Hollis, had borne
the brunt of the day, he vainly urged Essex to convert,
by a decisive forward movement, a doubtful issue into a
victory. Had his advice been followed, it would probably
have much shortened the war.

It is not, however, our province to give a history of the
contest. It is sufficient to say that Hampden became as

distinguished for energy in the field, as he had been for
decision in Parliament. Failing in his efforts to arouse
his superior to some great enterprise, he was, nevertheless,
exceedingly active in a smaller way; and it was in the line
of such duty that he received his death-wound. On the
evening of the 17th of June, Prince Rupert, with about
two thousand men, surprised and burned two villages occupied by parliamentary troops. As soon as Hampden
heard of this, he set out with a body of cavalry, which
volunteered to follow him, to endeavor to delay the Royalists
until Essex could occupy the passes of Cherwell, and cut
them off from Oxford. Rupert drew up on the field of
Charlgrove to receive the attack. The action had not
fairly commenced, when Hampden received two bullets
from a carbineer. These shattered his shoulder bone; his
arm hung powerless at his side, and in agony he rode off
the field.

His first impulse was to seek the village of Pyrton,
where thirty years before he had married the wife of his
affections, but Rupert's cavalry interposed. He then rode
to Thame, about ten miles from the fatal field on which he
was wounded, and found refuge in the house of Ezekiel
Brown. Here, after six days of excruciating pain, he expired. His last words were, " Oh Lord, save my country!
—Oh, Lord, be merciful to—"

Macauley, speaking of the death of Hampden, thus
concludes: " He had, indeed, left none like him behind
him. There still remained in his party many acute
intellects, many eloquent tongues, many brave and honest
hearts. There still remained a rugged and clownish
soldier, half fanatic, half buffoon, whose talents, discerned

20

as yet only by one penetrating eye, were equal to all the
highest duties of the soldier and the prince. But in
Hampden, and in Hampden alone, were united all the
qualities which at such a crisis were necessary to save the
State—the valor and energy of Cromwell, the discernment
and eloquence of Vane, the humanity and moderation of
Manchester, the stern integrity of Hale, the ardent public
spirit of Sidney. Others might possess the qualities which·
were necessary to save the popular party in the crisis of
danger ; he alone had both the power and the inclination
to restrain its excesses in the hour of triumph. Others
could conquer ; he alone could reconcile. A heart as bold
as his, brought up the cuirassiers who turned the tide of
battle on Marston Moor. As skilful an eye as his watched
the Scotch army descending from the heights over Dunbar.
But it was when, to the sullen tyranny of Laud and
Charles, had succeeded the fierce conflict of sect and fac-
tions, ambitious of ascendency and burning for revenge,
it was when the vices and ignorance which the old tyranny
had generated, threatened the new freedom with destruction, that England missed that sobriety, that self-command,
that perfect soundness of judgment, that perfect rectitude
of intention, to which the history of revolutions furnishes
no parallel, or furnishes a parallel in Washington alone."

The following splendid description of the Cavaliers and
Roundheads is from Hartley Coleridge's Lives of Distinguished Northerners :—" Fifty thousand subjects of one
king stood face to face on Marston Moor. The numbers
on each side were not far unequal, but never were two
hosts speaking one language of more dissimilar aspects.
The cavaliers, flushed with recent victory, identifying their

quarrel with their honor and their love, their loose locks
escaping beneath their plumed hemlets glittering in all the
martial pride which makes the battle-day like a pageant
or a festival, and prancing forth with all the grace of
gentle love, as they would make a jest of death, while the
spirit-stirring strains of the trumpets made their blood
dance, and their steeds prick up their ears; the Roundheads, arranged in thick dark masses, their steel caps and
high crowned hats drawn closely over their brows, looking
determination, expressing with furrowed foreheads, and
hard closed lips, the only working rage which was blown
up to furnace heat by the extempore effusions of their
preachers, and found vent in the terrible denunciations of
the Hebrew psalms and prophecies.

" The arms of each party were adapted to the nature of
their courage: the swords, pikes and pistols of the Royalists, light and bright, were suited for swift onset and ready
use; while the ponderous basket-hilted blades, long hal-
berts, and heavy fire-arms of the parliamentarians were
equally suited to resist a sharp attack, and to do execution
upon a broken enemy. The Royalists regarded their ad-
versaries with that scorn which the gay and high-born
always feel or affect for the precise and sour-mannered:
the soldiers of the covenant looked on their enemies as the
enemies of Israel, and considered themselves as the elect
and chosen people—a creed which extinguished fear and
remorse together. It would be hard to say whether there
was more praying on one side, or swearing on the other,
or which, to a truly Christian ear, would have been most
offensive. Yet both esteemed themselves the champions
of the church; there was bravery and virtue in both: but

with this high advantage on the parliamentary side—that
while the aristocratic honor of the Royalists could only
inspire a certain number of *gentlemen*, and separate the
patrician from the plebeian soldier, the religious zeal of the
Puritans bound officer and man, general and pioneer, together in a fierce and resolute sympathy, and made
equality itself an argument for subordination. The captain
prayed at the head of his army, and the general's oration
was a sermon."

Hannah More.

Residence of Hannah More.

BY MRS. S. C. HALL.

IN the month of January, 1825—during a fall of sleet and snow, we left Bristol to pay a visit to Hannah More at BARLEY WOOD, her then residence, close to the pretty and retired village of Wrington, in Somersetshire.

Trembling on the threshold of a Life of Literature— quivering with apprehension as to what our fate might be, if we dared to pass its iron gates, and ask to sit in the awful presence of those who had raised the veil of the Inner Temple,

> "whose names
> In Fame's eternal volume live for aye!"

a note of invitation from Hannah More, written by her own hand, was an event that made the heart thrill with delight—not altogether unallied to fear: and even now, after the lapse of nearly a quarter of a century, with its mingled burthen of triumphs and depressions, it recalls one of the most impressive memories of a long and active career of authorship to which that valuable and admirable woman was the earliest, if not the strongest, prompter.

(235)

We had previously made acquaintance with many memorable women of the epoch: we had bowed to the turbaned head of Miss Benger; gossipped with Miss Spence; been affectionately greeted by the excellent and accomplished sisters, Jane and Maria Porter; attracted, as by a golden link, to the lofty genius and generous heart of unhappy Lætitia Landon; corresponded with Felicia Hemans; been stirred to activity by honored and venerated Maria Edgeworth; and received from good Barbara Hofland encouragement to "appear in print"—notwithstanding the too popular opinion which refuses faith in the possibility that women may think and write, and yet keep their homes in order, and augment the comforts of all around them.   But none of these had inspired us with the awe which seemed inseparable from the idea of an interview with Hannah More, whose great work in life had been accomplished before we entered it; whose lessons had been our guides from youth upwards, and whose friends were the now buried immortalities of a gone-by age.   Her "Strictures on Female Education" had been our polar star from infancy; and its author could not fail to be, in imagination, so wise, so lofty, so self-contained, so far above, and so different from, all other women, that while we eagerly desired, we feared to meet her.

The snow was deep on the ground, and the friends with whom we sojourned said it was "madness" to set out for Wrington on such a morning, particularly as the venerable lady's hours for reception were but from twelve till three; but we were decided, and the journey of some ten miles was passed in speculations as to what she would say, how she would look—and also as to what we should say!

"Say?" why nothing; how could *we* speak to Hannah More, or before Hannah More! who had depicted so truthfully the character of "Lucilla Stanley," in "Cœlebs," and of course expected every woman to be a Lucilla; who had written "Practical Piety," and "Christian Morals;" who had suggested to Royalty how a Princess should be educated, who had been complimented by Dr. Johnson, who had sat to Sir Joshua Reynolds, exchanged wit with Sheridan, enjoyed the social eloquence of Burke, had sufficient bravery to set Walpole in the right path, and been the honored counsellor of Porteus and Wilberforce, and the familiar friend of David Garrick!

We had too much faith in the righteousness of her name—we honored her too devoutly to imagine her—Mrs. Hannah More—anything like any other human being we had ever seen; we recalled to memory how she had been fêted, and "embroidered for," * by Royalty, we could hardly conceive how she could have put off the "stiff stays" of such "grand" society to wander amid the Mendip hills, enduring—not the rusticity, for *that* might interest, or the vulgarity, for *that* might be pardoned—but the deep, and dark, and dangerous ignorance which had sent her humble neighbors to a fortune teller, to discover if the lady who wanted them to learn to read and work was not a "methodist:" while some expected to be paid for permitting their children to attend a Sunday School, and others suggested that she wanted to sell them as

* The late Duchess of Gloucester was so charmed by Mrs. Hannah More's work, "Hints on the Education of a Princess," that she gave a fête for the purpose of introducing her to the nobility, and embroidered a dress for her with her own hands.

slaves for the colonies! But the darker the ignorance, the greater became the necessity for her exertions,—such exertions as she never wearied of, until physical strength gave way beneath mental energy. All that she had written, and all we had heard of her, gathered about our memory, as the wheels rolled softly in the snow, or sinking still deeper, crackled upon the frozen paths. We knew that her mind, when she resided with her sisters in Bristol, engaged in the actual business of scholastic education, had drawn inspiration and health from her visits to the beautiful neighborhood in which she was now spending the twilight of her radiant day; we attempted to rub our frozen breaths from off the starry glass, and look out, but we could only discern lofty hedges through the mist of snow; we knew that we were in the centre, round which her "Practical Piety" had been evidenced by the perpetual exercise of universal benevolence; whose liberality, true as it was to the Divine precepts of her Master, was in advance of her period; we counted up the schools which owed their existence not only to her money and influence, but to her actual bodily exertion, and that while struggling with infirm health, and years that will exact augmented toll as they roll on. Her friends had told us she was totally unspoiled by the flattery and attention of the great; escaping from the society she never loved more than when she quitted it, but which she left from *a sense of duty;* zealous, without bigotry; and liberal, with a Christian spirit; and the more we recalled her excellencies, the more did we desire that the interview, so longed for, might be over—simply from a deep sense of our own unworthiness. At length we saw the chimneys of Barley

BARLEY WOOD

(240)

Wood above the trees, and driving along between high hedges of evergreens, whose bright leaves occasionally pierced through masses of snow, we drew up with a frosty crash at the door of the schoolmaster's daughter.*

It was a pretty cottage—simply and purely rustic; even in winter it looked cheerful, with its eaves where swallows build, its covering of English thatch, and its many homely props—pillars hewn from the adjacent wood, which the axe of the woodman had not desecrated by fashioning. It has been accurately copied by Mr. Tucker of Bristol, to whose graceful pencil we are indebted for these valuable aids to memory.

A country serving girl gave us entrance; and we stood for a moment in the hall. We had pictured to ourselves an old lady shrouded in black velvet, of a stately and severe presence, leaning (if she might rise to receive us) on an ivory-headed cane, and resuming quickly her seat on a carved and dignified high-backed chair; and we fancied that a large Bible, clasped with silver, should rest on a table beside her: we were kept waiting for a few minutes in the parlor, in which were hung several old and interesting engravings. The stillness and torpor of a frosty atmosphere had hushed all external noise, save the cold chilling whistle that moves no leaf—monotonous and

---

* Barley Wood was built by Hannah More in the year 1800; she purchased the site—about half a mile from the village of Wrington. Previously, her dwelling had been at Cowslip Green, about two miles from Wrington, which, until she resided there, had never heard the sound of a Bristol post-horn. Mrs. H. More's father was a man of respectable family, who kept a boy's school in the neighborhood of Bristol: he left four daughters, but no son; and as they all died unmarried, the direct family is extinct.

21 Q

dull; the snow was cleared away from the porch, and food
for the wild birds had been strewed within the circle;
several songsters, their feathers all on end, looking like
fuzz-balls, were still there, and the earth's white covering
was marked with the impress of their feet; the long
slender toes of the fragile lark, the broad foot of the wood-
pigeon, the deliberate prints of the thrush and the black-
bird—told of the considerate charity that ministered to
their wants: once a glittering shower of crystals fell from
a spangled bough, and a flock of starlings wheeled up,
but to return again to the same spot.   While watching
these stranger birds, a demure-looking servant ushered us
up-stairs, and though all was so still without, within we
heard voices and the very merry laugh of a child—a glowing fire diffused through the half-opened door the heat
and light which are so delightful after a chilling drive.
When we entered, a glance showed that the room was
not too large for comfort, that the walls were lined with
books, and that a group consisting of three ladies and a
little boy were round a table, upon which there was an
abundant supply of cake and wine; to the cake the little
fellow was doing ample justice, and a diminutive old lady
was in the act of adding another piece to that already upon
his plate; she moved to meet us—it was the least possible
movement, but it was most courteous.   Instead of black
velvet, Hannah More wore a dress of very light green
silk—a white China crape shawl was folded over her
shoulders; her white hair was frizzed, after a by-gone
fashion, above her brow, and that *backed*, as it were, by a
very full double border of rich lace—the reality was as
dissimilar from the picture painted by our imagination as

anything could well be ; such a sparkling, light, bright—
"summery"-looking old lady—more like a beneficent
fairy, than the biting author of " Mr. Fantom," though in
perfect harmony with "The Shepherd of Salisbury Plain."
The visitor and her son took their leave ; "Mrs. Hannah"
stooped and kissed the boy, not as old maidens usually
kiss children—with a kiss of necessity, or a kiss of compliment : she took his smiling, rosy, fearless face between
her hands, and looked down upon it for a moment, as a
mother would ; then kissed it fondly more than once.

"And when you are a man, my child, will you remember me?" The boy's eyes glanced from her to the remnants of the cake. "Well, remember the cake at Barley
Wood," she said, reading his thoughts by the light of her
own, and laughing.

"Both," replied the little fellow, with enviable fearless-
ness—"It was a nice cake, and you are so kind."

"That is the way I like the young to remember me,"
she replied, " by *being kind*—then you will always remember old Mrs. Hannah More?"

"Always, ma'am," he answered, his face at once becoming serious, as he returned her gaze with his large
well-opened eyes—indexes of truth and honest purpose ;
" I'll try and remember it always," he repeated, and then
there was another kiss.

"What a dear child," said Mrs. Hannah, after they
were gone, "and of a good stock—that child will be as
true as steel ! I so enjoyed his glance at the cake, it was
so much more natural he should remember *that* than an
old woman so very little taller than himself—children
always connect size with respect—a dear child—I hope

he may be spared to his lonely mother"—and her eyes were in an instant suffused with the light of coming tears, as if there had been something sad in that young mother's history.

There were some South Sea curiosities scattered about the room, as if they had been recently examined; the lady who was residing with Mrs. Hannah More, her tried friend and companion, directed our attention to these things, and while the venerable lady drew nearer to the fire, seeing that our interest proceeded not from curiosity but veneration, this friend showed us translations of many of her works into various continental languages; the eleventh edition of one, the tenth of another, and so on: every spot in the room was distinguished by having some treasure in its keeping, and every article of virtù had its story: one in particular attracted us—an inkstand made of Shakspeare's real mulberry tree, the gift of David Garrick. It was impossible not to congratulate her on the possession of such mementos.

"Yes," she said, "this place is in itself a great blessing from the hand of Heaven, and the trees you praise are well grown, and have taken deep root; and old as I am, there are times when I feel it a duty to be careful lest I become too deeply rooted myself in a soil sanctified by friends and friendships!" Her voice had a pleasant tone, and her manner was quite devoid of affectation or dictation: she spoke as one expecting a reply, and by no means like an oracle. And those bright immortal eyes of hers—not wearied by looking at the world for more than eighty years, but clear and far-seeing then—laughing, too,

when she spoke cheerfully; not as authors are believed to
speak—

> "In measured pompous tones,"

but like a dear matronly dame, who had especial care and
tenderness towards young women. It is impossible to
remember how it occurred; but in reference to some
observation we had made, she turned briskly round, and
exclaimed, "Controversy hardens the heart and sours the
temper; never dispute with your husband, young lady;
tell him what you think, and leave it to time to fructify."
Her friend said she had been fatigued sooner than usual
that morning by visitors, but would recover and "be herself" presently: she drew close to the fire, and seemed
inclined to repose or to muse, we could hardly tell which.

Of all women, Hannah More combined in the happiest
manner the perfection of spiritual existence and temporal
good. Her hopes were with the future, her activity with
the present. She lost no friends, no fame, no homage, by
living for the *future*, because she never neglected the
work of the *present;* her sympathies were as active as
her benevolence, and thus she carried conviction with her.
She established her Schools, her "Female Associations,"
with as firm a hand as that with which she wrote—despite
much that is impracticable, and the introduction of some
conventionalities inseparable from the period—the best
religious work we have on female education—the most
difficult of all subjects, from the mere fact that no two
children in the same family require the same training.
The only undeviating rule to secure this right training is
instant, unreasoning, and implicit OBEDIENCE; and if this

21*

task be commenced in infancy, both child and parent will be spared an infinity of after sorrow.

No woman was ever so universally acknowledged as the reformer of education, the interpreter of morals, the expositress of piety :* these distinctions shed around Hannah More a lustre far eclipsing that which dimly points out the memories of the Sewards, the Piozzis, and the Montagus. It was a privilege to look at her for the few moments she "rested," and to think of all she had done; when so far from "Education" being, as it is now, "the fashion," it was something so new as to be considered dangerous, particularly to women, and to the born "thralls" of humble life. Her brow was full and well-sustained, rather than what could be called *fine;* from the manner in which her hair was dressed, its formation was distinctly visible ; and though her eyes were half-closed, her countenance was more tranquil, more sweet, more holy—for it *had* a holy expression—than when those deep intense eyes were looking you through and through. Small, and shrunk, and aged as she was, she conveyed to us no idea of feebleness; she looked, even then, a woman whose character, combining sufficient thought and wisdom, as well as dignity and spirit, could analyse and exhibit, in language suited to the intellect of the people of England, the evils and dangers of revolutionary principles. How bravely had that woman stood in the gap during the crisis of England's moral as well as political peril, and sent forth in the "Cheap Repository"† tracts after tracts, that were de-

---

* Life of Hannah More, by the Rev. Henry Thompson, Curate of Wrington.

† In a degree originated by that Children's Friend, Mrs. Trimmer.

voured by the people with more than the avidity with
which they now swallow the paper pellets whose best
apology is, that they do no harm! How fine, and brave,
and true was her exposure of the speech of M. Dupont,
ringing, as it did, with the hideous clangor of atheism
throughout Europe; and how noble her sacrifice of the
sum produced by its sale (240*l*.) to the relief of the
French emigrant clergy—a charity again proving her
practical piety—for her dislike to the tenets of the church,
whose ministers she succoured and protected, was well
known. There were no traces of the sarcasm she evinced
in her clever story of "Mr. Fantom" upon her most
peaceful face; perhaps the mouth had the power of satire,
yet it was softened by time and religion. Alas! the race
of "Fantoms" are by no means extinct; there are still
plenty such, who, like this hero of false philanthropy,
neglect every duty of common humanity, and leave their
neighbors' cottage and children to burn, and poor way-
farers to perish of hunger, while devising plans to extin-
guish the fires of the Inquisition, or to drag the wheels
from off the chariot of Juggernaut.

It had ceased snowing, and though the sun cast what
seemed rays of fire through the atmosphere without dis-
pelling the thick rimy substance that hazed the air, we
resolved to brave the cold, and see the monuments erected
in the pleasure-grounds to the memory of Locke and
Porteus. We felt as if breathing icicles, but we persevered, and knew that beneath that expanse of snow lay
the lawn, where Mrs. More had assembled, at stated
periods, those best monuments of her Christian love—the
schools born of her will, and perfected by her example—

perfected according to the light of the period; and a beautiful sight it must have been, when some of the most able and best in the country came to witness the gatherings of these hitherto poor uninstructed children there.*

The very humbler classes of society have, it is to be feared, gained but little by the exchange which modern theories have put in motion—of the coldly moral for the warmer inspirations of spirit teaching. We are in this northern land of ours more prone to reason than to feel, and do not like to be too much troubled by emotions of any kind; we are becoming altogether material, and a few years more will test the good or evil of such training on our national character. One thing is certain: as far as it went, nothing could be better than the plan pursued by Mrs. Hannah More; and certainly, one of the perfections

---

* We copy one of several beautiful sonnets commemorating many places and incidents connected with the career of Hannah More— written by her esteemed friend and biographer, the Rev. Henry Thompson.

> When every vernal hope and joy decays,
>   When Love is cold, and Life is little worth,
>   Age yields to Heaven the thankless lees of Earth,
>   Offering their Lord the refuse of his days:
> O wiser She, who from the voice of Praise,
>   Friendship, Intelligence, and guiltless Mirth,
>   Fled timely hither, and this sylvan hearth
>   Rear'd for an altar! not with sterile blaze
> Of Vestal fire one mystic's cell to light,—
>   Selfish devotion; but its warmth to pour
>   Creative thro' the cold chaotic night
> Of rustic ignorance; thence, bold, to soar
>   Thro' hall and regal tower with radiant flight,
>   Till peer and peasant bless the toils of More.

of her system, for all classes, was her upholding of the *useful* as preferable to the merely *ornamental*. This is a theory which, when broached in the upper classes of society, is sure to meet approval; but it is not one mother in ten, who, finding that her daughter has only capacity for the more ordinary business of life, is content to cultivate that only, and not force her mind into what is called the higher range of intellect—forgetting altogether what a noble field for all that is of truest value in woman, is that which is connected with the ordinary business of life.

THE MONUMENT TO PORTEUS.

Mrs. Hannah More had a thoroughly English hatred to the unreal—to the untrue—and the useless; her total *deadness* to the heavenly enjoyments of music rendered her somewhat hard upon an accomplishment which her want of ear must have taught her to think waste of time; but the balance of education can be well preserved, even where a taste for this most enviable talent predominates. It is very rarely indeed that persons can appreciate—not so much what they do not understand, as what they do not feel.

THE MONUMENT TO LOCKE.

The two monuments we spoke of are in the grounds, each surrounded by shrubs and arched by trees. That to the good Bishop contains this inscription:—

" To BEILBY PORTEUS, late Bishop of London. In grateful memory of long and faithful friendship. H. M."

That to Locke is thus inscribed :—

"To JOHN LOCKE, born in this village, this monument is erected by Mrs. Montagu, and presented to Hannah More."

We returned, shivering, from our scramble through the snow ; our venerable hostess had become quite herself— vacated her seat by the fire, and insisted upon our occupying it.   She spoke with fervor and affection of the advantages she received from her long friendship with Porteus, and laughed while she said that Lord Oxford had called him her Father Confessor ; she seemed quite alive to the *on dits* of Clifton, and referred to her long residence at Bristol more than once ; she spoke with animation of Wilberforce, and his exertions on behalf of the Negro.   Her friend drew her back from what she called " modern times" to Mrs. Thrale, and Mrs. Carter, and Dr. Johnson, who, she said, was never at all " savage" to her, though once he nearly made her cry concerning an apology she offered for Popery ; then she spoke of Garrick, and the expression of her countenance became more earnest, more affectionate, than it had been at the mention of any other name. Certainly, her eyes in youth must have been glorious ; for even then they were dark, and, almost painfully, penetrating, except when softened by emotion : when she spoke of this great Master of his art, they expressed the utmost tenderness—" Ah," she said, "if HE had been alive, it would have been indeed a trial to have retired from the world !" She considered him in every way a man of extraordinary genius : her reverence for Garrick was the true " Hero-Worship:" his very faults she looked upon as accessories to his perfections.   How beautiful it is to see this en-

thusiasm outliving its inspirer, and animating with fresh
life the slow pulsations of age.   "I should have liked,"
she said, "to have looked upon his face once more, but
they only showed me his coffin."   Her friendship for
Mrs. Garrick only terminated with that venerable lady's
life.

After a moment's silence, she smiled, and observed, "I
must show you some mementos of my wicked days."   She
opened a *bureau,* and took out some cards and a play-bill:
the cards were admissions for the *new* play of "Percy;"
the bill, the list of the players who performed therein—
amongst them, David Garrick!   It was curious to see these
in the hands of the author of "Percy" after the lapse of
so many years.   "It was a great temptation," she said,
"to write for such an actor; no one now can form any
idea of what it was.   He not only was all you could imagine, but the *reality* of whatever he undertook.   Then
such a face!   Can you wonder at me thinking so seriously
of the passing away of all these things, when I believe I
am the only one living of all who are named on this
paper?"   She folded the play-bill and cards together as
they had been, and replaced them carefully.

More than once we rose to depart.   Our awe had subsided into an affectionate respect towards the fragile
woman who had held fast to what she believed right—un-
flinchingly.   We do not now adopt her opinions quite so
implicitly as we did then; though we would gladly, for
the sake of one so great in her day, and who must ever
deserve a high place amongst the bravest and best of the
women of England, do pilgrimage anew to the houses she
occupied—particularly to Barley Wood, the real home of
her affections.

Some time after our visit, circumstances to which it is needless to refer induced her to leave Barley Wood and to reside at Clifton. She lived for about four years at 4, Windsor Terrace, Clifton, receiving the most marked testimonies of affection and veneration from persons of all sects and classes.   Her end, in the 89th year of her age, was peaceful as her life was pure; and if strangers had seen the numbers who congregated to attend her to the grave—had heard the tolling of the bells from the Bristol

THE TOMB OF HANNAH MORE.

steeples, and observed that every shop was closed as the procession passed on its way to Wrington—if they had noted the mingling of yeomanry, clergy, and gentry, accompanied by the children of the Wrington Schools—if they could have been told that the lessons conveyed in the

22

"Cheap Repository" were as familiar to the people as "Thoughts on the Manners of the Great" were to their noble fellow-mourners—they would have honored those who so honored the virtues of a lady of humble birth; who, by her own exertions, had realized enough to enable her during many years of her life to devote 900*l.* a-year to deeds of charity, and leave a noble property to be divided among the most useful of our Institutions.

Mrs. Hannah More died on the 7th of September, 1833; and in Wrington churchyard, within view of Barley Wood, she was buried. A flat stone, with iron railing, beneath a gnarled yew—aged, yet vigorous with branches and leaves—marks the spot which contains her honored dust; and not hers alone, but that of her four sisters, each of whom was worthy to repose beside one of the truly excellent of the earth.* It is a quiet and retired spot—meet resting-place for one so good and pure; who had quitted the world long previously—except for the holy ties which linked her to it for its service. But of her, in truth, it may be said, "Blessed are the dead which die in the Lord; for they rest from their labors, and their works do follow them." She has made posterity her debtor, for all time: her precepts and her example are alike lessons that will lead to active benevolence and practical piety. The stone contains this inscription:—

---

* The fame of Hannah More has absorbed that of her four sisters—all admirable women, who labored heartily and continually with her in the great work of improvement. Will Bristol ever erect a monument to commemorate her excellencies—or will it be content to trust her memory to the immortality of her works?

BENEATH ARE DEPOSITED THE MORTAL REMAINS OF FIVE
SISTERS.

MARY MORE, died 18th April, 1813,
aged 75 years.

ELIZABETH MORE, died 14th June, 1816,
aged 76 years.

SARAH MORE, died 17th May, 1817,
aged 74 years.

MARTHA MORE, died 14th September, 1819,
aged 69 years.

HANNAH MORE, died 7th September, 1833,
aged 88 years.

THESE ALL DIED IN FAITH;
ACCEPTED IN THE BELOVED.
Heb. ch. xi. ver. 13.
Ephes. ch. i. ver. 6.

In these our times, unfortunately, women have in many
instances been so busied about their RIGHTS, as to be for-
getful of their DUTIES: as they cannot destroy, they endeavour to set aside the laws of God and Nature; untuning
the sweet and gentle voice, given for the expression of
prayer, of supplication, of mercy, charity, patience, hope,
and faith, in "screaming" for more liberty: proving their
unfitness, by the very temper of their demand for an impossible equality, they lose sight of the beautiful balance
which constitutes civilized society; and forget that even in
savage life, it is the man who seeks the hunting-ground,
while the woman remains in the wigwam to nurse the
infant, and prepare the food. It is solely by the soften-
ing influence of the Christian faith that women are elevated to the position they hold in Christian lands; and
the only course beneficial to them is, by increasing those

qualities that will enable them still more to cheer and enlighten the social system, which it is their peculiar province to guide and to adorn. A well-organised and properly harmonised woman has so much occupation in the sphere so clearly defined in the Book of Life, that she appreciates the high privileges of womanhood, in the several relations of daughter, friend, wife, and a "joyful mother of children," too highly, to exchange them for "advantages" unseemly, out of keeping, and out of character. She values the power of forming the minds of those who are to be the great acting principle, the mental mechanists, the heroes, statesmen, rulers of our land, hereafter. Her proper sphere is so extensive, that she only fears her life may be too short, her power too limited, to fulfil its duties. What a spirit of harmony pervades her dwelling! Be her means large or small, she has still something to bestow: her humanity extends to all around her; she never keeps the seamstress waiting for her work or for her pay, and is too just to beat down the value of a necessary to obtain a luxury. A knowledge of her own defects instructs her to be merciful to those of others, and though her servants at first are not better than those of her neighbours, her patience and good management render them so at last: she has so early taught the infant at her bosom the duty of obedience, that his pliant will bends without distortion, and instead of rebellious brawls racking his father's heart, the well-trained child already imparts the consciousness of future happiness to his anxious parents: woman in the quiet, noiseless circle of her domestic and social duties, has even more to do with the future character of empires, than the mighty man, whose bolder brain and stronger muscle must fight life's battle till his life is done: for, after all, perhaps it is scarcely an exaggeration to say that

"Those who rock the cradle rule the world."

If woman but knows herself, she can work miracles; be she high or low, rich or poor, her influence is unbounded, if it be properly exercised: it is possible to combine a perfect fulfilment of arduous, literary, or other labor, with a devout and fitting attention to the more pleasing duties of a home-cherishing life; still, those women are certainly the happiest whose occupations and pleasures are strictly of a domestic nature; but no woman pursues a safe course who calculates her happiness to consist in any but the path of duty, while she remembers that the road to *real* renown lies not through mental endowments, however brilliant, or intellectual achievements, however great. The whole career of Mrs. Hannah More is a striking example of what can be effected by *one* woman—a woman, neither high-born, nor wealthy, nor beautiful, nor, in what is understood to constitute genius, as highly gifted as many others whose names are histories: her dramas have had no sustaining power to keep the stage, and her poems, as poems, are little more than amusing trifles; but her "Cheap Repository," her book on "Female Education," her "Thoughts on the Manners of the Great," her "Christian Morals," her "Spirit of Prayer," "Hints on the Education of a Princess," "Character of St. Paul," and her "Practical Piety," despite, as we have said, some occasional conventionalities, are the temples in which her memory is enshrined; and when we recall the formation

22 *   R

of those Poor Schools,—when we remember that neither
the time bestowed upon them, nor upon her literary pur-
suits, prevented her fulfilling her duty to the

"Great Father of all,"

in whom " she lived, moved, and had her being,"—when
we learn how faithfully her domestic duties were discharged, while she was the benefactor of the poor, and
the instructor of the ignorant,—when we remember what
she was to society, and recall the kind, playful, unostentatious womanliness of her nature, we do greatly rejoice
in the triumph of *usefulness;* we gaze with reverence
upon the clear beacon-fire she kindled, so different from
the phantom lights that dazzle and betray; and we recommend most earnestly to our countrywomen the study of
such a life, and its consequences, as opposed to the
malaria of those unhealthy influences which, born of a
degraded woman of genius, have, of late years, crawled
from France into the literature of England.

Hannah More.

BY PROFESSOR JAMES RHOADS.

Hannah More

HANNAH MORE was the favorite of Dr. Johnson, the admired of Sir Joshua Reynolds, the witty and eloquent companion of Sheridan and Burke, the brave monitor of Walpole, the honored counsellor of Porteus and Wilberforce, and the familiar friend of David Garrick; she was one of the most voluminous and successful writers of her time, extensively engaged in works of practical benevolence and educational reform. Of a woman so distinguished, of such fertile mind and such active industry, there is much more to be said than can be compressed within the limits of an article like this. A short Sketch of her life and character will, however, though necessarily imperfect, be both interesting and useful.

She was the youngest of the five daughters of Jacob More, a respectable village school-master, and was born at Stapleton, in Gloucestershire, England, in the year 1745. Her remarkable talents developed themselves at an early age. About 1773 she made her entrance into society in London, where she was cordially received by the most distinguished men of the day. Of her first interview with Dr. Johnson, we have the following vivid sketch from the lively pen of one of her sisters.

"We paid another visit to Miss Reynolds; she had sent to engage Dr. Percy (Percy's Collection, now you know him), quite a sprightly modern, instead of a rusty antique, as I expected; he was no sooner gone than the most amiable and sprightly of women, Miss Reynolds, ordered the coach to take us to Dr. Johnson's very own house: yes, Abyssinian Johnson! Dictionary Johnson! Ramblers, Idlers, and Irene Johnson! Can you picture to yourselves the palpitation of our hearts as we approached his mansion. The conversation turned upon a new work of his just going to the press (the Tour to the Hebrides), and his old friend Richardson. Miss Reynolds told the Doctor of all our rapturous exclamations on the road. He shook his scientific head at Hannah, and said "she

was a silly little thing." When our visit was ended, he
called for his hat, as it rained, to attend us down a very
long entry to our coach, and not Rasselas could have
acquitted himself more *en cavalier*. We are engaged
with him at Sir Joshua's on Wednesday evening—what
do you think of us? I forgot to mention that not finding
Johnson in his little parlor when we came in, Hannah
seated herself in his great chair, hoping to catch a little
ray of his genius : when he heard it, he laughed heartily,
and told her it was a chair upon which he never sat. He
said it reminded him of Boswell and himself, when they
stopped at night, as they imagined, where the weird sisters
appeared to Macbeth. The idea so worked on their enthusiasm, that it quite deprived them of rest. However,
they learned the next morning, to their mortification,
that they had been deceived, and were quite in another
part of the country."

About two years afterward, the same sister, after the
publication of Hannah's "Sir Eldred of the Bower,"
alludes thus to the increased intimacy between her and
the great man. "If a wedding should take place before
our return, don't be surprised—between the mother of Sir
Eldred and the father of my much-loved Irene ; nay, Mrs.
Montagu says if tender words are the precursors of con-
nubial engagements, we may expect great things, for it is
nothing but 'child,' 'little fool,' 'love,' and 'dearest.'"
This friendship of Johnson thus pleasantly described, was
not a transient feeling, not a momentary whim, but a settled and permanent affection, founded upon a right appre-
ciation of the talents and characters of Hannah and her
sisters. There was, perhaps, nothing in connection with

them which struck his mind more forcibly, than the perfect harmony and love which subsisted among them. Upon one occasion, on parting with two of them, he thus characteristically alluded to it. "I love you both," he said— "I love you all five. I never was at Bristol—I will come on purpose to see you. What! five women live happily together! I will come and see you—I have spent a happy evening—God for ever bless you! you live lives to shame duchesses."

The last, or nearly the last, of her published poems was entitled *The Bas Bleu*, or *Conversation*. It was written to eulogize the Blue Stocking Club, a literary assembly that met at Mrs. Montagu's. This singular appellation, Blue Stocking, which was given to the club in consequence of one of its most admired members, Mr. Benjamin Stillingfleet, always wearing blue hose, has since been generally adopted in our language, as the distinctive family name of pedantic, or affectedly literary ladies. This poem was very highly complimented. Johnson called it a great performance. The following couplets may be quoted as a sample of its terse and spirited character:—

> "In men this blunder still you find,
>   All think their little set mankind."

> "Small habits well pursued betimes
>   May reach the dignity of crimes."

Soon after the publication of "Bas Bleu," Hannah retired from the gay world, and went again to live with her sisters, who kept a flourishing boarding-school near Bristol. In 1788, appeared her first prose work, *Thoughts on the Importance of the Manners of the Great to General Society.*

This was followed three years afterwards by an *Estimate of the Religion of the Fashionable World*. Her next important work was a series of political tales, advocating or instilling conservative doctrines, and designed as an antidote to the democratic sentiments which became prevalent at the time. These tales appeared in monthly numbers, and are said to have attracted so much attention, that there were sold upwards of a million of each. With respect to her other works, I must content myself with merely giving the titles and dates of publication of some of the principal, hoping at the same time, that some at least, of those who may honor this hasty memoir with a perusal, will make themselves better acquainted with many of them. *Village Politics*, about 1794; *Strictures on the Modern System of Female Education*, 1799; *Hints towards forming the Character of a Young Princess*, 1805; *Cœlebs in Search of a Wife, comprehending Observations on Domestic Habits and Manners, Religion and Morals*, 1809; *Practical Piety, or the Influence of the Religion of the Heart on the Conduct of Life*, 1811; *Christian Morals*, 1812; *Essay on the Character and Writings of St. Paul*, 1815; *Moral Sketches of Prevailing Opinions and Manners, Foreign and Domestic, with Reflections on Prayer*, 1819. Cœlebs in Search of a Wife, one of the best of her performances, was so popular that it ran through ten editions in the first year after its publication, and it has run through almost innumerable editions since. It is a remarkable fact that this master-piece of its kind, was written while the author was confined to her bed, with a disease which caused excruciating pain, and had afflicted her for a long time previously.

The great success of her works placed her pecuniarily
in an independent position, enabling her to live at her ease,
and to dispense liberal charities to the poor around her.
About 1800, she and her sisters purchased a property of
considerable extent, in Somersetshire, and built upon it
Barley Wood Cottage, in which they afterwards resided
for many years, and in view of which they now repose in
Wrington Churchyard. Among other interesting objects
in the Barley Wood grounds are two monuments, one to
Locke and one to Porteus. The neighborhood of this
country residence soon became the scene of labors on the
part of the sisters, even more honorable than all literary
triumphs. Within a circuit of eight or ten miles of their
new abode, a concurrence of unhappy circumstances had
reduced large numbers of the inhabitants to a state of
ignorance, almost inconceivable to an American, accustomed to the universal intelligence which pervades his own
country. Among these, the sisters determined to endeavor to diffuse the blessings of education and religion.
After many difficulties and vexations, not the least of
which proceeded from the perverseness of the ignorant beings themselves, some of whom demanded pay for sending
their children to school, they were so far successful that,
" on the hills of Cheddar, they had the gratification of witnessing the celebration of a yearly festival, where upwards
of a thousand children, and numerous members of the
female clubs of industry, after attending church service,
were regaled at the expense of their benefactresses."

Not the least interesting part of the life of Mrs. More
is yet to be noticed,—her green old age. Without being
entirely free from the infirmities of temper and disposition

so commonly attendant upon advanced years, she retained, in a remarkable degree, that youthful freshness of heart, which, in a person of her age, like the autumn rose, exhales a fragrance grateful in itself, and still more so because it is so rare.

23

Reminiscences of Hannah More.

BY GRATTAN.

The first literary lady whom I ever remember to have seen, was one whose works yet remain to improve and edify her own sex in particular, and the world in general. She was invested, too, with a particular degree of interest, owing to the fact that she was among the latest remnants of the blue stockings of the last century. She had, in her youthful days, mingled in the gay circles of *ton:* had listened to the oracular sayings of Dr. Johnson; echoed the lively sallies which burst forth in Mrs. Delany's little circle; bandied elegant trifles with that brilliant literary butterfly, Horace Walpole; had been p tted by David Garrick; and in her middle age, and in later years, had been the centre around whom bishops, princes, philanthropists, and many of meaner name and note revolved. I refer to Hannah More.

I was but a little fellow when I first saw this celebrated woman; but although then scarcely seven years of age, I retain as vivid an impression of her person and manners, as if the interview had occurred only yesterday. Twenty-eight years have rolled over my head since then, and during the interval, I have watched, on the disc of life's camera, hundreds of busy and noticeable figures go by, and then disappear in darkness forever; but my impressions of the learned old lady are as vivid as ever: and as I sit noting down this reminiscence, I can, by a very slight exercise of fancy, see her precise form, and hear her low-toned musical voice as distinctly as I did when the sober reality engrossed my attention.

My mother had, for many years, been on terms of great intimacy with Hannah More and her sisters; and I remember frequently having heard her, in our family circle, read letters which she had received from the celebrated authoress. My two sisters were then about commencing their education, and my mother, who had a great reverence for the occupant of Barley Wood, presuming on the strength of an old acquaintanceship, had written to Hannah More to ask her advice respecting a course of study. This led to a friendly correspondence, and at length to an invitation to the "little girls" to spend a week, during the hay-making season, at Barley Wood, which was, I need scarcely say, accepted.

At this time Hannah More's "sacred dramas" were very popular—and from hearing my sisters' recitations of them, and occasionally enacting a part in them myself, I became pretty familiar with these compositions. Their author's name, too, was so frequently mentioned in terms of admiration, and almost reverenced in my father's house, that I felt a growing desire to see the individual whose lines I so often repeated, and who was so looked up to. It was, therefore, with no little degree of childish delight, that one morning I set out with my mother for the purpose of bringing home my sisters, who had been spending the promised week at Barley Wood.

I had very vague ideas then about people who wrote books; they were mysterious personages to me—and in proportion to my delight in any particular work, was my estimate of the outward and visible appearance of its author. I could hardly realize, when I did think about the matter, the writer to be an actual flesh and blood reality. I used to think of him or her more as a spirit communing with my spirit than anything else; but I have lived to know better, and to experience the sad reality, that many, whose written productions are of an almost imperishable nature, have themselves been, emphatically, but of the earth, earthy.

There were no iron roads in those days, so intersecting the country in all directions, that, viewed from a height, it appeared as if a monstrous gridiron had been laid on the earth, and on the road to Barley Wood, not even a stage-coach ran, so that my mother and myself journeyed towards the place of our destination in what is called a tilted wagon. I had scarcely ever been in the country before, and oh! how keenly I enjoyed that homely ride in the early morning; for we were on our way soon after sun-rise, as we intended to make a long day of it. In antici-pation of the visit, I had, with a childish vanity, *crammed* myself with scraps of Hannah More's poetry—and I well remember I had learned by heart, in the hope that I should be asked to recite it to the authoress, " The Foolish Travel-ler," or, "A Good Inn is a Bad Home." As we ascended the high Somersetshire hills, I would alight from the cart, and, running on before it, gaze far into the hazy distance, expecting to view some such imposing looking house as I anticipated seeing at the end of our journey: and I would ask many questions about Hannah More of my mother, until her patience was almost exhausted; and then I would recite to make sure I had not forgotten the fable—and so things went on, till at length my mother held me, whilst I stood on the front seat of the vehicle, and pointed out the long wished-for spot when we were yet two miles from it.

We were on the turnpike road, and Barley Wood lay about the distance I have mentioned to our left. It was a picturesque cottage residence on a hill side, embosomed amongst trees. Behind it rose a gently sloping hill, richly wooded; in front was a lawn of emerald verdure, enclosed by shrubbery, from which the ground gently declined, until it blended with the valley of Wrington. On our left were the Mendip Hills and the Quantock Range, (famous because of the wanderings of Coleridge, Lloyd, Southey, and Wordsworth among them—it was among the Quantock Hills that the "Ancient Mariner" was composed,) rose in the blue distance. The houses of the little village of Wrington lay beneath us, and its pretty tower formed a conspicuous object in the landscape. As we descended the hill, my mother told me of Locke, and when we reached the village and quitted the tilted cart, she led me towards the church, still speaking. of the great man. The sharp air of the morning had made me hungry, so we went into a cottage near the church-yard—indeed it was in the pathway leading to it—and I got a draught of milk and a piece of brown bread and butter, and after I had dispatched these creature comforts, I was informed that I had taken my morning meal in the very room in which John Locke

23 *

was born. The great philosopher was buried in the adjoining church.

Barley Wood was but a short distance from Wrington, and we determined to walk it. At eight o'clock we quitted the village, and when we had nearly reached the house, my two sisters, who had been watching us from the lawn, came dashing down the lane to meet us, their curls streaming in the wind, and their cheeks glowing with exercise. They were in raptures with Hannah More, and in five minutes told me all that had occurred during the week. As we neared the gate, they would have dragged me triumphantly into the "Presence"—but my half awe for learned people came over me, and grasping my mother's hand, I entered the shrubbery door and walked up the lawn. We had scarcely reached the house when an elderly lady approached and welcomed us. She was plainly dressed, and presented nothing extraordinary in her appearance. This was Martha More. She invited us to follow her to the garden, where she said we should find Hannah.

At the back of the cottage was a flower-garden, arranged with exquisite taste, and surrounded with a privet hedge—which hedge, by the way, exhibited one of the absurd fashions of the time—a fashion not even yet altogether exploded in some of the retired rural districts of England. I mean that of clipping the foliage into fantastic shapes of birds, vases, &c. With this exception, Hannah More's flower-garden was faultless in arrangement. Near one of these deformed vegetative barriers, we encountered the object of our search.

Hannah More did not perceive us as we approached, for

her back was turned towards my mother and myself, as we walked up the garden pathway, and she was busily employed too, in trimming one of the before mentioned vegetable specimens of ornithology. She was dressed in a black silk gown, with a remarkably high waist, according to the fashion of the day—so high indeed that it seemed to be just beneath the arm-pits; this gave an appearance of unusual length to her figure, and afforded a striking contrast to the hour-glass contractions of the present time. Both fashions strike me as being equally ungraceful. Her shoulders were covered with a thick shawl, deeply edged with black lace, for she was an invalid, and her feet were protected by substantial shoes, worsted stockings and pattens. On her head she wore what was called a high mob cap, with ample bordering of lace, nicely plaited and tied in a monstrous bow under the chin. On her hands she had black cotton gloves, with long sleeves, the tips of the fingers having been cut off. As soon as she heard our voices, she turned round, and held out her right hand (in her left was a pair of garden scissors) to welcome us.

This celebrated woman was past seventy, of very feeble health, but her face had a surprisingly vivacious expression. Pickersgill's, prefixed to the English edition of her works, is the best, but that is too *flashy* in detail, for its somewhat staid subject. Her features were small, and furrowed with the lines of age, but her complexion was remarkably clear—almost pure red and white, owing no doubt to her long residence in the country. Her forehead was nearly concealed at the sides by an abundance of false hair, which was disposed in the shape of two huge bundles and bunches of long spiral curls—but in the centre, where these appendages met, or rather from whence they diverged, there was visible an ample cerebic development. The nose had evidently at one time been short and thick, but it was now thin and slightly hooked. The mouth was but slightly retracted, and the lips wonderfully plump for so old a woman—her chin was double and dimpled. But the most striking part of her countenance was the expression of her eyes, which were coal black, deep set, and very brilliant. None of the fire seemed quenched, and in earlier days they must have been very expressive; indeed they were so when I saw her, despite the drawback of a faded set of features to match them. Altogether she was in appearance very plain, very prim, and very precise. After the usual civilities and courtesies had been exchanged, we adjourned into the house, and were ushered into a neat little parlor, the windows of which commanded a fine view of the delightful vale of Wrington. Here a breakfast, consisting of tea, coffee, rashers of bacon and eggs, and rich clotted Somersetshire cream, was laid, and we all sat down to it, including a very plain stiff looking body, whom Hannah More introduced as Miss Frowd, and said, "She is my right hand." Elsewhere she describes her as her "domestic chaplain, secretary, house apothecary, knitter, and lamp-lighter; missionary to her numerous and learned seminaries, and without controversy the Queen of Clubs" —alluding to the charitable institutions where she took the place which her aged friend could no longer occupy.

For breakfast, Hannah More merely took a little milk and water, in which she placed some plain bread, and of this simple fare she partook very sparingly. "I live almost entirely on physic," she said to my mother, and

am the best patient Dr. Lovell has.   This, however, is no
trial for me; for many years ago I had a violent illness,
whilst visiting Mr. Thornton in London, and on recovering
from it, lost entirely both my smell and taste.   Indeed,"
she continued, "I never knew a year to pass over my
head, a considerable portion of which was not spent in
bed, to which I have been confined by illness."

The room in which she sat was decorated with a number
f portraits, most of them of dignitaries of the church.
I noticed that one of the frames contained no picture, and
with very childish curiosity, asked the reason of it.   "Oh,"
said the lady, "that frame contained the portrait of an old
•friend of mine; but as I thought him hardly fit to hang in
such good company as bishops, I have removed Davy
Garrick to my study."   Now I had often heard the saying,
"*As deep as Garrick*," and I inquired whether her friend
Davy Garrick was the person alluded to.   Miss More
turned to my mother and said, "Of all the persons I ever
knew, poor Davy was the last whose nature I should have
thought would have been associated with the idea of design.
Excepting in his art, he was simple almost to silliness."

Talking of Garrick reminds me of an anecdote which I
heard Hannah More relate on a subsequent occasion.   It is
well known that Mrs. Garrick was most devotedly attached
to her "dear Davy," as she called him.   When the great
tragedian died, she would not allow a single article in his
room to be removed from its place : and as soon as the
coffin was borne from the house, the room in which he
died was locked up, and for thirty years no one was permitted to enter it.   At the end of that time, Hannah
More happened to be visiting her old friend Mrs. Garrick,

S

whom she described as a little bowed down old woman, who went about leaning on a long gold headed cane, dressed in deep widow's mourning, and always talking of her "dear Davy." Some circumstances occurred which rendered it necessary that she should quit her residence, and Hannah More was present with her when the long closed room was opened. She said that when the door was thrown back on its hinges, and the window shutters unbarred, the room was actually darkened by millions of moths, which arose from the mouldered bed and the hangings of the room—every square inch of the bed furniture was eaten through and through, and on the air being admitted, dropped to pieces. The solid articles of furniture alone remained uninjured—but the mouldy smell of everything around was so unendurable, that the place had to be fumigated before it was habitable, even for a short time.

Breakfast having been dispatched, the domestics were summoned to family devotions, a custom rigidly observed by Hannah More every morning and evening. There were eight servants, a large number it may seem, for two or three maiden ladies to keep; but it must be remembered that, almost, from morning until night there was a constant influx of company at Barley Wood. Hannah More conducted the service, which consisted of a portion of the Liturgy; and after this had been read, we all knelt down, and the venerable lady offered up a short extemporaneous prayer, in the course of which she mentioned every individual present by their given names, aptly introducing, where it was practicable, texts of Scripture applicable to their condition or circumstances. Her enunciation was slow, solemn and very distinct. It was a fine and impressive sight to see that pious woman, whose fame had literally gone out unto the ends of the earth, bowing before the mercy seat, and humbly soliciting for the meanest one in her household those blessings which make rich and add no sorrow.

Attached to the residence was a large room, in which it was her custom every evening to receive the recipients of her bounty, and where she occupied many hours in the manufacture of articles for the use of the poor, and for charitable purposes: to this place we accompanied her, and there remained some time witnessing her labors of love, and a pleasant thing it was to witness the quiet way in which she did good; there was no ostentatious parade; the poor came to her as to a friend for assistance and advice, and never went away unrelieved. The number of garments she gave away that morning was really surprising. To most of these articles was pinned a scrap of paper, on which a text of Scripture was written with her own hand; sometimes a tract was added, and in no case without an order on the housekeeper for a supply of food. During the time my mother was closeted with Hannah More, I rambled with my sisters about the house and garden, and I well remember our being attracted to the front gate, by the arrival of a carriage, from which two gentlemen and a lady alighted, and inquired for the lady of the mansion. One of the strangers was a personage far advanced in years, and of a very venerable appearance. He was evidently in ill-health, and coughed dreadfully. As he walked up the broad gravel path, he dropped his stick, and I ran to pick it up for him. When I had done so, he took me by the hand, patted me on the head, and asked me my name. The lady who was with him called my little sisters to her, and they soon got friendly, as they rested on a rustic seat. She was also in years, and dressed quite in the old style. I have a distinct remembrance of her light, flaxen hair, which she wore in large curls, and of her faint but pleasant smile, as she took some sweetmeats from her pockets and gave us children, which quite won our hearts. The third stranger was a middle aged gentleman, of harsh and rugged features. His hair was dark, and his eyes of a light grey color; when he spoke it was with a broad Scotch accent, and a harsh, disagreeable sounding voice, quite different from the winning tones of the old lady and gentleman I have just described. I did not know who either of them were, and soon left to proceed with my play.

It was really astonishing what a number of visits Hannah More had that day; and I afterwards was informed, that every day, in this respect, was alike. How she managed, with all this visiting, to get through her extensive correspondence, and her charitable engagements, I cannot imagine. She herself says, in 1825, "I think I never was more hurried, more engaged, or more loaded with cares, than at present. I do not mean afflictions, but a total want of that article for which I built my house, and planted my grove. I mean retirement. It is a thing I know only by name. I think Miss Frowd says I saw eighty persons last week, and it is commonly the same every week. I know not how to help it. If my guests are old, I see them out of respect; if young, I hope I may do them a little good; if they come from a distance I feel as if I ought to see them on that account; if near home, my neighbors would be jealous of my seeing strangers and excluding them. My levee is, however, from twelve to three—so that I get my mornings and evenings to myself—except now and then an old friend steals in quietly for a night or two." At this time, too, Hannah More had been confined to her apartments seven years and two months. It was no want of strength, however, but the fear of an exposure to cold, which often threatened to be fatal to her.

The dinner hour at Barley Wood was four o'clock: and as a special favor we children were allowed to dine in the same room as the great people—a little table being set for us in one corner. I must mention, however, that prior to dinner, whilst taking a turn with my mother and sisters in the garden, the former asked me if I knew who the old gentleman was who had patted me on the head in the garden? I replied in the negative, of course.

"Don't you remember the 'Evenings at Home?'"

"Yes, that we do," exclaimed all three of us.

"Well, my dears, that old gentleman, and the lady who was with him, wrote them."

"What! was that old gentleman Dr. Aiken, and the kind lady who gave us the barley sugar, Mrs. Barbauld, mamma?"

"The same," was the reply. And oh how proud I then felt to have been noticed by such learned folk.

"And pray who was the other gentleman who was with them?"

"That," said my mother, "is a Scotch minister, and his name is Chalmers." It was even so—but the since celebrated divine did not interest us half as much as the chil-

24

dren's book makers. I believe when we returned home that we did little else for a week than read Evenings at Home and Barbauld's poems, and tell every one that we had seen the writers.

I was of course too young to appreciate the conversation at and after dinner, but I greedily drank it in, and I well remember that anecdotes of Dr. Johnson, Mrs. Thrale, Miss Barry, Garrick, and many others, were related. I wish now that I had been old enough to have remembered them. But as it is, a very slight recollection of them remains. All through the day Hannah More was exceedingly kind to us, and after dinner we were allowed to sit at the dessert,—when, for the edification of the company, my sisters and myself recited a portion of one of her sacred dramas, with which performance, I believe, both ourselves and the audience were very well satisfied—at least I know I was. Then we were asked sundry questions, and our kind hostess, having ascertained that I had a liking for poetry, gave me, with a kiss, a copy of Campbell's "Gertrude of Wyoming"—it was of quarto size, and a presentation copy from the author. The kiss soon evaporated, but the book I retain—with my name written in it by her own hand,—to this day, and it is needless to say I highly value it.

Such was my first interview with the author of "Cœlebs." In 1828 she removed from Barley Wood to Clifton, where, at her residence on Windsor Terrace, I frequently saw her. And as my parents resided near, she would often send for me to read to her the newspapers of the day. Many is the anecdote she has told me of her early days; and graphically would she describe the brilliant society in

which she moved, whilst a young woman, in London. Of
Dr. Johnson she was in the habit of speaking in very enthusiastic terms: and frequently said that there never was,
and never would be, his equal for solid acquirements. Sir
Joshua Reynolds, she said, was a pompous and somewhat
disagreeable companion, in consequence of his excessive
hauteur—but I might fill columns with her coloquial personal criticisms, which were exceedingly delightful to listen
to, but might prove tedious on paper.

In talking with Hannah More one seemed to be living
in the brilliant time of Chapone, Montague, Walpole, Pri-
ors, "noble lovely little Peggy" (the Duchess of Portland,)
and others of the blue stocking coteries of the last century.
She was very anecdotal, and told a story or an anecdote
with much point—and her having been a member and a
star of the celebrated circles of which Madame D'Arblay's
Diary gives us such delightful and sprightly glimpses,
added greatly, of course, to the interest of her narrations.
She was nearly, if not quite, the only survivor of those
re-unions, and when Hannah More passed away, the
last link which connected those times with our own was
broken.

The last time I saw Hannah More was in the autumn
of 1833, when she was lying on her death-bed. My
mother went to bid her old friend farewell, and I accompanied her. But the venerable woman was then a mere
wreck. Her frame had long been enfeebled, and now the
fine gold of her mind had become dim. She knew no one,
and took so little nutriment that it was wonderful how she
survived so long. She was greatly altered from what she
was when I first saw her—indeed I should not have known

her. I took a last glance, and quitted the chamber. Three days afterwards she died, and in a week from that date, I saw all that was mortal of Hannah More laid in a vault in Wrington Church, near the spot where John Locke was buried.

Andrew Macvel.

The House of Andrew Marvel.

A FEW months ago we had been strolling about Palace-yard, and instinctively paused at No. 19, York-street, Westminster. It was evening; the lamp-lighters were running from post to post, but we could still see that the house was a plain house to look at, differing little from its associate dwellings; a common house, a house you would pass without a thought, unless the remembrance of thoughts that had been given to you from within the shelter of those plain, ordinary walls, caused you to reflect; aye, and to thank God, who has left with you the memories and sympathies which elevate human nature. Here, while Latin secretary to the Protector, was JOHN MILTON to be found when "at home;" and in his society, at times, were met all the men who, with their great originator, Cromwell, astonished Europe. Just think of those who entered that portal; think of them all if you can—statesmen and warriors; or, if you are really of a gentle spirit, think of two—but two; either of whom has left enough to engross your thoughts and fill your hearts. Think of JOHN MILTON and ANDREW MARVEL! think of the Protector of England, with two such secretaries!

Evening had deepened into night; busy hands were closing shutters, and drawing curtains, to exclude the dense fog that crept slowly and silently, like an assassin, through the streets; the pavement was clammy, and the carriages rushing through the mist, like huge-eyed mis-shapen spectres, proved how eager even the poor horses were to find shelter; yet, for a long while, we stood on the steps of this building, and at length retraced our steps homeward. Our train of thought, although checked, was not changed, when seated by a comfortable fire. We took down a volume of Milton; but "Paradise Lost" was too sublime for the mood of the moment, and we "got to thinking" of Andrew Marvel, and displaced a volume of Captain Edward Thompson's edition of his works; and then it occurred to us to walk to Highgate, and once again enjoy the sight of his quaint old cottage on the side of the hill just facing "Cromwell House," and next to that which once owned for its master the great Earl of Lauderdale.

We know nothing more invigorating than to breast the breeze up a hill, with a bright clear sky above, and the crisp ground under foot. The wind of March is as pure as champagne to a healthy constitution; and let mountain men laugh as they will at Highgate-hill, it is no ordinary labor to go and look down upon London from its height.

Here then we are, once more, opposite the house where lived the satirist, the poet, the INCORRUPTIBLE PATRIOT.

It is a peculiar-looking dwelling, just such a one as you might well suppose the chosen of Andrew Marvel—exquisitely situated, enjoying abundant natural advantages, and yet altogether devoid of pretension; sufficiently beautiful for a poet, sufficiently humble for a patriot.

It is an unostentatious home, with simple gables and plain windows. In front are some old trees, and a convenient porch to the door, in which to sit and look forth upon the road, a few paces in advance of it. The front is of plaster, but the windows are modernized, and there are other alterations which the exigencies of tenancy have made necessary since Marvel's days.

The dwelling was evidently inhabited;—the curtains in the deep windows as white as they were when we visited it some years previous to the visit concerning which we now write, and the garden as neat as when, in those days, we asked permission to see the house, and were answered by an elderly servant, who took in our message, and an old gentleman came into the hall, invited us in, and presented us to his wife, a lady of more than middle age, and of that species of beauty depending upon expression, which it is not in the power of time to wither, because it is of the spirit rather than the flesh; and we also remembered a green parrot, in a fine cage, that talked a great deal, and was the only thing which seemed out of place in the house. We had been treated with much courtesy; and, emboldened by the memory of that kindness, we now ascended the stone steps, unlatched the little gate, and knocked.

Again we were received courteously and kindly by the lady we had formerly seen; and again she blandly offered to show us the house. We went up a little winding stair, and into several neat, clean bed-rooms, where everything was so old-fashioned that you could fancy Andrew Marvel himself was still its master.

"Look out here," said the old lady; "here's a view! They say this was Andrew Marvel's writing closet when he wrote *sense;* but when he wrote *poetry* he used to sit below in his garden. I have heard there is a private way under the road to Cromwell House, opposite; but surely that could not be necessary. So good a man would not want to work in the dark; for he was a true lover of his country, and a brave man. My husband used to say, the patriots of those times were not like the patriots now;—that then they acted for their country,—now, they talk about it! Alas! the days are passed when you could tell an Englishman from every other man, even by his gait, keeping the middle of the road, and straight on, as one who knew himself, and made others know him. I am sure a party of Roundheads, in their sober coats, high hats, and heavy boots, would have walked up Highgate-hill, to visit Master Andrew Marvel, with a different air from the young men of our own time,—or of their own time, I should say,—for *my* time is past, and *yours* is passing."

That was quite true; but there is no reason, we thought, why we should not look cheerfully towards the future, and pray that it may be a bright world for others, if not for ourselves;—the greater our enjoyment in the contemplation of the happiness of our fellow-creatures, the nearer we approach to God.

It was too damp for the old lady to venture into the garden; and sweet and gentle as she was, both in mind and manner, we were glad to be alone. How pretty and peaceful the house looks from this spot. The snowdrops

were quite up, and the yellow and purple tips of the cro-
cuses bursting through the ground in all directions. This,
then, was the garden the poet loved so well, and to which
he alludes so charmingly in his poem, where the nymph
complains of the death of her fawn:—

> " I have a garden of my own,
>   But so with roses overgrown,
>   And lilies, that you would it guess
>   To be a little wilderness."

The garden seems in nothing changed; in fact, the entire
appearance of the place is what it was in those glorious
days, when inhabited by the truest genius and the most
unflinching patriot that ever sprung from the sterling stuff
that Englishmen were made of in those wonder-working
times. The genius of Andrew Marvel was as varied as it
was remarkable;—not only was he a tender and exquisite
poet, but entitled to stand *facile princeps* as an incorruptible patriot, the best of controversialists, and the leading
prose wit of England. We have always considered his as
the first of the "sprightly runnings" of that brilliant
stream of wit, which will carry with it to the latest posterity the names of Swift, Steele, and Addison. Before
Marvel's time, to be witty was to be strained, forced, and
conceited; from him—whose memory consecrates that
cottage—wit came sparkling forth, untouched by baser
matter. It was worthy of him; its main feature was an
open clearness. Detraction or jealousy cast no stain upon
it; he turned aside, in the midst of an exalted panegyric,
to Oliver Cromwell, to say the finest things that were ever
said of Charles I.

The Patriot was the son of Mr. Andrew Marvel, minister and school-master of Kingston-upon-Hull, where he was born in 1620; his father was also the lecturer of Trinity Church, in that town, and was celebrated as a learned and pious man. The son's abilities at an early age were remarkable, and his progress so great, that at the age of thirteen he was entered as a student of Trinity College, Cambridge : and it is said that the corporation of his natal town furnished him with the means of entering the college and prosecuting his studies there. His shrewd and inquiring mind attracted the attention of some of the Jesuit emissaries who were at this time lurking about the Universities, and sparing no pains to make proselytes. Marvel entered into disputations with them, and ultimately fell so far into their power, that he consented to abandon the University and follow one of them to London. Like many other clever youths, he was inattentive to the mere drudgery of University attendance, and had been reprimanded in consequence ; this and the news of his escape from college reached his father's ears at Hull. That good and anxious parent followed him to London, and, after a considerable search, at last met with him in a bookseller's shop ; he argued with his son, as a prudent and sensible man should do, and prevailed on him to retrace his steps and return with him to college, where he applied to his studies with such good-will and continued assiduity, that he obtained the degree of Bachelor of Arts in 1638. His father lived to see the fruits of his wise advice, but was only spared thus long, for he was unfortunately drowned in crossing the Humber, as he was attending the daughter of an intimate female friend, who, by this event becoming childless, sent for young Marvel, and by way of making all the return in her power, added considerably to his fortune.

This accession of wealth gave him an opportunity of travelling, and he journeyed through Holland, France and Italy. While at Rome he wrote the first of those satirical poems which obtained him so much celebrity; it was a satire on an English priest there, a wretched poetaster, named Flecknoe. From an early period of life Marvel appears to have despised conceit, or impertinence, and he found another chance to exhibit his powers of satire in the person of an ecclesiastic of Paris, one Joseph de Maniban, an abbot who pretended to understand the characters of those he had never seen, and to prognosticate their good or bad fortune from an inspection of their hand-writing. Marvel addressd a poem to him, which, if it did not effectually silence his pretensions, at all events exposed them fully to the thinking portions of the community.

Beneath Italian skies his immortal friendship with Milton seems to have commenced; it was of rapid growth, but was soon firmly established: they were, in many ways, kindred spirits, and their hopes for the after destinies of England, were alike. In 1653 Marvel returned to England, and during the eventful years that followed we can find no record of his strong and earnest thoughts, as they worked upwards into the arena of public life. One glorious fact we know, and all who honor virtue must feel its force,—that in an age when wealth was never wanting to the unscrupulous, Marvel, a member of the popular and successful party, continued POOR. Many of those years he is certain to have passed—

25   T

"Under the destiny severe
　　Of Fairfax, and the starry Vere—"

in the humble capacity of tutor of languages to their daughters. It was most likely, during this period, that he inhabited the cottage at Highgate, opposite to the house in which lived part of the family of Cromwell, a house upon

CROMWELL HOUSE.

which we shall remark presently. In 1657 he was introduced by Milton to Bradshaw. The precise words of the introduction run thus, "I present to you Mr. Marvel, laying aside those jealousies and that emulation which mine own condition might suggest to me, by bringing in such a coadjutor." His connection with the State took place in 1657, when he became assistant secretary with Milton, in the service of the Protector. "I never had," says Marvel, "any, not the remotest relation to public matters, nor correspondence with the persons then predominant until the year 1657."

After he had been some time fellow-secretary with Milton, even the thick-sighted burgesses of Hull perceived the merits of their townsman, and sent him as their representative into the House of Commons. We can imagine the delight he felt at escaping from the crowded and stormy Commons, to breathe the invigorating air of his favorite hills, to enjoy the society of his former pupils, now his friends; and to gather, in

"—— a garden of his own,"

the flowers that had solaced his leisure hours when he was comparatively unknown. But Cromwell died, Charles returned, and Marvel's energies sprung into arms at acts which, in accordance with his principles, he considered base, and derogatory to his country. His whole efforts were directed to the preservation of civil and religious liberty; in perpetual opposition to him, whom

"Virtue's nurse, adversity, in vain
Received, and fostered in her iron breast!"

It was but a short time previous to the Restoration that Marvel had been chosen by his native town to sit as its representative in Parliament. The Session began at Westminster in April 1660, and he acquitted himself so honor-

ably that he was again chosen for the one which began in
May 1661. Whether under Cromwell or Charles, he
acted with such thorough honesty of purpose, and gave
such satisfaction to his constituents, that they allowed him
a handsome pension all the time he continued to represent them, which was till the day of his death. This was
probably the last borough in England that paid a representative.* He seldom spoke in Parliament, but had
much influence with the members of both Houses;
the spirited Earl of Devonshire called him friend, and
Prince Rupert particularly paid the greatest regard to his
councils; and whenever he voted according to the sentiments of Marvel, which he often did, it used to be said by
the opposite party that "he had been with his tutor."
Such certainly was the intimacy between the Prince
and Marvel, that when he was obliged to abscond, to
avoid falling a sacrifice to the indignation of those enemies among the governing party whom his satirical pen
had irritated, the Prince frequently went to see him, dis-
guised as a private person.

The noted Doctor Samuel Parker published Bishop
Bramhall's work, setting forth the rights of kings over

---

* The custom of paying members of the House of Commons for
the loss of time and travelling expenses, was common in the seventeenth century; constituencies believed such equivalents necessary
for the attention to their interests and wishes, which a Parliamentary agent was expected to give. In the Old Corporation books of
provincial towns are many entries for payments to Members of Parliament, and in some instances we find them petitioning to Government for disfranchisement, because they could not afford to pay the
expenses of a member.

the consciences of their subjects, and then came forth
Marvel's witty and sarcastic poem, " The Rehersal Trans-
posed."*   And yet how brightly did the generosity of his
noble nature shine forth at this very time, when he forsook
his own wit in that very poem to praise the wit of Butler,
his rival and political enemy.   Fortune seems about this
period to have dealt hardly with him.   Even while his political satires rang through the very halls of the pampered
and impure Charles, when they were roared forth in every
tavern, shouted in the public streets, and attracted the
most envied attention throughout England, their author
was obliged to exchange the free air, apt type of the freedom which he loved, for a lodging in a court off the Strand,
where, enduring unutterable temptations, flattered and
threatened, he more than realized the stories of Roman
virtue.

The poet Mason has made Marvel the hero of his " Ode
to Independence," and thus alludes to his incorruptible integrity :—

* Marvel's first *expose* of Parker's false logic was in 1672, in the
poem named above, which was immediately answered by Parker
and re-answered by Marvel, who appears to have had some private
threat sent him, as he says his pamphlet is occasioned by two letters ; one the published " Reproof" of him by Parker, in answer to
his first attack ; " the second, left for me at a friend's house, dated
November 3d, 1673, subscribed J. G., and concluding with these
words :—" If thou darest to print any lie or libel against Dr. Parker,
by the Eternal—I will cut thy throat."   This last reply of Marvel's,
however, effectually silenced Parker : " It not only humbled Parker,
but the whole party," says Burnet, for, " from the king down to the
tradesman, the book was read with pleasure."

25 *

> "In awful Poverty his honest Muse
> Walks forth Vindictive through a venal land;
> In vain Corruption sheds her golden dews
> In vain Oppression lifts her iron hand;
> He scorns them both, and arm'd with Truth alone,
> Bids Lust and Folly tremble on the throne."

Marvel, by opposing the ministry and its measures, created himself many enemies,* and made himself very obnoxious to the government, yet Charles II. took great delight in his conversation, and tried all means to win him over to his side, but in vain; nothing being ever able to shake his resolution. There were many instances of his firmness in resisting the offers of the Court, in which he showed himself proof against all temptations.

We close our eyes upon this peaceful dwelling of the heroic senator, and imagine ourselves in the reign of the second Charles, threading our way into that "off the Strand" where Marvel ended his days. We enter the

---

* No stronger satire could be penned than that descriptive of the Court of Charles, in the poem called "Britannia and Raleigh:"—

> "A colony of French possess the Court,
> Pimps, priests, buffoons, in privy chambers sport;
> Such slimy monsters ne'er approach'd a throne
> Since Pharaoh's days, nor so defil'd a crown;
> In sacred ears tyrannic arts they croak,
> Pervert his mind, and good intentions choak."

But not only do the courtiers feel the lash, for when Raleigh implores Britannia to urge his duty on the king, and save him from the bad who surround him, she interrupts him with—

> "Raleigh, no more! for long in vain I've tried
> The Stuart from the tyrant to divide."

house, and climbing the stairs, even to the second floor, perceive the object of our warmest admiration. He is not alone, though there is no possibility of confounding the poet with the courtier. Andrew Marvel is plainly dressed, his figure is strong, and about the middle size, his countenance open, and his complexion of a ruddy cast; his eyes are of a soft hazel color, mild, and steady; his eyebrows straight, and so flexible as to mould without an effort into a satirical curve, if such be the mind's desire; his mouth is close, and indicative of firmness, and his brown hair falls gracefully back from a full and noble forehead. He sits in an upright and determined manner upon an uneasy-looking high-backed chair. A somewhat long table intervenes between him and his visitor; one end of it is covered with a white cloth, and a dish of cold meat is flanked by a loaf of bread and a dark earthenware jug. On the opposite end is placed a bag of gold, beside which lies the richly-embroidered glove which the cavalier with whom he is conversing has flung off. There is a strange contrast in the attitude of the two men. Lord Danby lounges with the ease of a courtier and the grace of a gentleman upon a chair of as stiff and uncomfortable an appearance as that which is occupied after so upright a fashion by Andrew Marvel.

"I have answered you, my lord," said the patriot, "already. Methinks there need be no further parley on the subject; it is not my first temptation, though I most fervently desire it may be the last."

The nobleman took up his glove and drew it on. "I again pray you to consider," he said, "whether, if with us, the very usefulness you so much prize would not have a

more extensive sphere.　You would have larger means of
being useful."

"My lord, I should certainly have the means of tempt
ing usefulness to forsake duty."

The cavalier rose, but the displeasure that flushed his
countenance soon faded before the serene and holy expression of Milton's friend.

"And are you so determined?" said his lordship, sor-
rowfully.　"Are you really so determined?　A thousand
English pounds are there, and thrice the sum—nay, anything you ask——"

"My lord! my lord!" interrupted Marvel, indignantly,
"this perseverance borders upon insult.　Nay, my good
lord, you do not so intend it, but your master does not
understand me.　Pray you, note this: two days ago that
meat was hot; it has remained cold since, and there is
enough still for to-morrow; and I am well content.　A
man so easily satisfied is not likely to exchange an approving conscience for dross like that!"

We pray God that the sin of Marvel's death did not
rest with the great ones of those times; but it was strange
and sudden.*　He did not leave wherewith to bury the
sheath of such a noble spirit, but his constituents furnished
forth a decent funeral, and would have erected a monument to his memory in the church of St. Giles-in-the-Fields,
where he was interred; but the rector, blinded by the dust
of royalty to the merits of the man, refused the necessary

---

* "Marvel died in 1678, in his fifty-eighth year, not without the
strongest suspicions of having been poisoned; for he was always
very temperate, and of an healthful and strong constitution to the
last."

permission. Marvel's name is remembered, though the rector's has been long forgotten.*

Wood tells us, that Marvel was, in his conversation, very modest, and of few words; and Cooke, the writer of his life, observes that he was very reserved among those whom he did not know, but a most delightful and improving companion among his friends. John Aubrey, who knew him personally, thus describes him: "He was of a middling stature, pretty strong set, roundish cherry-cheeked, hazel-eyed, brown-haired." He was (as Wood also says) in conversation very modest, and of a very few words. He was wont to say, that he would not drink high or freely with any one with whom he would not trust his life.

Marvel lived among friends at Highgate; exactly opposite to his door was the residence of General Ireton and his wife Bridget, the eldest daughter of Oliver Cromwell; and which house still bears his name, and is described in " Prickett's History of Highgate," one of those local topographical works which deserve encouragement :—" Cromwell House is supposed to have been built by the Protector, whose name it bears, about the year 1630, as a residence for General Ireton, who married his daughter, and was one of the commanders of his army; it is, however, said to have been the residence of Oliver Cromwell himself, but no mention is made, either in history or in his biography, of his having ever lived at Highgate. Tradition states, there was a subterraneous passage from this house to the mansion house which stood where the New Church now

---

* On the death of this rector, however, the monument and inscription was placed on the north wall of the church, near the spot where he is supposed to lie.

stands, but of its reality no proof has hitherto been adduced. Cromwell House was evidently built and internally ornamented in accordance with the taste of its military occupant. The staircase, which is of handsome proportions, is richly decorated with oaken carved figures, supposed to have been of persons in the general's army, in their costume; and the balustrades filled in with devices emblematical of warfare. On the ceilings of the drawing-room are the arms of General Ireton; this, and the ceilings of the other principal apartment, are enriched in conformity with the fashion of those days. The proportion of the noble rooms, as well as the brick-work in front, well deserve the notice and study of the antiquarian and the architect. From the platform on the top of the mansion may be seen a perfect panorama of the surrounding country."

The staircase above described is here engraved. It is a remarkably striking and elegant specimen of internal decoration, of broad and noble proportion, and of a solid and grand construction suitable to the time of its erection; the wood-work of the house is everywhere equally bold and massive; the door-cases of simple but good design. There are some ceilings in the first story which are in rich plaster work, ornamented with the arms of Ireton; and mouldings of fruit and flowers, of a sumptuous and bold enrichment. The house altogether has that pleasant and instructive air of antiquity, which, combining comfort with convenience, gives a peculiar character to houses of the olden time in England; they exhibit a happy mingling of confidence with domestic tranquillity.

Out of the series of figures which stand upon the newels

of the staircase, there are ten remaining of twelve, the
original number; the missing two are said to have been
figures of Cromwell and Ireton, destroyed at the Restoration. They stand about a foot in height, and represent
the different soldiers of the army, from the fifer and drum-

STAIRCASE.

mer to the captain, and originally to the commanders.
They are curious for more reasons than one; their locality,
their truthfulness, their history, and the picture they help
us to realize of the army of Cromwell are all so many
claims on our attention.

Dr. Isaac Watts.

Residence of Dr. Isaac Watts.

BY MRS. S. C. HALL.

THERE is but to look into our own hearts, to scrutinise our own habits, to close our eyes on the tumultuous present, and recall, by a simple effort of memory, the past, to be convinced of the immense influence which the literature of infancy, so to speak, has exercised over our whole lives. Servants, in nine cases out of ten, are considered admirable care-takers of children, if they are good-tempered, clean, and careful; but they are suffered to remain altogether ignorant of *moral training;* they pet the child to keep it quiet; disorder its stomach by sedatives, or what is worse; and foster its evil passions, rather than either cause its tears to flow, or tell to parents the truth. However disposed we may be, and ought to be, to deal leniently with the errors of our fellow-beings as we advance in years—the judicious mother knows that the fault of a young child should never be passed over without reproof; for as surely as it is, it will be strengthened by repetition—

"The child is father to the man."

What ill passions may be nursed—what dangerous habits

contracted—what ruinous prejudices fostered—what bitter bondage to evil may be signed and sealed during the first years of life; while the unthinking and uneducated argue, that as the "child knows no better," no mischief can ensue. Yet moral as well as physical diseases may be contracted in childhood, nay, in infancy, which time and reason can never entirely eradicate.

The great first lesson for the infant is *obedience:* it should be taught firmly, yet tenderly, before the rebellious spirit strengthens. The mother will, and must suffer during the great sacrifice to duty she is called upon to make; but perseverance will go far to secure the happiness of both, and that of all with whom the future of the child may be associated or connected. The more difficult the task, the more needful that it be discharged faithfully.

Blessed privilege! not only to bring forth heroes, but to arm them for the battle of life with the shield of endurance—a sure defence only when tempered by self-restraint! We could enlarge upon this theme—a theme often suggested to us by some line from the divine and moral songs of Dr. Isaac Watts, as it rings upon our heart. Memories they are of verses learned almost before we could lisp them, but which, second in value only to maxims of Holy Writ, have come to us, like angels' whispers, amid the labors, and trials, and struggles—ay, and amid the pleasures and triumphs—of life.

We do earnestly record our belief, that we never *thought* a complaint against the destiny that commands the daily and nightly toil of the inventive faculty, without "the witness,"—as the "Friends" call it—"within our breast," taunting us with a reproach borrowed from Watts' Hymns or Moral Songs. Sometimes, when inclined to repose at the wrong time, "the little busy bee" will remind us of our duty, or "The Voice of the Sluggard" rise up against us, and call to mind that terror of the wise, *the consequences* of indolent dreaminess. We might, indeed, quote such suggestions from nearly every page of his writings.

It is extraordinary how a thinking people, as we are believed to be, can neglect, as we do, the infant training of the upper classes. We supply infant schools to "the people," and we admit none but teachers properly instructed in the duties they engage to perform, and yet we confide the children of the higher and most influential middle orders, to the care of persons who, in most cases, failing in every undertaking, with broken means and shattered reputations, become the Mentors of "Preparatory Establishments :" the blue board or brass plate seeming sufficient to satisfy the credulous parent, that those who offer to conduct the great business of education are worthy of the trust they seek. Parents are not unfrequently content if the nursery governess be able to attend to the children's wardrobe, and is content with less as a "salary" than the cook as "wages." "She does very well for the children at present, and is not at all particular," is a general observation:—"any one does for the first seven years who keeps them out of mischief."

Why, the "first seven years" are the most important years of human life ! There are plenty of "superior" women engaged in what is called "finishing," and they will tell you that the greater portion of the time which ought to be dedicated to completing a young lady's education, is of necessity devoted to undoing what has been

26 *   U

done: bad habits to be got rid of, bad accents to be displaced, bad manners to be set aside, and what is worse, evil principles uprooted, so that when these things are accomplished in a degree, " the time is up :" the daughter is required to take her station at home or in society ; and the whole fabric, instead of presenting the result of a good foundation upon which a solid, as well as an ornamented, structure has been raised, is dilapidated and incongruous ; exhibiting odds and ends of accomplishments—bits of gilding amid early mildew and decay, and the wrecks of half-developed systems. All this could be avoided were *infant moral training* attended to, and not confided to thoughtless or incompetent teachers. It is only a clear and comprehensive mind that can understand the " workings" and demonstrations of childhood; they are so varied, that but for their impulse and truthfulness, they would be incomprehensible from the very ductility—creating confusion—with which they fall into each other. The truly great never disdain to become, not only the instructors, but the playmates of children. None have, as yet, written down to the comprehensions they sought to elevate, so perfectly in prose, as Maria Edgeworth, or in verse, as Dr. Watts. There is a sublimity in the simplicity of childhood, which is almost divine ! we see every moment as observation developes effects around it, the tint of the world soiling the purity of its nature. To prevent this— and what a task it is !— should be the chief care of the mother or her delegate ; to impart knowledge, but not worldliness, her object ; to see that nothing is implanted that must be uprooted ; nothing encouraged that must thereafter be cast forth ! Government may found Universities

and sustain Colleges, but until teachers, either for public or
private purposes, are themselves taught beneath the State's
eye, and are able to answer to competent and fixed judges,
as to their fitness for the onerous duties they undertake,—
until schools are placed under the surveilance of persons
appointed to see that schoolmasters and schoolmistresses
are fit for their now voluntary task; until every private
teacher is responsible to the State, and until a code of
infant education is arranged and adopted, under the sanction and guardianship of "authority," we shall continue
to pursue a perpetual course of doing and undoing.   We
are increasing the power of the people over the aristocracy
by this negligence of the first principles of education; we
are strengthening *them*—pouring new ideas into their
minds, while aristocratic education stagnates.   We are
tardy in giving the educator a position.   As long as the
brainless and disreputable commence our children's education, it is of comparatively little consequence by whom it
is finished.

The task of training infant minds would not degrade a
Socrates; our Divine Master honored children—he would
have them come to him; he did not even send them to his
disciples for instruction; he said, "*Suffer little children to
come unto me.*"   The eagle that soars highest can also
stoop lowest; those must be strangely blind, indeed, to the
means of dignifying and purifying human nature, who neglect infant training.   We may be considered enthusiasts,
but we are none the less resolved to call aloud for the re-
generation of the nursery, by means of a totally different
class of nursery teachers.   We would intreat others to
demand that Government take this weighty matter into

consideration. It is not only for the lower orders that teachers should be trained in Normal Schools. The training of subjects is the duty, the power, the privilege of the State; and its neglect an unpardonable *State negligence.* If the Educator were fitted for the great moral and intellectual duty of his, or her, calling, we should have none of the educational mistakes which strike at the foundations of Social Order. .If properly conducted through infancy and childhood into youth, much that is evil would be altogether swept away from among us. No means should be neglected—not of preaching or lecturing a child—but of saturating its mind with that which must be of vital importance to its high moral existence. The moral maxims in our copy-books, which those of the early part of the present century often now recall, have been set aside for an accumulation of heavy strokes and hair strokes, conveying no definite idea to the young learner of the Caligraphic Art. The infant should have an idea sown in the mind, and left there to fructify; all its organs are capable of receiving impressions for afterthought, and all should be brought into active employment; the senses are its ministers of intelligence before it can give words to its sensations; they are, so to say, the great mental pores through which it receives food. The subject is one for grave consideration and for enlarged space; but it may not be inaptly introduced in reviewing the life of Dr. Isaac Watts, who, in "condescending to things of small estate," has been a large benefactor to mankind.

It is a curious classification, but the simplicity of Watts and the cavern-like profoundness of Young, furnish the best of good thoughts for every-day existence. When a

great authority said that Dr. Watts was a poet with whom
Youth and Ignorance might be safely pleased, the tribute,
properly considered, was of a *high order.* The office of
teacher having its origin in Heaven, what so god-like as
to instruct the innocent and enlighten the ignorant! Sublime names went before the Minstrel of Childhood; great
names have followed since his time: acting upon the spirit
of the modest introduction to his "Moral Songs" ("such
as we wish some happy and condescending genius would
undertake for the use of children, and perform much better.") Many have written lyrics for the young upon his
plan, borrowing, as he recommended, "subjects from the
Proverbs of Solomon, from all the common appearances of
nature, from all the occurrences of civil life, both in city
and country." Some, as Mary Howitt, and the Taylors,
have done excellently well; but still, "Watts' Hymns,"
"Watts' Moral Songs," have been encountered by no rival;
they nestle into the softest places of the heart, and hover
with the visions of Childhood round the bed of Age. It was
but lately we heard of the passing away of a great spirit
—learned, and of account; a man of strong mind, though
very old as we count years; his intellect never became
filmy, it was clear to the last, and discoursing with his
friends, with true Christian hope and cheerfulness as to
the prospect of the Future, he said, "It is very singular
how Watts' Hymns crowd my memory; I had forgotten
them for years, but now they are my companions, mingling with other things, and then coming forth distinctly; I
welcome them as old friends."

Dr. Watts' collected works deserve a place in every
library, and the Dissenters owe him a deep debt of grati-

tude, for he showed them that zeal and charity might be expressed and enforced in polished diction. His "Improvement of the Mind" ought to be regarded with the trust and veneration due to a domestic physician ; and it is impossible not to acknowledge and venerate the man, who, at one time, combated Locke, and, at another, made a " Catechism for children in their fourth year." But after all, his popularity is based on the universal knowledge of his " Divine and Moral Songs ;" and never was popularity more widely diffused, better merited, or productive of more glorious results.*

It is now about eight years ago, a rumor reached us that it was determined to pull down the dwelling-house of Abney Park, where Dr. Watts spent the last thirty-six years of his life, in a prolonged and harmonious " visit" to Sir Thomas and Lady Abney.† To literary persons,

---

* His works in prose and verse, published by himself, together with his manuscripts, revised and corrected by Dr. Jennings and Dr. Doddridge, were collected and published in six volumes, 4to, in 1754, by Dr. Gibbons, who prefixed to them a short account of his life and character.

† Sir Thomas Abney was knighted by King William III., and he served the office of Lord Mayor in 1700. He was bred up in Dissenting principles, and it is related of him as an instance of his strong sense of religious duties, that upon the day of his Mayoralty dinner, " he withdrew silently after supper from the public assembly at Guildhall, went to his own house, performed family worship there, and then returned to the company." Sir Thomas's loyalty was displayed in the pageant which was carried in the procession that day, when "a person rode before the cavalcade in armor, with a dagger in his hand, representing Sir William Walworth, the head of the rebel Wat Tyler being carried on a pole before him."

ABNEY PARK.

(311)

"visits" are not always "relaxations." The unceasing labor of Literature requires seasons, however short, of perfect unrestraint,—of entire calmness and repose. Society demands either novelty or a new dressing of old thoughts; and, to some sound thinkers, conversation—the light and sparkling conversation of "the world"—is intensely laborious. But Dr. Watts' friends really permitted him to be free beneath their hospitable roof, and his small independence during his latter years, though not more than a hundred pounds a-year, prevented his feeling even their loving tenderness a burden.

We had been warned not to delay our pilgrimage to his residence too long, and a desire to visit the Shrine of the sweet Psalmist of Childhood, drove us forth during the darkness of a London fog. It is foolish to pack and unpack a resolution too often, so away we went; the horses looking dim and spectral, and the human beings flitting along in the murkiness like demons in a pantomime. We certainly detest a fog, creeping and breathing around us like a mighty incubus that cannot be shaken off—entwining our limbs, and chilling us to the very heart—so mysterious in its monotony—giving ample scope to the very imagination which it chills—etching, as it were, the public buildings and solemn churches, and leaving it to the traveller to fill up the gloomy outlines. We never saw a fog painted, and though the peculiarity of English atmosphere, it is very un-English in its sly, insidious ways; we hear such hollow coughs in foggy weather; the horses suffer so much; the fairest face obtains a thick bluish tone of color; and little blacks descend upon our noses, or sit on our eye-lashes with dignified indifference. As much as we

27

can hate anything that God sends, we *do* hate a fog, particularly a yellow fog, which is the very embodying of
suspicion and ill-feeling. Iagos and Iachimos, men of
that *ilk*, are, we opine, born in foggy weather; at such
time, murderers are seen to creep about; and the air,
instead of being "voiceless," is filled with cruel whisper-
ings. We were so ill at ease, that, truth to say, we
thought we had chosen an evil day to visit Abney Park.
We remembered when half way through the city, that we
had no introduction to its present proprietor; and of all
awful things, the meetings of unintroduced English people
are the most embarrassing! It was not for some little
time after we had entered it, that we discovered the house
was occupied as a college for the instruction of youths of
the Wesleyan Society; but we had only to declare our
desire to inspect the house, hallowed by the memory of Dr.
Watts, to be cordially received. It was, indeed, a spacious
dwelling, standing in what was once a noble park, but a
greater portion of which had been converted into one of
those cemeteries that now abound in our suburbs, and are
so auxiliary to the preservation of health of body and mind
to the living; it was to increase its size that they designed
pulling down the noble mansion that had for so long a
time sheltered the poet. The trees were remarkably fine,
adding much to the beauty and solemnity of the grounds—
then only partially dotted with memorials of those who
have exchanged time for eternity. Before we describe
the house to our readers, we must mention that many
honored persons have resided in Stoke Newington—which
we of the West-end affect to consider a semi-barbarous
region. Isaac Watts wrote much of his poetry beneath

THE GROVE OF CEDARS AND YEWS IN ABNEY PARK.

(315)

the avenues of yew-trees, and upon the mound consecrated by his name, and which a vague tradition tells us, covers the ashes of the mighty one of England—CROMWELL ! * A large portion of Abney Park, ranging from the magnificent cedar of Lebanon, in the part once called the Wilderness, and continued to the southern extremity, where the mound is placed, and all the land east of that line, extending as far as the principal entrance to the cemetery, was, during the Commonwealth, and after the Restoration, the

---

* Many are the traditions of Cromwell's resting-place.   After the Restoration of Charles II., the bodies of Cromwell, Bradshaw, and Ireton were, with the characteristic meanness of that king, "dragged out of their superb tombs among the kings in Westminster, to Tyburn, and hanged on the gallows there from nine in the morning till six at night," and then thrown in a deep hole under the gallows, their heads being set upon poles on the top of Westminster Hall. The head of Cromwell, which had been blown down, and carried off by a passer-by, afterwards re-appeared, and was made a public exhibition of in the early part of the present century, but although it was affirmed to be his very head, its authenticity was questionable.   It was a favorite tradition with his partisans, that his body was not subjected to the indignities intended for it, but that, fearing desecration, his friends had re-interred the body, and changed its place with that of Charles I.   Hence it was a favorite saying with them, that the king suffered greater indignities at the hands of the Cavaliers than he had done from the Roundheads.   The exhumation of the body of Charles at Windsor, however, settled the fact of his identity.   That Cromwell's body received but a mock funeral at Westminster, and was really peaceably reposing elsewhere, was still a favorite belief with his partisans ; and Ireton's residence at Newington, and the circumstance of his marriage with Bridget, Cromwell's eldest daughter, as well as the important position he filled as head of the Republican party in the army after the death of the Protector, may have easily led to the tradition above mentioned, however unfounded.

27 *

property of General Fleetwood.   The eccentric Thomas
Day, whose amusing letter forms so interesting a portion
of Miss Edgeworth's life of her father, Lovel Edgeworth,
dwelt in the immediate neighborhood.   Daniel De Foe
occupied a house in the village.   John Howard, the Man
of Prisons, who lived in darkness that the darkness might
be made light : and, some few years ago, Dr. Aikin, with
his sister, the gentle child-loving Mrs. Barbauld, combined
to give a higher interest to this locality than it is in the
power of mere fashion to bestow.   Our glance at the park
was anything but satisfactory.   The fog was hanging
round the trees, and imparted that air of desolation and
chillness to the landscape which is so very much at variance
with our feelings and desires.   It was refreshing to enter
the warm and comfortable house, to feel the glow of heat
and again receive the courteous welcome of the benevolent
gentleman, the Superintendent of the establishment, whose
name is honored among his own people.   The house, with
its oak panellings and grave aspect, reminded us of Sir
Christopher Wren's, at Camberwell.*   Perhaps it was
not quite so old, nor was the Hall so handsome, but it was

---

* The house was a square, substantial, red-brick building, with
stone quoins.   The roof was flat, with a balustrade around it ; and
had a central turret, from which an extensive view of the surrounding country could be obtained.   The entrance-gate was richly carved
with flowers and fruit.   The interior was entirely walled with oak
panelling, and the staircase and rooms were all large and stately.
There was one "painted room" on the first floor, the panels of
which were filled with landscapes and figures, and which must have
originally been gorgeous in its effect; but the general character
of the house was that of unostentatious solidity and wealthy
plainness.

a noble house, and rendered deeply interesting as the scene of one of those acts of disinterested friendship, which we have already mentioned—not growing out of whim, nor kept alive by the love of praise, or the love of novelty or adulation, but springing from an exalted religious principle, loving a brother in Christ because of his fervor and excellence in that which Christ loved. Isaac Watts, his slender frame worn to a shadow by illness, and helpless as an infant, was invited by Sir Thomas Abney, of Abney Park, to visit him. As a visitor for a few weeks he was received into the house, where he was treated, for thirty-six years, with all the kindness that friendship could prompt, and all the attention which respect could dictate. Sir Thomas dying about eight years after the commencement of his visit, he resided with Lady Abney and her daughter until his own death.

On the right, as you entered the hall, was the small library, which the poet and logician was permitted—nay, that is too cold a word to express the noble hospitality exercised for *six-and-thirty years* towards the weak and quivering life of Isaac Watts—was compelled rather, by words and deeds of unchanging kindness—to call his own.

We could not avoid picturing the little trembling man moving from that very door, bowing at every third step as he advanced to meet old Lady Huntingdon, who once came to greet him there—and saying, while offering his hand to conduct her into his library, " Madam, I came to this hospitable house on a visit for three weeks, and I have remained here thirty-and-three years." "And," added Lady Abney, curtseying with all the dignity of hoop and highly-mounted head—as suddenly she stepped forth from the small oak parlour—"it is the shortest visit a friend ever paid."*

We entered the library, and all the gloom of the day vanished while considering the uniform but useful life of

THE LIBRARY OF DR. WATTS.

Dr. Watts. We conversed about him as we would of an old and cherished friend, whose memory was still "green in our souls." He was born at Southampton, in the sunniest part of the year 1674—the month of July. Some say his

* We heard this characteristic anecdote on the spot, from the gentleman who received us with so much kindness.

father was a shoemaker, others that he was a schoolmaster; it matters little which; he suffered persecution for his religious opinions, and maintained his firmness in them as befits a Christian, for one of his son's biographers tells us a family tradition has recorded that, during his imprisonment, the youthful and sorrowing mother has been known to seat herself on the steps of her husband's prison-house, suckling this child of promise—this child cradled in meekness amid controversial storms.   The adversities of Isaac Watts' early years were remembered by him in after life, and doubtless originated that deep and ardent attachment to civil and religious liberty which marked his character, and led his muse to hail its establishment with exultation, when the dynasty of the vacillating Stuarts was driven from the throne.   He was a remarkable lover of books from infancy, and the proficiency of the pale, delicate little boy, when at school, was so extraordinary, that a subscription was proposed for his support at the University; but he declared his resolution of taking his lot with the Dissenters.   Doctor Johnson, in the brilliant and generous biography—which is in fact a dissertation upon the moral and spiritual beauty of the man—pays him a most marked compliment on this head:

"Such," says the Doctor, "he was as every Christian church would rejoice to have adopted."

It was very gratifying to sit silently in this room for a few minutes—and think! We have been in many houses where the high and mighty, and the brave and wise, have lived and died; but never beneath any roof for which we felt greater reverence than this, where there was nothing, either in the past or present, of the noisy, gaudy world,

V

nor of the show and parade of fanaticism or learning—
everything was real and true, simple and holy.

He quitted the academy at the age of twenty, spent two
years in study and devotion, beneath the roof of his father,
and then became tutor in Sir John Hartopp's family. It
is as interesting as curious, to remark how events come
round—foredoomed, as it were, to work out great purposes. Sir John Hartopp married one of Fleetwood's
daughters; this lady is stated not to have been the fruit
of the general's marriage with Cromwell's daughter, (Ireton's widow,) but by a former wife; she resided in the
house adjoining Abney Park;* and as tutor to their children, the grandchildren of Fleetwood, whose name Dr.
Watts says, "is in honor among the churches," he came
there; and thus began his friendship with the Abneys.
It would seem that his tutorship did not interfere with his
ministry, for he had a "church," an independent church,
then meeting in Mark lane, first as assistant to Dr. Isaac
Chauncy; subsequently, after much hesitation, he accepted
the invitation to succeed Dr. Chauncy in the pastoral

---

* This house, still known as Fleetwood House, is standing close
beside the iron gates which led to Abney Park, and which are
remaining, as well as the circular drive that led to the house, which
stood at a considerable distance further back than its neighbor,
Fleetwood House. Here the famous Republican general was fortunate enough at the Restoration to be permitted to retire with life
and liberty, and here he died in 1692. The house has been much
modernised, and presents so few external features of antiquity, that
it is only by looking narrowly at some small portions, which, owing
to their unobtrusiveness, have been left untouched, that its age
could be guessed at. After Fleetwood's death it was inhabited by
his descendants, the Hartopps and Hurlocks.

office !   He retained this ministry until the last ; devoting
a third part of his small stipend to the poor.   *Here* the
remainder of his life was spent, in a family which, for
piety, order, harmony, and every virtue, " was a house of
God."   To this happy circumstance the world is mainly
indebted for the many rare and estimable productions of
Dr. Watts.   Ease of mind, with graceful relaxations from
laborious studies—domestic quiet and competence—were
matters upon the obtaining of which even his existence
depended.   The history of his life, from the time of his
entering this home, is merely a history of his works.   He
continued actively employing his pen, producing his
" Logic," which, having been received at the Universities,
needs no higher praise ; his ennobling " Improvement of
the Mind," sermons, discourses, prayers, essays, and
poems ! all !—most blessed distinction !—all tending to
one great and one exclusive object—the glory of God and
the benefit of human kind.

Dr. Johnson—that unshorn Samson of our faith—as if
he could not bear to enter on controversial points with one
whose memory he treated with a gentleness foreign, not to
his nature, but his habit,—Dr Johnson says, " With his
theological works I am only enough acquainted to admire
his meekness of opposition, and his mildness of censure.
*It was not only in his book, but in his mind, that ortho-
doxy was united with charity.*"   Charity, indeed, was one
of his favorite themes.   " I find," he says, in one of his
harmonious discourses, "a strange pleasure in discoursing
of this virtue, hoping that my very soul may be moulded
into its divine likeness ; I would always feel it inwardly
warming my heart ; I would have it look through my eyes

continually, and it should be ever ready upon my lips to soften every expression of my tongue ; *I would dress myself in it, as my best raiment ;* I would put it on, upon my faith and hope, not so as entirely to hide them, but as an upper and more visible vesture, constantly to appear in amongst men ; for our Christian charity is to evidence our other virtues !"   Although his stature was but five feet, he was in his pulpit of a presence at once sweet and dignified, and his elocution was remarkable for its grace and intonation ; his eyes were both firm and brilliant, and his voice full of music.

We followed our conductor to the top of the house, where, in a turret upon the roof, many of Dr. Watts' literary and religious works were composed. We sat upon the seamed bench, rough and worn, the very bench upon which he sat by daylight and moonlight—poet, logician and Christian teacher. We were in some degree elevated above the dense and heavy fog, for the heavens were clear and blue ; but all beneath us was shrouded in a sea of mist, that would sometimes clear away, and then press its yellow folds more closely round every object of interest. This was very provoking : we desired to see what HE had seen : but we remembered how, out of this good man's naturally irritable temperament, he had become gentle, modest, and patient. We could almost fancy the measured yet dulcet tones of his sweet, eloquent voice reproving our unthankfulness for what we had already enjoyed. Considering the unostentatious and righteous nature of the man, we could not agree with Dr. Johnson in thinking it at all wonderful that he condescended to lay aside the scholar, the philosopher, and the wit, to write little devotional songs, poems, and systems of instruction, adapted to the wants and capabilities of children ;* the more he combated with Locke, the greater necessity he perceived for making a Catechism for children of four years old.

The chamber upon whose walls hung the parting breath of this benevolent man might well be an object of the deepest interest to all who follow, however humbly, the faith of Jesus. We were told of a little child who, knowing every hymn he had written, was taken into his room, having some vague but happy idea that she should meet him there. Learning, as she eagerly looked round, that the author of "Watts' Hymns" was dead, she burst into bitter tears, which did not cease while she remained in the house. Many of his works are said to have been produced in this room, which, though small, was lofty and pleasant. The greater number of his poems are devotional. His nature and education both prompted him to employ his talents in the service of his Creator. Poetry with him was but the giving a more delightful and inviting dress to that which is naturally grand, dignified and beautiful. We remember in his preface to his "Lyric Poetry" he seems to think it almost necessary to apologise for spending the time thus. He says, if he seized these hours of

* Doctor Southey, in his "Life," says that he composed rhyming lines for copy-books, containing moral instruction, and beginning with every letter of the alphabet; copies composed of short letters, for teaching to write even; and others, each line of which contained all the twenty-four letters. Can any of our publishing or other readers inform us if these proofs of Doctor Watts' knowledge of the importance of having a fixed object in all that is written for children, are in existence now?

28

THE STATUE IN THE CEMETERY.

leisure wherein his soul was in a more sprightly frame, to entertain himself or his friends with a divine or moral song, he hopes he shall find an easy pardon. These "Divine Songs for Children" seem to have achieved the perfection of their intent. To this hour, when fretful, or in pain, or indisposed for occupation, a line—as we have said—a verse of those hymns, learned in our childhood, set us "all right again." No wonder, then, that we class the "Divine Songs for Children" among the rarest and most valuable works to which genius has given existence. If the earliest impressions are of the greatest importance, because the most effective and the most enduring, how essential is it that the bias of the young mind should be towards virtue, honesty, industry, humanity and moral courage? There is no lesson in either which Dr. Watts has left untaught. Children lisp his verses long before they can read them— the moral fixes upon the mind through the active medium of the imagination, and is retained for life. "The Divine Songs" are neither too high nor—what is less easy of attainment—too low for the comprehension of a child; and they tempt perusal and thought by the graces of easy rhyme. They are simple without being weak, and they reason without being argumentative; they are just of sufficient length to be committed to memory, without being long enough to become wearisome as tasks. We do indeed regard their author as one of the great benefactors of the human kind, and have searched in vain amongst the tomes of poets of far loftier pretensions for so many golden verses as are to be found in the " Divine Songs for Children."

Eight years have passed since this visit was paid to the dwelling-place of Dr. Isaac Watts. Eight years! which, as they rolled on, have left us much, and taken much from us! And it is good and right to be able to bless God both for what he took and what he left, knowing that the bitter has become sweet, and our foolish repinings have been silenced into wisdom. One, tried and trusted, who was with us then—the heart-friend of our youth, the dear companion of our thoughts and hopes—has been perfected in heaven; and we never missed her ever cheerful voice, or sunny smile more, than when we revisited Abney Park but a short time ago. Our very affections become selfish when not tempered by the spirit of charity and love; the most acceptable homage we can render to the righteous dead, either in the sight of God or man, is by walking to our own graves in their footsteps!

THE MOUND IN THE CEMETERY.

Abney Park is now part of a large cemetery. The iron gates by which we entered the drive leading to the house in 1842, are still there; and the trees, the avenues, preserved with a most delicate respect to the memory of the poet are so well kept—there is such an air of solemnity, and peace, and positive "beauty" in the arrangement of the whole—that if spirits were permitted to visit the earth, we might hope to meet his shade amid his once favorite haunts. There is nothing to offend us in such receptacles for the perishing away of humanity, but everything to soothe and harmonize the feelings of the past and present. A statue in pure and simple character of this high-priest of charity, stands (we were told) upon the "exact spot" where the house stood; but we think it has been placed rather farther back than was the dwelling.* Perhaps the site is more ostentatious of display than would have met

---

* The inscription on the pedestal of the statue to Watts, which was executed by E. H. Baily, R. A., and "erected by public subscription, September, 1845," is as follows:—"In memory of Dr. Isaac Watts, D. D., and in testimony of the high and lasting esteem in which his character and writings are held in the great Christian community, by whom the English language is spoken. Of his Psalms and Hymns it may be predicted in his own words:—

> " ' Ages unborn will make his songs
>   The joy and labor of their tongues.'

"He was born at Southampton, July 17th, 1674, and died November 25th, 1748, after a residence of thirty-six years in the mansion of Sir Thomas Abney, Bart., then standing in these grounds.

"Few men have left behind such purity of character, or such monuments of laborious piety; he has provided instruction for all ages, from those who are lisping their first lessons, to the enlightened readers of Malbranche and Locke. He has left neither corporeal nor spiritual nature unexamined: he has taught the art of reasoning and the science of the stars; such he was, as every Christian church would rejoice to have adopted."—DR. JOHNSON.

28 *

the Doctor's taste had he been consulted; and had it been hid away in a wilderness, where the nightingale sung to the rose, and the cushat converted melancholy into music, he might have liked it better. But all honor to those who honored the teacher of their childhood: he would pardon them this genuine homage. "The mound," too, from whence he loved to overlook the green and fertile country, (for London at that period had not escaped from Shoreditch) is walled in, fenced round, and guarded as a sanctuary. We have said that one dreamy tradition affirms that the bones of CROMWELL sleep beneath the tablet which records the love of Isaac Watts for that which was in his time lovely and solitary—looking over a large pond, where the heron sat musing by

"The sedgy shallow;"

and commanding, beyond, extensive views of the surrounding country. The cemetery is also ornamented by a picturesque little church, from which a funeral procession was passing as we entered.

Many of the monuments are remarkable for truth and simplicity, and numbers of the graves were enriched by early flowers in full bloom. The old trees are invaluable to the Abney Park Cemetery, and so suggestive of memories of Dr. Watts, that his home seems still there; though, in reality, his remains—now a mere handful of ashes—are interred in the burying ground of Bunhill Fields, opposite the chapel where John Wesley preached, when past the age of eighty, to the many missionaries who have since carried his name over the universe.

We visited this crowded place of interment for Dissenters: the walk through its thickened tombs is literally paved—like the chancels of our old cathedrals—with tombstones; and our feet frequently recoiled as our eyes caught the name of some time-honored gospel minister.*

Such a brotherhood of graves is full of profit! The city din sounded like distant thunder; but yet, though the rain splashed on the tombs and sunk into the thickly-matted grass, all seemed silent. We thought upon the memorable words of the old man, "waiting God's leave to die!"—how he had said, "that the most learned and knowing Christians, when they come to die, have only the same plain promises of the Gospel for their support as the common and unlearned; and so," he added, "I find it."

The tomb is square. Southey calls it "handsome." He could hardly have seen it; for it is humble, unpretending, even Quaker-like in its plainness. The epitaph,

---

* Bunhill Fields was known as the city burial-ground in the reign of Charles I., and here was buried the son of his successful opponent—the mild Richard Cromwell. General Fleetwood, Cromwell's Lord Deputy of Ireland from 1651 to 1654, was also buried here. The ground was walled in at the expense of the city during the Great Plague of 1665, and was some time afterwards purchased by Mr. Tindal, who appropriated it as a burial-ground for persons of any religious persuasions who chosed to avail themselves of it. It has hence become the favorite "resting-place" of eminent Protestant Dissenters; and here rest John Bunyan, Dr. Watts, Dr. Price, Dr. Lardner, Dr. A. Rees, author of the "Cyclopædia," and a host of others celebrated for their learning and piety. An avenue of trees adds to the appearance of this cemetery, which has been recently enlarged by the removal of some houses at the farther extremity. An idea of the immense number of dead here deposited may be formed from the fact, that in the twenty-four years previous to 1821, no fewer than 35,000 bodies had been interred in it.

written by himself, is an index to his humility. He does not tell his age, but counts his years by the length, as it were, of his Gospel Ministry:—

"Fifty years of feeble labors in the Gospel."

It records his death, on the 25th November, 1748, and adds, that the monument was erected to his memory by Sir John Hartopp, Bart., and Dame Mary Abney: having been "replaced in 1808 by a few of the persons who met for worship where he so long labored."

The tomb is on the right-hand side of this great burying-ground, which, doubtless, when first enclosed, was in the country, but now is surrounded by houses. It is well and carefully kept, but lonely and uncheerful, though the sun came out and turned into crystal the rain-drops which hung from the leaves of the young trees. One man was giving a date and a name to a fresh tombstone; and another told us, when we said how full of death was the enclosure—that there was room enough for many more. We could not avoid wishing that Dr. Isaac Watts had been buried amid the stillness of the groves he loved so well.

Life and Genius of Dr. Watts.

BY THE REV. JOEL PARKER, D.D.

THERE is a natural alliance between genius and infancy. Simplicity is a leading characteristic of both. The sublimest poets advert to their recollections of childhood with a pleasing interest. Men like Moore and Byron go back to those "sunny hours," because they furnish to their minds the only just conceptions of purity and innocence. Their latter experience would, probably, lead them to deny the existence of such qualities. Yet childhood is, to society at large, what the mission of the infant prophet was to the house of Eli, a mission of reproof. But men love not to be rebuked, and hence, happily, none but such as have retained the simplicity and virtue of "life's young dawn," care to spend their hours amid the charms of the nursery. Wordsworth deemed it good to be there, because his philosophic and gentle spirit was akin to infancy. Maria Edgeworth loved to converse with children, because she saw all noble qualities closely folded in their germs in infant minds, and waiting for some genial influence to develope them. Dr. Watts discovered all these and more. He saw that sentiments of virtue and piety were most easily infused in the very dawn of intelligence. He per-

ceived that poetry was the most natural vehicle for introducing such sentiments, and the most efficient means of
keeping the thoughts that nourish them ever green in the
memory.   He possessed an affinity with childhood, because he was child-like in his character; and children
have a conscious affinity with him, because all children
possess poetic qualities.   The child who discovered that
the stars were gimlet-holes bored through the solid sky,
and made on purpose that streams of glory might be let
down from heaven to earth, was prepared to sympathize
with a poet like Watts.   The little girl of four years old,
who recollected distinctly an event that had occurred six
years before, and who modestly combated her mother's
declaration that she could not remember what had taken
place previous to her birth, evinced true poetic genius,
when raising her tiny hands, and clasping her little neck,
she exclaimed, with the ardour of an undoubting faith in
the visions of her own glowing imagination, "You forget,
dear mother, you forget; I know I was not born, but God
had made my head, just as far down as to here, and I
peeped out of that cloud and saw it. You did not see me,
but I saw you, and I remember it well."   Not inferior to
either of these was the confidential disclosure of a young
lad to his playmates, that he had discovered the use of
those fleecy clouds piled up by the horizon, at nightfall,
and overhung with red and blue curtains.   They were
couches on which the angels sleep.   He had seen one who
had become weary and gone to bed at an unusually early
hour.   He saw him at the going down of the sun stretched
out in gigantic dimensions, with a bright face, having one
foot and leg sheathed in a crimson stocking, the other

bare, and an orange-colored satin counterpane drawn over his shoulders. If these are extraordinary instances, still children generally are full of faith, and gifted with warm imaginings. A poet like Watts turns their own thoughts into verse, and no small portion of his power consists in doing for them what every teacher that is most skilful does for his pupils, when he makes them feel that what he has accomplished, was the expressing of their views better than they could have done it themselves.

Doctor Watts was a great man. True, he did not place himself at the head of any one department of science or literature. Yet he was highly distinguished in more respects, perhaps, than any man of the age in which he lived. He was a general scholar; a skilful logician, a profound divine, an acute metaphysician, a sublime poet, and a charitable and devout Christian. There is not a more attractive grace in human nature than condescension, and one knows not where to find a more beautiful instance of it than in him who composed a Logic for the Universities, combated the philosophy of John Locke, framed a catechism for children in their fourth year, and wrote "Divine and Moral Songs" for the nursery. It may be justly doubted whether the world's history furnishes a parallel, except it be in Him who claimed the heavenly hierarchies as his servants, and took little children in his arms, and laid his hands upon them, and blessed them.

Isaac Watts was born in 1674 at Southampton. His father was a schoolmaster. He suffered persecution for his dissenting opinions, and tradition says that "the youthful and sorrowing mother has been known to seat herself on the steps of her husband's prison-house, suckling this child of promise—this child cradled in meekness amid controversial storms." He was a very precocious child, as is seen in the fact that he commenced the study of Latin at the early age of four years. He was a great lover of books, and was wont, when any of his friends had given him a penny, to cry, "A book, a book," and never to rest till he held in hand the only commodity for which he thought money well expended.

His precociousness, instead of being regarded as an intimation, as a wiser philosophy teaches us it should have been, that mental development should be cautiously repressed, was looked on only as an encouragement to stimulate to the utmost his already over-active brain.

The pale and expressive features and manly actions of a delicate boy like him, could not but awaken a deep interest in his education. He was first intrusted to the care of a worthy clergyman of the established church, the Rev. John Pinhorne, master of the free grammar school at Southampton; of whose able attention to his improvement the Doctor bears honorable testimony in a Latin ode inscribed to him. It was written at the age of twenty, and published among his Lyric Poems. While he was yet a lad, his sprightliness, and wit, and extraordinary attainments in learning, attracted the attention of neighboring gentlemen. Dr. Speed, a physician of Southampton, proposed a subscription for his education at one of the universities, but his sympathy with the suffering non-conformists would not allow him to avail himself of the generous offer. "I am resolved," said he, "to take my lot with the Dissenters."

In the year 1690, at the age of sixteen, he was sent to

London for academical education, under the Rev. Thomas Rowe, to whom also he has inscribed an ode among his Lyric Poems. His conduct while at the academy was inoffensive, not only, but also such as to be continually presented by his tutor as a model for others. Having spent four years at this institution, he returned home, and for two years prosecuted that course of study which was deemed necessary for the sacred office. It was during this time that a circumstance occurred which led to the composition of his sacred lyrics. He attended worship in the same church with his father. Complaining one day of the untasteful character of the compositions employed in sacred praise, his father, knowing his poetical turn, suggested that he should try if he could do better. He did so. Thus, one after another, a considerable portion of his hymns were produced during these two years, though they were not published till some time after.

From his father's house he went to reside in the family of Sir John Hartopp, at Stoke Newington, to superintend the education of his son. Here he spent five years very agreeably and usefully, and by a revision of his elementary studies and extensive reading, laid the foundation for his subsequent eminence. During this period he studied extensively the Scriptures in the original tongues, and on the day which completed the twenty-fourth year of his age, he was chosen assistant to Dr. Isaac Chauncy, pastor of the Dissenting Church in Berry Street, London. Upon Dr. Chauncy's resignation in January, 1702, Mr. Watts was called to succeed him in the same church, of which the famous Dr. John Owen had formerly been pastor. After much delay and modest diffidence, he at length accepted the call on the 8th of the March following,—the very day on which King William died,—a day regarded as very alarming to the dissenting interest.

In 1707 his Hymns were first published, and the copyright sold for only ten pounds. Their sale, if they could have been retained, and the copyright perpetuated, would probably have yielded more than twenty times that amount per annum. The copyright for Milton's "Paradise Lost" was sold for fifteen pounds. It would afford an interesting view of the benefactions of genius to the world, if we could estimate the amount of what is deemed a copyright compensation of all the copies of their works sold. A small copyright tax paid on each copy of Homer, of Virgil, of Paradise Lost, of the Pilgrim's Progress, and Watt's Psalms and Hymns, would exhibit an immense accumulation. Yet these writers gave their works to the world, to be used at the bare expense of manufacturing the books, and many of them will thus be given for thousands of years.

In 1712, Mr. Watts was seized with a most alarming illness. This sickness so prostrated his nervous system that he never entirely recovered from its effects. Yet it was the means of one of the most fortunate occurrences of his life. It was the means of introducing him to the acquaintance of Sir Thomas Abney, Knight and Alderman, and, at that time, Lord Mayor of London. In this refined and opulent family, at Newington, he spent the remainder of his days, enjoying every comfort which the most abundant wealth and liberal munificence and kind affections could supply. Here, for thirty-six years, his mature powers produced and sent forth the greater portion of

those works with which Dr. Watts blessed his own and
subsequent times.

He went thither at the invitation of Sir Thomas, to
make a brief visit. The time of his stay was insensibly
prolonged, till the congeniality subsisting between the
Doctor and this excellent man bound him to the spot,
and rendered him ever after the "genius loci" of Abney
Park.

The place is replete with interesting associations, besides
its being the shrine of "The sweet Psalmist" of England,
we had almost said of Christendom: for Watts is little
less conspicuous as a composer of songs of praise for the
modern gentile church, than David had been in the Jewish.

The gifted Daniel De Foe had once occupied a house in
the village. Here, also, had resided John Howard, who
acquired by his compassionate endeavors to illumine
dungeons by the spirit and beneficence of the gospel, the
honored name of "The Philanthropist." And here, also,
but a few years ago, dwelt Dr. Aiken, with his sister,
"the gentle, child-loving Mrs. Barbauld."

Still, a peculiar sanctity was imparted to the house, by
the recollection that many of those beautiful poetic versions
of the Psalms were penned within its walls. The building
itself seemed to possess characteristics analogous to the
spirit and qualities of the guest which it so long sheltered.

On the right, as you entered the hall, was the library,
where the logician and poet thought and wrote; where his
mind passed back and forth from earth to heaven, from
contemplating the glories of the Godhead, to a survey of
the wants and the attractions of infant minds. Here he
often rehearsed his songs of praise. One would like to

stand in the same room, and listen to one's own voice, and
to fancy that he heard mingling with it the reverberations
of the mellifluous tones of the poet dying out in a continually weakening whisper, but still all the holier because
remote in time from the salient points of their original
impulse.

In this room he had conversed with the celebrated Mr.
Whitefield, and had ventured to chide gently the overaction
which is almost sure to mar, in some degree, a character
of such generous and warm impulses.   Here also he met
the Lady Huntingdon, who desired to greet with a holy
urbanity all that possessed talents thus consecrated to the
cause of true piety.   After the usual salutations, the
Doctor thus accosted her : "Madam, your ladyship has come
to see me on a very remarkable day.   This day thirty
years ago I came hither to the house of my good friend
Sir Thomas Abney, intending to spend but one single
week under his friendly roof, and I have extended my visit
to the length of exactly thirty years."   Lady Abney, who
was present, replied : "Sir, what you term a long thirty
years' visit, I consider as the shortest visit my family
ever received."   "A coalition like this," says Dr. Johnson, "a state in which the notions of patronage and
dependence were overpowered by the perception of recip-
rocal benefits, deserves a particular memorial."

Abney House has been removed, but the grove of cedars
and yews under whose shade the poet loved to linger, and
the mound from which he used to survey the park and its
green environments before the city had encroached upon
them, as at present, still exist.   They have been preserved
with jealous care, and while dilapidated walls and decay-

ing marble tell of perishing humanity, the living branches of those trees, with their enduring verdure, as they sigh in the breeze, whisper of the "green memories" of this great and good man.

The genius of Dr. Watts makes less impression, because he sought by varied studies to be useful rather than to shine pre-eminent in any individual walk of literature. Yet his poetry plainly indicates that he might have risen to the very highest style. Some of his verses are harsh, but no writer conceives of grander objects, or invests them with a richer drapery. Marble monuments and statues are poor mementoes of such a man. One prefers to think of him as associated with the green yews and cedars of Abney Park, with the rich cloud palace, which the setting sun and his own imagination has changed into walls of sapphire surrounded by an emerald sea, and surmounted with golden turrets; or, better still, one would think of Watts after listening to a full choir in the sanctuary, singing from his second version of the twenty-fourth Psalm those three sublime stanzas:

> "Our Lord is risen from the dead,
> Our Jesus is gone up on high;
> The powers of hell are captive led
> Dragged to the portals of the sky.
>
> "There his triumphal chariot waits,
> And angels chant the solemn lay,
> 'Lift up your heads, ye heavenly gates;
> Ye everlasting doors, give way.
>
> "'Loose all your bars of massy light,
> And wide unfold the eternal scene;
> He claims these mansions as his right—
> Receive the King of Glory in.'"

29 *

Still, if the lasting fame of Watts were staked upon any one species of composition, it should be his *Divine and Moral Songs for Children*. We know of nothing of human inditing which has exercised a deeper and more abiding moral and religious influence over us than these little poems. While they are simple, and thus adapted to childhood, they are replete with the profoundest truths, and much of their imagery is worthy to be embroidered upon the vestments with which we would desire our souls to be dressed for immortality. Where in all our English literature can be found a similitude containing more beautiful moral analogies, or richer associations with which to fasten a valuable impression on the mind, than that contained in his "*Summer Evening.*"

Though written for children, it will repay any mind for the labor of fixing it in the memory; and we cannot avoid citing it, in the hope that it may furnish some reader who is not familiar with it, the same lasting pleasure which it has given to ourselves.

"How fine has the day been! How bright was the sun,
How lovely and joyful the course that he run!
Though he rose in a mist when his race he begun,
    And there followed some droppings of rain;
But now the fair traveller comes to the west,
His rays are all gold, and his beauties are best,
He paints the sky gay as he sinks to his rest,
    And foretells a bright rising again.

"Just such is the Christian: his course he begins,
Like the sun in a mist, while he mourns for his sins,
And melts into tears, then he breaks out and shines,
    And travels his heavenly way;

But when he comes nearer to finish his race,
Like a fine setting sun, he looks richer in grace,
And gives a sure hope, at the end of his days,
    Of rising in brighter array."

The usefulness of such a man can never be estimated. His "Psalms and Hymns," and his "Divine and Moral Songs," have been published by millions. Yet they are by no means antiquated. No better sacred lyrics—no better songs for children have yet arisen to supplant the productions of Watts. Of his person little need be said. He was scarcely more than five feet in stature. Yet he possessed a dignity of manner, a bright countenance, and a piercing eye. In the pulpit, his manner was quiet, seldom moving a hand, but his voice was distinct, and his intonations sweet and attractive. His last days were peaceful and happy. He was heard to say, "I bless God that I can lie down with comfort at night, not being solicitous whether I awake in this world or another." In conversation with a friend, while he was patiently waiting his departure, he observed, "That he remembered an aged minister used to say, that the most learned and knowing Christians, when they come to die, have only the same plain promises of the gospel for their support, as the common and unlearned; and so," said he, "I find it." He died on the 25th of November, 1748, little more than one century ago. He was honorably interred among the worthies of Bunhill Fields. Six clergymen, two from each of the different dissenting churches, bore his pall. Dr. S. Chandler pronounced the oration at the grave, in which he delivered the following just commendation: "We here commit to the ground the venerable remains of one, who being intrusted with many excellent talents by Him who is the giver of every good and perfect gift, cheerfully and unweariedly employed them as a faithful steward of the manifold grace of God, in his Master's service, approving himself as a minister of Christ in much patience, in afflictions and distresses, by pureness, by knowledge, by long-suffering, by kindness, by love unfeigned, by the word of truth, by the armor of righteousness, by honor and dishonor, by evil report and good report, and who, amidst trial from within and from without, was continued, by the kind providence of God and the powerful supports of his grace, to a good old age, honored and beloved by all parties, retaining his usefulness till he had just finished his course, and being, at last, favored according to his own wishes and prayers, with a release from the labors of life into that peaceful state of good men, which commences immediately after death.   Oh, how delightful is that voice from heaven, which has thus pronounced: *"Blessed are the dead who die in the Lord, yea saith the Spirit, that they may rest from their labors, and their works do follow them."* Dr. Jennings preached the funeral sermon from Hebrews xi. 4, *"He being dead yet speaketh."* He observes in his discourse, "I question whether any author before him did ever appear on such a variety of subjects as he has done, both as a prose writer and a poet. However, this I may venture to say, there is no man now living, of whose works so many have been dispersed both at home and abroad, that are in such constant use, and translated into such a variety of languages; many of which will, I doubt not, remain more durable monuments of his great talents than any representation I can make of them, though it were to be engraven on pillars of brass."

Grave of William Penn.

The Grave of William Penn.

BY MRS. S. C. HALL.

A DISTINGUISHED American observed to us, not long ago, that "of all lawgivers there are none whose names shine so brightly on the page of history as do those of George Washington and William Penn," both of whom he claimed for his country. The former was, indeed, truly a great man; perhaps of all patriots who ever lived he is the one most "without spot or blemish" —pure, faithful, unselfish, devoted; yet, all things considered, it may be that William Penn is entitled to even higher admiration: the one, nurtured in liberty, became its high priest; the other, cradled in luxury, lived to endure a long and fierce struggle with oppression; and yet, amid sore temptations and seductive flatteries, he passed with the innate consciousness of genius, and a human desire of approbation, conquering not only others but himself, and finally doing justice among the "Red-men" of a new country, whom all his predecessors had sought to pillage and destroy. The sense of right must indeed have been of surpassing strength in the nature of William Penn. In an age fertile of slander against every act of virtue, and of calumny as regarded all good men, the marvel is, how his reputation has descended to us so unscathed ; living, as he did, with those who make us blush for England, and often in contact with the low-minded and the false, who were ever on the watch to do him wrong, still the evil imputed to him is little, if it be any, more than tradition ; while his goodness is to this day as a beacon, casting its clear light over the waves of the Atlantic, and his name a watchword of honor, and a synonyme for probity and philanthropy.

It is a joy and a comfort to turn over the pages of this great man's life ; to view him as a statesman, acting upon Christian principles in direct opposition to the ordinary policy of the world ; and it was to us a source of high enjoyment, to reflect upon this eventful career while spending, during the past summer, some sunny days wandering amid scenes in Buckinghamshire,—in places which bear his honored name.   In Penn Wood there are trees yet in the vigor of a green old age, beneath the shadow of which the peaceful lawgiver of Pennsylvania might have pondered on the true and rational liberty he would have gladly died to establish.*

There is one spot—the most hallowed of them all—of which we shall write presently : a simple, quiet resting-place, for those who have gone to sleep in peace ; but, ere we pause at this Shrine, we must recall the lawgiver, amid the billows of life, buffeting the waves which in the end floated him into a haven of rest.

* Further traces of this family are to be found in Penlands, Penn-street, Penhouse, all in the same county. The name given in after years to the American colony—Pennsylvania—is but a remembrance of the locality.

The family of William Penn were of Buckinghamshire, and from them sprang the Penns of Penn's Lodge, on the edge of Bradon Forest; from the Penns of Penn's Lodge *our* William Penn came in direct descent. His father was, by profession, far other than a man of peace. He was one of England's rough bulwarks, braving

"The battle and the breeze;"

obtained professional distinction while almost a boy; commanded (in 1665) the fleet which Cromwell sent against Hispaniola; and, after the Restoration, behaved so gallantly in a sea-fight against the Dutch, that he was knighted, and "received," runs the chronicle, "with all the marks of private friendship at court." Charles II.'s "private" friendship could have been of small value to Admiral Penn; indeed, he seemed to have cared little which was in the ascendant—King or Commonwealth; but his sailor-nature *did* care for the glory of England, and he improved her navy in several important departments. Admiral Sir William Penn married Margaret, the daughter of John Jasper, of Rotterdam, and in due time the fair Dutchwoman's son became the "Proprietor" of Pennsylvania.* William was born in the parish of St. Catherine's, Tower Hill, on the 14th day of October, 1644;†

* This phrase is copied from the tomb of one of his grandsons, in the Church of the Village of Penn.

† This district has entirely changed its aspect; twenty years ago it was densely and not very reputably populated. The Collegiate Church and Alms Houses stood in the midst of dirty streets, down which few strangers ventured: the Hospital of St. Catherine was removed to the Regent's Park; and the parish cleared away to an enormous extent to form on its site the Docks which bear the same name.

30

doubtless his mother left her home at Wanstead, in Essex, to be confined in London, although the neighborhood of the Tower could not have been a very quiet retreat. The beat of the drum and the blast of the trumpet must have often disturbed the couch of the young mother. The fashionable world of those days knew nothing of the "west end," except from the salubrity of its fields and mulberry gardens, and the locality of Tower Hill was well adapted to suit the taste and calling of the Admiral, who had there chosen his "town house."

In due time the mother and child returned to Wanstead; and the Archbishop of York having a little time previously founded a grammar-school at Chigwell,* the embryo law-giver was sent there at a very early age, where he was sufficiently near the family residence to give his mother the opportunity of frequently seeing her beloved son.

The localities thus connected with the early life of Penn are on the borders of Epping Forest, and although but a few miles from London, lie in a district but little visited. Wanstead is a picturesque spot, and the village green, with its thickly planted over-arching trees, and large red-brick houses, give it even now an air of old-fashioned dignity. We were pleased with the aspect of the place,

---

* The free schools at Chigwell were founded in the year 1629, by Archbishop Harsnet; one for teaching children reading, writing, and arithmetic, the other for their instruction in the Greek and Latin tongues. There is a fine brass to the founder in the church here; he commenced life as master of the grammar school in his native town of Colchester, and became successively Bishop of Chichester and Norwich, and ultimately Archbishop of York. He died in 1631.

WANSTEAD, IN ESSEX.

(351)

and left it with regret to journey on to Chigwell. The latter is an old and silent village; the church, with its row of arching yews; the large inn opposite, with its deep gables and bowed windows, and the entire character of the village carried the mind insensibly back. The school is an ivy-covered building; and the room in which the after governor of Pennsylvania was educated bears traces of considerable antiquity.

INTERIOR OF CHIGWELL SCHOOL.

The temperament of William Penn was sensitive and enthusiastic; and must have caused his parents much anxiety. It is certain, that while at Chigwell, his mind

EXTERIOR OF CHIGWELL SCHOOL.

358

became seriously impressed on the great subject of religion. The Admiral, we may suppose, if he knew of this impression, would not have regarded it favorably; and if it were known to him, it made him hasten his son's departure from Chigwell, for the following year we find him at school near his birthplace on Tower Hill, and most likely at a *day* school, for his father, to augment his scholarship, kept a private tutor for him at his own home. Sir William had high hopes for this darling child. His talents were of a lofty order, his accomplishments were many, and he won all hearts by his captivating manners. When fifteen, he entered Christ Church, Oxford, as a gentleman commoner. There, without neglecting his studies, he took great delight in manly sports and in the society of his companions, numbering among his friends Robert Spencer and John Locke; but though the seed may remain long in the earth and give no sign of life, if the soil be but favorable, it will spring up as surely as it has been sown—to "bring forth fruit in due season."

About this time a certain Thomas Loe was drawn into what his college considered the heresy of Quakerism, and, like all sincere men who believe they have discovered truth, he sought to win others over to his new faith, or rather to a purifying of the old. Accordingly, the meetings and devotional exercises of him and his friends gave offence to the heads of the college, who fined all of them for nonconformity. This opposition strengthened their determination to persevere; and those who had been simply devotional, rushed into fanaticism. While these youths were fusing in the fire of increased zeal, a command from Charles II., to Oxford, directed that the surplice should be worn according to the custom of ancient times. His majesty loved to see religion in full dress—outward pomp seemed to him a good excuse for absence of the vital principle—but William Penn, his friend Robert Spencer, and others who believed that the robe would impair the spirituality, fell upon the students who appeared *en robe*, and tore the dresses to pieces—for which they were all expelled. There was much more of the father's spirit than of the mother's gentleness in this outbreak; but his father was not moved to approbation thereby; on the contrary, he was sorely grieved; the Admiral was terror-stricken at his son's becoming "religious;" he knew that Quakers were men who professed to hold all worldly distinctions in contempt—whose political principles were hardly defined, but who refused to remain uncovered in the presence even of royalty—whose plain speech, and uncompromising faith, left no loop-holes for "excuses" or "expedients"—whose nay was nay—whose yea was yea—without "*compromise ;*" and, above all, who were men of peace. It was not to be expected that a hero such as Admiral Penn could have endured the idea of his son—endowed with all the accomplishments that charm society, and the high qualities which engrave their possessor's name on the page of history—subsiding into Quakerism in the days of his youth; hiding his fortunes beneath a broad-brimmed hat; and abandoning forever the graces of society—the established learning of the schools; and what was far more dear to the Admiral, the sword—then the badge and birthright of the English gentleman.

Even in this more tolerant age, when no sorrow or misfortune visits our country without testing and proving the social value of the Quakers, as most faithful laborers in the cause of charity, and most loyal and peaceful subjects —even we can fancy the rage of some old Admiral—the very Hotspur of the ocean—if his son were found guilty of going over to sectarianism; quitting his church being, in his eyes, almost as criminal as deserting his gun.   Admiral Penn was so annoyed at William's conduct that he turned him out of doors, well-beloved as he was.   There is no record of William Penn's conduct at this time; probably he had not been sufficiently schooled into forbearance to endure patiently; and yet, when his father's wrath subsided, his mother's tears and entreaties prevailed : overcome by his own affectionate nature on the one hand, and her expostulations on the other, the father forgave the son, who was again sheltered beneath his roof; but not long destined to remain there.

The unenviable distinction which France enjoys, of being the country where no serious thought can arrive at maturity, tempted Sir William to send his son to Paris. Foreign travel was then considered indispensable to the gentleman, and he, doubtless, thought that the gaieties of Paris would do more towards emancipating young Penn from the thraldom of sectarianism than the reproof of the college, or his repented-of severity.   It is believed that for a time his father's wishes were gratified; but only one anecdote is preserved of his conduct there, and that tells greatly to his honor.   He was attacked one night by a person, who drew his sword upon him in consequence of a supposed affront.   A conflict ensued, proving that the youth had not in all things conformed to the habit of those whose influence was so dreaded by his father.   William disarmed his antagonist, but spared his life, when, according to the record of all those who relate the fact, he could have taken it; thus exhibiting, says Gerard Crosse, a testimony not only of his courage but of his forbearance.

But if touched by the dissipations of Paris, he was not tainted by them.* In 1662 and 1663, we find him residing with a Protestant minister of Calvinistic faith, the very learned M. Amyrault, of Saumur, whose character and works recommended him to the notice of Cardinal Richelieu, who imparted to him his design of uniting the two churches.

The privilege of receiving instruction from such a man was appreciated as it deserved by William Penn; the teaching of the schools is widely different from the knowledge communicated by the wise and true to a docile and eager pupil, in the comparative silence and solitude of a private family. At Saumur, Penn pondered over "the Fathers," became more deeply interested in theology, and labored diligently to acquire a perfect knowledge of the

---

* It has been said, indeed, that at this period of his life he dallied with the enervating pleasures of the time; we have not only no evidence of this, but the supposition is inconsistent with his indignant exclamation, when before the Lieutenant of the Tower, Sir John Robinson, who charged him with having "been as bad as other folks," "abroad and at home too," which elicited from William Penn the following:—"I make this bold challenge to all men, women, and children, upon earth, justly to accuse me with ever having seen me *drunk*, heard me *swear*, utter a *curse*, or speak one *obscene word* (much less that I ever made it my practice); I speak this to God's Glory, that has ever preserved me from the power of these pollutions, and that, from a child, begot an hatred in me towards them;" concluding his outbreak thus—"Thy words shall be thy burden, and I trample thy *slander* as *dirt* under my feet."

French language; from thence he proceeded to Turin, where he received a letter from his father informing him of his taking sea against the Dutch, and commanding his immediate return to England. The Admiral was perhaps too busied to inquire much as to the state of his son's mind ;—satisfied, as many are, with the ease and grace to which foreign travel seldom fails to mould the young, he commended his improvement, and Lincoln's Inn had the honor of receiving William Penn as a student for a year, when the "great plague" set him free from the dry, but —as regarded his future—useful study of the law.

The sacred fire, kindled in his bosom, though it smouldered for a time, was never extinguished. The awful visitation that had driven him from Lincoln's Inn was well calculated to revive his more serious thoughts, and lead them from the present to the future. The fatal pestilence had not subdued the restless spirit of religious controversy; men cried more loudly than ever, "I am of Paul," "and I of Apollos." But, for a time, he spoke less and pondered more; he had completed his twenty-first year, and with his manly robe, assumed a grave and manly bearing. His father returned from the expedition flushed with glory and triumph; but his proud pulses beat less quickly when he noted the gravity of his son, and his evident leaning towards serious matters. Again he determined to change the scene, and draughted him to the viceregal court of Ireland, then glowing with the brightness and animation of the accomplished Duke of Ormond. The means were too violent for the end: the young man grew disgusted with the court and courtly doings. The Admiral, fertile

in expedients, then turned over to him the management
of his Irish estates in the county of Cork.*

The task was after his son's own heart, and he performed it to admiration ; this occupation most likely
sowed the seeds of his wisdom in territorial management,
and, as there were no gaieties to annoy or perplex him,
he might have continued long to delight his father in this
capacity, but for the accident of his hearing WILLIAM
LOE, the layman of Oxford, preach at a Quakers' meeting
in Cork, from the text,—" There is a faith which over-
comes the world, and there is a faith which is overcome by
the world."   This convinced him of the necessity for religious vitality ; and at length he was, according to the
custom of those " rare old times," apprehended at a
Quakers' meeting in Cork, and thereupon committed to
prison ; but thanks to Lord Orrery, his term in " the dark
prison-house " was not long. His nature was strengthened
in his new faith, as all noble natures are, by the invigorating power of persecution ; for

> " —who would force the soul, tilts with a straw
> Against a champion cased in adamant."

From this time all wavering and indecision passed away,
and he was considered a confirmed Quaker.   Sir William,
refusing to believe that every means he had taken to dispel,
had but established his son's faith, commanded his return ;
it would seem that at first William Penn desired to meet

* " He had large estates in Ireland, one of which, comprehending
Shannigarry Castle, lay in the barony of Imokelly, and the others
in the baronies of Ibaune and Barryroe, all of them in the county
of Cork."—*Clarkson.*

his father's wishes, were it possible to do so. His adherence to what was called the ceremony of the " hat," and his communion only with those of the same faith, convinced the Admiral that he embraced the " heresy " more fondly than ever. The stormy and sorely-tried father used every means in his power to induce his son even to appear to the world what he was not. The great point of dispute, the wearing or not wearing the *hat* in the presence of royalty, may seem to us a light matter ; but it was not so to the " Friends," and is not so to this day.* And so the father again turned the son from beneath the shelter of his roof, a homeless and moneyless wanderer ; his situation would have been most pitiable, but for his mother's watchful tenderness and affection.

The young Quaker now put forth his faith in printed books, and was not slow in disputation ; evincing occasionally rather more of the fiery zeal of Peter, than the discretion of Paul ; combating the attacks of certain Presbyterians with marvellous intrepidity, and attacking in his turn, which attacks ended in his being committed to the

---

* Clarkson has very clearly summed up the reasons of the early Quakers for discarding *hat-worship*, as they termed it. Taking it for granted that the ceremonious removal of the hat was intended to be indicative of honor, respect, submission, or some similar feeling of the mind, they contended that, used as it then was, it was no more a criterion of these than mourning garments were criterions of sorrow : hence, they argued, the falsity of the custom. If used as indicative of respect, they contended that it was more generally applied to the purposes of flattery, and equally objectionable. But the strongest reason of the three, was that which declared, that the removal of the hat in the worship of God, precluded the possibility of giving any of his creatures an equal amount of honor.

Tower. His imprisoment was rigid, but he wrote continuously; and in one tract, "Innocency with her open Face," explained away the anti-christian charges made against his faith. After seven months' incarceration he was liberated; it is believed, by the intercession of the Duke of York, to whom, from this or some other cause, he was personally attached. Certainly, in nothing did his purpose waver, for he left the gloom of the prison to attend the death-bed of Thomas Loe, his friend and guide. And then the heart of his father yearned towards him; the Admiral could not but respect his son's earnestness and consistency of purpose; the chords of both were the same, but they were tuned in different keys, and for different ends. He relented gradually, giving permission to the *mother* again to receive her son, and sanctioning his resuming the management of his Irish property.

He performed to admiration the duties with which he was entrusted; and on his return to England was received with open arms by a father no longer stern or unforgiving; his mother had the joy of seeing them once more united. Nor does it appear that his son's after disputations, or preachings, or imprisonments, caused any new breach between them, though we find the young "Friend" preaching in Gracechurch Street, and expressing his opinions so freely upon various matters—especially the famous Conventicle Act passed in 1670, prohibiting dissenters from worshipping God in their own way—that he was, with another of the Society, one William Mead, seized upon by constables, conveyed at once to Newgate,* where

* Newgate had been a prison since 1218, and was used for persons of distinction even before the Tower. It was a most miserable

they were left until the following session, and then had the good fortune to be tried by one of the most steadfast **and**

OLD NEWGATE PRISON.

honest juries ever empanelled, even in England.* The indignities endured, both by prisoners and jury, can hardly

dungeon, originally termed Chamberlain's Gate; and when re-constructed by Whittington was called New Gate, it being then one of the gates of the city. It was destroyed in the great fire.

* The trial of Penn is an extraordinary picture of the legal

be credited; but ultimately the Quakers were liberated
upon the payment of a fine, which was privately discharged by Sir William Penn.

When William Penn was freed from the Tower, he had
passed from its walls to the death-bed of his spiritual father,
William Loe, and he hastened from the loathsome cells of
Newgate to the deathbed of his earthly father, whose
career was terminating, at an age when men calculate on
length of days to enjoy the repose which is so needful as
the evening of life approaches.   At the age of forty-nine,
his warring but chastened spirit passed to the God who
gave both peace and Christian wisdom to his latter days.
It throws, however, a good deal of light on the "king-
loving" habit which was made a cruel reproach to William

tyranny of the times.   It took place at the Old Bailey, in September, 1670.   The indictment was for preaching in Gracechurch
Street.   Penn's conduct was most heroic.   He argued manfully and
well against the persecution to which he and others were subjected,
and appealed to the jury so powerfully, exhorting them to preserve
their integrity of action uninfluenced by the lawyers, that they
would only bring in their verdict "Guilty of speaking in Gracechurch Street."   And, although sent back to re-consider this verdict frequently, "until," as the Recorder told them, "they brought
such a one as the court would accept," they continued firm for two
days and nights.   The court indulged in brutal language toward
them, and the infamous Recorder lamented the want of the Inquisition in England, declaring England "would never be well" till
something equal in "policy and prudence" to it was established.
When finally pressed to deliver a verdict,—guilty, or not guilty,—
they, to a man, returned an answer in the negative; for which
they were each fined forty marks and sent to Newgate, as also were
Penn and Mead, for refusing to pay the fines.

Penn's after course, by those who could not separate the *man* from the monarch—to remember, that in his last illness, indeed towards its termination, Admiral Penn, foreseeing that, while the existing laws of the country remained, his son would have many trials and much suffering to undergo, sent one of his friends to the Duke of York, to entreat him, as a death-bed request, that he would endeavor to protect his son as far as he consistently could, and to ask the king to do the same, in case of future persecution.   The answer was such as the Admiral deserved, and for once the *Stuart* promise was faithfully kept.   Be it also remembered, the Duke of York had previously befriended the young Quaker, who was personally attached to him; and all know that every member of the house of Stuart possessed an extraordinary power of attaching to them those they desired to bring under their influence.

Now that he was his own master, with a fortune of fifteen hundred pounds a-year, it would be impossible, within our limits, to trace his career abroad and at home, remarkable as it was for spiritual zeal, activity of body and mind, close penmanship in his closet, and so many perils and imprisonments, that he might compete with holy Paul in the eloquent list of perils and trials.   At one time, he publishes "The People's Ancient and Just Liberties Asserted;" then he disputes with Jeremy Ives touching Baptist matters, at Wycomb; then he lets fly a barbed arrow against Popery: is again taken up, and sent first to the Tower, and then to Newgate, for preaching; yet imprisonment no way damped his zeal, but seemed only to give him time for letters, essays, pamphlets,

addresses.*   He was never more fluent—never more
industrious than when in bonds; his spirit of endurance,
his hope, his enterprise, were astonishing.   He no sooner
quitted Newgate than he travelled into Germany and
Holland, seeking and making converts.   Returning, when
in the twenty-eighth year of his age, he sought and found
a loving and lovely wife, Gulielma Maria Springett,
daughter of Sir William Springett, of Darling, in Sussex.
For a brief time he enjoyed the quiet of domestic happiness at Rickmansworth, in Hertfordshire; but he would
not, perhaps could not, give up for domestic tranquillity
the life of excitement wherein he had cast his lot; and in
those days there was always something fresh to stir up
the spirit of an independent mind.   Charles II. had issued
a declaration of indulgence to tender consciences in matters of religion, in consequence of which five hundred
Quakers were released from prison; but William Penn
again went forth on a self-imposed mission, accompanied
by his lovely wife, and behold, amid the rant and turmoil
of Bristol fair, they encountered George Fox, the great
fountain of Quakerism, who had just then landed in Bristol,
after a sojourn in America.   Though subsequently much
engaged in very stormy controversy, there can be little
doubt that this meeting determined William Penn to investigate human nature in the New World.   We may diverge
a little from our subject to introduce two engravings, interesting as associated with this period of the history of
William Penn.   With Fox he travelled much; and in the

* In a catalogue of "Friends' Books" (J. Soule, 1708) we find a
list of his written productions from 1668 to 1700, in number no
fewer than *one hundred and nine.*

31 *

Journal of that celebrated man he is frequently referred to. They visited each other's houses; and while we know that Fox resided at Worminghurst, we have the traditional certainty of his visiting Fox, at his house, Swarthmoor Hall, on the borders of Lancashire. This

SWARTHMOOR HALL.

mansion was his by marriage with the widow of Judge Fell; and in the memoirs of Margaret Fox, she records his first visit there in her husband's lifetime, in 1652, who, from being opposed to Quakerism, became a convert on hearing Fox, and she says—"He let us have a meeting in his house the next first day after, which was the first public meeting that was at Swarthmoor; our meetings being kept at Swarthmoor about thirty-eight years, until a new meeting-house was built by George Fox's order and cost, near Swarthmoor Hall."

In 1676, Penn became "manager of Property concerns"

SWARTHMOOR MEETING-HOUSE.

in New Jersey; invited settlers, sent them out in three vessels, and occupied himself in the formation of a constitution, consisting of terms of agreement and concession. Perfect religious liberty was of course established, and William Penn left on record that "he hoped he had laid the foundation for those in after ages of their liberty, both as men and Christians, and by an adherence to which, they could never be brought into bondage but by their own consent."

How evident it is that such-like exercises qualified him for his after-charge of "his property" of Pennsylvania! In these days it is little more than a pleasure trip, to those who like, or do not absolutely dislike, the sea, to cross the Atlantic; but in the time of William Penn it was a serious undertaking; yet nothing obstructed his progress;

when once he fixed within his mind, that it was *right* to act, the act was "a-foot." It would be the PILGRIMAGE of a life to follow his steps; we have taken but a condensed view of his movements, yet what space it has occupied; and still his journeyings are only commenced! What meetings and preachings in Holland and Germany —what disputations abroad and in England—what petitions on behalf of the peaceful, but most persecuted Quakers—what answers to libels, and what loving epistles to God's people! Stimulated by the hot blood of his father, which at times boiled within his veins, he for a time forgot his consistency, and made common cause with Algernon Sidney in his contested election at Guildford; but his "plainness" did not move the people "more than eloquence," for Sidney lost his election, and Penn was forced from the hustings. And all this time his mighty head was projecting, and his mighty heart beating with plans for the good of New Jersey: mingling the divine and secular in a way which cannot be comprehended by those who have not known what it is to contend with the restlessness and suggestions of an enterprising and fervent spirit. His heart was rent asunder by the persecutions endured by his people—especially in the "rough" city of Bristol—and anxious as he then was for the grants, which he in aftertime obtained, the fear of "great ones" never prevented his raising hand and voice against tyranny.

At length one of his great objects was attained; the Charter, granting him the tract of land which he himself had marked out, bears date the 4th of March, 1681. Let none suppose this was a free gift from the Majesty of England to the Quaker,—not at all;—he had petitioned for land in "the far West," where brethren might dwell together in unity, in love, and in security, chiefly as the liquidation of a debt which the government owed his father.*   And when his petition was granted, then commenced the career by which his name is chiefly known and honored; his sayings and doings, his writings, his wearyings and journeyings, are only parts of the political and religious contention which disjointed England in those days, and show forth the restless and truth-seeking spirit of one whose aim was to keep alive the purer and simpler forms of religion, while contending manfully for its liberty. Happily, the spirit of persecution—at least of legalised persecution—has been extinguished in our age; and now, instead of sitting in terror under our own "vine and fig tree"—

> "We rather think, with grateful mind sedate,
> How Providence educeth, from the spring
> Of lawless will, unlooked-for streams of good,
> Which neither force shall check, nor time abate."

But the grand feature—the climax—the crowning of the capital—is PENN at PENNSYLVANIA; the just man, rising above all temptations. Let quibbles be raised, and old rumors revived,—the facts of Penn's legislation prove the greatness of his mind and the purity of his intentions. He had the strong feelings, passions, and thoughts inseparable

---

* "His father had advanced large sums of money, from time to time, for the good of the Naval service, and his pay had been also in arrears. For these two claims, including the interest upon the money due, government were in debt to him no less a sum than £16,000."—*Clarkson.*

Y

from a large brain ; and the wonder of all who look upon him dispassionately, must be, not that some evil has been asserted of one who accomplished what he desired, and commanded the respect of the voluptuous, as well as the affection of the good, but that so little has been found or written to his discredit.

Gathering "a favored people" together from wherever he had preached "the word," we find that at a very early period he freighted two ships with Irish Quakers.

Mercurial as the Irish are, there is no country where Quakers are more beloved and trusted to this day, than in Ireland; and well they may be so! At all times the Quakers stand forth between " the people" and destruction; no matter whether the peasantry are assailed by pestilence or by famine, the firm, calm, unpresuming, but steadfast Quaker,* comes forward with his store of wealth, and energy, and industry, and charity, (pure charity, in its most comprehensive sense,) and *mind*, ready to save, and employ, and instruct.   We have met with some who remember having heard from their parents, that their grandsires remembered the wailing of the poor when the "great law-maker," William Penn, induced so many of the "neighbors" to go to the New World.   The "conditions," as it pleased him to call his code of laws,—laws made as much for the advantage of a people given carelessly into his hand by a power which evidently thought little of the " Peltries," or "hunting-ground" of the red-men—as for the good of those who sought a home in an unknown land,

---

* It is worthy of record, that, during the rebellion of 1793, there was but one instance of a Quaker being put to death by the rebels; and that act was perpetrated in ignorance of the calling of the victim.

in full reliance upon their leader,—the " conditions" are all stated in Clarkson's life of Penn.*

The closeness, and simplicity, and wisdom of his legislation are admirable commentaries on the multitude, and mystery, and involvements which sepulchre our laws. It is evident that in all he did he sought not only that his own people should be well treated, but that they should treat others well. He put far away all attempts at religious persecution; and strove rather to make men upright and just in their old faith, than to tempt them into a new one.

The embarkation of this Quaker colony must, if we recal it by help of imagination, have formed a strange contrast to the going out of an "emigrant ship" in our own day. The well-clad, well-organised, steadfast, earnest, subdued, yet hopeful people, taking leave of those whom they loved, yet left, subduing, as is their custom, all outward indications of anguish, and seeming ashamed of the emotion which sent tears to their eyes, and tremors to their lips! Two of the good ships—well ordered, well appointed, well provisioned—sailed from London; another from Bristol. How different from those wretched hulks which are now sent staggering across the seas, to convey a diseased, half-naked, and enfeebled multitude to the promised land!

Penn's letter to the Indians, transmitted by one of the earlier ships, is a master-piece of what worldlings call

* Philadelphia, the name which Penn gave to his new city, is a compound from the Greek, signifying brotherly love. The "conditions" were also published in French, German, and Dutch, in 1682, and were extensively circulated over the Continent, inviting adventurers of all nations, creeds, and tongues, to join him in his enterprise at the city of " Brotherly Love."

policy, but which is simply justice and right feeling. This letter preceded his visit, and was well calculated to excite the confidence and curiosity of the red-men, who must have felt deeply anxious to see the "pale-face" who addressed them, and was disposed to treat them as brethren.

The death of his mother at this time spread a gloom over his loving spirit, and delayed his departure; but the interests of the new world summoned him from the Old. IIis letter to his wife and children, written on their separation, is such a record of pure love and true wisdom, that we should like to see it published as a tract, to find place among the treasures of every young married woman, and be unto her and her children a guide through life. He dates this letter from Worminghurst, where his family resided some considerable time.

He at length sailed for the new colony, in the ship " Welcome," and was there greeted by his future subjects, consisting of English, Irish, Dutch, and Swedes, then in number about 3000. He had people of many creeds and many lands to deal with, as well as an unseen and almost unknown nation, but he commenced with so noble an act of justice, in *paying* the Indians for the lands already *given* him in *payment* by the king of England, that "Pale-faces" and " Red-Skins" were alike convinced of his certain honesty of purpose. There are few persons whose pulsations are so numbed that they will not beat the quicker when they hear of a generous action; the soul is revived, even in a worldly bosom, by the throbs of immortality which tell us there are great and righteous deeds prompted by God himself. With what an upright gait and open brow must William Penn have met the tribes at

Coaquannoc—the Indian name for the place where Philadelphia now stands—foremost of a handful of Quakers, without weapon, undefended, except by that true protector which the Almighty has stamped on every honest brow.

Here the peace-loving law-maker awaited the pouring out of the dusky tribes.

PENN'S TREATY GROUND.

Amid the woods, as far as eye could reach, dark masses of wild uncouth creatures, some with paint and feathers, and rude, but deadly weapons, advanced slowly and in good order; grave, stern chiefs, and strong-armed "braves" gathering to meet a few unarmed strangers, their future friends, not masters! There was neither spear nor pistol, sword nor rifle, scourge nor fetter, open or concealed,

32

among these white men; the trysting-place was an elm-tree of prodigious growth at Shackamaxon, the present Kensington of Philadelphia.* Towards this tree the leaders of both tribes drew near, approaching each other under its widely spreading branches; front to front, eye to eye, neither having a dishonest or dishonorable thought towards his fellow-man—comprehending each other by means of that great interpreter—Truth! How vexatious that history should be so mute as to this most glorious meeting, and there is little but tradition—that faintest echo of the mighty past,—to tell of the speeches made by the Indians, and replied to by William Penn, after his first address had been delivered. The Quaker

---

* Penn, in his letter to the Earl of Sunderland, thus describes the great event which gives this spot celebrity: he says—"In selling me this land they thus ordered themselves: the old in a half-moon, upon the ground; the middle-aged in a like figure at a distance behind them; and the young fry in the same manner behind them." "We have thus," says Watson, in his Annals of Philadelphia, "a graphic picture of Penn's treaty, as painted by himself; and to my mind the sloping green bank presented a ready amphitheatre for the display of the successive semicircles of Indians." The large elm under which Penn concluded his treaty is seen to the right in the foreground of the cut on p. 373; it was blown down on the 3d of March, 1810. In its form it was remarkably wide-spread, but not lofty: its main branch, inclining towards the river, measured 150 feet in length: its girth around the trunk was twenty-four feet, and its age, as it was counted by the inspection of its circles of annual growth, was 283 years; it stood on the edge of the bank, which sloped to the river. The avenues of trees seen in the view, and Fairman Maurian opposite, was constructed in 1702. Penn greatly desired to purchase it as a country residence for himself, but failed to do so

used no subterfuge, employed no stratagem, to draw them
into confidence; imposed not upon their senses by a display of crown, sceptre, mace, sword, halbert, or any of
the visible signs of stately dominion or warlike power, to
which, like all wild men, they were inclined to render
homage;—and this is a thing to look at with pride and
thankfulness, when man in a righteous purpose, and with
simplicity, and steadfast intent, becomes so completely
one of Heaven's delegates, that he is looked up to, and
respected by his fellow mortals, who are not so richly endowed by God. It must have been a sight of exceeding
glory when Penn, whose only personal distinction was a
netted sash of sky-blue silk, cast his eyes over the mighty
and strange multitude, who observed him with an unde-
fined interest, while his followers displayed to the tribes
various articles of merchandize, and he advanced steadily,
towards the great *Sachem*, chief of them all, who, as Penn
drew near, placed a horned chaplet on his head, which
gave his people intimation that the sacredness of peace
was over all. With one consent the tribes threw down
their bows and arrows, crouched around their chiefs, forming a huge half-moon on the ground, while their great
chief told William Penn, by his interpreter, that the
"nations were ready to hear him."*

* Watson, in his *Annals of Philadelphia*, tells us—"After the
death of the great lawgiver of Pennsylvania, his family appear to
have much degenerated. One member became remarkable for dissolute and ungovernable habits, and ultimately the property passed
into other hands. The settlers, however, still retained a sense of
respect for his descendants, and upon a visit of one of them in the
early part of the eighteenth century, who had been a shopkeeper,

32 *

This scene has never been either recorded or painted as it might be. The great fact that he there spoke fearlessly and honestly, what they heard and believed—pledging themselves, when he had concluded, according to their country's manner, to live in love with William Penn and his children as long as the sun and moon should endure— is more suggestive than any record in modern history.

After arranging all matters as to the future city, well might William Penn write home, "In fine, here is what Abraham, Isaac, and Jacob would be well contented with, and service enough for God, for the fields are here white with harvest. Oh, how sweet is the quiet of these parts! freed from the anxious and troublesome solicitations, hurries, and perplexities of woeful Europe!"

But much as the lawgiver* eulogised the "quiet" of his new colony, he was not content to remain there. His mind was anxious; his affections were divided between the two hemispheres; his ardent, restless nature longed to act wherever action was needed. If the English government had hoped to get rid of him when they sold him the land

they received him with so much general rejoicing and public honors that the poor man, totally unused to it, was frightened out of all propriety."

* Slate-roof House, the city residence of William Penn and family while in Philadelphia, on his second visit in 1700, is remarkable as the birth place of the only one of the race of Penn born in the country. Here John Penn, "the American," was born one month after the arrival of the family. After Penn's decease, the house was retained as the governor's residence; and John Adams and other members of the Congress had their lodgings in "the Slate-House." We give views of the Slate-roof House not only as it was, but as it at present stands altered to suit the purposes of business.

for an inheritance, they were mistaken; several of those
he loved were in sorrow and imprisonment; the Stuarts
gave liberty of conscience one day and withdrew it the
next; he therefore returned to England. Charles II. was
trembling on the verge of the grave, which soon closed
over him, leaving nothing for immortality but the fame of

SLATE-ROOF HOUSE, PHILADELPHIA.

weakness even in vice. William Penn records James telling him, soon after his accession, that now he meant to
"go to mass above board:" upon which the Quaker
replied quaintly and promptly, "that he hoped his Majesty
would grant to others the liberty he so loved himself, and
let all go where they pleased." His renewed intimacy
with James strengthened the old reproach of "time-serv-
ing," and "trimming," and William Penn was frequently
32 *

called Jesuitical. Those who so reproached him had forgotten the long friendship which had subsisted between the King and himself, and the fact that never had his influence in high places been used except for right and righteous purposes. Whatever was said against him either then or now lacks proof, and is no more history than the bubble on the surface of the stream is the stream itself. He resided then in a house at Charing Cróss, most probably one ready furnished, as it has not been pointed at as a residence. His journeyings to and fro were resumed, and as he was known to be affectionately attached to James, (who certainly showed him great favor), when William came to the throne he was persecuted nearly as much as in the old times. Pennsylvania, too, became disturbed, not by the discontent of the Red-men, but by discontent with another governor. The wife of his bosom died in her fiftieth year, and soon after his son, in the prime of youth and hope, was taken from him. He married, however, again, feeling it hard to superintend a household without the overlooking care of a steadfast woman. From those of his own people who could not comprehend his liberal views he experienced great opposition and reproof, some of them thinking he entered too much into the world of politics.

"Time and the hour run through the longest day."

Penn outlived evil report and persecution. After a lapse of seventeen years he again sailed with his family to Pennsylvania; again was received by "white and red" as their father and their friend; dispelled many differences, healed many sores, saw the city he had planned

rising rapidly on every side. These seventeen years
seemed to have done the work of seventy, and the pros-
perity of Pennsylvania was secured. He had shown the
possibility of a nation maintaining its own internal policy
amid a mixture of different nations and opposite civil and
religious opinions, and of maintaining its foreign relations
also, without the aid of a soldier or a man-at-arms. The
CONSTABLE'S STAFF was the only symbol of authority in
Pennsylvania for the greater part of a century!

He had still abundant vexations to endure. His circumstances had become embarrassed. He returned with
his family to England, an aged man, though more aged
by the unceasing anxiety and activity of his life, than by
years.

There are traditions of his dwelling at Kensington and
Knightsbridge; but it is known that he possessed himself
of a handsome mansion at Rushcombe, near Twyford, in
Berkshire.* Here a stroke of apoplexy numbed his
active brain, and rendered him unfit for business. That
such "strokes" were repeated, until he finally sank beneath them, is also certain; but those who visited him

---

* Rushcombe is a quiet little village on the boarders of Berkshire;
it lies in a valley, and the gently-rising hills afar off add to the
placid beauty of the scene. Some very old cottages and farms constitute the homes of its inhabitants, which remain much as they
must have been when Penn was here resident. The house in which
he died was destroyed nearly twenty years ago; and an old countryman, who noticed our scrutiny of the village, and entered freely
into the interest of our visit, described it as a large and quaint old
mansion, which stood opposite the church, and commanded the view
exhibited in our wood cut; a view entirely unaltered by moderniza-
tion, and upon which the eye of Penn must often have rested.

between the periods of their infliction, bore testimony to his faith, and hope, and trust in the Lord, and of his unfailing loving-kindness and gentleness to those around him. Thus, through much faintness and weakness, he had but little actual suffering, though there was a gradual pacing towards eternity, during six years; and on the 30th day of July, 1718, in the seventy-fourth year of his

RUSHCOMBE.

age, he put off the mortal coil which he had worn, even to the wearing out, and joined in heaven those he had loved on earth. There was an immediate and mighty gathering of his friends and admirers, who attended his remains to the burying-ground of Jordans. It must have been a thrilling sight; the silent and solemn people wending their way through the embowered lanes leading from

Rushcombe into Buckinghamshire, that hallowed land of Hampden, consecrated by so many memories, of which Penn, if not chiefest, is now among the chief! The dense

THE GRAVE OF WILLIAM PENN.

unweeping sorrow of a Quaker funeral once witnessed can never be forgotten.

The sun had begun to make long shadows on the grass, and the bright stems of the birch threw up, as it were, the foliage of heavier trees, before we came in sight of the quaint solitary place of silence and of graves. The narrow road leading to the Quakers' Meeting-house was not often disturbed by the echo of carriage-wheels, and before we alighted, an aged woman had looked out with a perplexed yet kindly countenance, and then gone back and sent forth her little grand-daughter, who met us with a self-possessed and quiet air, which showed that if not "a friend," she had dwelt among friends. The Meeting-house is, of course, perfectly unadorned—plain benches, and a plain table, such as you sometimes see in "furniture-prints" of Queen Anne's time. This table the little maid placed outside, to enable Mr. Fairholt to sketch the grave-yard, and that we might write our names in a book, where a few English and a number of Americans had written before us;—it would be defamation to call it "an album," —it contained simply, as it ought, the names of those, who, like ourselves, wished to be instructed and elevated by a sight of the grave of William Penn.

The burying-ground might be termed a little meadow, for the long green grass waved over, while it in a great degree concealed the several undulations which showed where many sleep; but when observed more closely, chequered though it was by increasing shadows, the very undulations gave an appearance of green waves to the ver-dure as it swept above the slightly raised mounds; there was something to us sacred beyond all telling in this green place of nameless graves, as if having done with the world, the world had nothing more to do with those whose sta-tions were filled up, whose names were forgotten!—It was more solemn, told more truly of actual death, than the monuments beneath the fretted roofs of Westminster or St. Paul's, laboring, often unworthily, "to point a moral or adorn a tale," to keep a memory green, which else had mouldered!

The young girl knew the "lawgiver's" grave among the

many, as well as if it had been crushed by a tower of monumental marble.

She pointed it out, between the graves of his two wives. Some pilgrim to the shrine had planted a little branch, a mere twig, which had sprouted and sent forth leaves, just at the head of the mound of earth,—an effort at distinction that seemed somewhat to displease the old woman, who had come forth looking well satisfied at what she called the "quiet place" being so noticed. "All who came," she said, "knew the grave of William Penn; there was no need of any distinction; *there it was*, every one knew it; yes, many came,—especially Americans.—Ladies now and then plucked a little root of the grass, and took it away as a treasure; and no wonder, every one said he was a man of peace,—a GOOD MAN!"

We walked along the road that leads to the upland, and leaning against a style, saw the shadows of the tall trees grow longer and longer, as if drawing themselves closer to the hallowed earth. The Meeting-house had a solemn aspect; so lonely, so embowered, so closed up,—as if it would rather keep within itself, and to itself, than be a part of the busy world of busy men.

How still and beautiful a scene! How grand in its simplicity; how unostentatiously religious,—those green mounds, upon which the setting sun was now casting its good-night in golden benisons, seemed to us more spirit-moving than all the vaunted monuments of antiquity we had ever seen. How we wished that all lawgivers had been like him, who rested within the sanctuary of that green grass grave. We thought how he had the success of a conqueror in establishing and defending his colony, without ever, as was said of him, drawing a sword; the goodness of the most benevolent ruler in treating his subjects like his own children; the tenderness of an universal Father, who opened his arms, without distinction of sect or party, to the worthy of all mankind;—the man who really wishes to establish a mission of peace, and love, and justice to the ends of the earth, should first pray beside the grave of William Penn.

"The manor of Stoke," the present residence of the members of the Penn family, says J. Jay Smith, "consists of one thousand acres, four hundred of which are in park, very finely wooded, where ranges considerable game, including two hundred and fifty deer. Here reigns that rural ease enjoyed by the wealthy English in so very remarkable a degree. The noble trees are venerable; every luxury of wood, lake, fine views, an excellent and large library, await the fortunate guest. Windsor Castle and forest are seen through numerous beautiful vistas from the library, drawing-rooms, extensive pleasure-grounds, and park. The collection of family pictures, historical portraits, and statuary, is highly interesting. The original picture of Penn's Treaty with the Indians, by West, ornaments one of the drawing-rooms.

" 'Gray's Church,' as it is called, is situated in Granville Penn's noble park. The steeple is in full view from the principal drawing-room windows. His tomb is of brick, surmounted by a plain blue marble slab, immediately in front of the chancel window."

THE END.

www.ingramcontent.com/pod-product-compliance
Lightning Source LLC
Chambersburg PA
CBHW021530110726
47902CB00004B/823